RAVE REVIEWS FOR
EYES OF PREY AND BARRY HOFFMAN!

"A shout of outrage and frustration at the way things seem to be. An urban nightmare for the millennium—psychic powers, soulless criminals, victims of abuse trying to reinvent themselves, even a conspiracy theory underneath everything—but throughout all this Barry Hoffman stays close to his protagonists and sees them through to their unforgettably unexpected ends."

—Ramsey Campbell, author of
The Last Voice They Hear

"*Eyes of Prey* is a compelling novel with an unpredictable plot that's rich in detail and peopled with fully fleshed characters you care about."

—F. Paul Wilson, author of *Legacies*

"Hoffman's characterization transcends the simpleminded killing-machines who populate the genre."

—*Publishers Weekly*

"Barry Hoffman's characters come to life on the page and resonate long after the story is done."

—Poppy Z. Brite, author of *Lost Souls*

"Barry Hoffman can really tell a story. Once you begin *Eyes of Prey,* I'm guessing that, just as it happened with me, you won't be able to put it down."

—Charles de Lint, *Fantasy & Science Fiction*

"A new voice—and a telling one—in the horror genre."

—Richard Matheson, author of
I Am Legend

THE NIGHTWATCHER

"What's a fine looking bitch doing out this time of night?" he asked, his eyes taking stock of Lysette's skirt, which had risen high up her thigh, then checking out the cleavage exposed by her low-cut top, and finally the gold cross that dangled between her breasts.

"It's no business of yours what I'm doing," she said evenly, dropping her cigarette to the ground, and calmly crushing the embers with her shoe.

"A feisty one. I like that in a woman. We could have a good time," he said, his hand rubbing his crotch.

"I don't think so." Her eyes locked with his.

"Bitch," he said. Then he smiled. "I don't have to fight for pussy. Tell you what. Give me that fine jewelry and you can be on your way."

"Why would I give you my fucking jewelry?" she asked, without emotion, and saw a cloud of doubt cross the man's face for a moment.

He'd been moving steadily toward her as he spoke, and now his hand touched the gold cross, his palm resting on her breast. She heard the click of a switchblade, which he held up to her face. He wasn't smiling anymore. She saw cockiness, arrogance and determination.

"So I won't cut you," he answered. "I'm going to get the jewelry one way or another. Matter of fact, I don't give a fuck whether I take it from you dead or alive. Your choice, bitch."

Lysette stepped back, raised the arm covered by her coat, exposing her gun, which she fired once at the man's head.

Other *Leisure* books by Barry Hoffman:
HUNGRY EYES

BARRY HOFFMAN

EYES OF PREY

LEISURE BOOKS NEW YORK CITY

With love, respect and gratitude
to my children—
Dara, David and Cheryl

A LEISURE BOOK®

August 1999

Published by

Dorchester Publishing Co., Inc.
276 Fifth Avenue
New York, NY 10001

ISBN 0-8439-4567-2

ACKNOWLEDGMENTS

Thanks to Anna Rodriguez of the Philadelphia Police Department, and homicide detectives who clued me in; to Don D'Auria, my editor, for all his help; to Richard Christian Matheson for his encouragement; to Harry O. Morris for his wonderful art; to the woman at the Fantasy Showbar in Pennsauken, New Jersey, who put a human face on strippers; and to my children, Dara, David and Cheryl, for being there—always.

EYES OF PREY

Prologue

What I'd give to be a fly on the wall . . .

Lysette's father had used the expression all too often during the three-hour conversations his thirteen-year-old daughter, Laura, had on the phone. *Now* she knew what he'd meant; lying on a hospital bed in a coma, she *was* a fly on the wall. Sitting . . .

—*cowering*

. . . in the attic of her mind, too weary . . .

—*too terrified*

. . . to venture out, as the nurses and doctors talked about her ordeal as if she weren't there. And she listened . . .

—*a fly on the wall.*

"Animals. Goddamn animals."

She recognized the voice as LaToya, relieving Heather. If it was LaToya, it must be morning, Lysette thought to herself.

"Look at the poor child," she heard the woman say, her voice husky and filled with concern. "I heard Dr. Paul say she was hit upside the head with a marble ashtray or lighter. Same as her sister. Don't know if it's a curse or a blessing she wasn't killed like the others. Could end up a vegetable . . . "

Images floated past her as Lysette peeked out the attic door, tuning out the nurse's patter. Pat's Steaks. They had gone to dinner— the four of them. Mom. Dad. Her big sister, Laura. And Lysette, two years younger than her sister. Once a week they'd all go out for dinner. More often than not, it was to Pat's Steaks; the *best* Philly cheese steaks in the city. Laura covered hers with onions.

"Some steak with your onions?" her mother joked.

Lysette passed on the onions and slathered mustard over hers, to her sister's consternation.

"Yuck! Mustard. You put mustard on *everything*."

11

"Do not."

"Do, too. Lysette puts mustard on her cereal, Mom," she said, ignoring her sister.

"Do not, onion breath."

"That's enough, girls," her mother admonished, not too sternly, as she tried unsuccessfully to stifle a smile.

The attic door closed abruptly, and Lysette could hear LaToya speaking again.

"Heard the police talk when she was brought in. Poor child was beaten and left for dead with the rest of her family. Was found lying under her mother *twelve* hours after they was attacked."

"Good thing she was comatose," Heather, the night nurse, answered. "Imagine being conscious with the rest of your family bludgeoned to death."

Lysette *had* been awake. *Had* been aware. She had tried to move, but couldn't, lying beneath her mother. Saw her father with his throat slashed, his head bent back at an impossible angle. Felt her mother's blood seeping through her blouse. Saw the dent in Laura's head that reminded her of the top of a bowling pin. Smelled the blood and urine and number two . . .

—"Stool," her mother would call it.

—"My morning constitutional," her father labeled it, going into the bathroom with the morning paper.

—"Crap" or "shit," Laura told her. "Gotta take a shit," Laura liked to say lately.

. . . and something more she couldn't identify right then.

—*Death*, her mind screamed now.

It was then she crept into the attic of her mind, hardly aware when she was lifted, put on a moving bed . . .

—"*stretcher, you fool*," she could hear Laura chastise her for her ignorance.

. . . and carried from the house.

There was a rustle of paper, then LaToya was talking again. "You haven't seen this yet, have you?"

It must be the *Daily News*, Lysette thought. Every morning LaToya brought in the tabloid, which for the last two days had been trying to piece together the crime which had shaken the city.

"The paper quotes an unidentified police source saying they are considering the possibility of a triple murder, with the distraught father committing suicide."

"Right. The father kills his family, *then* slits his throat, *then* disposes of the knife. Police source, my ass. Probably some secretary. Give me a break."

"More likely the dude from the paper had *no* police source," La-Toya added. "Made up the story to see if the police would refute it. Just out to sell papers. God, they make me sick."

More pictures, as Lysette peered from the safety of the attic into her memory. Dad opening the door. A man—a stranger—in the living room. Another behind the door grabbed Laura, put a knife to her throat. For the life of her she couldn't make out their faces. The harder she tried the more blurry they became, as if a fog had rolled in.

The man in the living room grabbed her and told everyone to keep quiet . . .

—*"Shut your fucking mouths or we'll cut their throats."*

. . . and sit on the sofa. The other man made Dad sit in the easy chair that faced the sofa, and began questioning him.

"Where does the bitch keep her fucking jewelry; the *good* stuff?"

She saw Dad telling him they didn't have any expensive jewelry, just his wife's engagement and wedding ring. The man—angry now—hit Dad in the face.

"Wrong answer, shithead. Gimme your wallet."

The man rifled through the contents, took out some bills and flung the wallet across the room.

"Forty-two fucking dollars! Now don't tell me that's all you keep in the house. You don't want to make me angry. Where's the safe?"

"There is no safe," her father said, slurring his words, as blood streamed down his chin.

The man hit her father again.

"Wrong again, asshole. People like you always got safes. Give it up, man. You don't want us fucking with your wife or daughters, do you, now?"

The images came faster, almost in a blur. Lysette didn't like this game of reliving that night like a full-length movie. She willed everything to move faster. She wanted to close her eyes, but she had to see *everything* . . . over and over.

One of the men hitting her mother while the other yelled at her father.

The man ripping her mother's blouse off, pushing her down on the couch on top of both her and Laura, pulling something out of his pants . . .

13

—"*His penis, stupid*," Laura would have admonished, but now she was crying.

. . . and sticking it into her mother.

They were having sex, she thought to herself. Why were they having sex?

—"*Fucking*," Laura would have corrected her, just like on some of the movies on HBO she wasn't supposed to watch. When she'd question Laura, her older sister explained patiently about *making love*. Lately, though, she'd tired of the endless questions and told Lysette to close her eyes. "They're fucking now. You're too young to see." Lysette ignored her, of course.

The man with her father yelling at him so loud, she wondered why the neighbors didn't hear.

"Do it man. Finish her off. Show this asshole we're not fucking around."

Lysette, frozen with fear, saw the other man holding her mother. Yanking her head back. Drawing a knife across her neck. Blood, like a blanket unfolding, covering her mother's chest.

Laura screaming. Trying to run. The man who cut her mother grabbing her hair from the back. He held the knife in front of her face. Laura bit him and the knife slipped from his grasp. Cursing, he picked up a lighter made of marble . . .

—The one Laura dropped on the glass table when she'd decided to smoke her first cigarette; the glass cracking, looking like a jigsaw puzzle.

. . . and hit her on the head three, four, five times until Laura stopped screaming. Stopped crying. *Stopped moving*.

"Last chance, asshole. Where's the safe?" the other yelled at her father.

Her father mumbled something Lysette couldn't make out, but saw it angered the man.

"Do the other bitch," he yelled to his friend. "Let this shit see them all die."

Lysette was huddled against her mother, her mother's blood covering the right side of Lysette's face and dripping into her eye so she had trouble seeing. The man with the marble lighter . . .

—*Red eyes*. He had red eyes. Or was it the blood in *her* eyes distorting everything?

. . . grabbed her by her sweater and swung the hand with the lighter at her head, hitting her just above her eye.

Woozy. She felt woozy. And nauseous, like she was going to throw up.

Saw him lift his hand in what seemed like slow motion to hit her again. Instinctively, she moved slightly to the left and his hand came crashing down on her temple.

Mama who had been still . . .

—*Dead*.

. . . all of a sudden was crawling to cover her.

"What the fuck?" she heard the man say, then saw him hit her mother with the lighter. Again and again. Then the lights seemed to go out and everything was quiet.

When Lysette opened her eyes the men were gone. She saw her father sitting in the chair, his throat slit like her mother's; his white Phillies shirt crimson. The gash in his neck smiled at her.

"Are you happy, Lysette?" she thought the new mouth said. "Didn't we have fun, tonight?"

"Are you happy."

"Are you happy . . . "

"happy . . . happy . . . happy . . . "

It was then she crawled into the attic of her mind. Anything to get away from that voice.

Back in the hospital, Lysette heard Dr. Paul. He came by every day after Heather left. Sometimes alone; usually with other doctors . . .

—*Residents*, Dr. Paul had said once.

"How's our patient, today?" Dr. Paul asked LaToya, as he felt her wrist, then shined a light in each of her eyes.

"Same-o. Same-o. Will she ever come out of it, Dr. Paul?"

Today he was alone. He and LaToya talked as if she weren't there.

—*A fly on the wall*.

"As a neurologist, LaToya, yes, she should. Her head looks like a cracked egg, but it's superficial damage. She'll have scars, but there appears to be no serious brain damage. Won't know for sure, though, until she wakes up. She's still in shock. She's got to want to wake up. And that's easier said than done."

—*Don't want to wake up*, Lysette wanted to shout.

"I'll be praying for her, Dr. Paul," LaToya said.

"You do that," he answered. His voice sounded far away. He must be leaving the room, Lysette thought.

15

Still later another man entered.

"Morning, officer," LaToya said. She sounded a bit fearful, Lysette thought. It must be the policeman who stopped by each day. LaToya didn't like the police. She told Heather and Sara, the afternoon nurse, they made her feel like she had something to hide. She'd become angry, though, when the man asked if Lysette was faking.

"Now why would she be faking? You think she up and killed her parents and sister, then hit herself upside the head? You want her to wake up so you can arrest her? She'll wake when she's good and ready. Leastways, that's what Dr. Paul says. Then you can arrest her."

"No one's going to arrest the child. We *would* like to question her. Get a description, you know, of her attackers."

"You leave this child alone and go do your job. When she wakes up, last thing she needs is a policeman barking questions at her. . . . "

Lysette was bored. Every day it was the same with these two. Every day it was the same with *everything*. She could wake up. *Should* wake up. But she didn't want to answer his questions. Didn't want to tell him she couldn't describe the men who attacked her family. He'd think she was a baby. Anyway, when she thought about waking up she'd hear another voice in her mind.

—Don't leave me, Lysette. Come and find me and we can play.

She thought it must be Laura, and she couldn't leave Laura. But try as she might, she couldn't find the voice in the attic they shared. She'd looked all over, but the voice never stayed in the same place long enough for Lysette to locate it. It was just like Laura to play the tease.

Finally, after a few weeks, Laura, or whoever it was, left. Lysette heard the attic door open and close. She was alone, and soon the movie would begin again. She didn't want to see it alone. Didn't want to see it *at all*.

So four weeks after the attack she left the attic and rejoined the world.

Chapter One

The subway car smelled of urine, feces . . . and death . . .

—*Just like the night your family died*, a long-dormant voice spoke to Lysette, in her mind.

. . . as she tried to capture its rhythm, as it swayed to and fro. It was like finding the groove to the music she danced to at work. Let it inside you, become one with it, and *you* controlled it.

Lysette was anxious to read the paper she had found beside her when she'd transferred from the trolley at 69th Street, but not until she flowed to the rhythm of the subway.

She normally drove to the Genesis Club in Media, a suburb of Philadelphia. A thirty-minute drive. Less at night, going home. But, like clockwork, six months after replacing them, her brakes were shot. Her '86 Dodge Charger was often more hassle than it was worth, but it had two redeeming features that made it priceless. Its age and assorted dents and scratches made it as theftproof as if it had an expensive alarm system; no small feat in a city where you were in the minority if your car *hadn't*, at one time or another, been stolen or broken into. And it drove like a tank in the winter. While others skidded and wheels spun, going nowhere in ice and snow, Lysette's little engine that could moved effortlessly.

Today, though, it was public transportation. She had gotten a ride to the club, but after four hours, her boss had sent her home at ten PM.

She'd been a wreck, her mind on Rose Santucci, her body totally out of sync with the music. Negative vibes emanated from her, and she knew her customers felt them. Her dance routine was sloppy, and even regulars for whom she would Table Dance shied away from her.

"Lys, they can tell you're distracted," Jil had told her. "You

17

should be home grieving. Take the rest of the night off; tomorrow, too, if you need to. I want you here, but like I want you *here*, if you catch my drift."

"Are you sure?" she had protested, though not too vigorously.

"Call it a business decision," Jil had said, not unkindly. "Tonight you're no good for business."

If she'd waited for the end of her shift, she would have had a ride home. Or she *could* have splurged and taken a cab. But she'd made squat in tips as it was, and wasn't about to throw it away on a blood-sucking taxi.

Leaving the club, she regretted her decision immediately; a mid-September wind penetrated her coat, as if it were crepe paper, as she first walked the four blocks to the trolley stop, then waited fifteen minutes for the trolley. She had changed at 69th Street, and would have to do so again at Broad Street, but at least she would have time to think about her neighbor; come to grips with her sudden death.

—63rd Street stop

The story took up the top half of page three of the *Daily News*.

One Sister Killed, Another Injured
Trying to Stop Carjacker

One sister was killed, another seriously injured when, while loading groceries in their car, a carjacker sped off from a South Philadelphia shopping center with their 1993 Oldsmobile Cutlass last evening.

The incident occurred between 9:00 and 9:30 PM as Rose Santucci, 72, and Mary Cirillo, 64, were leaving the Acme Supermarket at Snyder Plaza. As Cirillo tried to get the keys from the suspect—described as an African-American, 5 feet 10 inches, slim, between 18 and 22 years of age—Santucci ran around to the back of the car. The suspect threw the car in reverse, knocking Santucci to the ground, dragging the victim 30 feet beneath the automobile. The woman was released when the man shifted the car and drove off.

Santucci, mother of seven, with sixteen grandchildren, was pronounced dead at the scene. Cirillo was listed in serious condition with a broken hip, dislocated shoulder and numerous cuts and abrasions. . . .

—60th Street stop.

Lysette read the cold, bare facts and once again tears welled in her eyes. While she knew both women, Rose Santucci lived directly across the street from her, and Lysette had known her all her life. The two sisters had owned a bakery, and as a young child Lysette would sit on her stoop waiting for Rose to come home.

A heavyset woman, obviously fond of pasta and the pastries she sold, she was nevertheless light on her feet. Lysette could never remember seeing her without a smile. Even when attempting to act stern, her eyes betrayed her. While her life hadn't always been easy, it had been generally good to Rose Santucci.

"You been a good girl today, my little Lysette?" she'd ask.

"Yes, ma'am."

"Finish your homework?"

"Yes, ma'am."

"Help your mama with the housework?"

"Yes, ma'am."

"I wouldn't want to spoil your dinner . . . ," she'd begin, a smile playing across her face.

"We've already eaten. But I didn't have dessert," Lysette would interrupt excitedly.

"In that case, I guess a cannoli wouldn't hurt," and she'd produce two out of the huge shopping bag she held. "One for my little Lysette, and one for your sister. See that she gets it now."

"Yes ma'am. Thank you, Miss Rose."

—56th Street stop.

When Lysette's family had been killed, she spent as much time with "Gramma Rose" as with her real grandparents, who had taken her in. She would help at the bakery after school, rewarded with spending money and all the pastries she could eat.

And while Rose wasn't thrilled by her dancing, she had accepted Lysette's "career" choice, just as she had those of her own children.

"If it makes you happy, I'm happy."

She had become even more of a mother hen when Lysette moved back into her parents' house across the street. While the bakery was now run by one of her daughters, Rose always had some pastries for Lysette.

"You're all skin and bones, child. All skin and bones," she'd say, shaking her head in worry. "Gotta take better care of yourself."

"All skin and bones, my foot," Lysette would reply, sticking out her more than ample chest for Rose to see.

"Tits and ass, that's all you ever think about. Tits and ass. That's all the men you dance for look at. The *rest* of you is all skin and bones," she would say stubbornly.

Lysette knew better than to argue with the woman. She could weigh two hundred pounds, and it wouldn't be enough for Gramma Rose.

Over the past three years Rose had finagled a key from Lysette . . .

—52nd Street stop.

. . . and Lysette was never wanting for a hot breakfast, lunch or dinner, depending on her schedule. She would wake to wonderful smells, eat every morsel with Rose keeping a watchful eye on her, and find all the pans and dishes washed and in their allotted cupboard before she was off to work.

And now she was dead; some crackhead, no doubt, had stolen and sold what he could for his next fix. Their neighborhood, which had been insulated from the crime that plagued the city, had been defiled and would never be the same.

When Lysette had gotten home at two-thirty the morning before, the entire neighborhood was still awake, shaken and grieving. Lysette had been shattered by the news, and for a moment thought she might retreat into the attic of her mind that had protected her as a child. . . .

—A fly on the wall.

She listened listlessly at the venom spewed forth by others.

"Damn niggers. Aren't there enough of their own they can feed off of?"

"Catch him? And what if they do? Fucking DA will cut a deal. He'll be out of jail before Rose is cold in the ground."

"Used to be you didn't have to lock the doors. Now, I keep a gun next to my bed—and I damned well know how to use it."

On and on they'd ranted until bitterness gave way to exhaustion—even resignation—and they returned home. They had talked of a march or candlelight vigil to City Hall demanding more of a police presence. Lysette said nothing to dissuade them, but felt it would be fruitless. Promises would be made, then broken when their anger subsided. Rose Santucci would end up as just another statistic, until crime touched their neighborhood yet again. Soon they'd forget about Rose.

—Just as they had forgotten about her family.

Yes, it was a terrible thing, but life would go on.

—46th Street stop.

The story below caught Lysette's eye, as well, and further fueled her anger. At a local high school, one girl had stabbed another to death several months earlier. At her trial the defense was attempting to make the *killer* the victim.

—No father
—Mother hooked on drugs
—Molested by one of mother's boyfriends
—Brothers involved in gang activity
—Truancy leading to poor grades leading to further truancy and low self esteem.

A description of the "code of the streets" had followed. This child had adapted to the failure of society and her family to meet *her* needs, a local college professor had testified on the stand.

—40th Street stop.

She'd been "dissed"—put down by another girl—and if she didn't respond she would lose respect, the professor explained. So, she brought a knife to school and showed all her friends who was boss, who was big and bad. And with the victim—no saint herself—her life bleeding away at her feet, she showed no sign of remorse. She gloated, "No one gonna mess with this girl and live to tell about it," then walked back to class until the police came.

The defense, with its expert witnesses, patiently explained the cycle of poverty . . .

—34th Street stop.

. . . asking society to blame itself, not this "other victim" of abuse and neglect.

Hell, Lysette thought, even if she were found guilty, the seeds had been planted for a lenient sentence. What's the world coming to, she wondered, when you can wantonly kill and be considered the *victim*?

—30th Street Station.

All but six passengers got off here, and a black youth with an attitude got on. He didn't walk; he strutted. Dark-skinned, hair cropped close, eyes glazed like he was on drugs, rail-thin and short, he looked no older than sixteen.

He looked at each of the other passengers, his gaze daring one of them to challenge his authority. All but an old man, sitting across from Lysette, averted their faces. The old man, his face buried in a wiry beard of Brillo, shook his head and chuckled to himself.

21

"You got a problem, shithead?" the boy asked, sauntering over to the man.

"Don't want no trouble, son," he answered with quiet dignity.

"What was you looking at, then?"

"Didn't mean no harm, boy," he said, weary, as if this were not the first such confrontation he'd had.

"Who are you calling *boy*, old man?" he asked, drawing the last words out slowly and derisively. Without waiting for an answer, he took out a gun and looked around to see if anyone dared to intervene. A smile played at his lips as he saw the other black passengers sink deeper into their seats.

He totally ignored Lysette directly behind him.

"This *boy* got a piece, old man. Maybe you wanna give this *boy* your wallet—right, *old man*?"

"Son, I didn't mean—"

"Your wallet, old man. This *boy* wants your wallet and none of your lip."

Resigned, the old man gave the youth his wallet.

The boy took out a few wrinkled bills and flung the wallet halfway across the car. "Six dollars. Sheeeet," he said drawing the expletive out, "I know you got more than that. Give it up, now!"

The old man slowly pulled each of his pockets inside out, to show he had nothing more, then shrugged.

"I travel light, son. What you got is all I've got."

Infuriated, the boy swung the gun, hitting the man across his face.

Lysette, watching, no longer saw a boy with a gun, but a man with a marble lighter swinging it at her sister.

"You old fart, think you can fuck with me," the boy said and swung his gun at the man again.

—swung the lighter at Laura.

Without thinking, Lysette was on her feet, and as the boy raised the gun a third time, she grabbed it.

The boy turned on her, a look of bewilderment momentarily making him look terribly vulnerable.

"What the fuck you want to do that for? Give me back my piece, bitch." His voice was now high-pitched.

—An angry child throwing a tantrum, Lysette thought, and hardly threatening.

She shook her head no, not wanting her voice to betray the fear that now overcame her.

—What the fuck have you gotten yourself into? a part of her questioned. More to the point, how was she going to get out of it in one piece?

The old man moaned softly, ribbons of blood dripping down his forehead and cheek, and fixed her with a thoughtful stare.

—Don't back down; show strength, she could almost hear him cautioning. *You've humiliated him. He'll kill you if you give him the chance.*

The boy seemed to regain his swagger. "Last chance, bitch," he said, pulling a closed knife from his pocket, pressing a button to expose a blade. He was smiling, now. Totally in control. "Be a good little cunt, and hand over my piece. I'll finish my business and we'll forget you lost your fucking mind."

"You're not going to hurt anyone. I'm warning you, I know how to use this," she heard herself say to her amazement.

—To the man who'd hurt Laura.

—To the punk who dragged Rose to her death.

She did, too, having learned after she had recovered from her wounds. Therapy hadn't chased away the nightmares or fears that the men would return. Her grandfather had taken her to a shooting range and taught her how to use a gun. Slowly the dreams had receded.

"Then I'll just have to cut you, bitch," the boy responded coldly. His eyes, though, were ablaze, his nose running. Crack and wounded pride . . .

—She'd dissed him and the code of the street wouldn't allow him to back down. Lysette could almost hear an expert for the defense describe her death at his trial.

. . . propelled him, as he advanced on her, swinging the knife in a slow arc, hypnotizing her.

Lysette looked around quickly, willing someone to come to her aid, but the others sat transfixed.

—Like they were watching a goddamn movie.

She heard their voices, though; inner voices goading her on.

—"Do it."

—"Shoot him."

—"Kill the fucker."

He lunged, and she fired instinctively, aiming for his head and hitting the mark.

—The man hitting Laura dropped the lighter and fell.

—The man dragging Rose slumped down and the car stopped.

23

The youth in front of her toppled backwards like an old oak hit by lightning, hit the floor of the car and was motionless.

"Holy shit, she did it."—a voice behind her.

Lysette stood motionless.

—Yeah, I did it, she thought.

"Saved that there man's life, she did." Another voice.

—Guess I did that, too, Lysette thought.

Movement behind her, then someone feeling for the boy's pulse. "He's dead." A hint of surprise at the words.

This time Lysette *did* speak. "This isn't the movies. In real life you aim to kill or end up being killed."

"Damned straight," another voice said from behind.

Lysette bent down to the old man. "How are you doing?"

"Not bad, thanks to you. Not bad at all."

"Let me wipe some of the blood off," Lysette said.

"No! Not you. No time." The train was slowing down—Broad Street. "If you don't leave now, you'll have to answer to the police, reporters and what all. No matter how we tell it, they'll make it racial. White woman shoots black boy. If I were you, I'd stay out of the glare. Let us do the talking for you. Tell them what happened. You saved my life. Maybe theirs, too," he said looking at the other passengers. "Let us protect you."

Lysette didn't know what to do. Run? Why? It was clearly self-defense. But the old man was right. When it came to a white shooting a black—a black *boy*, no less—she'd have to prove *her* innocence. There were too many axes to grind and hidden agendas within the black community to accept the truth at face value. The old man was right; no need to endure the agony of proving her innocence.

She looked at the old man one more time; another passenger was wiping the blood off his face with a handkerchief. She needed confirmation; his blessing.

"Are you sure?"

The subway came to a stop. The doors opened.

He shook his head. "Go, girl. We'll pull the emergency brake at the next station."

—*Go*, Laura said.

—*Yes. Now!* It was Rose.

She fled.

Behind, she heard the man. "Don't run, now. Just draw attention. And do something with that gun."

Lysette had been unaware she still held the gun as she left the subway car. She considered throwing it in the trash.

—*Keep it*, Rose told her.

She slipped it into the pocket of her coat. She was in no frame of mind to make decisions. She'd think what to do when she got home.

Chapter Two

Just north of Allentown, in a small town that barely warranted a dot on a map, Shara Farris awoke with a start; the sound of a bullet reverberating in her head. Her body was drenched with sweat; her hands clenched into fists. Someone had been shot . . .

—*Killed*

 . . . not here. Back in Philly, she knew someone had been shot . . . shot dead.

She slipped on a robe, went outside and sat on the steps leading to her front door. She marvelled at the display of fireworks in the sky; stars so bright she could reach out and touch them. In Philly there were no stars; none at least she had ever noticed. A curtain of smog hid the beauty of the night sky in the city she'd left just over a year before.

She should be happy, she knew. Her personal demons—the brother she had killed—no longer tormented her dreams. She slept, *really* slept for the first time in a year and a half. She was a deputy in the local police department, no longer tied to a desk and computer.

Yet she was just as much a prisoner as if she had been locked in jail. She was just living a new lie in a new town. She seldom dated; never more than once or twice with the same man. She had too much to hide and had told so many lies, she feared she would betray herself if she ever opened up to anyone here.

She had no interest in sex; there were still too many memories to overcome. Someday, maybe, but not yet. She dated mainly for appearances. Though she'd rather be alone, a life of solitude would arouse suspicions, and she just wanted to blend in. Trying to blend in, though, added to her sense of being a prisoner. She couldn't just be herself. There were things she just had to do—for appearances.

26

While not tied behind a desk, her job held no real challenge. Traffic tickets, rowdy teenagers, the odd fight at the pub Friday or Saturday night. She had been a predator on the prowl for a year and a half before coming here and there was an inner urge to hunt again. Not kill. But the chase. It had been the most exhilarating period of her life, and only now did she acknowledge its allure. And she was good at it; something that had only recently dawned on her. She had chased six men—no, six *animals*—to the ground *and* eluded the police.

—But not Deidre.

Face it, she told herself, you're bored. You're not a country girl. The quiet—interrupted only by the incessant chirping of insects— left her uneasy. For twenty-three years she had been a city dweller. In her case you couldn't take the city out of the girl. She didn't want to take the city out of the girl.

In many ways this quiet town had healed her over the past year, and she would be eternally grateful. But she couldn't make a life here. She could never marry or have a meaningful relationship. There was too much she would have to hide, and she'd have to be constantly vigilant lest she let something of her past slip. She just couldn't see growing old here. And in such a small town, sooner or later if she didn't get serious about someone, marry, settle down and produce a brood of rug rats, there would be talk; then suspicions. She'd stick out like a sore thumb.

She needed the city with its foul smells, the hustle, bustle and jostle of people moving to get somewhere; the potential for danger that lurked around every corner; and its anonymity. She longed for a Philly cheese steak, soft pretzels and *real* pizza dripping with oil; not the pale imitation they served at Pizza Hut several miles outside of town.

And what of the debt she owed? One that constantly preyed on her mind. She had strung Deidre along, convinced her to hide what she knew, which had cost Deidre her job. Deidre was back with the newspaper; no longer the Mayor's press liaison.

—*Because of her.*

Used and abused her, then threw her to the dogs. Why did she care?

—*Because she was your friend*, her mind answered. You don't shit on your friends, if you really care for them.

Shara stood and sighed. She was stuck here; in this prison of boredom. There were too many demons in Philly for her to return. And Deidre. How could she ever repay her for the years of duplicity?

She went back inside, the gunshot she had heard forgotten. She had to get some sleep. There was . . . nothing for her to do tomorrow.

Chapter Three

Deidre Caffrey tossed uneasily in the throes of another nightmare; actually the same nightmare she'd had off and on since she had allowed Shara to escape.

In the nightmare she was looking down at a man; his mouth was taped shut, his unseeing eyes blinded with acid. Only it wasn't Shara's brother, Bobby Chattaway. It was Jonas, Deidre's father-in-law; Shara's *next* victim.

Looking at Jonas, a scream pierced the night. She thought it was her, but as it continued intermittently, she realized it was the phone and fumbled for the receiver.

"Dee, sorry to bother you, but I need a favor."

It was John Ralston, who manned the overnight desk at the *Daily News*. A fellow reporter whose family she'd had over numerous times for barbecues . . .

—Before *her* family was taken from her.

He'd recently been promoted. She knew he sorely missed the action of catching a story, but with a growing family, excitement played second fiddle to a larger paycheck.

" . . . a fire in the Northeast, an overturned eighteen-wheeler on I-95 with chickens fleeing for their lives . . . "

She had missed part of what he was saying, but knew where the conversation was leading.

"John," she interrupted, "you know I don't—"

"And a shooting on the subway at the 13th and Juniper Street station," he hurried on, interrupting her before she could reject him. "A kid's been shot. Killed. Look, I'm strapped, you're close and with a kid involved, I thought . . . " He let the thought hang.

"You're good, John," she answered after a moment of thought. "Hook me with the kid; a possible victim." Another pa

29

the fuck? I won't be able to fall asleep anyway. You owe me big time, and you can bet your ass I'll collect." She hung up on him, happy to have gotten in the last word . . .

—Like Shara.

. . . and began to throw on some clothes.

A lot had changed in the last year.

—Since Shara had left.

She had changed a lot in the last year, after Shara had gotten the best of her.

She had quit as the Mayor's press liaison and convinced Ralston's boss, Ted Mahoney, to take her back at the *Daily News* . . . on her terms. She would do "occasional" special investigative reports, though she had agreed to be available in a pinch if he didn't abuse the offer. Her stories would deal with victims, much as they had *before* she left the paper . . .

—When her husband and son had died.

. . . but with a different slant. What had become of victims who survived as they entered adulthood?

Kids at a school where an honor student who had flunked his first test had burst into class, shot his teacher in the head, then stuck the gun in his mouth and taken his own life.

Kids in Florida, uprooted by a killer hurricane, their small town literally wiped off the map.

A busload of students abducted—a number of them viciously raped—before a police sharpshooter had shot the kidnapper.

She had covered these and many other stories when they had first broken, but Shara had opened her eyes to a bigger story. She had reported on how these children and adolescents had suffered and coped; had given life to faceless names. It had been her forte: champion of the victim.

But what if the victims turned into victimizers years later, as Shara had? Her stories had been incomplete; like a short story, an isolated moment in time. Life went on, but until her confrontation with Shara she had just been caught up in the moment. Now she wanted to know what had become of the victims.

Some were relatively unscathed. Others had turned to booze or drugs; some recovering—two steps forward, one step back. Too ⸺ ⸺ere dead, incarcerated, homeless or had just dropped off ⸺ earth. Some—again, too many—had married, but ⸺tain a successful relationship. They had become abusive, or had affairs, or were just too into themselves and were now divorced.

Deidre had written about those, but there had been others—like Shara—who had been so emotionally crippled they had crossed over from victim to victimizer.

Joseph had joined a cult, become disillusioned and become a de-programmer—exit counsellor, in P.C. terms, she'd been corrected. He had "kidnapped" a young woman at the urging of her parents, but unknown to them his therapy consisted, in part, of repeated rapes. Deidre had documented the abuse, told the families who had gone to the police. Joseph was put away for a good long time.

—As Shara should have been, a voice chastised.

Her reports had led to two others who were now behind bars solely because she had dug for the truth; the means justifying the ends. Illegal wiretaps, unauthorized searches, even physical intimidation. She used her many contacts to do whatever was necessary, when her suspicions were confirmed but evidence was lacking. Unlike the police, she didn't have to operate under their constraints of probable cause—as long as she wasn't caught.

New victims were being spawned daily by some of those who had been victimized, and she had no compunction at all against turning them in. At the paper she had been playfully dubbed a bounty hunter. It was closer to the truth than they knew. Though she wasn't in it for the money or publicity, she had become a hunter; a predator . . .

—Like Shara.

. . . and though she was saddened by what she exposed, the stories needed to be told, and punishment meted out by the courts, regardless of the circumstances that led them to cross over that invisible line that separated the law-abiding from broken souls who no longer lived by society's rules.

Shara would have been proud, though Deidre was uncomfortable with the warm feeling the thought gave her.

Dressed, she picked up her keys she had left by the fishbowl—Leon, Too—a present from Shara. Shara had inadvertently killed her first goldfish; the original Leon. She had named the new fish Leon, Too as yet another reminder of how Shara had shaped her life.

—Where was she?

—What was she doing?

—Had she come to terms with her past?
—Had she killed again?
—Killed again?
—*KILLED AGAIN!*

That last question most gnawed at Deidre, as she walked out the door. She really didn't want to know the answer.

—*Yes you do*, an inner voice told her.

Chapter Four

Lamar Briggs surveyed the organized chaos of the crime scene before him. Forensics bagging every scrap of evidence in the subway car; uniforms interviewing witnesses; the ME examining the body; a police photographer patiently awaiting further instructions. He had taken pictures of the body from every conceivable angle, but knew with Briggs' arrival more might be necessary. Paramedics administered to the old man who had been pistol-whipped.

Briggs was no happy camper, for any variety of reasons. It was twelve-fifteen in the morning, and by all rights he should have been in bed. This was his second day on the eight AM–four PM shift; his favorite. For two weeks he would feel like a regular working stiff. Then he would be back on the four PM–midnight shift; his body clock having to adjust to the change in routine.

Yet instead of snuggling under the covers next to his wife, he was at a homicide scene.

Because of politics.

Because he was black, as was the victim—a boy no less.

Because the alleged killer was white.

Because *someone* at the "highest of levels" had specifically asked for *him*.

He had gotten the call from his squad sergeant, Estefan Morales, at 11:45 PM, who like Briggs had also been at home.

"Briggs. Morales, here."

"What gives?"

"Shooting on the subway at 13th and Juniper. Black kid shot by a white woman breaking up a mugging."

"So? *I'm* off duty. Hell, *you're* off duty," Briggs said with mild irritation.

"Someone up the ladder asked for you. Someone who doesn't

33

know what you've been going through or someone who doesn't care."

—*What I've been going through*, Briggs thought to himself. He had to put the thought out of his mind, though he knew it would be with him no matter how hard he'd try to tuck it away.

"Why *me*?" He knew the answer, but needed confirmation.

"They want a strong black presence due to the racial overtones."

"Assholes," Briggs whispered, not realizing he uttered his thought aloud.

"My sentiments exactly," Morales answered, "but we don't make policy. Just follow orders . . . even from assholes."

Briggs laughed. "You'll be there." It wasn't a question.

"Just to secure the crime scene. I *won't* be looking over your shoulder, if that's what you're afraid of. Look, get the facts, give them to the lieutenant at the scene so he can brief the press, then swing by the office and we'll talk." He paused a moment. "Ask off the case, then, and I'll do whatever's in my power to accommodate."

"I appreciate it, Sarge. Who you teaming me up with?"

There was another pause. "Rios."

"You're shitting me," Briggs said.

"Rios. And that comes from me," answered Morales.

"Jesus. You're busting my balls on this one, Sarge. Give me a case that shouldn't be mine in the first place. Keep me from my family when I'm most needed. And now *Rios*!"

His anger was beginning to get the best of him. Again. It was all he could do to keep from hanging up on his superior and going back to sleep.

"Don't bust my chops, Lamar. You're not marrying her. In your condition you need someone like Rios, and Rios it is."

Briggs knew better than to argue. The detectives of his squad learned to gauge Morales' degree of anger early on. If he asked you to close the door when you entered his office, he was pissed. "Have a seat," and you were in hot water. An offer of jelly beans he kept on his desk meant he could hardly contain himself; not that he ranted or raved. But use of your first name meant you were in deep shit. Bitch about Nina Rios now could easily mean he would be teamed with her for good, and that was a truly frightening thought to Briggs. So he bit his tongue and followed orders.

An hour and a half later, watching the frenetic activity around the crime scene, he sighed, wishing he were in bed where he belonged. He spotted Morales talking to his lieutenant, and tried to stifle a smile. The man was no happier being here with the brass breathing down his neck than he was.

Estefan Morales was a tall, gaunt, brooding man in his mid-forties. Several inches shorter than Briggs, an even six feet, his wavy salt-and-pepper hair was in constant need of a trim. His clean-shaven, olive-complected face was pock-marked, the result of a nasty case of chicken pox or some other childhood disease that had ravaged him in his late teens. He didn't try to mask the craters with a beard, as some would. No, Estefan Morales didn't give a shit if you couldn't look at him straight in the eye. As far as he was concerned, that was *your* problem, not his.

Tonight he wore a suit—newly pressed—white shirt, and a charcoal tie. Briggs knew he was uncomfortable. Morales would begin the day in a shirt, tie and jacket. Within half an hour he'd lose the coat, then the tie and shortly thereafter looked like he'd slept in his clothes. He'd rather *feel* comfortable than look good. Tonight he was dressed to the nines and most definitely uncomfortable.

Briggs sighed again and approached the senior uniform on the scene, Carl Jenkins. He had worked with Jenkins before and knew the man to be capable and thorough. Jenkins ran down the basics.

"Three items of concern," he concluded. "Initially we thought the woman who shot the kid got off at this stop and fled. Now we find out she got off at Broad Street."

"How's that?"

"That has to do with the second problem. Our witnesses are none too cooperative. One inadvertently let it slip about Broad Street. *After* we'd cordoned off this area. We pressed the others and they grudgingly agreed. We've got officers at Broad Street now. The woman's long gone, though, but we're hoping she ditched the gun in a trash can there."

"How's that?"

"So these people all consider the woman some kind of a hero," Briggs said.

"From their accounts, she is. Probably saved the old man's life," he said, gesturing to the man being treated by a paramedic.

"And your third problem?"

"We've got six different descriptions of the woman."

Briggs laughed. "These yo-yos didn't lift a finger to help the old man when he was being beaten. So now they're trying to make amends protecting the woman who may have saved their asses. Real cute. How's the old man?"

"Looks like he'll be okay. Tougher than he looks. Paras tell me he may need some stitches, but he says he's not about to spend the night at the hospital."

"He got a name?"

"Isiah Hayes. Sixty-six. Retired. Worked at the Navy yard."

"All right. Give me a minute, and I think we can get you a better description of the elusive suspect."

Briggs beckoned to his "partner," who had been examining the body of the dead youth under the watchful supervision of the medical examiner.

"A moment of your time, Detective Rios," Briggs said.

The two hadn't spoken since arriving separately. Briggs was struck by the many similarities between the twenty-ish detective and Morales. He could have been her father, Briggs thought. Both were Puerto Rican. If anything, Rios was thinner than their sergeant, and she wore his brooding demeanor. Her shoulder-length wavy brown hair was long and tied in a ponytail. Unlike Morales, though, her skin was smooth and the color of a pitcher of iced tea sitting in the sun. She wore little makeup. She had a thin nose, and a mouth a bit too wide for her long angular face. Reasonably good-looking, Briggs thought, if a bit on the bony side, and would be better without her perpetual pout.

"Nina," he said loud enough so all could hear. "Officer Jenkins has a problem we were wondering if you could help us out with," Briggs said, not trying to conceal his irritation at having to work with her.

"What might that be, La-mar," she said, intentionally dragging out his first name, which only his wife and his sergeant—when he was pissed—dared use. "Does he want to know whether to wash his hands before or after he takes a piss?" She gave him her best "fuck you" smile, telling him to give her respect or she'd treat him in kind.

Briggs looked at her thoughtfully for a moment. She had spunk, he had to admit. He would have to watch his tongue if he didn't want an ugly scene; which, with Morales there, was the last thing he desired.

"Our witnesses are giving different descriptions of the woman who killed the boy," Briggs said, ignoring her sarcasm, but softening his tone. "Think we can help him?"

"My pleasure." She turned to the passengers, who had been separated from one another while they were questioned, but were looking at the two cops with interest.

"You folks just about ready to go home?" she asked, loud enough so all could hear.

They stirred, some nodding affirmatively, others mumbling the same sentiment. One man began to rise. A woman reached for her purse.

"Well, the only place you'll be going is down to the Roundhouse for further questioning."

"What the fuck," a dark-skinned man in his mid-thirties murmured. "We told you all we know. We got families to go home to. We got obligations. . . . "

"Yes," said the woman who had reached for her purse. "I'm a single mother. The baby sitter will be worried. . . . "

Rios held up her hand. "Maybe we can expedite matters. Like you help us and we'll help you; one hand washing the other."

"What you getting at?" asked the dark-skinned man, who seemed to have become their spokesman.

Rios asked for Jenkins' pad and scanned the varying descriptions, then turned her attention back to the passengers. "We've got six of you who each saw a different person shoot that boy," she said, pointing to the youth covered with a black plastic bag. "Blonde hair, brown hair, black hair; long hair and short hair. Twenty-five years old, forty years of age, in her mid-thirties; tall, short, fat, thin. Need I go on?"

She paused a moment as it sank in that they had been caught with their pants down.

"All we want is to question the woman. I know you want to protect her, but there's no need. All your stories of the incident jibe. This woman's got *cojones*—balls—you wish you had. Your choice is simple. We're going to ask for a description of the woman. You can give it here, then be on your way home, or you can take a trip to the Roundhouse and be our guests until sunup. Understand?"

There was nodding of heads and general mumbling they did.

"Good. Now, these officers will question you again. We'll compare notes, and if you cooperate, we'll inconvenience you as little as possible."

She turned to Briggs, gave him a mock curtsy and then whispered to Jenkins, "Make sure to ask if she smoked. There are four butts under the seat she was sitting in. And see if anyone noticed if she was reading the newspaper we found." Then turning to Briggs she said, "Anything else, sir?" and snapped him a salute.

"Yeah, you can kiss my black ass," he said just loud enough for her to hear, but the hostility was gone.

"Lower your pants, bend down and I'll do just that." She tried to sound gruff, but couldn't stifle a smile. Then, to cover her embarrassment, "Forensics told me as soon as they dust the kid's wallet for prints, I can take a look. I'd like to hang a name on him. That is unless you have something else you want me to do. . . . "

"Just do your job, Rios. You don't need me babysitting you."

"Well, I do declare," she said in a high-pitched voice. "Almost a compliment," and she was gone.

Briggs shook his head knowing Jenkins was watching him. "Women," he said, exasperated, but didn't finish the thought. He paused and looked around. "I'm going to talk to Mr. Hayes for a moment. Let me know when you've got your description."

Isiah Hayes had been lying on the hard plastic seats of the subway car while a paramedic bandaged him up. He was swatting them away now, trying to sit up when Briggs approached.

Briggs identified himself. "How ya doing, Mr. Hayes?"

"Just wonderful," he said sarcastically. "If I don't get pistol-whipped at least once a month, I feel neglected." He glowered at Briggs.

Briggs knelt down so they were face-to-face. "Don't have much use for the police, do you, Mr. Hayes?"

"Truth be told, you can't find a cop when you need one. Been burglarized, mugged, had a car stolen and not *once* did the police do more than pay lip service, officer."

"Doesn't look like your fellow passengers were much help, either."

The old man smiled. "That be true, too. A white woman the only reason you ain't scraping me off the floor. Ain't that a bitch." His eyes clouded over for a second, and he put a hand on Briggs' shoulder to steady himself. "Feeling a bit woozy. Best let them take me to the hospital to stitch me up."

Briggs handed the man his card. "When you're feeling up to it, give me a call, and I'll have someone drive you to my office. We got some talking to do."

Briggs had the feeling the old man had snookered him. Briggs hadn't had the chance to ask for a description of the woman. *Feel-*

ing a bit woozy, my ass, Briggs thought, as he saw the old man walk under his own power out of the car with the paramedics.

Jenkins approached at that moment. "We've got a description of the woman, not that it will be of much help."

"Why's that?"

"Average height. Twenty-two to twenty-eight. Blonde, shoulder-length hair. Wore a black leather coat that obscured her figure, but . . . "

"Wasn't too fat, wasn't too thin," Briggs finished for him.

"Your average white woman," Jenkins concluded. "To them all white people look the same, uh . . . if you know what I mean."

"Your being white, if you were here you could have provided a better description?" Briggs shot back.

"I didn't mean any offense, sir," Jenkins backtracked.

"Try this. These people were scared shitless. When a punk comes into a subway car waving a gun you *don't* want to be a witness. You avert your eyes. The confrontation between the woman and the boy was bang, bang," Briggs said snapping his fingers. "If anybody got a good look at the girl, it was the old man, and he's just about out on his feet. Does that make any sense to you, Jenkins?" Briggs said, his anger mounting—as usual lately, for no good reason.

His voice had been rising, and some of the passengers and uniforms were staring at him. Even if Jenkins deserved a dressing down, his comments didn't warrant public humiliation. Before Jenkins could answer, Briggs tried to defuse the situation.

"Let's wrap this up. See that the passengers are driven home. Tell them we'll want full statements tomorrow."

Flushed, Jenkins began to move to carry out his orders. Briggs grabbed his arm before he could pass.

"Look, I didn't mean to get on your ass. Leastwise, not in your face in front of everyone. That's as close to an apology as you're going to get. We square?"

The other man's anger seemed to dissipate, and he shrugged. "No problem. Been a bitch of a night for all of us."

Briggs went over to Morales and filled him in. "You can tell the lieutenant he doesn't have to worry about racial implications. The passengers did all they could to protect the woman. She saved an old man—a *black* man—from a doped-up punk. The kid lost face and would have killed her. Self-defense."

"Then why did she flee?"

"Panicked, I imagine. Lay out the facts to the media and she'll probably give herself up by noon."

Morales scrutinized him, but said nothing of the blowup he'd had with Jenkins.

"You and Rios write up a full report. Details, no matter how insignificant. Basically make sure you cover your asses with this one. It's going to be scrutinized, possibly by the commissioner himself. It may not be racial, but you can be damn sure *someone* won't see it that way; won't want to see it that way. We'll talk soon as I can get away from here."

Chapter Five

Deidre caught up with Briggs before he got to the subway steps. She knew he had seen her and had quickened his pace.

"Trying to avoid me, Briggs?" she yelled before he could make good his escape.

He turned and she saw him attempt to show surprise. He was a lousy actor, she thought.

"Sorry, Dee, didn't see you . . . "

"Bullshit."

"What're you doing here anyway?" he asked. "This isn't your kind of story."

"A favor for a friend."

"Well don't try to pump me for information. No scoop for you on this one." He turned to leave, then turned back to her. "Look, don't sensationalize this. And don't go feeling sorry for the little shit who got offed." Again he turned to leave.

"How's your daughter doing?"

Briggs looked at Deidre hard, then his features began to soften. He seemed to see Deidre was sincere, not just making small talk to keep him from leaving.

"Not too good, Dee. Not too good." His voice trailed off. Then almost as an afterthought or maybe an apology for his earlier hostility, Deidre thought, he added, "Thanks for asking."

As they left, she saw Briggs' partner taking her measure; wondering how their paths had crossed.

There was movement behind her; the hustle and bustle of activity. A police spokesman had a statement to make and questions to answer. The media jostled for position. More than ever she was glad she was seldom part of this circus. They were like cattle, liter-

41

Barry Hoffman

ally stepping on one another's toes and elbowing for position. At home, she would sit fascinated . . .

—*no, nauseated*, she corrected herself.

. . . in front of the television, watching a horde of reporters chasing a lawyer or witness or converging en masse, yelling questions, jockeying for position in some perverted effort to impress their editors. It was a rat race she had seldom taken part in. When she had to she hung back, knowing she'd get the same answers as the rest of her colleagues without making a fool of herself.

There was *always* someone else to interview—without others around—who would provide the same, often more valuable information.

Now she only half-listened to the prepared statement and elusive answers being provided. She had seen the confrontation between Briggs and Jenkins; knew Jenkins well enough to know she could get more from him. A beat cop his entire career, he resented the likes of Briggs who let the uniforms do the grunge work, then bitched about their incompetence. Add to that the fact he'd been publicly humiliated and Deidre knew he would be more than willing to spill all he knew; more than the official line, to embarrass Briggs and the other suits he despised.

Deidre's mind strayed to Briggs. Just over a year ago, she had finally gained his confidence while acting as the Mayor's press liaison on the Vigilante case, only to betray Briggs in the end; a betrayal he was fully aware of, even if he couldn't prove it.

She had followed his career ever since from afar, guilt gnawing at her initially for the price he had to pay for her protecting Shara. His career had been like a yo-yo of late. There was the Vigilante fiasco and his dismissal as head of the task force, followed by a slow rise to good graces again, and some high-profile successes.

With the attack on his thirteen-year-old daughter four months before, his star had begun to descend again. Like tonight, he was a loose cannon, ready to erupt without warning. Still, he was held in high regard by the department.

She could easily empathize with his churning emotions. When her husband and son had died in a senseless traffic accident, she had totally shut down. It had been only four months since Briggs' daughter, Alexis, had been brutally raped and beaten and she could imagine him heaping blame on himself.

Their paths had crossed only once since the attack. Two weeks earlier he'd been taking his daughter to Jefferson Hospital for therapy; she had been leaving after another depressing visit with her father-in-law, Jonas Caffrey, who'd suffered a massive stroke.

It had started off awkward as hell, she remembered. Briggs dwarfed his daughter, who shuffled along as if she had a cramp in one leg; her small hand nestled in his huge hand, her head down, seemingly unaware of all around her.

"Hi, Briggs," she'd said tentatively. Then, "This must be Alexis."

The girl continued to stare at the ground, her body swaying gently back and forth, as if to some inner rhythm.

"She can't hear you, Dee. Maybe she can," he corrected himself. "But she can't or won't respond. You can speak openly."

The girl seemed to realize they were talking about her. She lifted her head tentatively, seemed to stare past Deidre, then was back inspecting the ground. Deidre could feel tears well in her eyes. She had seen pictures of Alexis on Briggs' desk when they'd worked together. Even in the photo the girl seemed vibrant; so full of life. The child in front of her now was a hollow shell of the one in the photos. From the right side she was still strikingly beautiful; dark-skinned, though not as dark as her father, but her face was as baby smooth as Briggs' was coarse. From the left, though, Alexis reminded Deidre of a grossly deformed pumpkin that sat forlornly on the shelf as the others were chosen for Halloween. Her head had been bashed in. Surely she was disfigured for life.

"I'm so sorry," she said, groping for words that eluded her. "Have they found the . . . her attacker?"

"Not a clue. She had just left a friend's house; two blocks from home. A neighbor found her in an alley, completely naked, curled up in a fetal position."

He paused, as if deep within himself.

"She fought back, though," he continued with pride. "There was skin under her nails. Scratched him good. If we ever catch the fucker . . ."

He tensed, unaware he was squeezing his daughter's hand hard enough to hurt. Alexis looked at him, not in pain, but she must have sensed his torment, Deidre thought to herself.

He finally became aware, and loosened his grip.

"Is the therapy helping?" Deidre asked tentatively.

"Physically, except for her head, she's made a lot of progress. God, I wish she could tell me what happened. What kind of animal would hit a child in the head with a brick? Not once, but repeatedly. And nobody heard."

He looked up at the sky, as if cursing the gods.

"The doctors still don't know the extent of the damage," he continued. "There's been brain damage, no doubt about it, but they feel she's also still in shock. She hasn't said a word, hasn't shed a tear. She's like a rag doll. We sit her down and she stays. Take her by the hand and she'll walk. Put mashed potatoes on a spoon and she'll eat. I'd taken her for granted while she was growing up. Now that I've lost her . . . " He paused. "I want to make amends."

"You haven't lost her," Deidre said. "She needs you now more than ever before."

"And what good am I? I feel impotent, Dee. Here I am a big shot homicide detective, and I can't even protect my daughter. Can't catch the fucker who did this to her. It's a cancer eating at me. All I can do now is try to be there for her, even if she's unaware. Ironic, huh. Took this to make me a good father." He shook his head, then looked at his watch. "Gotta go. She'll be late for her therapy."

As he began to walk away, Deidre called after him. "Maybe we can do lunch or something, if you want. Catch up, you know. . . . "

Briggs turned and gave her a hard look. "Sure. I'll call." He gave her a weak smile, then began walking again.

Deidre wasn't about to hold her breath waiting. Briggs was so deep into himself, she thought, she wondered how he was able to function at work. As bad as she felt for him, she couldn't help being a bit peeved at his not asking *why* she was at the hospital. Lamar Briggs wasn't the only one with problems, she'd thought to herself.

The lieutenant had finished his prepared statement and was taking questions; being evasive as hell with his answers. A waste of time, Deidre thought, as her mind wandered to Briggs again.

She couldn't get over the physical change in the man. Always stocky, a year ago she would have been charitable to call him beefy. Portly?

—Fat was more like it.

The beginnings of a beer belly . . .

—A paunch that all but obscured his belt was more precise.

An ever-expanding rump . . .

—A fat ass; no ifs, ands or buts about it.

She conjured up Bill Cosby's Fat Albert character, and remembered the ever-present Milky Ways he'd polish off in two bites.

The Lamar Briggs she had seen tonight—even two weeks ago— was hardly the man he had been. *Literally.* He had lost thirty,

44

maybe forty pounds if he'd lost an ounce. He hadn't just lost weight, though. His body looked chiseled, as if he'd been working out. She searched her mind for a word to describe him, and it dawned on her. Formidable. He still shaved his head, which made him look even more menacing. He was definitely someone you wouldn't want to fuck with.

She wondered, though, just how formidable he was with his daughter constantly preying on his mind. He was clearly guilt-ridden . . .

—"I feel impotent."

. . . and he certainly didn't have control of his emotions. . . .

—" . . . a cancer eating away at me."

She hoped he was able to come to grips with his demons. She had come to like the man when they'd worked together; his gruff exterior merely a shell protecting a sincere, sensitive man who felt passionately about his job. He was one of the good cops, and it would be a shame if he self-destructed.

The impromptu press conference broke up, and as she suspected, she was soon able to corner Jenkins, who was all too willing to give her some juicy morsels that might embarrass Briggs. He told her to call him in an hour and he'd be able to tell her just how extensive a rap sheet the late Jerome Brown had.

Driving to the *Inquirer* building, which also housed the *Daily News*, Deidre's mind drifted to the woman who had fled after saving one life and taking another. The woman would probably come forward tomorrow . . .

—But what if she didn't?

. . . have her picture taken with the old man she had saved . . .

—But what if she had something to hide?

. . . do the talk show circuit . . .

—What if she disappeared?

. . . shake the Mayor's hand . . .

—Could Deidre track her down?

. . . as he applauded her heroics.

—Was there more to the story than met the eye at first glance?

Nah, she decided. Just write it up. This Good Samaritan story had little allure to her. She had bigger fish to fry.

Chapter Six

When Lysette got home just after one, she finally gave vent to her churning emotions: fear, exhilaration, astonishment, pride and terror.

She had left the station in a panic. She couldn't walk home; it was too far and she'd probably be mugged. . . .

—But you got a gun, fool, an inner voice reminded her.

—Right, shoot someone else and carve yourself another notch, she answered herself.

She couldn't take a cab, even if one happened by, which was unlikely. The object, she told herself, was not to stick out like a sore thumb. No, a cab was out of the question.

Then her answer arrived in the form of a bus. It wasn't the perfect solution, but given the lack of an alternative, it was by far the best. Just another passenger. She would get off four or five blocks from home, so even if someone did remember her later, she wouldn't lead them directly to her door.

Once on the bus she thought she would have an anxiety attack. Was everyone looking at her? Why were they looking at her? There was no reason they should be looking at her. Or was there? No, they weren't looking at her, she concluded. Or were they?

Halfway home, it finally dawned on her that it didn't matter. What a fool she'd been. As long as she averted her face they could look at her all they wished. *She was wearing a wig*, the wig she wore at the club. The flowing blonde hair that trailed past her shoulders hid short-cropped black hair. More than once, other dancers had commented they'd never know her on the street without the wig.

—The wig . . .

Part of a persona she had created for the club. She wasn't Lysette Ormandy from South Philadelphia, but Cassandra Knight from the Big Apple.

She had been at art school when she had auditioned at the club four years earlier, having just turned nineteen. Even with a loan she had taken out, she was financially strapped. A friend told her she'd more than meet ends by exotic dancing.

"You're a *stripper*!" Lysette had blurted out without thinking. "I'm sorry . . . it's just . . . a stripper? Dancing *naked* in front of a bunch of leering strangers jerking off under the table?"

"It's nothing like that," Vicki had responded. "Well, not exactly the way you put it," she laughed. "It's an upscale club. If they jerk off they do it discreetly," and they'd both laughed.

A week later, she was auditioning, not in front of the manager, but on stage in front of a bunch of leering strangers. Vicki had given her advice.

"I know it's easy to say, but don't let them intimidate you. All they really care about is your tits and pussy. Pick out one guy. That's what I do. I dance for the one guy, make sure I make eye contact with him a lot. I'm letting him know I want to Table Dance with him later—"

"Table Dance?" she'd interrupted.

"Don't worry about that now. If you get the job, they'll fill you in. The main thing is to pick out one dude and dance for him. Kinda like he's your boyfriend, and you're at home; just the two of you. Before you know it, you'll be through."

That first dance had been the worst. An O'Jays song, but she couldn't remember which one. She hadn't been able to get its rhythm, and felt awkward as hell; caressing one pole, then another, dropping her bra . . .

—Exposing her tits!

. . . then her g-string . . .

—Exposing her muff

. . . caressing—no, *grasping* the pole for dear life. And as the song wound down the audition was over.

She had been hired. She didn't know how; it certainly wasn't her dancing.

Soon she found out why.

Jil St. Claire, the manager and part-owner, called her into her office. She wore tight jeans and a halter top and smoked a thin cigarillo. She had once been a dancer herself, Vicki had told her. She looked to be in her early thirties.

"I'll lay it on the line, kid," Jil told her. "I don't give a rat's ass if you can dance. The moves you'll learn. So don't flatter yourself. You got the job because you got big tits."

Lysette had remained silent. What could she say? *Thank you for liking my tits.*

"And, it takes balls, so to speak, to get in front of a group of strangers and take it all off—at least at the beginning," she said with a smile. "I like girls with balls. I don't want prima donnas working for me. I'm not looking to be your sorority mother, if you get my drift."

Lysette saw no reason to abandon her silence. *Thanks for telling me I got balls.* Silence seemed prudent, she thought to herself.

"There is one problem. That nasty scar over your eye. Like a horse kicked you or something." She held up a hand to stop Lysette from speaking. "Now don't go telling me how you got it. It's not germane to the issue at hand." She handed Lysette a wig. "Put it on."

Lysette did as she was told.

"Now cover the scar with the bangs. Good." Jil inspected her, then nodded, as if to herself. "With the lights down, like it's out there, with a bit of makeup, no one will notice."

Lysette had worn the wig, or a variation, ever since; donning it once she got to the club, not taking it off until she was in her car and had driven several blocks. She felt safer ensconced in her club persona until she was away from the club.

Tonight, without a car, she had forgotten all about the wig.

She willed the bus to move faster, as she lit up her third cigarette. The wig protected her *after* she got off the bus. If the police stopped the bus, however, it was a dead giveaway.

Getting off the bus, she slipped into an alley and removed the wig.

And now, locking her door with its three dead bolts, she could allow herself to dwell on what had happened, and more importantly, on what to do. It was ten to one. The news. It would be on KYW, the all-news station, at one o'clock. Good. She had ten minutes to check the windows. She was obsessive, she knew, but for good reason.

—Walking in on two strangers who had killed her family and left her to die tended to do that, she said to herself.

Even so, she knew the windows were locked, so why check? Why? Because she always did; a dozen times or more a day. She had put bars on the outside; special locks on the inside—the kind you couldn't open even if you broke the window.

"You really don't need these, lady," the locksmith had said. "With them bars, no one's gonna be able to squeeze through."

"Humor me," she had answered.

"Hey, it's your money. Just wanted to point it out. Don't want you to be telling anyone I'm ripping you off. I got a reputation, you know."

All the windows were locked. What about the front door? Lysette thought. She *knew* she had locked them when she came in. Hadn't she? In her state, had she forgotten? No harm in making sure, she decided. She checked them, and, yes, they were locked. Now what? A beer. She craved a beer. Twelve-fifty-eight. There was a radio in the kitchen. She turned it to KYW, lit a cigarette, popped open a can of Miller Lite and waited.

The headlines—a shooting on the subway.

The weather—"Get on with it," she said out loud.

Sports and business teasers.

All right already, get to the fucking news, her mind screamed.

And there it was. A sixteen-year-old boy fatally shot in the midst of a mugging by a woman who had fled the scene. The deceased, Jerome Brown. Sixty-six-year-old Isiah Hayes, the mugging victim, had been taken to Jefferson Hospital. Reported in good condition.

"In other news . . . "

That was it? Wham, bam, thank you ma'am, and now on to other news! she thought. Did the police consider it self-defense or was she wanted for some crime? Could she go to jail for fleeing the scene of a crime? Had the passengers and the old man told them she had had no choice but to shoot the kid?

—*Shoot for the head. Shoot to kill. This ain't the movies, baby*, an inner voice spoke to her.

Or had they conspired once she'd left to make her look guilty? She was white, after all—they were black; the boy . . .

—*A drug-crazed mugger*, she corrected herself.

. . . was black, too.

"Stop it!" She cried aloud. "You stupid, paranoid bitch. Don't go drawing conclusions. Calm down. Calm down. Calm down."

She had been pacing the room, running a hand through her hair, puffing on her fourth cigarette.

The report said the old man was being mugged, she remembered. The old man promised to protect her. She had looked into his eyes . . .

—Kind eyes.

—Trusting eyes.

—*Grateful* eyes.

. . . and knew he wouldn't backstab her.

But where did she stand? She'd have to wait until the morning. There would be a fuller report on the morning TV news; even more in the late-morning editions of the *Daily News* and *Inquirer*. Now certainly wasn't the time to make any rash decisions.

After checking the locks again she went to bed; the old man's grateful eyes staring into hers. "Let us protect you," he had said.

She knew he would.

Chapter Seven

Briggs and Rios were silently writing their reports, seemingly oblivious to one another, when Morales entered. He was clearly preoccupied. He gave a cursory wave and disappeared into his office. Through the frosted windows that afforded little privacy, Briggs could see he was on the phone. Though he couldn't make out the words, Morales appeared angry. He slammed the phone down and made several more calls. At two in the morning Briggs knew he wasn't shooting the breeze with his buds. Twenty minutes later he emerged from his office; his jacket off, tie gone, shirt disheveled.

He and Rios gave their sergeant their finished reports. Morales hardly glanced at them, as if he knew they'd be thorough.

"Nina. There's nothing more we can do tonight . . . I mean this morning. Go home and get some sleep. We've got to turn up this woman. The message, which I'm hopeful the media will convey, is we just want to question her. We're not contemplating any charges. That should bring her in unless she has something to hide."

"In that case . . . ?" Rios asked, letting the question hang.

"In that case be prepared for some long days and nights. We'll try to backtrack and find out where she got on the subway. And we'll see if anyone saw her after she fled. Prepare your boyfriend for some lonely nights." He gave her a weary smile.

She got up, looked at the two men as if she wanted to say something, shrugged and left.

"She's pissed," Briggs said after she'd gone. "Us boys making plans behind her back."

Morales acknowledged the comment with a nod, and sat down across from Briggs. "Let's talk."

He ran his hands through his thick hair, as if contemplating how

51

to begin. "This case may be over tomorrow," he said finally, "but my gut says otherwise. I've been making calls, calling in markers, but I'm hitting a brick wall. I don't know where it came from, but someone who doesn't know what's gone down with you lately wants you on *this* case on the off chance it turns racial."

Briggs knew better than to add his two cents. Morales was leading up to something, and he'd just have to wait him out.

"I won't beat around the bush. If you can't convince me you can take the heat—long days away from your family, *from Alexis*—or if you want out, I'll put you on extended sick leave. Then no one, no matter how high up, can do a fucking thing about it."

"I won't ask out," Briggs responded calmly, though inside his emotions were swirling.

"Then I'll tell you why you're not equipped for this case, and you can convince me I'm wrong."

Briggs knew Morales was going to put him on a guilt trip; make him feel that if this case was to be his he'd better not fuck up.

His sergeant was not an overbearing pain in the ass or a hollerer, nor an ass-kisser, for that matter. As a detective, he'd been a living legend of sorts. Before being assigned to homicide, he'd broken up a child kidnapping ring where girls six, seven or eight were shipped overseas and sold into slavery. Later he'd headed a task force that had tracked down Islamic Fundamentalist bombmakers, for which he'd received national recognition. That had led to a promotion and to the homicide unit.

Not too far removed from the streets, initially he had become part of every case, to the point his squad called him "The Commish," in reference to the TV character who was able to run an entire police department, yet still immerse himself in every case.

To his credit, though, as Morales got to know and trust his men, he backed off. He was a man with keen insight whose door was always open if you wanted to bounce a theory off him. He'd never ridicule, but subtly redirect you if you were off target, without making you feel the fool. If you made sense he'd simply say, "Run with it," and trust you'd do him proud. Do your job; keep him posted. That's all he asked.

Thus, you felt guilty if you screwed up. He wasn't one to rant and rave. He would quietly shake his head and spout cliches until you felt you'd personally let him down.

"I'm disappointed in you . . . " to a detective who failed to follow up a tip.

"I went to the wall for you . . . " when there was sloppiness at a crime scene.

"I let you run with this case." He'd shake his head, berating himself. "I stuck my neck out, and what do I get . . . "

Everyone knew it was part of his shtick, but it still rankled.

His men were fiercely loyal to him, as he was to them, and he had one of the best clearance rates in the unit.

Yet, there was an aura of sadness about him. He loved the action of an investigation, yet had to distance himself and act as a bureaucrat. He couldn't survive on a detective's salary with six kids and a seventh on the way. His wife, at barbecues she held, kidded that the only way she could keep him home was to get pregnant. Only then would he fuss over her like a mother hen. Briggs felt there was more truth than teasing behind her words.

There was no doubt Morales' tenure as sergeant would be brief. While he dreaded the thought, he would be moving higher up the ladder; more money and prestige, but even less contact with actual cases.

Now Briggs had to convince him—and at the same time he knew—why he should take on a case he didn't want. And Morales would tell him why he didn't want it, no holds barred.

"I saw the confrontation between you and the uniform," he began. He put up his hand to tell Briggs he didn't want an explanation.

"It's symptomatic of the stress you've put yourself under. I know when you're off duty, if you're not with your daughter, you're looking for the fucker that raped her. I could bust your balls for that; it's not a homicide, thank God, and you wouldn't be on the case even if it was. I understand it's your way of atoning for not being able to protect your child. As long as it doesn't interfere with your work here, it's no hair off my ass."

"Would you sit back and do nothing, if it was your kid?" Briggs asked irritably.

"That's not my point. It's eating at you like a cancer. You're so self-absorbed in your own tragedy, at times you're worthless to me."

"C'mon, Sarge, I'm pulling my weight," Briggs said. He hated being put on the defensive; having to prove his worth. He was no slacker. The cases he worked on might seem trivial compared to catching Alexis' attacker, but he did his job and did it well.

"It's *how* you're going about it that has me concerned. You're reckless; a loose cannon. Notice how no one jokes around you anymore; how that acid wit of yours has taken a vacation? This squad's an extension of your family. When you hurt, we feel the pain. You're aloof and distant with us. I guarantee it's like that at home. Vivian blames you, right?"

"Of course not," he started, but caught himself. He was bullshitting himself if he thought his wife didn't blame him. By city statute he had to live in the city if he wanted to work in the city. But, with both of them working, they earned more than enough for him to get a job and move to the suburbs. . . .

—Where kids don't get raped.

—Where kids don't get shot playing outside.

—Where kids aren't within arm's length of drug dealers and addicts.

He'd balked at looking for a job on one of the suburban forces; knowing full well he could get one with ease. The city was his turf, and until the attack on Alexis, he had felt personally invincible. No one was going to run him out of *his* city where his parents and their parents had been raised.

Yes, in a perverted sense his wife blamed him. He could protect himself. But he couldn't protect his daughter.

He looked at his superior; knowing he couldn't hide the truth.

"Our relationship's strained now. I won't deny it, but it's not affecting my work."

"Listen to yourself," Morales said. "Every time you look at your daughter, you take it as a personal defeat. You couldn't protect her, so you compensate by hunting the man down. Instead of supporting your wife in her time of need, you spend your spare time trying to find a needle in a haystack."

He wiped his brow with the sleeve of his shirt. Winter or summer, it was always hot and stuffy in the squadroom. Then, he continued.

"You don't confide in your friends, and you blow up at the drop of a hat. Would *you* want that man heading a potentially sensitive investigation?"

"Sarge, I'm not going to let you down. I'm on edge, I admit it, but I'm working my way through this thing."

He paused, deep in thought, wondering whether to tell Morales about his recurring dream, then plunged ahead.

"Every night I dream of finding the fucker, chasing him through alleys, over fences—things we did on the beat, but seldom anymore. Anyway, he's looking back at me and slowly his terror turns into a leer, and then laughter. I'm lagging behind him, wheezing, because I'm so out of shape. He turns and begins running backwards and still I can't gain on him. Then he flips me the finger, and he's gone.

"That's why I began going to the gym; why I run in circles around a track, though I hate it. Why I've sworn off all the fattening food I love so much. If I ever get the fucker in my sight, I want to be able to pounce and wipe that smile off his fucking face."

"That's supposed to inspire confidence?" Morales asked.

"What I'm getting at . . . how can I put it? I need to work to survive, is what I'm trying to say. Maybe this is the very type of case I need. One I must focus on totally. Most of what's on my plate I can sleepwalk through. There's no challenge, so my mind wanders. To him. If this woman doesn't come in, I'll want to find her, and I won't leave any stone unturned."

Morales leaned forward. "Before you blow this all out of proportion, keep in mind, all we want is to find her to question her. Then probably shake her hand. Can you maintain the focus you speak of knowing in the end you'll have spent countless hours for nothing?"

Briggs didn't have to think before he answered. "It's the hunt that's the challenge, Sarge. You know that better than I. We've learned not to expect justice. It doesn't matter what happens to her *after* she's caught."

Morales shook his head, showing he understood.

"The hunt, that's what it's all about," Briggs added, trying to hammer home his point. "It's those few cases a year that make all the other shit tolerable. Maybe it's what I need to get me out of this funk."

"All right," Morales said, grudgingly. "You've convinced me." Then a pause. "But you'll have to work with Rios."

"Jesus Christ, Sarge. It's going to be tough enough finding this woman as it is. Why can't you give me someone who I won't have to babysit?"

"Listen and listen good, Lamar. We disagree about Rios. You have it in for her because she's a woman. She can't pull her weight. That's bullshit, but I'm not going to argue with you. You've got Rios because she's the only one who won't take your crap."

Briggs looked at Morales quizzically.

"Look, before you bull your way into a China shop, she'll grab you by the balls so you know the consequences. The others, good as they are, they'll look the other way. I know my squad. That's how it is. You and Rios may never be buddies, but in your current frame of mind, she's the best partner you could have. Got a problem with that?"

Briggs knew better than to argue. A few hours earlier he hadn't wanted anything to do with this case. All of a sudden Morales had him salivating. Briggs had to hand it to the man. Morales had him expose himself for the first time since Alexis had been attacked. Verbalized his worst fears; thoughts he couldn't share with his own wife. And Morales made it sound like he was going out on a limb for him. . . .

—*He* was, an inner voice told him.

The man had played him like a drum. They both knew it. But for the first time in months, Briggs felt alive. He almost hoped . . .

—No almost about it.

. . . the Good Samaritan *wouldn't* show her face. He wanted to hunt her down and present her to Morales on a platter.

"No problem. You want me to work with Rios, I'll work with Rios."

Morales stood up.

"Sarge. Look, I appreciate the confidence you have . . . " He shrugged, unable to articulate the thought.

"Go home. Get some sleep. It may all be moot when you return."

"Soon," Briggs said. "I want to check this kid's rap sheet and give ballistics a kick in the ass before I go."

"Whatever," Morales said, seemingly without interest.

Motherfucker, Briggs thought, smiling to himself. You lit a fire under me, just as you planned.

Chapter Eight

Morales sat for a while after Briggs left. He could have gone to his office, but it wasn't much bigger than a broom closet, and made him feel claustrophobic. There was precious little privacy for anyone, actually. The detectives' work area, where he sat, consisted of a long table that ran the length of the room; something akin to cafeteria tables at school. Typewriters, pads, pencils, paper clips and unfinished paperwork were strewn over each work area. There were no desks, no drawers.

On the one hand, Morales felt he'd accomplished what he'd set out in forcing Briggs to come to grips with himself. More than a few he had worked with had told him if he wasn't a cop he'd make a damn fine priest. Father Morales was one of his many nicknames. His sometimes brooding silence somehow inspired confidence. As a detective he'd find his partners telling him their innermost secrets, knowing they would go no further. Moreover, questions he would ask, more out of curiosity than design, often forced his colleagues to look in a mirror or confront the real reasons for their grief, anger or frustration.

"Why do you have to play around when you've got a wife who's the envy of every detective in the squad?" he'd asked Furillo, after the man had told him about his frequent one-night stands, during a surveillance several years back. He was making small talk. All of a sudden, Furillo was telling him of his insecurities, having a wife who *was the envy* of men wherever they went. He questioned *her* fidelity. He was getting back at her for something she hadn't even done.

Morales seldom offered advice. He was no psychiatrist, he told himself, having no better credentials than a bartender to tell others how to run their life. He was content to lend an ear.

57

He didn't for a moment delude himself into believing Briggs' problem was solved by their little talk. Alexis would prey on him for months, even years to come. But he was content with the knowledge Briggs was now more aware he'd been slipping. Just like every working stiff, Briggs had a job to do, even in the midst of tragedy. Morales had no problem with Briggs taking some time off if that was what he needed. But if he planned to work through his grief on the job, he couldn't allow the man to torpedo an investigation because his mind wasn't on his work.

He was now satisfied Briggs could—*would*—do his job, or be man enough to admit to Morales if he couldn't.

More baffling and disturbing to Morales was the question of who was so insistent Briggs be assigned the case. It *had* to be someone far up the ladder, unaware of Briggs' personal problems. Answers to his many calls had been strangely evasive. In a department the size of Philadelphia's, politics ruled; especially in promotions. And this certainly wasn't the first case a specific detective had been requested. What bothered Morales was the secrecy. Whoever wanted Briggs on the case didn't want it known who it was. As a result, Morales was unaware of the man's agenda; for whoever wanted Briggs leading the case most certainly had an agenda.

The optimist in Morales told him it was all much to do about nothing. This was clearly a case of self-defense. There had been an instinctive overreaction when word came down that a white woman had killed a black youth. A red flag had gone up. But even the rabble rousers who'd like nothing better than to make this into a racial incident would find it tough. And the woman would in all probability pop up when she heard she had been exonerated.

Unfortunately, Morales wasn't an optimist, but a firm believer in Murphy's Law: if something could go wrong, it would. What if the woman had a prior criminal record or, worse, an outstanding warrant? Why come forward and risk exposure, even prison, for a crime not connected with the evening's events? On the other hand, it might simply be the woman didn't want the glare of the limelight; her personal life put under a microscope. There could be any number of reasons she wouldn't come forward.

In that case, Briggs had his work cut out for him, because the media would be all over the story like white on rice. In a city plagued by crime, where more often than not people turned their backs on their neighbors in times of need, this woman was a cause celebre, and even he had to admit a gnawing curiosity to learn more about her.

Briggs would do his job;

—*He'd best*, an inner voice implored, because if he fucks up the shit's gonna hit the fan and land squarely on you. The smartass who forced you to put Briggs on the case sure ain't gonna come to your aid.

. . . the man's dedication to his work, and Rios on his ass all but assured thoroughness, though not necessarily success. He smiled at the thought of the odd pairing. Working together might force Briggs to ameliorate his chauvinist views; another bonus.

And, a promotion was at stake. One he loathed as it would further distance himself from the streets and men working cases; with his ever expanding family, one he needed. He'd have to hope for the best.

How he wished *he* were working this case.

—*Any case*.

The juices would be pumping. Though he would never admit it, he would have gladly put in overtime without pay when such a case landed on his plate. It would be on his mind wherever he was; in the shower, on the can, even making love to his wife. The highs and lows that went with such a case were addictive. How he envied Briggs. If there was anything that could take his mind off his daughter, it was a case that was a ballbuster.

Unfortunately, the thought of Juanita's bloated belly, heavy with child, made it all wishful thinking. Hope that Briggs came through, accept a promotion and the pay that went with it and become even more of a bureaucrat.

"Fuck," he said aloud in the empty room. "Soon I'll be confessing to Father Morales about promotions I don't want."

Chapter Nine

Lysette awoke at five-thirty in the morning. While she had a clock radio, she never set the alarm. There was an internal clock within her that woke her at the prescribed time regardless of how much sleep she'd had. It had failed only once . . .

—Her grandmother's funeral.

. . . and that was only because she had subconsciously wanted it to fail.

As usual she didn't awake in bed, but in the corner of the room, as if she had been fleeing . . .

—*Hiding*.

. . . from her attackers. Even though the light of dawn should have filtered into the room, it was totally black. Lysette felt completely at ease. . . .

—As if in the attic in her mind.

She had had trouble sleeping upon leaving the hospital, after the attack on her family. She'd gone through a severe trauma, both physically and emotionally, a psychologist had told her concerned grandparents.

"She may have nightmares. She may talk or walk in her sleep. She's in a very fragile state. It's important to remember it's only temporary, though. Indulge her whims, cater . . . " He paused to relight his pipe. He had been talking about her while she was there, clutching her grandfather's hand. But just as when she was in a coma, he ignored her presence. " . . . to any unusual requests. Later we can wean her off bad habits she may develop."

The first night, at her grandparents' house, she had tossed and turned for hours, drifting into a troubled sleep due *only* to total exhaustion. She awoke as fatigued as when she went to sleep. It was too bright at night, she'd realized. The men, their faces still obscured by a shroud-like fog, were approaching, taking her where she belonged . . .

—*With her family*.

"It's too bright in my room," she had told her grandmother, a squat, solid woman, not the type to coddle her grandchildren.

"How can it be too bright, child? There's no nightlight. The shades are pulled down," she said, not trying to hide her exasperation.

Lysette could tell she was pissed. If she had her way, she would tell Lysette it didn't make no never mind to her if she slept or not, long as she didn't disturb anyone.

Her grandfather had been more understanding. He had replaced the faded orange shade with a black one.

"Grandpa, can I have my walls painted black, too?"

He had scratched his head in bewilderment. "I don't know, Lys. Black is so somber." But he'd given in . . .

—*Just as the doctor had suggested*.

. . . and soon the entire room was black: walls, carpet, bed-spread, sheets, pillowcase and blanket. He had even painted the dresser black. Lysette would hear her grandmother berating him for giving into her every whim.

"She's playing you for a fool. She says jump and you ask how high? How long are we going to let her rule this household?"

"It's only her room," he'd replied without any trace of pique, "and the doctor says it's only temporary."

Lysette found peace in the pitch black room. The intruders never entered her room devoid of light, and soon she slept peacefully through the night.

The only oddity was she never awoke in her bed, but in the corner, cuddled up in a fetal position as if she had been fleeing her tormentors. She reminded herself of a gerbil in school that constantly escaped from its cage. It was never hard to locate. It had built a nest in the coat closet, and it was there he invariably fled. Her corner of the room was her nest. Soon, she had made it more comfortable with a mattress, pillow and comforter—all black. Each night she went to sleep in her bed and awoke in the corner . . .

—*Her nest*.

. . . warm and cozy.

When she moved back to her house after her grandparents' deaths, she'd replicated the room, adding three deadbolt locks to the bedroom door for extra protection.

The night before, as all nights, she had followed the same routine. She lay in bed, on her back, absorbing the darkness of the room, shutting down all the systems in her mind. It was like when she had been in her coma. She would retreat into her mind, careful, though, not to venture into the attic. Once there, she feared, she might never awaken. She found a quiet place in her mind—a sitting room or library—found a comfortable rocker and gently swayed to Angela Bofil's "Intuition," which played on her tape deck . . . played so softly she could barely make out the words . . .

Her instincts had told her to become a stripper, when common sense dictated otherwise. Intuition had told her to flee that night as the old man had commanded.

Before the tune had finished she was asleep.

Now fully awake, she had time for a shower before the news. A hot shower daily . . .

—Ever since the ice bath.

. . . the scalding water soothing her, driving away unbidden memories . . .

—Of *the* bath.

Coffee, a cigarette and another cup of coffee, and she flopped naked in front of the tube in the living room. Before she had begun dancing she could never imagine herself sitting around the house unclothed. She could remember showering, more than once, the phone ringing and wrapping a towel around herself before she'd go to answer; as if whoever was calling could see through the phone.

"Hi, Lys. My God! You answer the phone naked?" she imagined someone on the other end asking, and she instantly felt foolish. She was so accustomed to television, where nudity was forbidden, she took it for granted *everyone* covered themselves before answering the phone.

At the club there was no such self-consciousness. The girls walked around naked as a matter of course in their changing room. Lysette had been shocked at first, but just as she got used to disrobing in front of a room of strange men, she soon felt comfortable talking with the other girls in the buff.

Five fifty-seven. Not quite time to turn on the TV. She could see her reflection in the screen. She was proud of her body; had every right to be. Not only was she naturally endowed with a great set of boobs, the dancing and daily exercising had done wonders for the rest of her figure. Just as a pianist or violinist was dependent on his or her hands, she had to keep her belly flat, and her legs toned and shapely. Expertly applied makeup transformed a relatively plain face into one alluring, if not beautiful. Her face a bit too rounded, her cheeks too chubby . . .

—Her father loved squeezing her cheeks, she vividly recalled.

Her large brown eyes complemented the overall look, even more so with a bit of makeup. Her nose was pert and turned up at the end, and her lips a bit too thin for the rest of the face. It was as if someone had sculpted her piece by piece, and when it came to her nose and mouth had run out of the proper pieces and put on what was at hand. Again, with makeup, she could make the lips fuller, though she could do nothing with her nose. . . .

—*No plastic surgery*, she had told one of the other girls when she complained of her nose. Makeup was one thing, but *no one* was going to cut her face.

The scar and indentation from being struck with the marble lighter stuck out like a sore thumb in the mornings. Though her black hair was short, she could cover the indentation with her bangs. Her wigs, with their exaggerated bangs, all but obliterated the scar above her eye, as well.

Enough admiring and analyzing yourself, she thought, and flicked on the television.

"A man is alive today, according to witnesses, due the courage of a woman who refused to be cowered by a sixteen-year-old mugger with a rap sheet of a hardened criminal," the report began.

Lysette was shocked. She was being portrayed as a *hero*; the passengers had made good on their promise. Lysette recognized one of the men being interviewed, by a haggard-looking reporter, from the train.

"If it weren't for that white woman," the man said, "the old man would have been pistol-whipped to death by that drug-crazed little pissant."

"We have heard rumors," the reporter continued, "the passengers were reluctant to provide a description of the woman to the police. Is that true, Mr. Hazzard?"

"Not exactly," the man said, looking uncomfortable. "We didn't get a real good look at her, you know. It all happened so fast, and as they say, all white people look alike." He laughed at his joke.

The reporter turned serious, now, facing the camera. "Jerome Brown, aged sixteen, according to those who knew him, led a troubled life."

The reporter went on to tell of a child with no father, brought up by a mother, herself a crack addict. A boy without supervision who seldom went to school, got into fights when he did attend class, hung with a rough crowd and was introduced to drugs at the age of eleven. Then the reporter surprised Lysette.

"But, while one can sympathize with the plight of such a child, one cannot excuse his actions. Jerome Brown spent time at a youth detention facility for selling crack to fifth graders. He was involved in at least three convenience store robberies, and pistol-whipped his own grandmother when she refused to turn over her welfare check. And this was not Jerome Brown's first subway holdup. A transit police source, who wishes to remain anonymous, identified Brown, saying he was being sought for *at least* six such robberies, including one where an elderly woman was beaten, three weeks ago, and remains hospitalized.

"Meanwhile," he continued, "police are asking the courageous woman who risked her life to save a stranger to come forward for questioning."

The reporter turned to a police officer he identified as homicide Lieutenant Frank Evans, and asked if the woman faced any charges.

"This was clearly a case of self-defense," the officer replied. "This woman managed to wrestle the gun from the assailant, and he came at her with a knife, according to witnesses, threatening to stab her. We have no intention of filing charges at this time. We encourage . . . we *implore* this young woman to come forward to aid in the investigation."

"Yes!" Lysette yelled joyously, pumping her arms in the air. She was in the clear.

The morning news show was an hour-long program, usually littered with trite filler stories. But its format allowed the station to devote more time than usual to a story such as this. They cut to another reporter who was getting man-on-the-street reactions from those on their way to work.

"It's about time someone stood up to the hoodlum element. Good for her," was the reaction of a black sanitation worker.

"I long ago gave up riding the subway," said a heavyset black woman, a manager of a McDonald's. "Especially at night. Crack dealers and crackheads *own* the streets at night. I'd sooner quit my job and go on welfare than have to travel at night."

"I'd like to give her a big hug," said a black crossing guard who was taking her daughter to a neighbor's house. "We have to get up at six in the morning so I can drop my little girl off at a friend's house. I'm scared to have her walk to school alone—and it's *only* four blocks away. This woman—this *white woman*—risked her life to save a brother. Hell, I'd like to have her over for dinner."

Lysette was beginning to feel uncomfortable. She didn't want to be a celebrity. She wanted to be left alone. If she turned herself in her life would never be the same. Her life would be dissected . . .

—" . . . tragic victim of a crime as a child . . . "

. . . her privacy invaded. Her career choice would be questioned and some would denounce her for dancing "ne-kid." Her boss, co-workers and neighbors would all be interviewed . . .

—*Hassled.*

. . . put under a microscope, judged and condemned. No wonder people don't get involved, she thought. She didn't want to be held up to public scrutiny; *wouldn't* allow it.

She was on the verge of turning off the television when there was yet another spin given the story. A police officer from a suburban Stop, Look, Listen and Protect Program was giving advice on how *not* to become a victim, addressing herself mainly to women.

"Too many women leave home with a sign on saying 'Attack me.' Don't go out with your gold all hanging out or your pocket-book hanging loose. You gotta watch what you wear. Let's face it, some women today dress provocatively, then wonder why they draw attention. Dress to avoid attracting attention . . . "

"What the fuck?" Lysette said aloud. "Why do we have to avoid attracting attention? Why don't they get the scum off the streets who are harassing *us*?"

The woman on the screen didn't hear her, though, and went on for another minute.

Still naked, Lysette went into her room and brought a box of jewelry with her to the living room. She put on several gold necklaces and began prancing around the room. "Here I am," she said to the television. "I pay my taxes. This is *my* city, and you're telling me not to wear my gold jewelry."

There was something missing, she felt. Lysette found her coat on an easy chair where she had left it the night before and took out the gun; a snub-nosed .38.

She *knew* guns, though she'd never owned one. The months after being released from the hospital after her family had been killed had been difficult, to say the least. She had been terribly depressed and angry. She'd gotten into fights at school and jumped at every sound in her grandparents' house. She'd had therapy sessions with psychologists twice weekly, but still her fear and anger festered; her nerves were frayed.

Then one day, her grandfather took her to a target range, and taught her to shoot. To twelve-year-old Lysette, her grandfather was *old*. She had to yell when she spoke to him. He walked with a slow gait, wheezing, with a cigar permanently in place at the corner of his mouth. When he sneezed, she thought he might break windows. And he would fart at the most embarrassing of times, especially at dinner. Long, loud, juicy farts . . .

—Flatulence, he called it.

. . . that almost made her gag and giggle out loud at the same time. She'd have to bite her tongue to retain control. Even her grandmother would give him a scathing glare, then shake her head in silent rebuke when he smiled self-consciously.

Still and all, she worshipped him, because he tried to understand her torment, and didn't make light of her fears. At the target range, the years seemed to recede. He was no helpless old man, but a man with strength.

"Lys, your psychologist would frown on this, but just between the two of us he's a waste of time and money. Me, I think you need to learn to protect yourself. I'm too old to teach you karate, but if you want, I'll enroll you for lessons. But I taught your dad and I'll teach you to protect yourself with a gun."

He put a gun in her small hand. "Listen, now. Man comes at you and you know how to use a gun, *he's* lying on the ground."

And he taught her to shoot; took her to the shooting range each week for a year, and saw her confidence grow. It was her grandfather who'd told her if she had to use a gun to shoot to kill.

"This isn't the movies, where you can shoot a knife or gun from another man's hand. *One shot*, Lys, is all you've got before *you're* dead. Make that shot count."

Now she stood before the television, the weatherman giving the day's forecast, but she wasn't paying attention. She had on her gold, and she had her gun at her side, and she imagined walking into that same subway car, as the night before. Even though she was nude, most of the passengers ignored her. She imagined Jerome-Fucking-Brown sashaying up to her, interested *only* in her jewelry.

"Hey bitch, gimme your gold," he said.

She heard the voice of one of the passengers—the woman from

the Protect Program—whisper, "It's her own fault. With that gold, she's attracting attention."

But now she raised her gun and pointed it at Jerome-Fucking-Brown. "Look, fucker," she said. "If I want to wear my gold, I will, and you best leave me the fuck alone. And if you don't like it, take this," and she pretended to unload her pistol. "Bam, bam, bam"; giving him three extra eyes in his forehead.

Suddenly the real world intruded on her vision. The news was over. She looked at the clock on the mantle over the fireplace and saw it was seven-thirty-five. Where had the last hour gone? she wondered. Had she been pointing the gun at the TV the whole time . . . ?

—At Jerome-Fucking-Brown.

One thing she knew. She wasn't going to the police *today*. She had to sort things out. . . .

—"The gun felt good, didn't it?" she heard the voice of her grandfather in her mind.

"Yes," she said aloud. "The gun felt good."

—"You can walk anyplace with that gun and you're in control." Her grandfather, again.

"Yes, I'm in control," she answered. "No one messes with me when I've got my piece."

—"Get a hold of yourself, Lys," her grandfather admonished.

"Oh yes, I've got to get a hold of myself," she said aloud to herself.

She decided she would go down to the shore for a few hours. Her car would be ready, and if she left at nine, she could stay until three, maybe even four, and get back in plenty of time for work.

She loved the beach, even in late September when the water was getting too cold for swimming. She had her own private beach she'd found at Cape May. Yes, she would go down and do some sand sculpting. At art school she loved sculpting in clay, and found sculpting in sand was not much different. A quiet day at the beach with no one to hassle her was just what she needed to figure out what to do.

Before she went for her car, though, she decided to take off her jewelry, hide the gun . . . and put on some clothes.

Chapter Ten

Briggs was surprised when at nine-thirty in the morning he was told an Isiah Hayes was downstairs and wished to see him. He was on his third cup of coffee; fatigue still squeezing at his eyes. He stifled a yawn and went to greet the man.

"Mr. Hayes," he said, holding out his hand when the man entered the squadroom. "I'm surprised to see you here."

"It's Zeke. Nowadays, the only time I'm called Mr. Hayes is when I attend a funeral for a friend." He paused for a moment. "Which, at my age, is too often. You told me you wanted to speak to me when I felt up to it. Feeling pretty chipper this morning, so here I am."

His voice was raspy from age and too many cigarettes, and he offered an engaging smile.

"We would have sent a car to get . . . "

The old man waved away the thought. "Walked down," he said proudly. "Rush hour, not too much chance of getting mugged." He gave Briggs a playful wink.

Isiah Hayes must have broken many a heart as a young man, Briggs thought. He was six feet tall, with only a slight stoop due to age. The white beard that enveloped his dark, weather-beaten complexion couldn't cover the twinkle in his eye, nor the smile that played at his lips. Briggs instantly knew he'd been a working man all his life. He hadn't dressed up to come down to be interviewed, but his clothes were clean. The man had self-respect. A bandage covered his forehead, right cheek and nose.

"Let's go to one of the interview rooms. Have us some privacy," Briggs said.

Once settled, both with a fresh cup of coffee, Briggs asked him about his hospital stay.

68

Again, the old man gave a dismissive wave.

"Hate hospitals. Spent too much time watching the missus waste away with cancer seven years ago. They made such a fuss last night, like I was some old man on my deathbed. I'm old, but I've had my share of scrapes and wasn't about to stay no night at no fool hospital. Stitched me up and I left; some fool doctor trailing down the hall telling me it was in my own best interests to stay the night."

He gave a hearty laugh. "Ever hear anything so foolish and stuffy? 'in my own best interests,' " and he laughed again.

The man had spunk, and Briggs liked him instantly.

"So what can I do for you, Detective?" he asked with a smile.

"Let's start at the top," Briggs said, hoping to put the man at ease with questions that had little relevance to what he really wanted— a description of the woman who had saved his life. "Where were you coming from last night?"

Hayes told Briggs he played cards with some friends twice a week in West Philly. "I'd bring twenty dollars with me, so I couldn't lose more. If I left with twelve dollars I considered it a good night. Most I ever took home was fifty-three dollars. Seldom cleaned me out, though." Again, said with a smile.

"And last night?"

"Lady luck took the night off," he chuckled. "Walked out with six dollars. The boy that attacked me was mighty pissed."

"How old are you, Mr. Hay—Zeke?" Briggs asked. In interrogations, Briggs jumped from subject to subject for no apparent reason to keep the suspect or witness on his feet. While he wasn't interrogating a potential perp or hostile witness, old habits died hard.

"Sixty-six," he said without hesitation.

"Retired?"

The old man nodded his head affirmatively. "Been going on six years, now."

"What kind of work did you do?"

"Worked lots of jobs. Loved boats. Sailed around the world more times than I can remember. Last twenty years, though, worked at the Navy yard." Now there was an added twinkle to his brown eyes. "They call us custodial engineers, nowadays, but I was a janitor, pure and simple."

"Ever been arrested?"

Hayes looked quizzically at the detective, then shrugged. "Got into a few bar fights when I was too young to know better. Nothing serious, though."

"You live alone since your wife . . . " Briggs paused, looking for the right word.

"Died? Passed on? Went to her maker?" the old man finished for him. "Been seven years, Detective. Not a day goes by when I don't think about her, but it's not like I'm still grieving."

"You live alone, then?"

"Shacking up with a twenty-year-old if you must know."

Briggs looked at him oddly for a moment, then smiled. "You're pulling my leg, aren't you, Zeke?"

He smiled broadly. "Say it all the time when someone's feeling sorry for me. Don't want their pity, so I make 'em feel like an ass. Yeah, I live alone, sorta."

"C'mon, Zeke. Sorta?"

"I got five children—all by the same woman," he said with pride. "They're scattered around, but two live in Philly. I watch my grandchildren so their parents can go out a couple of times a week. So, I'm only *sorta* alone."

"This the first time you been hassled on the subway?"

The old man's eyes hardened for a minute. "First time. Twenty years ago I would have ate that little prick and spat him out. Now, I consider it a good ride home if I don't fart up a storm and embarrass myself. No one's ever messed with me on the subway before, though."

"Never victimized by crime before last night, then," Briggs said incredulously.

"Didn't say that. Robbed twice of my social security check when I was first eligible. Now I use direct deposit. House been broken into . . . "—he paused to count—"seven, no, eight times—all in the past ten years. Neighborhood—hell, the whole city's going to hell in a handbasket, if you ask me."

"Ever seen the woman in the subway before?" It was time to get to the matter at hand.

"We meet regular, after my card games. Been screwing up the courage to hit on her for two months now," he said matter-of-factly.

Briggs was taken aback for a moment, then the other man burst out laughing. "Had you going for a minute, didn't I Detective?"

"Time to stop playing games now, Zeke," Briggs said, but he couldn't help chuckling. "Really. Seen her before?"

"Don't pay much attention to who's on the subway with me. Not healthy to be too nosy, if you get my drift. Apt to get knifed or shot if you look at someone too long; even someone who looks, you know, normal. All of us just keep an eye out for punks like the one hit on me, and keep our distance."

"So you never saw her before?"

"Not that I would know. No."

"Can you describe her for me?" Briggs asked neutrally.

The old man began to squirm in the straight-backed wooden chair, and Briggs knew, too late, he'd erred. The man wasn't going to rat on the woman who had saved his life. Briggs knew that was how the man looked at it.

"Well, you know, I was sitting down, and kinda preoccupied and bleeding, you know. I seen her. Seen two or three of her, if you know what I mean, but none too clearly."

"You're trying to protect her, but there's no need. She's not in any trouble, Zeke. Matter of fact, papers say she's a hero."

"Why can't you just let her be, if that's what she wants? Shit, if you spent your time going after the dealers that got that boy high, I wouldn't be here now, would I?"

"Couldn't agree with you more, Zeke, but I gotta do what my superiors tell me. Just like you had to when you worked. I'm low man on the totem pole. They tell me they want to talk to her. Just talk, understand. If it were up to me, I'd let it drop. But it's not my decision. So why not help me do my job?"

"Would if I could, yes, sir. All I knows is she was blonde and white. I was bleeding and woozy and *scared*. I'm trying to cooperate, but . . . " He shrugged and looked down at his shoes.

Trying to cooperate, my ass, Briggs thought, but he knew he'd lost him. No good trying to browbeat him. He had underestimated the man. Isiah Hayes knew just what he was doing. Probably came down early on purpose to keep me off guard, Briggs thought. No, this old man was one tough nut, and he wasn't about to break him. At least, not today.

"I appreciate your cooperation, Zeke," Briggs said, rising and extending his hand. "Here's my card. Call if you remember anything. Will you do that for me?"

"At my age, I tend to forget, not remember," he said, taking the card. The twinkle was back in his eyes. "You have a good day now, Detective," he said, rising.

"Want a ride home?" Briggs asked. No use antagonizing him, he thought.

"Appreciate the offer, but it's a nice day and the walk will do me good."

Briggs returned to the interrogation room after he'd escorted the old man out. It was one of the few places there was any semblance of privacy. A bare room with a desk and chair.

He'd been played for a fool, and he was angry at himself. He had learned long ago lying to the police came naturally. Most everyone had something to hide or their own hidden agenda. Why should Hayes cooperate? The woman had saved his life. If she wanted to come forward, she would. If not, she must have her reasons, Hayes must have thought, and he wasn't about to help give her up. If he had treated the old man as he should have . . .

—As you *would* have before the attack on Alexis.

. . . he would have gotten more out of him. What bugged Briggs was that his mind hadn't wandered. He *had* been doing his job, but he was a step slow, like an athlete coming off an injury. There was an art to an interrogation. He *hadn't* interrogated the old man. They'd had a nice conversation, but the old man had controlled the event from the very beginning. Briggs had learned a lot about Isiah Hayes, but nothing that could help him locate the mystery woman.

Worse, his gut told him good-old Zeke knew something he wasn't telling. He'd been too evasive, come on too strong telling him he couldn't describe her. And if he had something to hide, whatever it was, it obviously set her apart from the thousands of white blondes on the street that day.

Briggs wondered whether he should just go to Morales and take the extended sick leave he'd offered. He had left Vivian angry that morning and God only knew when he'd get home. He had slipped into bed at three in the morning, careful not to wake his wife. . . .

—Put off the confrontation.

At breakfast, he'd told her the truth. He had never hidden anything from his wife, which was one reason he hadn't joined the majority of cops who were divorced. She might not like what he was doing, but knowing was better than being kept in the dark.

The worst thing was she had just about gotten over blaming him for the attack on Alexis. . . .

—She'll *never* completely forgive you, he admitted to himself.

She'd commented more than once lately that now when he was home, *he was home*.

"There were times you were so distracted by a case it was as if we weren't here," she had told him. "But you don't bring your work home with you anymore. And don't think for a minute Alexis isn't aware. When you're with her, reading to her or just holding her hand, she's so much more relaxed. She feels safe."

"But the doctors . . . " he'd begin.

"Fuck the doctors. She's aware of your presence; the presence of her father who'll protect her."

And he knew it was true. Now, though, he was on a case where he might be working double shifts; when he wouldn't be home to comfort his daughter.

Vivian hadn't said anything; hadn't reminded him of recent promises that family came first. Didn't have to. He had learned the hard way. She had brooded, though, holding her tongue, he knew, lest she say something incendiary.

Deep down he knew taking a sick leave now would only postpone the inevitable. If he was going to remain a cop—and there was no doubt in his mind he was—there would be other cases like this sooner or later. Much as he wanted to believe otherwise, he knew Alexis' road to recovery would be painfully slow; with no guarantees she would ever be able to function independently at all. Vivian would have to take half a loaf. He'd learned not to take his job home with him; to be there for the both of them when he was off duty. She would have to accept the demands of his job on his time.

They would talk it out. He'd make her understand he *had* changed. Tough as it was, she'd have to come to grips with the reality of being married to a homicide detective.

When they would talk was another matter. If the mystery woman didn't turn herself in, he and Rios would be on the subway that night from ten PM until eleven-thirty, trying to find someone who had seen the blonde other nights. He'd get home late and tired; in no shape to convince his wife he hadn't abandoned her again.

He looked at his watch. Ten-forty-five. The first of the other passengers would arrive soon to be re-interviewed. These he'd *interrogate*, though he doubted they could give him what the old man wouldn't.

Chapter Eleven

Lysette, $189 lighter, drove her car along the Atlantic City Expressway to Cape May. Mike, her mechanic, forty-seven, with a paunch covering his belt, teased her, as always, about coming to see her dance.

"I'm going to surprise you one night, Lys, and show up to catch your act," he said with a sly wink.

"Sure, Mike. Why not bring Lydia with you," she said, referring to his overly possessive wife.

Mike flushed. "Was thinking more of a boy's night out on the town myself."

Lysette flashed a knowing smile. When she first began dancing, she dreaded the thought that some of her former classmates and neighbors might inadvertently stop by and see her at the club. Mike was all talk, though. Lydia kept him on a short leash, and *he* wouldn't be caught dead at a strip joint.

As for the others, Lysette no longer concerned herself with gossip, rumors or innuendos that would spread like wildfire if anyone from the hood "caught her act." While she hadn't openly spread the word, only Rose's condemnation would have unsettled her. And while Rose hadn't done cartwheels, she'd accepted her career choice graciously.

"Me, I could never undress in front of a crowd of men, but who am I to pass judgment on others? There's worse you could do."

Exotic dancing . . .

—*Stripping*, she said to herself, fuck the euphemisms.

. . . had done wonders to bolster her self-confidence, as nothing else had before. Outgoing and effervescent before the attack on her family, she had become inhibited, wary and self-conscious after.

She was particularly aware of the indentation to the side of her forehead, and the stares it drew. Fuck them, she thought, now. If anyone stared at her she would stare right back, making *them* feel uncomfortable. She also laughed at what Rose called her "salty" language. While she had heard kids use "gutter" words through school, she had for the most part abstained. At high school graduation, she had told a friend she had to "urinate" so bad, she couldn't hold it in, and had slipped out quietly; hearing her friend tell another, "She's gotta pee."

At the club, she not only heard epithets often, but came to understand that they gave power and a clearer meaning to a message. "Get away from me," could be misinterpreted, but "Get the *fuck* away from me," was so much more effective.

She didn't consider herself foul-mouthed white trash. Insert "fuck" five times in a sentence and the word loses its power. Judicious use of expletives, that was now part of her everyday vocabulary.

The closer she got to the shore, the more at ease she felt with herself. It all went back to rhythm; becoming one with her surroundings. She had made a tape of her favorite Pointer Sisters songs and played it loud, getting in touch with the music, paying little attention, right now, to the lyrics. The smell of the ocean slowly crept into her consciousness as she got onto the Garden State Parkway. She was going to *her* beach; one she had discovered quite by accident several years before.

She spent so much time around people at the club, she longed for isolation at other times. Ocean City's beaches were far too congested; Atlantic City's too touristy. She'd remembered driving by a pier passing through Cape May one day, seeing men getting ready to go fishing. She continued without stopping, made several turns and came to what she could only describe as the end of the world.

She felt like Charlton Heston in *Planet of the Apes*, gawking at what appeared to be a petrified forest. Tree after tree without a leaf in sight, the bark peeled away, as if destroyed in a nuclear holocaust. The wood looked almost bleached; parched, thirsting for the water within its grasp without ever quite reaching it. The branches were like tentacles, grasping at interlopers, frozen in mid-motion for all eternity in the blink of an eye.

Lysette stayed clear of the forest. There was something foreboding about it.

Beyond the trees was a beach, totally deserted. A horde of horseshoe crabs—tank-like shells; carcasses of crabs washed ashore—

littered the sand. They reminded her of soldiers who had attacked from the sea, only to be picked off by defenders one by one and left to rot in the sun.

Only the sounds of waves crashing ashore and the shrill screech of seagulls—scavengers who'd somehow withstood the nuclear blast—broke the unearthly silence.

Lysette immediately laid claim to the beach and hadn't seen another living soul the dozen or more times each summer she visited. While she had never come in late September, it seemed the natural place to be when she had the most important decision of her life to make.

She took her tools out of the car, placed them fifteen feet from the ocean and waded into the water just past her ankles. It was cold; far too chilly to comfortably go in further.

—*Come*, the water beckoned; *welcome the caress*, she could imagine the waves whispering, as they crested and reached out to her like probing fingers.

She discarded her cutoffs and baggy t-shirt, wearing only a thong bikini. Before she had begun dancing, she had never worn anything more revealing than a one-piece suit that covered as much of her body as possible. Still, she would feel naked, and to hide her boobs she wore a shirt atop the suit.

Now, the very thought of being ashamed of her body made her feel foolish. The thong allowed her to get a natural tan, and spend less time at the club's tanning booths. She would have gladly discarded that, too, but she wasn't about to take the chance a cop might pass by and arrest her for nude bathing—not *today*.

She hadn't come to sun herself anyway. An art student at college, she had found the greatest satisfaction sculpting life out of clay, and she learned to apply the same techniques to sand-sculpting. She never knew what she would create; she just let her mind drift as she made her preparations.

In a large drywall bucket, twice the size that held a gallon of paint, she built a mound, soaking it down with water and compacting it with a block of wood. To the base she'd build a tower with smaller buckets; the kind kids used at the beach to make sand castles. With a cement trowel, then a pallet knife, and finally a one-inch putty knife, she'd add details. Lately she'd sculpted variations of two figures making love in the sand; the young woman's . . .

—*You, Lysette*, an inner voice spoke.

. . . nipples taut, her face in the ecstasy of orgasm, as her lover strode above her.

Time to get yourself a man, she thought, the third time the couple had greeted her eyes.

Today, she worked tirelessly as ever, oblivious to the passing hours; her mind in a fog, her hands carving and kneading as if they had a life of their own.

She was startled out of her reverie by a voice.

"What ya making?"

Sitting several feet from her sculpture was a young girl of perhaps twelve, her bathing suit discarded next to her, her knees pulled up covering her genitals, but not quite hiding her just blossoming breasts.

"What are you doing here?" Lysette responded.

"It's *my* beach," she laughed, as if the question were silly.

"Do you live around here? I don't see any houses."

"I come here all the time," she answered evasively. "It's my beach." She wasn't being arrogant, just stating facts very much as Lysette would if someone asked her why she was there.

"Do you always take off your clothes in public?"

Without answering, the girl got up, dashed into the water up to her waist, then dived into the breaking waves. She was long-legged and slim; gangly, all arms and legs. A child going through her changes, coming into her own. Lysette remembered her mother talking about Laura after her period had begun. "The girl and the woman fighting for control of the body." There was just a hint of pubic hair covering her genitals and her petite breasts juggled just a bit as she dashed back to the shore. Her tan was a deep brown, enveloping her entire body; her light brown hair flowed behind her and came to rest halfway down her back.

"It's my beach," she said matter-of-factly, as she plopped down on the sand. No one *ever* comes here. No need for a bathing suit when there's no one to gawk.

"I'm here," Lysette said.

"You're a woman, silly, and you don't have much more on than I do. You can stay on my beach if you tell me what you're making."

"Thank you," Lysette said with a laugh. "My name's Lysette. What's yours?"

"That's a pretty name. I'm Angela, but everyone calls me Angel. Angel, cause of my devilish ways," she laughed. "Not as pretty as your name, though."

"Sure it is," Lysette said with a smile.

"So, tell me what you've made. I can't make heads or tails of it."

For the first time Lysette looked at her sculpture, and felt lightheaded. She assumed she had sculpted her two lovers, which this child might not understand, but it was nothing of the sort.

On the ground, in bas-relief, was the figure of a girl . . .

—Lysette, when she was eleven.

. . . her mouth open in a silent scream, one side of her head bashed in. Towering over her was a man . . .

—The man who had attacked her.

. . . holding an object . . .

—A marble lighter.

. . . over his head, ready to strike her again. There was a phenomenal amount of detail; trails that appeared to be blood on one side of the girl's head, tears falling from her eyes to her cheek. The man's clothes showed detail, as well; wrinkles in the jeans, several buttons torn off his shirt exposing a hairy chest.

But the face. It was blank; totally devoid of features. No eyes, nose or mouth. It was as if she had been interrupted before she had finished her creation, but she knew that wasn't the case. There was no face because she couldn't remember what he'd looked like.

Angel confirmed this for her.

"I wouldn't have bothered you, if I didn't think you were done. I mean, you were working, your hands moving real fast, and then you got to the face and stopped. I waited ten minutes before saying anything . . . honest. You just looked at the face totally frozen. Is it a secret, or will you tell me what it is? If it's a secret, that's all right. I've got secrets, too . . . " and her voice trailed off.

"No, it's not a secret. It's just . . . This sounds silly, but I don't remember sculpting *this*. The girl on the ground is me, when I was about your age. How old are you? Eleven, twelve?"

"Eleven. *Eleven and a half.*"

"I was eleven when some men attacked my family. This man," she said, pointing a shaking finger at the figure in the sculpture, "hit me on the head with a marble lighter. That's what he's holding."

"But he has no face. Everything else is so detailed, you know."

"I couldn't remember what he looked like. I was in a coma for a month. Doctors said I blocked it out. Today, it's like it was on the tip of my tongue, if you get what I mean, but just beyond my reach."

"Wow! It's . . . I don't know. Powerful. That's it. *Powerful.* I can almost feel your pain. And I can feel his rage, just looking at it. It's beautiful in a weird sort of way."

Lysette sat down next to Angel, and both of them stared at the sculpture.

"Why did you build it so close to the water? Look, the tide's coming in. It'll be destroyed in a few minutes." There was a sadness, almost panic in her voice.

Lysette smiled. "Don't worry. It's intentional. It's like . . . how can I put it?"

"You mean so a little kid like me can understand?" Angel said with some irritation.

"You're not so little," Lysette said, again noticing the girl's breasts. "No, I mean, how can I explain it, even to myself? Okay. I feel almost like a trespasser. And maybe I am because this is *your* beach," she said with a smile. "I'm taking something from the beach that belongs to the beach. Does that make any sense?"

"Like you're stealing a part of the beach?"

"Not exactly stealing. Using without permission. Like if you go into your mother's room and use her makeup without asking. Understand?"

Angel looked thoughtful for a moment. "It's not yours, and you feel . . . bad."

"Guilty would be a better word," Lysette said. "Anyway, if I build it close to the water's edge, the sea can reclaim it. I've gotten the pleasure from making my sculpture, but I'm allowing the ocean to take it back."

"It's a shame it has to be destroyed," Angel said as the water crept closer.

"I can always build another. And with this one, I'm not sure I'd want to preserve it. It gives me goosebumps."

Lysette looked at her watch. "Oh my God. It's almost four o'clock. I started building it at one and . . . I can't remember a thing until you started talking. I gotta be going. I've gotta drive to Philly, change and go to work."

Lysette got up. Angel did, too, and helped Lysette bring her tools to the car.

"Can I drop you anywhere?" Lysette asked, as she prepared to leave.

"No. I live just over the dunes," she said, pointing. "Anyway, I want to see the sea swallow your sculpture."

"Was nice meeting you, Angel," Lysette said, not knowing what else to add.

"You can come back to my beach, if you want. Just you. No one else. Maybe you'll build another sculpture."

"How will you know I'm here?" Lysette said with a smile.

"I'll know," Angel said, and without saying goodbye turned and ran into the surf again. As Lysette got into the car, she saw the child wave at her.

Driving home, Lysette's thoughts were churning. She always got into her sculptures when she began, but she was always aware what she was doing. This time, though . . .

—You blacked out, her mind screamed.

. . . three hours lost. She remembered standing in front of the television that morning, gun in hand and . . .

—Blacking out. For forty-five minutes.

The sculpture itself brought back such vivid memories; memories long suppressed. No, she thought, they had resurfaced after Rose's death. Brief, but vivid, flashes. Grabbing the knife from the boy in the subway, she'd seen the attack on Rose described in the paper, but also the man who had killed her sister.

Now, this sculpture, so real the side of her head ached, as if he had actually hit her with the lighter. And the featureless face . . .

—The face only a mother could love.

Why a face only a mother could love? she thought. The face was as elusive as ever.

And Angel. What a spirited child; a hint of mischief about her . . .

—Angel, because of my devilish ways.

So unlike herself *after* the attack. She hadn't thought of it before, but seeing Angel, she felt robbed of her youth and adolescence. In a way she had stopped growing emotionally after she awoke from the coma. She'd sleepwalked through sixth grade, junior high and high school; her emotions kept in check as her body went through its metamorphosis.

Angel, though, was just beginning to experience the agony and ecstasy of becoming a woman.

If the weather held up, she'd return to the beach in a few days . . .

—To Angel.

—To the beach they shared.

—Angel's beach.

80

—To the man without a face.

As she crossed the Walt Whitman Bridge to Philadelphia, she was also aware she'd decided not to go to the police. She didn't want the public scrutiny, praise or condemnation. Let it remain a mystery, she thought. No one would be hurt. She had been cleared of any wrongdoing, after all. She would just disappear.

The decision made, she felt content.

At home she decided to forgo a shower until she got to the club. She grabbed her things and on the way out noticed the answering machine blinking. She'd only got it—and reluctantly at that—so Jil, at the club, could contact her. Some days girls didn't show up and Jil would call to ask Lysette to work a double shift. To Jil's credit, she didn't abuse the privilege. One shift was hell on her feet, especially her ankles with the five-inch pumps she had to wear. A double shift was absolute torture. She rewound the tape.

"Hi Lysette. It's Angel. Don't be mad. I told you I was devilish. While you were staring at that blank face of the man, I got bored. So . . . " There was a pause. "I kinda went through your purse in the car and found your number. I didn't take anything," she added quickly. "Check and you'll see. I'm devilish, not a thief. Anyway, just wanted to tell you how cool I think you are . . . for an *older* woman."

Angel giggled, and Lysette couldn't stifle a laugh of her own.

—*Older woman, my ass*, she thought.

"Anyway, I hope you'll come back to my beach." Another pause. "*Our* beach." Barely above a whisper. "Gotta go now. See you soon. Okay?"

There was a bounce to Lysette's step as she left the house; a contentment she hadn't felt . . .

—Since you lost your big sister.

For some reason she'd felt instantly comfortable around Angel, and in spite of the intrusion into her privacy, she longed to see the girl again.

She felt almost like . . .

—A mother?

—No.

—An older sister?

—Yeah.

—*A big sister.*

Chapter Twelve

At the hospital, while Lysette was at the beach, Deidre told Jonas about the subway shooting, and the dismay on the part of the police that the mystery woman hadn't come forward. Her own story, for the *Daily News*, had been a straightforward factual account, with the added tidbit about the reluctance of the passengers to describe the woman. She was also the first to detail Jerome Brown's troubled past; thanks to Jenkins.

Her editor showed his appreciation by allowing her to beg off the inevitable followups: talks with the victim's family, neighborhood reaction, interviews with the passengers and Isiah Hayes; and the search for the woman herself—the proverbial needle in a haystack.

"Not my kind of story, Jonas. Everyone covering the same ground, bumping into one another to get a scoop. For me it's back to checking out what happened to high school students who witnessed their teacher shoot himself in the head six years ago."

There was no response from Jonas; not that Deidre expected any. The once vibrant reporter—her mentor, father of her husband and later confidant and friend after her husband and son's death, now lay silent in a hospital bed. Only sixty-seven, and in generally good health, he had suffered a massive stroke a month before.

It had been touch and go for a while, but he had survived, though Deidre knew he craved death. He was paralyzed virtually from head to foot, couldn't speak, couldn't even communicate with his eyes, which stared vacantly into space.

Worse, doctors told her he was fully aware of his situation. His hearing was seemingly unimpaired. Doctors were evasive about his prognosis for even a partial recovery. With time the paralysis *might* subside. Then again . . .

Deidre visited him daily, when she wasn't off on assignment, filling him in on the progress of her stories; telling him about the foibles of his beloved Eagles. Just talk. She liked to bounce ideas off him, and even though he couldn't respond, just being in his presence helped crystallize her thoughts. She'd even verbalize his responses in her mind, in his rapid staccato sentence fragments that hid from most the depth of his warmth.

"Why isn't this girl coming forth, Jonas? Think of all the accolades and attention."

Fool reporters probing into her life, she imagined his response. *Pick her apart. Open old sores. Judge her. Look for flaws.*

"You're right," she said aloud. "As a mystery woman she's bigger than life. A hero with no warts. A human steps forth and it bursts their balloon."

She farts. Has bad breath. High-pitched squeaky voice. Bunch of rug rats underfoot. Husband with a beer belly, belching and dribbling on his undershirt.

"You're bad, Jonas. So cynical," she said, repeating out loud what she knew he would say if he could. "But, yeah, she could never live up to expectations. Maybe it's better for the city she remains an enigma. Helped a fellow man in need and asks for nothing in return. *That is unusual*." She sighed.

"So, I guess you want me to read to you about your Eagles." Mondays were for reports of the game itself. This being Tuesday, there were three articles analyzing the latest loss. Dallas, of course, was in first place, and the Eagles inconsistent, with two pint-sized quarterbacks; neither of whom endeared themselves to the fans with their erratic play.

While reading, she thought of the loneliness that now enveloped her. If it weren't for my work, she thought . . .

—You'd turn back to booze.

She didn't think so. The booze, she knew now, hadn't helped her cope with her family's death. It simply allowed each day to pass without having to face up to life without her husband and only child. Jonas had been there, and with his prodding she had come to grips with her despair.

Now she was truly alone. An only child; her father had passed on six years before. One year later, her mother had succumbed to ovarian cancer. Jonas had been the one constant in her adult life; there when she was in college, where he took her under his wing; there to guide her through her first years as a reporter; there when her family was snatched away; there when Shara reentered her life; there when, with Shara, she had finally become a journalist.

With Jonas gone there was . . .

—*Only Shara.*

Perish the thought, she admonished herself. Shara was a part of her, but with Shara each truth she told hid another lie. Shara had used her . . .

—*But she's your friend.*

. . . then used her again . . .

—*You're all she's got.*

Ridiculous. I'm nothing to her.

"Oh, Jonas," she said aloud, after finishing the final story. "I need you so. I'm so alone. What will I do without you?" For deep down, she knew Jonas would never return.

There was no response. She kissed him on the forehead, then squeezed his hand, hoping for any kind of response. None. Why should today be any different? she thought to herself.

"Here I go pitying myself again," she said to him. "Selfish little bitch. *You're* the one going through hell, and I'm pissed you're not here for me. Forgive me, Jonas. I'm trying to be strong, but it's not easy."

She would go home and immerse herself in news clippings that might lead her to . . .

—*Another Shara.*

. . . a victim who had crossed the line and was victimizing others.

"Tomorrow, Jonas. Same time. Same place. Next time don't monopolize the conversation."

She gave him another kiss and left.

Chapter Thirteen

Driving to the club, Lysette tucked herself away and allowed Cassandra Knight to emerge. While her big tits had been a major asset in getting hired, she found out later her interview had been equally important. No family. No boyfriend. Jil later told her these averted many of the pitfalls in the business.

"Some of the girls don't tell their family. More than once a girl's father, brother or uncle dropped by and the shit hit the fan."

Jil hadn't been intrusive, though, refraining from asking what had happened to her family.

"Boyfriends are absolutely the worst," Jil said with a laugh. "At the beginning they can be supportive. I mean the money's so good. The girls end up buying *them* expensive presents and paying for dates. Eventually, though, they get possessive and jealousy surfaces. If a girl's half an hour late she must have been balling one of the customers."

During her interview, Jil had fielded two phone calls—cordial, but all business—and handled several minor crises.

"Boyfriends," she continued after one call, "also don't get the attention they expect from their women. You work an eight-hour shift in five-inch pumps and when you're through you want to slip into a bath and then under the covers—*alone*. You work six weeks, then have one off, but you'll find precious little time during those six weeks to get into mischief."

Jil extinguished her cigarillo in an ash tray, and popped a piece of gum into her mouth.

"I can understand," she continued, "how it breaks up relationships. Unfortunately some—*too many*—of the girls take a short-sighted view and give up financial security for their man of the moment. As far as I'm concerned, a man who can't tolerate the needs of a working woman will find other faults later on. With you, it's no problem. Leastwise, not at the moment."

She also liked the fact that Lysette was goal-oriented.

"I want to finish art school," she'd told Jil, "and maybe open up a shop on South Street to exhibit and sell the work of relative unknowns. I might even do some private teaching. If I can build a bit of a nest egg, I won't have to be so . . . I don't know. Commercial, I guess. Compromise my principles and sell garbage because that's what sells and without sales you lose your shop."

"Maybe you can call your shop 'Shit Sells,' Jil said good-naturedly.

Lysette almost winced at the woman's language. Her vocabulary was rife with expletives.

On the phone: "I don't give a shit what your problem is this time, Savannah. You know with me it's three strikes and you're fucked." Pause. "Don't bullshit a bullshitter, girl. Cramps. Your period. Give me a goddamn break. You're not dealing with the fucking village idiot. It's time to clean up your act." Another pause, her eyes looking at the ceiling as if she couldn't believe what she was hearing.

"Look, babe, call me in six months—when you've got your priorities in order—and I'll be happy to give you another shot. But that's the best I can do. You fucked with me once too often. Sorry," and she hung up.

To a hostess whose headset malfunctioned: "You ever hear of batteries, hon? Shit, sometimes I feel I have to do *everything* for *everybody*. God gave you a brain, hon. Why don't you fucking use it."

It was here that Lysette first saw the power of profanity, and told herself if she ever opened up a shop of her own she might use "Shit Sells" for a slogan. She thought others would frown on it as a name for a store. It wasn't until much later that she gained enough self-confidence to do what *she* wanted, and to hell what the others thought.

Driving down Route 1, Lysette put in a tape of club music she'd compiled to help get herself into the Cassandra frame of mind.

After she had been hired, Jil told her she needed a stage name.

"You don't want customers calling you or stopping by your house. Mind you, they will, if you give them a chance. We're selling fantasy here. You have to separate Lysette from your stage presence."

She took out a list of first names and asked if any sang out to her. They ran the gamut: Peaches, Shannon, Joey, Tina, Paradise, Sheena. Some were enough to make her laugh. "Hey Peaches," she tried to imagine a guy saying, "you're looking foxy tonight." It didn't work.

Then she saw Cassandra. The name exuded poise and self-confidence—without sounding trashy—qualities foreign to her. If she could *become* Cassandra, she would not only shed her own personality for the club, but might take on some of the qualities in her own life.

"Cassandra it is then," Jil said. "A last name is optional. You needn't come up with one right now; needn't come up with one at all."

"Cassandra Knight," Lysette said with confidence. She didn't know where she'd pulled it out, but once she said it, she knew it was right for her.

"I like the *night* best. In the dark I can shut out . . . shut out memories I'd rather not dwell on. *Night* with an *N* doesn't look right, but add the silent *K*, and you've got the new me."

Jil nodded in agreement. "After you've been working awhile you'll take on a persona that fits your name. That persona is important because in many ways Cassandra Knight won't be like Lysette at all. You've got to find a happy balance; you know, a dash of Lysette and a smidgen of a woman you've fantasized yourself being, yet isn't really you, to make a Cassandra you can comfortably slip into."

Jil now threw out the gum in disgust, and lit another cigarillo.

"One more thing and it's very important. When you're here you answer *only* to Cassandra. Even with the other girls. Later, when you make friends you'll tell some your real name, but you're Cassandra when you walk in the door. Again, it's for your own protection."

As Jil showed her around the club, her eyes wandering to assure herself everything was as it should be, she told Lysette about its history.

"This used to be a dance club that sold alcohol. The company I work for bought it and introduced topless dancing. With liquor, in this state, you can't have total nudity."

She stopped and complimented a dancer passing by on earning her high-school equivalency diploma.

"Where was I? Oh, well, when the club reopened there was an

uproar; pickets outside like we were a fucking abortion clinic. I mean these people needed to get a life. They pledged to return until we closed. The ace up their sleeves was our liquor license, which was due to expire in sixty days.

"We never wanted to serve liquor here. We had two other smaller clubs in operation which didn't serve alcohol. My bosses figured, let them picket for two months and wear themselves ragged. We'd give up the fight to get a new liquor license; give them a victory they could go home with."

Jil stopped and watched a girl dancing center stage. She crawled on the floor like a panther, and stuck her dangling breasts into the faces of one of the many customers who sat in chairs around the stage. The man produced a bill which the girl plucked with her teeth and deftly transferred to her garter belt. Jil smiled.

"A month ago a couple of the guys made some crack about her fat ass, and she left the stage in tears. Now look at her. Not every girl has the perfect figure. You see some girls here on the chubby side. Why?" she asked rhetorically. "Because every man has his own fantasy girl. Some want them thin with big tits, but others want girls big all over. Now she has them eating out of her hand. She's using *her assets* to *her* advantage. Dangle those boobs in some guy's face and they won't be looking at her fat ass."

Lysette marveled at the girl's confidence; couldn't fathom the woman fleeing the stage in tears.

"Back to our history lesson. We traded liquor for total nudity. Then they brought me in. The day we reopened without liquor, I confronted the pickets. It was opening night, so they were out in force again.

"They were caught off guard. If you saw me walking down the street, you wouldn't give me a second look."

"That's not true," Lysette said. "You're stunning."

Jil looked at her quizzically, then shrugged. "I'm good-looking, and I carry myself well; something I learned as a dancer. But I'm thirty-six, and I dress conservatively most of the time, so no one in the world would mistake me for a stripper.

"Anyway, I told the pickets they had no reason to worry. No liquor. No drugs. We were entertainers, I told them, not sluts or prostitutes. I explained about our staff security. They weren't happy, but I addressed most of their concerns, and we knew legally they couldn't do a damn thing."

She introduced Lysette to her head of security, as they passed, again, her eyes darting back and forth, taking the pulse of the crowd. Then it was back to her story.

"And not coincidentally," she said, "the liquor license expired at the end of November. Gets nippy in December; hardly weather for mass protests. Slowly we wore them down, even if we didn't win them over."

She stopped at the bar and ordered two soft drinks, giving one to Lysette.

"There were no serious incidents the first two months. We donated money to community groups. Eventually the pickets just went away. This is our fourth year, and we're tolerated by most, accepted, even welcomed, by others. Those who condemn us have gone onto new crusades."

Having toured the club, Jil took Lysette back to her office.

"When do I start?" Lysette asked, her voice more than a little nervous.

Jil smiled. "Tonight. I like to start girls right away. If you get through tonight, you can get through anything. Give you a night to mull it over, and all your misgivings will be magnified."

"But what do I do?" Lysette asked.

Again Jil smiled. "I'm not going to throw you to the wolves. All you do tonight is greet customers and observe. Tomorrow, one of my trainers will show you the ropes, one step at a time."

Lysette had relaxed. Greeting customers seemed simple enough. "Hi, I'm Cassandra. Enjoy your stay at the Genesis Club," she'd imagined herself mouthing forty or fifty times.

Greeting customers, though, in reality, was far different. Near the entrance to the club were three gold bars—from floor to ceiling. Topless, she danced and when a customer entered she gave him a titty hug; planting the man's face between her boobs and squeezing.

It opened her eyes to what lay in store. Newcomers were as embarrassed as she; more so as the night passed and she became more comfortable. Regulars knew she was new and welcomed her. One guy circled her nipple with his tongue. She was too shocked to respond; surprised even more when he stuck a bill in her garter belt.

By the end of the evening she had become brash. She'd hold a guy's hand after giving him a titty hug, plant it on her breast and help him massage it for a few seconds.

Two other girls, also new, had less success. One needed a break every fifteen minutes or so, complaining the whole time about her aching feet.

Lysette's feet ached, as did her back, and her head pounded from the constant music, but she was making good money. The complainer had barely enough in her garter for a Big Mac and fries.

Over the next few weeks and months Cassandra Knight evolved. "Brash and bold with an 'atti-toode,' " she told a girl she was given to train, in a thick exaggerated South Philly accent, not at all like the way she talked off the job.

"I own the floor when I'm down here, and the guys eat it up. I'm aggressive as hell. Remember, *we're* the ones who are supposed to be the intimidators."

Lysette drove into the club's entrance. By the time she got to the parking lot she *was* Cassandra; there was no more Lysette. She swaggered with confidence to a side door for the dancers, hugging Sam, one of the security guards, when she entered. . . .

—Not at all like uptight Lysette.

"Hi, honey," she cooed. "How's it hanging tonight?" She wasn't Cassandra *only* when she was on the floor. She became Cassandra the moment she stepped out of her car.

She ran into Jil.

"Baby, am I glad to see you," Jil said. "It's one of those nights. Samantha and Lana both called in sick. I thought you might take me up on my offer from last night and—"

Lysette raised a hand to cut her off. "I was shaky yesterday, but what's the good of sitting at home moping? Went to the beach and it did me a world of good. And I wasn't about to let you down. If I wasn't coming in, you know I'd have called hours ago."

Jil gave her a hug. "That's my girl. You're an angel." Then brushing herself off, she added, "You *did* go to the beach. Didn't take a shower after, did you?" she laughed.

"No time, if I didn't want to be late. Thought I'd do it here."

"Gotta run," Jil said. "Got to find a fill-in for at least one of the girls or I'll end up dancing. That *would* be getting desperate, wouldn't it?" and they both laughed.

Taking off her coat in the spacious dressing room on the second floor, Lysette felt the gun. Shit, she thought. I forgot to hide it at the apartment. A cloud crossed her face for a moment. She remembered taking the gun out in the morning, pointing it at the television. She didn't remember putting it back in her coat after awaking from her brief blackout. Fuck it, she decided. No sense overanalyzing.

Lysette would replay the scene backwards and forwards umpteen times and worry it to death. Cassandra, on the other hand, would feel the gun in her pocket and know she put it there. Case closed.

There was a strange electricity in the air that night. Seemed like everyone was talking about the mystery woman who had shot a good-for-nothing crackhead.

Every once in a while, Lysette noticed, some topic became the focus of just about everyone's attention. Even before she'd begun working at the club, she'd gotten a taste of it in her South Philly neighborhood.

Often it revolved around sports: the firing of Buddy Ryan as the Eagle's coach, the Charles Barkley trade, the angina the "Wild Thing" Mitch Williams caused during the year the Phillies went to the world series. The O. J. Simpson trial had similarly grabbed the populace by the crotch and wouldn't let go. Everyone had an opinion. Argue all you want, you'd never alter anyone's viewpoint. With the death of Princess Di, it seemed everyone but she was grief-stricken. Tonight, it was the subway shooting.

Lysette felt slightly schizoid from all the fuss. Lysette, buried deep within, was intensely interested in everyone's opinion. Cassandra, though, was out to make a buck and was pissed at anything that caused customers to lose their focus; the fantasy she not only provided, but commanded.

She gravitated, first, to the young kids—eighteen, nineteen or twenty. To them she was the older woman who showed interest. She was her most aggressive with them. Wearing only a bra and panties, she would plant her boobs right into the face of one of the guys.

"What's your name, hon." Not a question. A command.

"T-T-Tommy," the boy answered hesitantly.

"I'm Cassandra, and when I'm out here, you only have eyes for me. Now, how's about a Table Dance?"

He giggled, his friends egging him on. "I-I-I don't have the six dollars."

"What have you got?"

The boy dug into his jeans and produced two singles.

Unfazed, Cassandra turned to the boy next to Tommy, who was laughing his head off at his friend's plight.

"How much do you have?"

He pulled out three dollars, which Cassandra plucked from his hand and gave to Tommy. The other boy convulsed into further laughter.

"You got good friends, Tommy. They want to help you out."

"Won't you do it for five dollars?" a third boy said. "Being it's his first time and all."

"You got a job?" Cassandra asked the third, her eyes still fixed on Tommy.

The boy flushed. "I go to Drexel, but I work weekends at my father's butcher shop," he said with pride.

"And what if I came in for a steak that cost six dollars and all I had was five?"

"I'd tell you to blow off," he said giving his friend a high five at his wit.

"Just my point. The dance is six dollars. You want to help your buddy, or am I wasting my time?"

The others now laughed at him. Duped by a half-naked broad. The kid produced a dollar.

Cassandra not only had Tommy's attention, but his friends'. No doubt in her mind, they'd be back with more than a few singles. And they were hers.

A Table Dance consisted of standing on a stool so she towered over the customer, taking off her top and caressing her body, sometimes getting within inches of the customer without touching. Club rules mandated she let each customer know what was allowed. With Table Dancing, it was simple: They couldn't touch her. She performed. They looked.

The song began—one of the dozens of club tunes that sounded so much alike she couldn't differentiate between them or identify the performer. But since walking into the club, she had been at one with her character and the music, and just let the rhythm take her.

She deftly slipped three dollars to one of the men who circulated taking a percentage from every dancer. Slowly, she undid her top, placing it on Tommy's shoulder, as the other boys whooped it up. Tommy was transfixed; too caught up in his fantasy to do anything but gulp.

Cassandra ran her hands over her body, slowly caressing and kneading her breasts. She turned around, her almost bare ass within inches of Tommy's face, and moved seductively to the music.

Facing Tommy again, she played with her nipples. Then she bent over Tommy, her hands resting on the bar behind him, her breasts within inches of his face.

Softly she talked to him.

"Enjoying yourself, Tommy?"

"Oh yeah!"

"Are you hard, yet?" she whispered.

"Oh yeah!"

She stood up, her crotch now eye level with Tommy, and slid her hand into her panties, playing with her genitals without Tommy being able to see.

She bent over again.

"Want me to take off my panties, so you can have a good look?"

"Oh yeah!! Oh yeah!!!"

"Sorry, honey," she said, stroking his face, teasingly. "Now if we had a Couch Dance, there'd be nothing left to your imagination. Want a Couch Dance?"

"Oh yeah!"

"But you need fifteen dollars. Do you have it, Tommy?"

"Fuck no."

"A pity. I want to do it for you, Tommy, but you know the rules."

She gave him a titty hug before he could reply.

He was flushed; breathing deeply. His friends had gone silent.

"You come back with some money, just ask for Cassandra and I'll give you the time of your life. Okay?"

"Oh yeah!"

The song ended, and Cassandra donned her top. Tommy was still panting; his friends had been transfixed since she'd given him a titty hug.

She looked at them and waved, turned and circulated. If they could come up with enough money they were hers. If not, she'd bet the house they would be back soon. She quickly glanced over her shoulder and saw Tommy's two friends asking him what she'd said.

—My floor.

—Putty in my hands.

—*I* am your Fantasy Girl.

She hit on some of her regulars; guys she had captured with her aggressiveness and who she had established a rapport with. No matter how much money they spent she would get at least a Table Dance and Couch Dance out of them, with a nice tip management didn't share.

Her regulars liked to talk. Sometimes she felt like a goddamned Ph.D. as they told her their woes.

"Boss is out to get me . . ."

" . . . swear my old lady is having an affair."

" . . . we'd screw twice a night. Now she's got a headache. *Every night*."

" . . . on the pill. How could she get pregnant?"

Tonight, though, her regulars wanted to talk about Lysette; the Good Samaritan who saved one nigger and wasted another. Many of her regulars were blue-collar workers. She was far too aggressive for the suits; guys who she knew were bosses and control freaks. They wanted to dominate. Aggressiveness turned them off.

Blue-collar workers, on the other hand, didn't mind giving up control. The downside was they were often crass. Niggers, spics, kikes and chinks. Fuck this. Fuck that. *Lysette* would have been repulsed. Cassandra was not out to change the world. These men worked hard, played hard. Given the chance they would rather work in shit-filled sewers than go on welfare.

They might get sloshed Sunday watching the Eagles; might slap the wife upside the head for no good reason at all; might get into fist fights with their best friends. But you wouldn't catch them selling or using crack; wouldn't find them stealing their mother's television for a fix; wouldn't find them getting twelve-year-olds high so they could score one later on.

Cassandra accepted them for what they were. Anyway, their money was just as green as the suits'.

Tonight, though, as she Couch Danced with her regulars, all they wanted to talk about was Lysette.

Couch Dancing was similar to Table Dancing except she wore nothing. Couches were discretely out of the glare, giving some semblance of privacy. The customer would sit with his arms on a wooden bannister—"remember, no touching"—above the couch while she danced.

Here, though, Cassandra would get down and dirty. Her pussy, shaved—she would gyrate within licking distance of the man. She'd turn, her bare ass facing the customer, bend over, so he could see her snatch, then play with herself with her fingers.

When he was aroused, she would turn around, bend down with her tits in his face, and whisper sexy thoughts in his ears.

It was during these dances that her regulars would open up to her—a total stranger—asking for advice, and probably more often than not taking it.

She bent down to Jack, wondering what new horror story he had to relate about his wife.

"Can you believe the stones that woman had; yanking that gun from the punk and shooting him in his frigging head."

Tim was certain he'd be fired; had been for the past eight months, but tonight his mind was elsewhere.

"You wouldn't catch me dead in a subway at night. That girl, though, man she's fucking fearless."

Kent had been going out with a girl for nine months and they had yet to kiss, but tonight he didn't ask for advice.

"Who do you think she is? Why the disappearing act? I'd stand in line to shake her hand."

Two customers commented on her blonde hair, and one went so far as to ask for protection.

"Hey, hon, if someone messes with me, you gonna stand up to them?"

When he forgot to tip her, she wanted to shoot *him*.

On and on it went. And over the course of the night Cassandra lost the rhythm that made her so successful. She became bitchy, her dancing mechanical; her mind wandered. No one would pick up on it, but Cassandra was pissed that Lysette was intruding *on her time*.

Why couldn't she have just left well enough alone instead of playing Superwoman? she thought. If some old fart was stupid enough to take a subway at night, he was asking for trouble. Cassandra had money to make and Lysette's little escapade was costing her big time.

For the night she cleared $150; better than the blue-collar workers she danced for, but one of her worst nights in a long time.

She heard other girls bitching about their earnings, as well. God, was she pissed. She had worked her butt off for a measly $150.

In her car, she didn't take off the wig. Though her feet ached, she still wore the five-inch pumps. She felt the bulge of the gun in her coat.

She was in a foul mood and drove home putting her foot to the floor at every yellow light; driving fast, even recklessly.

Cassandra was driving, without any regard for Lysette, who fought for control.

Chapter Fourteen

Nina Rios had no desire whatsoever to work with Lamar Briggs, but knew it would be a waste of time trying to convince Morales.

The pairing, she thought, was counterproductive. The few times they had been paired together, each had worked in virtual isolation and often at cross purposes. As a result, each wasted precious time duplicating the effort of the other. It was odd that they thought so much alike, yet there was no common ground to break the hostility that engulfed them like a shroud.

Nina was content that at least she had made an effort, early on, but after being rebuffed several times, she had her pride and decided Lamar-Fucking-Briggs could go fuck himself. The next overture would be *his*.

In this case, if the shit hit the fan, it would land squarely on him. She was merely window-dressing. Rumors were already rampant that Morales had been *told*—from someone very high up—to assign the case to Briggs. Racial sensitivity with a white having killed a black youth or some such crap. She was merely an appendage. Briggs had center stage, and she was satisfied to remain in the murky shadows of the background. If he self-destructed, so be it.

When she had arrived at eight in the morning, Morales had taken her aside for a moment; not to his office, but to the coffee machine in the far corner of the office area. Everyone knew when Morales was at the coffee machine with one of his detectives to give them breathing room. It was far more private than his office, with its paper-thin walls.

He waited while she put cream and sugar in her coffee.

"I'm fully aware you and Briggs don't get along," he said between sips of coffee. "It's not a black mark against you. Briggs is

96

set in his ways. He can be an opinionated, self-centered, stubborn ass. He's also one of the best detectives you'll ever work with."

He finished his cup and poured another.

"We both know how tightly wound he is, what with his daughter and all, but that doesn't mean he can't do his job. I partnered you with him for one reason and one reason only. You won't kiss his ass."

He paused to let the impact of his words sink in.

"He'll get the job done, if humanly possible, *but* it's *how* he gets it done that concerns me. Do you understand where I'm coming from, Detective?"

"His hair-trigger temper since his daughter was attacked," Nina answered. "You want me to make sure he doesn't go off half-cocked; blow a gasket that will reflect badly on the department . . . on you."

"I don't give a rat's ass about the department or myself," he said and then paused, made eye contact with her and smiled. "That's not exactly true. My ass is on the line if he self-destructs. Granted." His tone then became grave. "But my main concern is Briggs. For reasons I can't go into, I'll survive. Briggs, on the other hand, may not. If it seems he's coming unglued, I want to know *before* the explosion."

He seemed to know that what he'd said hadn't come out exactly right.

"Look, you won't be ratting on him to a supervisor. You'll be protecting him from himself. He's highly vulnerable now. A case like this can be cathartic. On the other hand, with the outside pressures eating at him, it could be too much to handle. Any questions?"

She could think of no way to weasel out of the assignment, so she shrugged no.

"In that case, we never had this discussion. Just the luck of the draw you got the case."

He finished his coffee and went back to the pill box that was his office.

Nina was grateful his reasons for assigning her to Briggs had nothing to do with her being a woman. Glad he hadn't asked her to get him to talk about his daughter, because as a *woman* she could relate to his pain. Glad that he didn't want her to *mother* him. On the contrary, apparently she was the only one tough enough to stand up to him. For one of the first times since she had been a cop, she felt like *one of the guys*; not female officer Nina Rios, with the emphasis on female.

The only daughter among nine children, Nina had clawed her way through much of her life; a lone female trying to fit in in a man's world. Always bony—gaunt, scrawny, even emaciated was more like it—she had nevertheless been toughened by her brothers, who adored her.

She had been a tomboy, more interested in stickball and hoops than dolls and doubledutch. She had gotten tired of her brothers fighting her battles for her at an early age, and had taken karate lessons at a local Y. She'd followed that with boxing instruction at a nearby gym, in exchange for cleaning up the joint. She didn't mind the women's work, as long as it was a means to an end—in this case, self-preservation and self-reliance.

She didn't know why she decided to become a cop, though in part it was because she never became a *lady*. She never denied her femininity, and after losing her virginity in high school gave her body freely, willingly and often. Sex could be a great equalizer, she learned. Often the aggressor, it was another form of power and control. But a *lady* she wasn't. She had no desire to be dominated, domesticated or coddled.

As significant, she had continually been surrounded by crime and violence. Her father drove a cab, and had been robbed four times; badly beaten once. Two of her older brothers had been shot; both involved in gang-related activities. Hector, sixteen, had been killed when she was eleven. Carlos, two years older than she, had been paralyzed a year later. Her oldest brother, Luis, was serving time in jail for his part in a robbery, in which a store owner had been killed.

She and her other four brothers had literally fought their way through school. Only she and Alejandro, two years her junior, had graduated.

Her parents had done what they could, but violence so permeated their neighborhood—was such a part of their everyday lives—they couldn't be an island onto themselves. To their credit, her parents had steered them away from drugs, by their own example and force of will.

Nina had continued boxing through high school, giving as good as she got in competition with boys her weight. She had a crush on one of her instructors, Felipe, a cop who spent a good deal of his spare time trying to wean troubled kids off the street through boxing and martial arts.

One day after she'd been knocked flat on her ass by a boy with much quicker hands, he had taken her aside.

"What are you going to do with yourself, Nina? You're graduating this year. You know you've no future in boxing. You're a hell of a fighter, but girls fighting professionally is in its infancy, not a full-time occupation."

She had shrugged. She hadn't given it any thought.

"You going to get knocked up and be trailed around by a bunch of rug rats?"

That got a response.

"I'm *never* going to get married," she had answered, sounding more like a fifth grader than a high-school senior. "Not soon, anyway," she added. "I want more out of life than keeping house for a man. Look at Mama. Clean house and have babies; then see them die or go to jail."

She began pacing around the room, warming to the subject.

"But women's work, like being a secretary, is no better." She spat out *secretary*, like it was an expletive; akin to being a whore. "And, I have no desire to go to college to become a prooo-fessional," she said, dragging out the last word derisively. She seemed to have exhausted herself, and went silent.

"I happen to know the police department is actively recruiting women," he said, making eye contact with her. "Especially *minority* women." He smiled. "Payback time. To be honest," he added, "I wouldn't want to work with many of the women I've seen on the force. They're not physically equipped to be cops and can't command the respect of the community. You," he laughed, "You are one tough son-of-a-bitch. You could watch my back good as any man. It won't be easy, being a woman, but that never stopped you before."

She looked at him skeptically.

He raised his hands in surrender. "No more preaching. Promise. Just think of it as an option."

With no better options she took him up on his offer and went to the police academy, where she excelled. Not only were women being sought out at a time when feminists were demanding equal employment and being given a sympathetic ear, but advancement was swift. More than some women's performance dictated.

—*Payback*.

Just as blacks had earlier, she leapfrogged over officers with greater seniority, and after only four years on the street and two in vice, she became one of only a handful of female homicide detectives; one of the most coveted positions in the department.

That was the crux of the problem with Briggs, she knew. She hadn't paid her dues. She knew he also saw her as this scrawny woman he'd have to protect if things ever got rough. He had only been partially mollified when she had decked a uniform at Cavanaugh's—a cop hangout—when he tried to feel her up after one too many drinks.

Sooner or later, she knew, she would have to confront his prejudices. Given her druthers, she'd get him in a gym and bust his chops. Chauvinist that he was, though, he probably wouldn't take her up on a challenge.

That morning, after her talk with Morales, she and Briggs had interviewed the subway passengers. Briggs had been particularly sullen and pensive after his interrogation of Isiah Hayes.

The interviews were pretty much a waste of time, from the three she talked to. She learned they held the woman in awe. They'd sat back, content to let an old man be sacrificed so they might escape harm, and a *woman*—a *white* woman, no less—had come to their rescue. Their descriptions of her were still vague.

Forensics had matched fingerprints found on several cigarettes the woman had left behind to a set of those on a newspaper passengers said she'd been reading.

Unfortunately, the woman had never been arrested. The prints could identify her if she came in or was caught, but were of little use at the moment. They'd been sent to the FBI, State Police and the military, but as yet nothing positive had come back. At four PM, Morales sent them home to get some sleep, as they'd be canvassing the subways starting at ten that night.

With two detectives from the night shift helping, she and Briggs later spent two hours riding the subway back and forth trying to locate *anyone* who might have *ever* seen the women on the train. It had proved fruitless, exhausting and dispiriting.

She was surprised when Briggs took her up on her offer to buy him a round at Cavanaugh's before they headed home.

A few drinks loosened him up a bit.

"You did a pretty decent job today, Rios, for someone with so little experience," he ventured.

It was obvious to her he was having trouble making conversation.

"Am I supposed to take that as a compliment or a putdown?"

He looked at her sharply. "Take it anyway you want," and he took another sip of his beer.

"You got a real burr up your ass, Briggs," she said, warming to the subject. The drinks had loosened her up, too, she knew. Added to the fatigue she felt, she wasn't about to take any more of his shit.

"Is it because I'm a woman or because it didn't take me fifteen years to claw my way up to homicide?"

He was about to answer, but she went on.

"You've been on my case since day one, and you owe me an explanation." Her Latino temper, she could feel, was once again getting the better of her, but fuck it, she thought. Tomorrow, he'd go to Morales, ask for a new partner and that would be the end of it.

"I owe you squat," he said sourly.

"Pardon me," she said sarcastically. "You *don't* owe me shit, but if you're a man, you'll be straight with me. You got the balls to tell me why I don't belong in homicide?" Having lived in a male-dominated household, she knew the buttons to push to get a man talking.

"If you weren't a woman and a PR you'd still be on the streets," he said, looking her square in the eye. "You want straight. You got straight."

He paused, then went on.

"We got to maintain a proper balance, ain't that right? A woman left to go to law school, so they killed two birds with one stone: replaced her with a woman, who's also Hispanic. Does wonder for the stats," he added sarcastically.

He took another sip of his beer, but maintained eye contact with her.

"Now if you were gay, the department could appease another fucking special interest group. It's a wonder they don't have quotas for the handicapped. . . . "

"Don't you mean disabled?" she said teasingly.

"Physically impaired," he said, a slight smile breaking out, in spite of himself.

"Physically *challenged*," she countered and they both laughed.

"Look," he said, turning serious again, "Quotas and affirmative action is what this department is all about now. It's CYA—cover your ass. So many blacks, so many Hispanics, so many women—regardless of ability. What's sad is, it's gonna get cops killed. Competency will no longer get you in, if you're the wrong color or gender."

"It's promotions that really bug you, though," she said.

"Damn right. After there's the proper balance on the force, then you have to look at quotas according to rank and elite units. Good officers, damned good men—even white men—who've slaved for years get passed over because the powers that be decide a woman is needed in homicide. Nothing against you personally, but you *haven't* paid your dues, and I know guys who have. They got the shaft."

"It has everything to do with me, Briggs," she said, their eyes still locked. "Granted, I'm not a seasoned veteran, but can't you judge me as a cop and not as a Hispanic female who fills two advancement needs for the department?"

"You're not as competent—not yet as seasoned—as dozens who were passed over. Sorry, but that's a fact."

"You forget, Briggs, that affirmative action worked for blacks, just as it's working for women now. It wasn't too long ago that white officers were pissed that they'd been passed over because more blacks were needed in high profile positions. And the last two police commissioners have been black. Why?"

She wasn't about to let him answer.

"Because we have a white mayor and politics dictate a black, whether he's the most competent or not. So what's the fucking difference?"

"I'm not denying the inequities," he said. "What bugs me, though, is now more than ever it's not performance that dictates promotion, but politics."

"Weren't you helped out by affirmative action? Would you be in homicide without quotas?" she asked.

"Damn right, I would. *I* paid my dues; put in my time. *I* worked the streets for ten years, then had to prove myself in narcotics, robbery and vice before I finally got homicide. Not quite the path you took," he said derisively.

"What about Covington, then?"

"What about Covington?" Briggs asked defensively.

Covington was a male black cop with no more time on the force than Rios, who had recently been promoted to homicide.

"Did he pay his dues? No way, Jose. Must be a lot of white cops got passed over so a *brother* could meet some quota. I don't see you all over his ass. Don't see you give him the cold shoulder. He's a brother. Black *and* male. You're a fucking hypocrite, Briggs. It all comes back to my being a woman; not good enough even if I were black."

Briggs was silent for several moments. Nina thought he'd clammed up again; gone back into his shell. She was pissed they hadn't gotten to the crux of the matter; the underlying problem was still unresolved. She was about to speak when he did.

"Truth be told, I don't feel comfortable with women cops. When we were out on the subway, tonight, I felt I had to do my job *and* keep an eye on you."

"To see if I was doing *my job*?" she asked, barely able to contain her fury.

"No, no, that's not it. To see you weren't hassled. I go up to some punk, he's not going to give me attitude. You go up to the same little prick, he looks at you and sees someone he can intimidate. We all lose respect because you can't handle yourself like we do."

Briggs put up a hand to stop Nina from interrupting.

"There's a story that spread around recently that makes my point. Two female officers were called to an apartment where a three-hundred-pound woman had fainted. They couldn't move her, so they called for backup. Two male cops came and carried her downstairs. You should have heard the names the neighbors called the women. It set a bad tone for all of us."

"So all you males are he-men," she said. "Sorry, I know a lot of male officers so out of shape they couldn't chase a perp three blocks without wheezing.

"You want honest," she continued. "I saw you on the tube last year; that Vigilante Task Force. No way you could have caught *me* then. You were fat and out of shape. Did that make you a lousy cop?"

"Fat as I was," he answered without skipping a beat, "I still commanded respect—*and* fear—when I confronted some asshole who wanted to make his rep at some cop's expense."

Nina leaned forward, without thinking. "I grant you many women aren't fit to be cops," she said. "But judge us as individuals. Guaranteed, someone messes with me, they'll get more than they bargained for. I grew up with eight brothers who would have loved me to be the cook and maid. I fought all of them . . . *literally*. I earned their respect. I may look all skin and bones, but even though you're in shape now, I'd lay odds I could whup your ass or give a good account of myself trying."

Briggs laughed, his smile the first genuine one she had seen from him since she had been promoted to homicide.

"Tell you what, Rios. I'm not going to change my opinion of women cops, but I'm willing to give *you* the benefit of the doubt. You're one tough cookie. And what you lack in experience, you make up for with thoroughness.

"I'm set in my ways," he went on, "I admit it, but maybe I've judged you too harsh. Maybe I'll cut you some slack. Then again," and he flashed that engaging smile again, "tomorrow when I'm not mellowed out from drinking on an empty stomach, maybe I'll think of you as a good-for-nothing bitch who needs me to look out for her."

It was Nina's turn to smile. "You're not as tough as you want others to think, Briggs. I'm wise to you, drunk or sober. You got the experience. Let me learn from you. But be assured, I'll protect your back as well as any male partner you've had. Maybe better. Guaranteed."

"You're a real piece of work, Rios. Now let me finish my drink and get home before my wife gets suspicious."

They finished their drinks in comfortable silence. Nina was determined to prove herself to Briggs. Show him she was a good cop and merited her position in homicide. If she could gain his respect, trust would follow and maybe he'd open up. Then maybe, just maybe, she could help rid him of the demons eating at him due to his daughter's attack.

Shit, she thought, I must be sloshed. I'm actually glad Morales teamed me with Briggs. Next, we'll be in the midst of a torrid affair. She saw Briggs looking at her quizzically, as if reading her mind, flushed, and decided it was best she get home.

Chapter Fifteen

Try as she might to shed Cassandra, Lysette couldn't as she drove home. She was fully aware she and Cassandra were the same person. She hadn't created Cassandra; the woman who worked the club was a part of her personality she had hidden. . . .

—Since the attack.

She was aware, too, that Lysette was acting more like Cassandra in her personal life; showing a good deal more self-confidence than she had previously. The Lysette walking around naked in her home that morning was Cassandra's doing. She'd lost many of her inhibitions the past four years. By the same token, Cassandra had chilled out. She was as aggressive as ever, but she could now deal with customers who didn't want Cassandra's flamboyance. It was a delicate balancing act, and tonight Lysette couldn't quite shake Cassandra.

She had been surprised to find she had packed a provocative black leather skirt and red silk blouse after coming home from the beach. Usually, she left the club in jeans and a t-shirt; a security guard walking her to her car. But tonight . . .

—*Another blackout*, her mind screamed, when she had looked in the gym bag and seen she'd brought Cassandra clothes.

Randi, her trainer, just after she was hired, had helped her purchase Cassandra clothes. She had told Lysette that you don't just create a stage persona. You have to actually *live* it. She told Lysette to take stock of herself and point out her best assets.

That was simple. Her legs and her tits.

Then she had to accentuate the positive.

Despite misgivings, she allowed Randi to help pick out a Cassandra wardrobe of short, short tight skirts that gave anyone who

105

looked plenty of leg to see, and low-cut blouses that also left little to the imagination.

Randi called it "the not-quite-a-slut look" and the two of them went barhopping so Lysette could capture the essence of Cassandra.

With Cassandra now ingrained as part of her, she had little use for the Cassandra wardrobe, as she seldom dated or went out with the other girls.

Tonight, though, she had inadvertently packed Cassandra clothes in her haste to get to the club. Cassandra clothes *and* one of the gold necklaces she had worn that morning; necklaces she had purchased for Cassandra. She had brought a gold cross on a chain that hung between her breasts. Lysette thought it slightly sacrilegious. Cassandra reveled at the stares it drew.

She hadn't even brought sneakers. She took off her pumps and drove barefoot. She also kept on her blonde wig. Why? she thought to herself. It went with her Cassandra clothes. Nothing more.

She further surprised herself by passing her home in South Philly, driving up Broad Street, maneuvering onto Benjamin Franklin Parkway, then onto Kelly Drive. A few minutes later, at two-thirty in the morning, she found herself at Smith playground just off the drive, her coat in her hand, necklace in place, her pumps on her feet. Her ankles ached. . . .

—But the pain felt good.

She had never been to this playground, but remembered having read about it in the papers a few days before. She saw some of the yellow police tape that marked crime scenes strewn on the ground, but for the life of her she couldn't recall what had happened.

She went over to the swings, put her coat on one swing and sat on another. She didn't swing high, just moved lazily back and forth, her feet kicking at the ground, as she had done when she was young. . . .

—After the attack.

Before she'd lost her family, she had been a bundle of energy. . . .

—A little Cassandra.

At the playground her mother would look on nervously as she pumped to the heavens; her feet just missing the trees. She'd find a rhythm and be one with the swing. At the apex of the arc she sometimes thought of letting go and flying. But common sense, and her mother's pleadings to slow down, prevailed, and all she did was pump until she could feel the swing all but come out of its moorings.

After the attack, she had no desire to soar to the heavens. A part of her warned that if she did, without her mother's presence, she might give way to temptation and let go when the swing was at its highest and fly. . . .

—To her mother.

—To Laura.

—To her father.

—*To her death*.

She had decided to stay clear of her classmates after her fifth fight and third suspension a mere eight months after she was discharged from the hospital.

For those eight months her grandmother had reluctantly deferred to both the psychologist and her husband. While she hadn't coddled Lysette . . .

—Grandma was not the coddling type.

. . . she had tolerated the girl's moodiness, tantrums and insolence.

With her third suspension, however, the principal lost patience and told Lysette's grandmother that *one* more incident meant a transfer to a special school for emotionally disturbed students.

"Mr. Steadman, there will be *no* further problems with my granddaughter," she had said emphatically.

He looked at her doubtfully, then looked at Lysette, who sat pouting.

The old woman bent closer to him, but didn't lower her voice. Lysette knew she wanted her to hear.

"I've let the goddamn shrinks have their way for eight months, and they've failed miserably." She almost sounded vindicated. "This child knows just what she's doing. She's getting attention. Well, grieving's over. From now on, *I'll* be administering therapy," she said derisively. "And mark my words, when this child returns to school in three days, you won't hear a peep out of her."

Lysette watched transfixed. And scared.

Grandma lit a cigarette the minute she'd left the principal's office. A cigarette almost *always* dangled from the woman's wafer-thin lips. At sixty-one, her voice could have been mistaken for a man's. She had the solid frame of a man, too. None of the curves of Lysette's mother. Close-cropped hair, no makeup, earrings or trace of femininity. She wore jeans and a drab flannel shirt, even in the summer. Lysette pictured her at the pool hall with other men smoking and coughing and being spiteful.

When they got home her grandmother sent her to her room, while she talked to her husband. Lysette heard little snatches of their argument.

" . . . she's not a bad child," her grandfather.

" . . . I've been patient . . . no more . . . it's my turn," her grandmother.

"But the psychol—"

"Fuck them and fuck you, too. At my age, I won't have a little bitch running this household."

She heard her grandmother coming up the stairs.

"Into the bathroom with you," she commanded.

Once there, "Take off your clothes and be quick about it."

Lysette complied. She was filled with dread. Her grandmother had dropped all pretenses of compassion.

"Get into the tub. No tears. It'll only make it worse on you."

Lysette did as she was told.

Her grandmother turned on the cold water. "Add any hot and you'll be sorry." With that she left.

It was winter, and the water stung like bees as it rose past her knees to her stomach. She shivered. Her hand reached for the hot water . . .

—*Stopped*.

She remembered the look in her grandmother's eyes and knew what it meant. *Add any hot and you'll be sorry*. Her teeth chattered.

—Her grandmother *wanted* her to add hot water.

Her legs numbed.

—Wanted Lysette to defy her.

She waited. Soon her grandmother would return and let her out. She'd learned her lesson.

Her grandmother returned . . . with a bucket. Dumped ice into the tub. She didn't repeat her warning. Her eyes told all.

The water rose to Lysette's chest, to her neck; almost to the rim of the tub.

Her grandmother returned with another bucket of ice. Dumped it in. Turned off the water. Left. Returned. Left. Returned. Each time with more ice.

Finally, she entered without ice. Lysette was even more terrified.

"Cold enough for you?" She didn't expect an answer, Lysette

knew from her tone. Didn't want one. Children should be seen and not heard, a cliche she had often spouted when over for a family dinner.

—Not heard.

—NOT HEARD.

"Cat got your tongue?" Her grandmother was teasing her. *Taunting* her. Now she wanted an answer.

"N-n-no, ma'am," Lysette said, stumbling over her words, her tongue a wad of cotton unable to obey the commands of her brain.

Her grandmother grabbed Lysette's long hair. Pushed her head into the freezing water. Held it there. Lifted it out.

"Children show respect for their elders." Dunked her again.

"No more sassing your teachers." Again.

"No more fights." Again. This time longer.

"Understand me?"

Lysette's brain said, "Yes," but her tongued refused the command.

Her head went under yet again, even longer this time, until she began to go limp.

"DO YOU UNDERSTAND ME, YOU LITTLE BITCH!"

Lysette was staring into her grandmother's eyes now. She knew if she didn't respond, the old woman would kill her. And enjoy it. Lysette could feel her grandmother willing her to defy her. She wouldn't give her the satisfaction.

"Y-y-yes, m-m-ma'am," she stammered.

Lysette saw the disappointment in the old woman's eyes, then she left.

Lysette sat in the tub another hour. Her grandmother finally returned, dragged her by the hair to the kitchen and listed chores she expected to be completed.

"You'll mop the floor, clean the stove—inside and out—then the refrigerator. Do it right or it's back into the tub."

Naked, Lysette cleaned.

The next day Lysette cut her hair. Cut it short. No one commented. No one cared.

It was evil. It was wrong. It eventually robbed her of any meaningful childhood. But it *worked*. Lysette never got into another fight at school, and any grieving she did was in her room. She became a loner, and only began to come out of her shell her junior year in high school.

On the swing, now, a cigarette dangling from her mouth, the memories were as vivid as if it were yesterday.

Lysette was startled out of her reverie by the approach of a man; a tall, lean, light-skinned black who swaggered toward her.

Lysette stood up, took something out of her coat pocket, put the coat over her arm and waited. She wasn't afraid. She was Cassandra being hassled by a customer. No one intimidated her.

"What's a fine-looking bitch doing out this time of night?" he asked, his eyes taking stock of Lysette's skirt, which had risen high up her thigh, then checking out the cleavage exposed by her low-cut top, and finally the gold cross that dangled between her breasts.

"It's no business of yours what I'm doing," she said evenly, dropping the cigarette to the ground, and calmly crushing the embers with her shoe.

"A feisty one. I like that in a woman. We could have a good time," he said, his hand rubbing his crotch.

"I don't think so." Her eyes locked with his.

"Bitch," he said. Then he smiled. "I don't have to fight for pussy. Tell you what. Give me that fine jewelry and you can be on your way."

"Why would I give you my fucking jewelry?" she asked, without emotion, and saw a cloud of doubt cross the man's face for a moment.

He'd been moving steadily toward her as he spoke, and now his hand touched the gold cross, his palms resting on her breasts. She heard the click of a switchblade, which he held up to her face. He wasn't smiling anymore. She saw cockiness, arrogance and determination.

"So I won't cut you," he answered. "I'm going to get that jewelry one way or another. Matter of fact, I don't give a fuck whether I take it from you dead or alive. Your choice, bitch."

Lysette stepped back, raised the arm covered by her coat, exposing her gun, which she fired once at the man's head.

In slow motion, she saw surprise register on his face when he saw the weapon, and like the boy the night before, he was dead before he hit the ground, the knife still in his hand.

"You talk too much, shithead," she said to the still figure. "You don't prove you're big and bad with your mouth. You prove it with your actions. You can take that lesson to hell."

She put on her coat, lit a cigarette and walked back to her car.

A solitary jogger passed her, Walkman earphones glued to his head. He gave her a quick glance, but nothing more, and never broke stride.

At home, twenty minutes later, Lysette went right to her room without checking the locks. While *Lysette* would have checked the locks, Cassandra wasn't the least concerned. In her unlit, pitch-black room, Lysette finally shed Cassandra as she stripped off her clothes.

Chilled, she put on a robe, turned up the thermostat, then locked the front doors and made her inspection of the windows. Before going back to her room, she rechecked the front door once again.

Not the least bit tired . . .

—Still wired.

. . . she took a hot shower and considered what she had done. *She had killed a man.* No, her mind snapped. You protected yourself, just like in the subway. She had no doubt the man would have cut her, left her dead or dying. But hadn't she set herself up, being in a deserted playground at two-thirty in the morning, dressed . . .

—Almost-like-a-slut.

. . . in Cassandra's clothes? *No*, she had every right to be in the playground or anywhere else for that matter, without having to fear for her life. And what she wore was irrelevant. The night was hers, as much as it was his.

She felt no remorse, moreover, at having killed. It hadn't been her intention, but a woman had to protect herself. The police, sure as hell, wouldn't have come to her rescue.

One thing was certain. There was no going to the police now. This time there were no witnesses to the shooting; to the attack on her. She could envision their questions: Why did she have a gun? Why was she dressed so provocatively? Why in the playground in the dead of night; a time that belonged to these vile predators. Why? Why? Why?

"Because it's my fucking right," she said aloud, hot water cascading over her, "to go where I want, when I please, without fear of being hassled."

After her shower she lit up a cigarette and checked the locks again. She lay in bed naked for fifteen minutes, the gun tucked between her breasts, giving her comfort, as she replayed the night's events. Slowly she shut down, dozed, then fell asleep; a smile on her face.

Chapter Sixteen

Briggs arrived at Smith Playground at four AM. The call had come twenty minutes earlier, and as he dressed he fought the headache of an oncoming hangover. He hadn't had much to drink with Nina, but then again, he hadn't had as much as a beer since Alexis had been attacked.

Intuitively, he knew why he had been called, but sought out Morales for confirmation once he arrived at the playground.

"What gives, Sarge?" he said, without greeting. There were already two detectives on the scene, as well as their sergeant. None looked too pleased at his arrival.

"Rios is on her way," Morales replied.

"That's not what—"

"Another call came in specifically requesting your presence. Passed down through channels, so I have no idea where it originated."

"Why this time?"

"You must have a clue," Morales said.

"Is it our mystery woman?" Briggs asked gesturing to the figure on the ground.

"Around two-thirty this morning, Lester Washington was shot. Once in the head. There's a knife in his hand. No one witnessed the shooting, but a jogger saw a blonde leaving the vicinity around the same time."

"Did he hear anything?"

"He was wearing a Walkman. A uniform passing by found the body and radioed it in. The MO and woman's description apparently triggered the call to me."

"Adds an interesting wrinkle," Briggs said, surveying the scene. "And changes the whole complexion of the case."

"We also have one pissed-off detective over there," Morales said, pointing to a heavyset man with red hair standing morosely with his sergeant. "The lieutenant filled the sergeant in, but neither he nor his detectives seem too pleased."

"It's Flannery," Briggs said. "We've worked together. Let me handle him." He saw Rios approaching. "You fill Nina in. Ask her to question the jogger."

He began to walk away, then paused. "Sarge, if you hear me raise my voice, I'm not out of control. It'll be calculated. Like I said, I know Flannery."

Morales shook his head in understanding.

James Flannery was a fifty-year-old Irishman who had been passed over for promotion numerous times, though he was a competent detective. He wasn't black, Hispanic or female. He was one of those white cops he'd referred to when talking with Rios earlier.

He also wore a chip on his shoulder for all to see. He wouldn't like a case being yanked from him after he'd done the preliminary workup. Truthfully, Briggs didn't blame the man. Flannery was methodical and thorough, deserving of promotion. Diplomatic he wasn't, which was why he'd retire a detective; a bitter one at that.

As Briggs approached Flannery, his sergeant said something to him, then turned and left. Briggs laughed to himself. The man didn't want to be caught in any crossfire.

Flannery didn't give Briggs a chance to start a dialog.

"What the fuck is going on, Briggs? I was on the wheel when this was called in. I work my ass off for an hour, then my sarge tells me it's no longer mine. I tell you, man, it's not kosher."

Briggs had to stifle a laugh. "Kosher" from an Irishman. From what he knew of Flannery, the man had little good to say about Jews, blacks or even Italians, for that matter, but like a lot of cops he knew, they'd begun using the jargon of other ethnic and racial groups.

Throw around the lingo of minorities and you prove you're not a bigot. Five years ago, Briggs remembered ruefully, only Jews ate bagels. Now bagels were American as apple pie; you could even get them at Dunkin' Donuts. Briggs could abide change, but couldn't imagine himself saying something wasn't "kosher."

"It's mine, though I'd give it to you in a heartbeat," Briggs told Flannery. "I just put in a full day and four hours of overtime. I barely hit the sack when I'm called again. You think I wanna be here? Think again." He purposely added an extra touch of bitterness. He had to make the man understand they were both being used; low men on the totem pole.

"Just because it looks like a white woman killed a black man doesn't mean I can't handle the heat," Flannery bemoaned.

"Someone thinks differently, and neither you nor I have a say in the matter."

"Yeah, but you'll get the bust. You'll get the promotion. . . . "

"Because I'm black, right, Flannery? If I wasn't black I'd still be a uniform walking the streets. That what you think, Flannery?" Briggs said, his voice rising intentionally so all could hear.

"You got me wrong, Briggs. I mean," he sputtered. "You're a good cop who's black—"

"But there are a lot of good-for-nothing black cops getting plum assignments and promotions because they're black. Is that it?"

"Matter of fact, yeah, that's it," Flannery said, warming to the subject. "Wasn't like that ten years ago."

"Bullshit. Politics have always ruled. The Irish had their day. Italians theirs too. Now it's blacks. Tomorrow it'll be women. C'mon," he said, putting an arm around Flannery's shoulder, and lowering his voice. "Let's get away from all these prying eyes."

A minute later, under a tree, Briggs laid it on the line for Flannery.

"You don't want this case, man. It's a ballbuster with no promotions in the offering. This lady's already a hero. We arrest her, there'll be no cheers. Meanwhile, I've got seven open cases, three or four I could clear within a week. But my Sarge wants me on this full time cause someone got to him. You see where I'm coming from?"

"Didn't mean no offense," Flannery said, somewhat mollified. "Just, you know, I'm fucking sick of favoritism and politics and bending to the pressure of the . . . the community," he said.

Of the black community, Briggs knew he wanted to say. The situation, however, was defused. Flannery would bitch to his buddies, but truth be told Flannery wouldn't want the case. Briggs didn't want it. He could see it as all-consuming, and, yes, a no-winner. Catch the lady and catch heat from the average Joe applauding her actions. Fail to nab her and get strung up by the balls by the press, and the brass.

The two men shook hands, and Briggs told him to go home, get some sleep, ball his wife or get plastered. He could be as crass as the next guy when it suited his purposes.

He went over to Rios, who was checking out the body.

"What we got, Nina?"

She looked at him oddly. There were circles under her eyes, and she looked hesitant.

"About this evening," she said tentatively.

"We both had a bit too much to drink," he cut her off, "but I meant what I said—all of it. Understand?"

She smiled. "Thanks. Everything square between you and Flannery?" she said, looking at the other detective walking out of the playground with his partner.

"We had a meeting of the minds. He'll get over it. Not the first time he's been given the shaft." He paused. "So, you been doing your job or what?"

She smiled, then pulled back a sheet of vinyl exposing Lester Washington's head. "Bullet's no more than a few centimeters from that of Jerome Brown. He had a knife in his hand. By the looks of it, he was the aggressor, and she shot him in self-defense. That's the way the press will play it up, anyway. I'll stake my pension ballistics will match this bullet with the one that killed the Brown boy."

"Any kind of identification by the jogger?"

She looked at her notes. "Terrence Lofton, junior at the University of Penn. Broke up with his girl, couldn't sleep, so he went jogging. Didn't get a good look at the woman who passed him. She was definitely white and blonde, with a black leather coat."

"Our girl certainly gets around."

"One more thing. They found three cigarette butts by the swings. Same brand as last night. My guess, the prints will match."

"All right. Let's say it's the same woman. Why am I bothered?" Briggs asked.

" 'Cause it makes no sense. The woman on the subway acted instinctively to save another passenger. This looks like she almost lured the perp. Like she was lying in wait. Plus, how did she get out here?"

"Did the jogger see a car?" Briggs asked.

"No," she said. "You think she drove here?"

"Drove or had someone drive her. My gut tells me we haven't heard the last of her, either. It's a jigsaw puzzle, and until we get additional pieces, we're pretty much flying blind."

"By the way," she said, suddenly remembering, "Morales wants to see us."

They went over to their sergeant and laid out what they had, and what they thought.

"We got a loose cannon out there," Briggs finished. "We're no longer looking for a Good Samaritan to question and pat on the back. She's killed twice, and she'll do so again."

"My thoughts exactly," Morales said. "You're not going to like this, but you're on this case full time until she's caught. I'll reassign your other cases, and take you off the wheel. Even if I don't, I'm sure I'll be ordered to, so it's kind of a pre-emptive strike. I'll also assign you additional manpower, after you come up with a plan of attack." He looked at Briggs and smiled. "Go on, get it off your chest. I know what's coming."

"You can read me like a damned book, can't you? I don't think you should reassign our other cases. I don't know about Nina's caseload, but I'm best equipped to handle those on my plate. Hell, three or four are close to being closed. Reassign them, and it's back to square one."

"You're right, but when this story breaks tomorrow, I know what I'll be told. So, you're going have to live with it. Look, with the three or four that look most promising, you brief the guys who'll be getting them. The others aren't going anyplace anyway. Close this case and you'll get them back, if you want. This is not the way I'd handle things, if I had my way, but someone above is pulling the strings. We can make the best of it or fight it and lose anyway. Are we on the same page?"

"I guess so," Briggs said, without enthusiasm. Rios only nodded.

"Go fill in the lieutenant, Briggs. The press will have a field day with this. Then get some sleep. You look like shit."

As Briggs sauntered off, the sergeant put a hand on Nina's arm. "Can I speak with you a moment, Nina?"

She looked at him quizzically, wondering if she had done something wrong. Morales usually only called you by your first name if he was pissed at you, but probably because she was a woman, he often used her first name. He could say what he wished, but she wasn't one of the guys, yet. She was long past the stage where bitterness crept in at every slight. She couldn't shrug off the sadness, however. And it rankled, not knowing if he was using her first name because he was pissed, or because she was female. At least the men could read Morales by how he treated them. She felt blind.

"You and Briggs clear the air at Cavanaugh's tonight?" He asked, as if he were just shooting the breeze.

"How did you know?" she asked, genuinely taken aback.

"I get paid the big bucks to know what's bugging my detectives and how I can help," he said keeping his tone light, as if it were no big thing.

For Nina, it *was* a big thing. Didn't she have any goddamn privacy? Maybe, if she and Briggs met in the john . . .

"Christ, it's been, what, three hours?" she answered when she had calmed herself down. "I don't understand."

"No mystery. Briggs hasn't been out since his daughter's attack. The two of you together at Cavanaugh's." He shrugged, as if she could put two and two together without his help.

"The owner? A bartender? Not another cop. Not in the middle of the night."

He shrugged again.

Suddenly it dawned on her and she was furious again. "You didn't pair me with Briggs to make sure he didn't go off. He's vulnerable. He was never comfortable with female cops. You knew that. Put us under a lot of stress and we'd either be clawing at one another or iron things out. You set us up. You son-of-a—"

"Hold it right there, Detective. You don't want to say anything you'll regret."

"How could you?" she said, ignoring him. "You build up my hopes; treat me as a cop, *not a female officer*, then burst my bubble. You used me as a *woman*, just like all the rest. I expected more from you." She could feel tears forming, and turned away to compose herself.

"Nina, I paired you with Briggs because you *were* the only one who would stand up to him. I didn't deceive you. At the same time, sure, I hoped you could get him out of his shell, as only a woman or best friend could. Briggs has no best friend. He has his family. You're not Miss Popularity in the unit yourself, though it's not your fault. The two of you are more alike than either of you would want to admit. My teaming you was no conspiracy. If you two found common ground, so much the better."

She faced her superior, anger, hurt and confusion radiating from her eyes.

"I don't know what to believe. I do know I refuse to be used. I fight for respect every day, and still I'm resented because I don't have a pair of balls."

"Your problem, Nina, is you doubt yourself—"

"That's not true," she interrupted.

"You believe you were promoted to homicide because you're a woman," he said, ignoring her, "but in fact you're part of my squad because of your capabilities. Yes, there was pressure to fill the vacancy with a woman, but I'd never accept anyone who wasn't qualified. And believe what you want, you weren't the only female to choose from. You were the best. Not just the best female. The best. Period."

She was shocked. She'd never considered there were competitors. How naive of her.

"So stop feeling sorry for yourself. Stop looking for hidden meanings were there are none. I asked how things were going with you two because I'm concerned. This is turning into a major investigation, and I need the both of you in top form. *So*, how did things go?"

She smiled tentatively. Her thoughts and emotions were still churning . . .

—Just like a woman, she thought.

. . . but she knew she'd at least proven herself worthy to him. From his reputation, she knew to be accepted by Morales was no easy feat, and should not be taken lightly.

"Let's say we cleared a hurdle, and leave it at that."

"I won't insult you and ask if Briggs can handle this case—"

"You don't have to worry," she interrupted. "He's not bringing his problems to the office. If you want my humble endorsement, you've got it. And if he can't handle the pressures, he'll be the first to tell you."

"Thanks for the candor," he said and paused. "I do value your judgment. Take to heart what I said. You're not on this case just for the ride. Briggs needs your input. No one can work in a vacuum. Follow your instincts, and tell Briggs your thoughts. He's stubborn, but he's not stupid. Now go home and get some rest. Can't have you dozing on the job," he said with a smile, one she felt was truly genuine.

Nina didn't know if he'd meant to give her a pep talk, but she felt a lot better about herself as she drove home. As tough-skinned as she had appeared at Cavanaugh's, a part of her questioned whether she warranted her promotion to homicide. She *did* want to be judged on her ability, not her gender. A promotion to fill quotas was just as abhorrent to her as the prejudice she encountered because she *was* a woman. And, while Briggs was clearly the point man on this case, she was determined to prove herself invaluable; someone he'd come to view as an equal—a partner in more than name only.

Her eyes heavy, she just hoped she could reach home without wrapping her car around a telephone pole.

Chapter Seventeen

For the second night in succession Shara awoke to the sound of a bullet; a bullet she couldn't possibly have heard. She's killed again, Shara knew. In Philly—a good seventy miles from where she now lived.

Getting out of bed, Shara went to the desk that held her computer and turned on a desk lamp. She had never believed in the supernatural or ESP or in psychics who had the power to locate missing kids who were kidnapped.

On the other hand, the death she had envisioned the night before had been confirmed on television, and of greater significance to her, by a story Deidre had written.

The shot she had heard had been the one that took Jerome Brown's life. And she knew the woman had struck again, this morning.

The questions that gnawed at her were twofold. Why was she aware of the killings and what was she to do? She felt an urge to rush to Philly . . .

—To Deidre.

—To repay her debt.

. . . but under what pretense? It wasn't time yet, some instinct told her. But the time would come. *Would come soon.* She would know when it was time to return home.

—To Deidre.

—To help her track down this mystery woman.

The thought gave her the rush of a narcotic. Helping Deidre. The chase. Making amends. The chase. Ending her exile. The chase.

—The chase.

—*The chase.*

Chapter Eighteen

Deidre received a wakeup call from Carter Hastings at eight in the morning. Groggily, she picked up the receiver.

"Looks like our mystery woman struck again overnight," he said, without a greeting.

"No shit," Deidre responded, instantly awake. As he filled her in, her mind drifted to this man of contradiction. South Philly born and bred, at first glance one would take the forty-two-year-old as a Main Line Patrician, who'd gotten his job through influence.

Impeccably dressed in expensive suits and an ever-present bowtie, he could be at the office eighteen hours straight, yet look like he had just arrived; no tie askew, no creases in his coat or trousers. Every hair of his thick, graying hair was in place and his delicate fingers and manicured nails gave him the air of a dandy.

His voice, though, belied the caricature. He had a thick South Philly accent, much like the punchdrunk Sylvester Stallone in *Rocky V*.

He was very much a chameleon. He would get down in the gutter with the guys from maintenance, yet more than held his own with Ivy Leaguers, who now, like himself, played golf over lunch at exclusive clubs on the Main Line.

Deidre knew him to be an overachiever; a man who worked his ass off to get where he was; hence the eighteen-hour days. Though he lacked the keen insight and instincts of Jonas, so crucial to success in the business, there was no one better at spotting talent and delegating authority. His reporters gave the City section its distinctive flavor, and their loyalty to him was unquestioned. He let them write in their own unique styles, without the heavy hand of most editors who were themselves frustrated writers.

121

His call this morning was more than just informative. Deidre waited for the other shoe to drop.

"Looks like there's more to this woman than we thought. Any interest in pursuing it?"

Before she could say no, he sweetened the pot.

"I don't want another beat reporter. I've got someone assigned to the nuts and bolts. When I say pursue the story, I mean pursue the *woman* any way you see fit. My gut tells me this woman is a creature from your closet of horrors. If anyone can get into her head, it's you."

"Let me get this straight," Deidre said. "You want me to treat this like my other pieces. I scrounge around *on my own* and when I've got something to say I give you a story. No deadlines."

"More or less."

"Carter!" she said, allowing irritation to slip into her voice. "Don't string me along. Lay it out—your 'more or less.' "

"You run with the woman, as you want, but I'd also like some commentary on the reaction of the man-on-the-street and the media."

"I don't understand."

"The story's just starting to unfold and already it's captivated the city. On WWDB it's the *only* topic for discussion, and all the local TV shows are scurrying for fresh angles. One promo has even labeled her the Angel of Death."

"Give me a break," Deidre said.

"My thoughts precisely. She's more than that. The point is, within a day or two she'll have a moniker. She's this bigger-than-life figure because no one can get a handle on her. Find her, but at the same time gauge the pulse of the city, as only you can."

"You flatter me, Carter," she said teasingly.

"I'm serious. Listen to the talk shows. Philadelphia has taken on a Dodge City mentality without a Wyatt Earp. The outlaws run the town. The people are angry . . . and frightened. This woman could be a rallying point. For what, I don't know. But she sure ain't taking no shit. So, interested?"

"How could I turn down my favorite editor?" Deidre said, trying not to betray her excitement. Carter was right. This was a big story. A potentially important story. Allowed to approach it as she wished, she couldn't say no.

"That's my girl. Look, I gotta go. See if you can come up with some commentary for tomorrow's edition. Other than that, just keep me abreast. Oh, and give my best to Jonas. Everybody's pulling for him." With that he hung up.

Son-of-a-bitch, she thought to herself. He played me. Gave me the story on my terms, then snuck in the zinger about an article for the next day. No deadlines my ass. And before I could respond, changed the subject to Jonas and rang off.

She wasn't really angry, though. She knew the media would overreact. Hell, the city, starving for a knight in shining armor, might well be caught up with the avenger's exploits. Here was a real life Lone Ranger; a one-woman assault on crime.

Carter was right, she thought. Crime was rampant and law enforcement seemingly paralyzed. This woman could rally the city into meting out frontier justice. Take back the streets. Take back the night. Take back the city. That's what the people wanted. Fear had held them hostage, but this one woman could be the spark to fuel their courage.

Listening to callers on talk shows only reinforced her views. The hosts, sensing their need to let it all hang out, let them speak with little input of their own. One caller, an elderly man, in particular, seemed to epitomize the bunker mentality of urban city dwellers.

"Drug dealer right on my corner got carted away by the police yesterday. Wouldn't you know by evening he was right back on the street peddling his wares. This damn prison cap gives them license to do whatever they damn please. With prison overcrowding, they know they won't serve no jail time. So they strut they stuff like they own the streets. And you know what? *They do*. Leastwise, they *did* until this woman came along. . . ."

So who was this woman? Deidre thought. She jotted down thoughts on a legal pad; the talk show on as background.

Fact: The first killing wasn't planned.

The second killing? She put a big question mark after it. Assuming the first wasn't planned, but the second was, something had to trigger her to action.

Triggering mechanism? Another big question mark.

Fact: Both killings took place late-evening/early morning. Again, assuming the first was unplanned, what could she infer?

Worked at night? Another question mark. Except for work, why would a woman, alone—a white woman at that—be on the subway so late at night? Coming or going to work made sense. But what of the second killing? If she took public transportation, how did she get to and from the playground off Kelly Drive?

A car? Another question mark, but it made sense. And with the time discrepancy, if she was at work, she was coming *from* work. The three hours between made the inference no great leap.

Motive? For now she had no idea. Again, the first killing seemed instinctive. From news reports, she had learned the same weapon killed both victims. She used that gun a second time because she didn't have one of her own. She didn't want notoriety or she would have come forth after the first killing. At the least she would have contacted the media, even if she didn't want police scrutiny. But she'd gone underground. What the hell did she want???? She wrote a series of question marks after this question.

A loner. A victim herself. No question marks. These were guesses on her part; the first based on the facts, the second on her research into victimization.

Someone could have driven her to the Kelly Drive playground, but instinct told her no. This woman internalized without normal outlets. She could envisage her getting home after the first killing. She had no husband to mull over what she should do; no boyfriend or confidant she could trust. Surely, if she had spoken to someone, she wouldn't have killed again.

And the second killing meant she had no children. This was no single parent. She could have gotten away with the subway shooting and vanished into the woodwork. But a second killing? Now she was aggressively being sought by the police. No single parent would imperil her children by striking a second time.

A victim of what? A definite question mark. Something recent; she or a friend or relative had been the victim of street crime. Something in her past that had been triggered by the subway incident. Or a combination of the two.

Deidre sat back, letting her mind drift. She was getting nowhere. Speculation and conjecture with precious few facts. Okay, her description. White female, long straight blonde hair. Age twenty-two to twenty-eight from the witnesses on the subway.

Again she looked at the paper disapprovingly. She had really narrowed it down, hadn't she?

Avenues of investigation? She wrote a series of question marks after this. Where to start, she thought? She stared at the page for a good five minutes, and in exasperation wrote another long series of question marks.

Now, more than ever, she needed Jonas. How empty her life had become. Her husband, also a reporter, had been much more ambitious than she was. He had covered trouble spots all over the world, but no matter where he was he found a means to call her. He'd always ask about *her* stories, and it wasn't just lip service.

In turn, when home writing magazine articles, putting the stories he had submitted for dailies into a context, he would have her edit them to help put everything into perspective, without the trappings of sensationalism or his own self-importance seeping in.

After his death, his father, Jonas, had been there when she felt adrift in a sea without a navigator. Now with Jonas unavailable . . .

—Dying.

. . . there was no one.

—Shara.

No one! her mind screamed.

She looked at the long string of question marks again, and sighed. For the moment there was no avenue of investigation. She feared the woman would have to kill again to add new pieces to her puzzle.

In the meantime, Carter's suggestion of a commentary on the mood of the city became more intriguing. She would put away the trappings of a reporter and venture out to see if the pervasive fear and apathy of Philadelphians had been altered by the actions of an elusive woman.

Chapter Nineteen

The building on 20th and Chestnut Streets had been vacant for three years now. A weathered sign hung in the window with a phone number for inquiries. For anyone calling, the rent was exorbitant. In light of the fact that foot traffic had been greatly reduced by the opening of Liberty Place several blocks east, no one in their right mind would make such an enormous investment in the property.

That was as it was intended, for the basement—a soundproof bunker that could withstand a nuclear attack—was the home of the most exclusive group in the city; a group dubbed The Fist by its founder in 1897. The founder never explained the choice of name, and no one bothered to ask.

The moniker never appeared on any letterhead, nor could one find a listing in the phone book, Chamber of Commerce or the IRS, for that matter. For all intents and purposes, The Fist didn't exist.

Richard Ashley, its titular leader for close to four years now, sat at one of four chairs in the near barren room. The chairs were of the finest oak, upholstered to afford the greatest comfort. The table, on the other hand, could have been from the Salvation Army or a local bar. It was cheap, stained, but serviceable. Much like a police interrogation room, the rest was bare; the walls painted institutional pea green.

As the group's leader, one would have expected him to enter last, having made the others wait so as to acknowledge his dominance. Richard Ashley, however, *always* arrived early. He had no need to flaunt any superiority. All four men were equal. He was the group's leader solely because someone had to chair the meeting.

Even if this were not the case, Ashley had never flaunted his dominance by arriving "fashionably late" nor did he keep those waiting to meet with him sitting in an outer office because they were less influential than he was. Powerful as he was, he had no need to massage his ego with such juvenile stunts.

As Ashley waited for the others to arrive, he recalled how he had been drawn into The Fist seven years earlier. His mentor had just learned he had lung cancer. He not only needed to find a replacement for himself when the disease ravaged him; he wanted to elevate that person to his position of leadership. Much as he respected his fellow members, they didn't have the combination of ruthlessness and common sense for his taste.

He had asked Ashley to meet him at Rittenhouse Park one day. The two had had business dealings with one another, but were hardly friends.

"Have you ever heard of The Fist, Ashley?" he'd asked.

Ashley had replied no.

"You're one of the wealthiest, most influential men in Philadelphia, yet you've never heard of The Fist?" he asked in surprise.

Again, Ashley admitted he hadn't.

"That's how powerful we are," he said with a smile.

"Tell me about it?" Ashley had asked.

"No. I'll show you. I don't do this casually, Richard. You'll see why later. Now, tell me someone you want destroyed—within days. Someone with impeccable credentials. Someone beyond reproach."

Ashley had. The old man was not known for playing games. He had always been direct and to the point. He was deadly serious, now, and Ashley didn't take his request lightly.

Three days later, the President of the University of Pennsylvania was indicted for making obscene phone calls from his office. He denied any knowledge, but the telephone company had calls logged from his office and a number of women identified his voice. He subsequently resigned in disgrace.

Shortly after, the two men met again.

"We can do almost anything, Richard. My demonstration speaks volumes, but it is only the tip of the iceberg. We have created bogus bank accounts to discredit judges. We have been responsible for the death of one mayoral candidate, whose election would have been unacceptable, and several elected officials who—how should I put it—had gotten out of hand.

"Our power is awesome; more so because it is devoid of conscience. Our only allegiance is to the goals of the group."

He had gone on to tell Ashley the group's aim was to maintain an equilibrium; so that those like himself could continue to prosper.

"We allow events to run their course until our financial interests are threatened. We restore the balance when it's askew. We don't interfere often, but when necessary we do what we must."

He told Ashley intermediaries were always used. Ashley, himself, was living proof how successfully they'd insulated themselves.

"We've created a buffer, so The Fist can never be exposed. We operate through organized crime, the political infrastructure, labor unions, corporations and academia. The few times there have been investigations into activities we've sponsored, others were held accountable. *We don't exist.*"

He paused and lit a cigar.

"We keep no records, no minutes of our decisions, actions or their consequences. Any history we have is passed orally as one member prepares to step down and another takes his place. It's a lifetime commitment, Richard. One does not retire and live out his golden years in Florida," he said with a gleam in his eye.

"How do you know I'll join?" Ashley had asked.

"Two reasons. Stability. You need it to prosper. And power. You want to influence events without the notoriety that goes with being in the public eye."

Though near strangers, the old man indeed knew Ashley well.

He had joined. It was not a hard sell. Before his mentor died, he made it known Ashley was to replace him as their leader. While they made their decisions in unison, the others now deferred to him even though, at fifty-seven, he was the youngest of the group.

The others arrived, and without fanfare Ashley got down to business. There were no regularly scheduled meetings. When a crisis arose they gathered. Sometimes a year went by without a meeting. At most, they had met six times in the course of a year.

Jonathan Spears, Henry Lassiter and Nathaniel Holcomb listened as Ashley outlined the problem. Had they wished, each, with one phone call, could cause the financial ruin of the city. Yet, like Ashley, none of their names appeared atop the stationery of any major corporation or foundation.

"The balance is threatened by this woman," Ashley finished in less than five minutes. "Initially, we considered the subway shooting an event that might further polarize the black and white communities. That was not the case. Still, I have no qualms with the detective assigned the case. He is relentless. He will succeed."

It was as close to an admission of an error as Ashley would make.

"On the contrary," he continued, "it is possible this woman may unify various factions within the city, and we may have a civil war of another sort; the criminal elements involved in the drug trade fighting off those who would banish them. In that case, we would have anarchy, gentlemen," he said dispassionately.

"What is being done to locate the woman?" Lassiter asked. At eighty, he was the oldest at the table, but Ashley wryly thought there was a good chance, robust as he was, he would outlive them all.

"The Police Commissioner will make sure those in charge of the case have every resource at their disposal. This woman is not a professional. It is only a matter of time before she is caught."

"And then what?" Lassiter prodded.

"I suggest we let the courts handle the matter, without obstruction."

Now Nathaniel Holcomb, who was intimately familiar with the judicial system, interjected.

"Without guidance, I believe a jury might well acquit her of all charges. Shouldn't we intervene?"

Ashley shook his head no. "We don't want to create a martyr by, say, having a judge overturn a jury's decision."

"Then we can't have her killed," Jonathan Spears said.

Ashley had learned it was Spears who had convinced the others a mayoral candidate had to die a year before he had been recruited. For Spears, literally wiping out the problem was the best course. Fortunately, he was sensible enough to be dissuaded in most instances.

"Let's put it this way," Ashley said, because he knew the woman's death would end the threat, under the proper circumstances. "If she was killed prior to her capture, it would send a clear message to the city. The status quo would remain in place."

He took a sip of water from a plastic cup.

"However, she appears quite resourceful, and if not caught quickly, others may follow her lead. Once in custody, though, she cannot be harmed. If a jury acquits her, we must accept the judgment."

Ashley allowed himself the briefest of smiles.

"There are contingency plans, however, should this occur." He then explained what he thought should be done in just such a case. At the conclusion of his presentation he could sense a lessening of tension.

"Questions or comments?" Ashley asked.

There were none.

"Are we in agreement, then?"

The others nodded affirmatively.

"Anyone for a hand of poker, then?" Ashley said, and the others chuckled and prepared to leave.

Ashley never adjourned a meeting; a meeting which officially never took place needed no formal closure. He had introduced a bit of levity to signal a meeting's end inadvertently, and it had become his hallmark.

He knew it was presumptuous of him, but he could imagine thirty or forty years down the line a new recruit being told how Richard Ashley would end a meeting with a suggestion they go to a bar for a celebratory drink, or a cake be wheeled in to celebrate one of their birthdays. Ashley gave a lot of thought to how he would close each meeting. Spontaneity was not his forte.

Pleased with the outcome, like the rest of the city, he eagerly awaited the unfolding of events.

As always, he was the last to leave.

Chapter Twenty

Lysette woke up at eleven in the morning, the cold metal of the revolver cutting into her side. She was momentarily disoriented. Why had she gone to bed with the gun? Why hadn't she awakened in the corner . . .

—Her nest.

. . . as she almost invariably did? Why had she gone to bed naked? Not the least self-conscious any longer, she didn't mind parading around the house nude, but she always slept in silk pajamas that seemingly allowed her to melt into the mattress.

And why hadn't she programmed herself to wake up at a decent hour?

Recalling the scene in the playground, she knew. She hadn't completely shed Cassandra when she fell asleep. Cassandra wouldn't scurry to the corner out of fear of an imagined assault. Cassandra enjoyed the feel of her naked body against the sheets. The gun was Cassandra's protection from real or imagined demons. Cassandra didn't care when she awoke. And Cassandra had killed last night.

Over her second cup of coffee and third cigarette, Lysette modified her last thought. *Cassandra* hadn't killed; *Lysette* had. "Don't dump that punk's death at Cassandra's feet," she said aloud, angry at herself; annoyed at Lysette for not accepting responsibility for her actions.

She was aware, and not at all displeased, that her Cassandra persona and Lysette were merging into one. The fact of the matter, though, was she was *becoming* Lysette; the Lysette she would have been if the attack on her family and her grandmother's vindictiveness hadn't stunted her emotional growth. She was becoming whole, and part of Lysette was Cassandra. Lysette would have to

131

learn to co-exist with the Cassandra in her. If she could rid herself of the extremes of both—Lysette's inhibitions and Cassandra's lack of discipline—she could strike a happy medium.

Waking up in bed was comforting. She could easily adapt to sleeping in the nude. She'd simply buy silk sheets, and meet both Lysette's and Cassandra's needs. Cassandra would have to accept Lysette's interior alarm clock, though.

And the killing? That wasn't Cassandra's doing. Cassandra may have been foolish to be outside when the city sold its soul to pipers, dealers, rapists and muggers, but Lysette had pulled the trigger to defend herself, and had no regrets. Cassandra was right not to be intimidated by the night and the sewage that claimed domain. Lysette had simply protected the Cassandra in her when attacked.

Whether she would venture out again, Lysette didn't know, but if she didn't it wouldn't be out of fear.

Having come to grips with her two selves, Lysette dressed and purchased the *Daily News* and *Inquirer* and read accounts of the shooting while waiting for the noon news on Channel Six.

As she guessed, Lester Washington, twenty-four, was no saint. Spouting cliches, the *Daily News* said Washington had a "rap sheet as long as his arm." In the past three years alone, Lysette was surprised to read he had been arrested for three car thefts, possession and sale of crack cocaine, and two burglaries. As all were nonviolent offenses, he'd served no jail time. Each time he had been set free, pending trial, without having to post bail, the paper said. Each time he had failed to show up for his trial. And, each time a bench warrant for his immediate arrest and incarceration had been issued, but with tens of thousands of such warrants pending, and precious little manpower to execute them, Lester Washington had little fear of arrest.

The paper explained, at length, that the city's prison cap was the culprit. Nonviolent offenders were not jailed, and were released without bail, in most cases. "Lester Washington," the paper continued, "was milking the system for all it was worth. He finally met someone who meted out punishment to fit the crime."

According to the police, Washington was found with a switchblade in his hand. Speculation was he attacked the young woman, seen leaving by a jogger, and she had fatally shot him once in the head. Five hundred dollars and an unspecified amount of cocaine had been found in his pockets. He was survived . . .

Lysette lost interest, and turned to the *Inquirer*. The Inky, as its many critics referred to it, had two stories; one focusing on the mystery woman who police believed was implicated in both shootings, and another on Lester Washington; a victim of "abuse, neglect and the cycle of poverty."

The Inky referred to her as the Angel of Death, a clear attempt to pin an instantly recognizable moniker on her. The jogger hadn't heard anything . . . his Walkman . . . a brief glimpse . . . white, blonde with a black leather coat . . . blah, blah, blah, blah, blah.

The story of Lester Washington was heartrending; at least the reporter made it appear so. No father, mother a heroin addict, the poor child was often left alone as a baby, which was better than when his mother was home. At those times she beat the baby with an electric cord when he cried. "Which only made him cry more, which only made her beat him harder."

He stayed with various relatives whenever his mother was arrested or enrolled in a rehab program. An uncle had reportedly sexually abused Lester when he was six. Often truant from school, he had been retained three times, and read at a fourth-grade level when he stopped coming to school at sixteen.

By this time he had a long juvenile record. "Lester found that he could make more money selling drugs and boosting cars than his teachers, who had given up on him. Blah, blah, blah, blah, blah, blah . . .

Lysette was about to toss the paper when she spotted an editorial, "Another victim of crime." It was written by the same bleeding heart who had written the article on Lester Washington.

"In two days, a young boy and man became victims of urban neglect, paying the ultimate price with their lives." The entire editorial focused on these "victims" who turned to crime because the "system had failed them."

"What a crock of shit," Lysette said aloud. "The system failed *them*. What about the old man who was pistol-whipped? What about me, if I hadn't had a gun? Give me a fucking break."

Furious, she turned on the television, expecting to hear more of the same. But she was mistaken. A reporter was talking to the noon anchor, Monica. "The mood on the street from our unscientific tally fully supports this mystery woman who, as one gentleman told us, once and for all put an end to the criminal activities of two worthless punks.

A pretty young Latino, no more than eighteen, holding her three-year-old daughter by the hand and sounding like Rosie

Perez, told the reporter: "It's about time someone stood up to this scum. The police ain't doing nothing. There are dealers on *my* block. They waves to the police when they drive by. Laughs at them. I don't let my baby outside, and I don't go out after dark. Maybe some of these fools will think twice before they mess with people. They might be the next with a bullet in the head."

"Tell them, sister!" said a young black youth behind her, who was then joined by a dozen others.

"Tell them, sister!!"

The reporter then spoke with a black construction worker.

"I don't know why the police are dogging this woman, like *she's* done something wrong. If I'm on the subway I want *her* watching my back. You know," the man said, laughing, "maybe we should all put on blonde wigs when we go out at night. Make those mothers think twice about messing with us then."

Finally, back to the reporter. "One paper, Monica, has dubbed her the Angel of Death," she said contemptuously. "But those we spoke to have another name for her—the Nightwatcher, and the people of this beleaguered city seem to have taken this mystery woman, this Nightwatcher, to heart. Reporting from Tenth and Market Streets, this is Lauren James."

"Holy shit!" Lysette said aloud, pacing the room. "I'm a goddamn hero." At least on TV, she thought. But what of the newspaper articles? They were written *before* the support for her came in from the common Joe on the street. The Inky, especially, seemed to be completely out of touch with its readers. The people, ravaged by crime, didn't want to hear about victims who themselves became victims. The people—the only ones who really counted—were not about to condemn her. On the contrary, they felt as she did. They wanted to take back the streets. They wanted to take back the night. They wanted to rid themselves of the fear that followed them like a plague.

Other, more practical concerns, soon intruded. Blonde. White. Black leather coat. If she went to work with her blonde wig, and black leather coat, *someone* was bound to make a crack, in jest of course. But others might think it more than mere coincidence.

The black coat was her newest; the one she had bought for the fall. Fortunately, she was a pack rat, who kept everything even if it was no longer in style, stained, or no longer suited her taste. That was the Lysette in her, practical to a fault.

She found any number of coats in her closet she could substitute, and chose a red leather coat to wear that night. As for the blonde hair, that, too, was no problem. She had a large array of wigs and regularly changed them, telling the regulars she had dyed her hair. For awhile, then, she'd be a brunette.

She flipped on WWDB, the all-talk station, and found the majority of callers were fed up with crime, corrupt and incompetent police, and an overburdened judicial system.

Talk show hosts seemed to sense a collective outrage among the masses; at least those who called in, and went with the flow—even at times led the charge.

One caller who felt the Nightwatcher—the name had caught on, Lysette noted—was a white racist bitch was blown off by the host in mid-sentence.

"This is not about race," one caller, who was obviously black, said passionately. "This woman came to the aid of a brother. When she was attacked in the park last night, her attacker was also a brother. This woman wouldn't have taken crap from anyone. As far as I'm concerned, she's color blind. She's not going to give a white dude the benefit of the doubt and find a knife slitting her throat. He'll end up with a hole in his head, too, if he messes with her. . . . "

At one point Lysette looked at the clock and, with a start, saw it was three in the afternoon.

—*Another blackout*, her mind whispered.

No, she said to herself. She had just been so absorbed in the callers' support for her street justice she had let the time get away from her.

It was time to shower and get ready for work. Up until a year ago Jil had just two shifts at the club—10 AM–6PM and 6PM–2AM. There were times, though, when there weren't enough girls and other times there were too many for slack periods. So, she had added a third shift, 4PM–midnight. It covered the club's busiest times, and those who came on at four were fresh. Shifts changed every Thursday. Tonight, she began the 4PM–midnight shift. Usually, she didn't care, but getting off earlier would allow her to get a decent night's sleep, and get to the beach early the next day.

She had considered going to the beach . . .

—To Angel.

. . . today, but getting up at eleven had made that impossible. She wanted to see Angel, sure. She was a spunky kid and all, but she also wanted to see if her last sand sculpture figure had been an aberration brought on by the stress of Rose's death and the subway shooting.

* * *

Applying her makeup at the club, Lysette marveled at how easily she had slipped into Cassandra. She hadn't had to psyche herself up, as she normally did. Once behind the wheel with her blonde wig she was Cassandra. . . .

—A lean, mean, *killing* machine.

No, Lysette reminded herself. *Don't* lay the killing at Cassandra's feet. She was Cassandra; tough, aggressive and totally uninhibited.

What was interesting about the 4PM–midnight shift was Lysette got to see girls who had been working seven hours. From four to five, she would just put on her makeup, and prepare herself for an uninterrupted seven hours of work. Around 4:45, she'd wander around the club, with her bra on, hugging some of her regulars, telling them to stick around—she'd be out soon. She tried to catch the club's rhythm. She couldn't explain why, but each night was unique. Become one with the rhythm and no one would turn Cassandra away, she thought to herself.

Looking at the other girls, she knew who would make it and who would be gone in a few months. Randi had pointed out such girls when she had trained her.

"See Tabitha. Two hours and already her shoulders are slouched. Watch her go ask that guy for a Table Dance. See, she's meek, her body language tells it all. He says no, and she accepts it."

"What's her problem?" Lysette had asked.

"You can teach them to be aggressive, but you can't teach them to be confident. That's something you acquire, and some don't get it. You can only kick them in the butt so many times before they lose it."

Self-confidence Cassandra had, and now so did Lysette. Although she had easily slid into her Cassandra persona, she realized she was looking at the club—*at Cassandra*—from Lysette's perspective. Yes, she thought, not at all displeased, she and Cassandra were becoming one.

Now watching the other girls, with an hour to go in their shift, she saw those who lacked the self-assurance needed to succeed.

Thea wouldn't be around long. She was a bit heavy, which some guys liked, but she was too self-conscious about her weight. *Accentuate the positive*, Randi had told her. Thea couldn't or wouldn't.

Paris, on the other hand, could and would stick it out. She was Thea's opposite; one of the few girls Jil hired without big jugs. Lysette . . .

—*Cassandra*.

. . . had asked her why.

"Like I said when I hired you," Jil explained, "every man has his own fantasy girl. Paris is twenty-one, but she looks fifteen. Has the tits of a girl just blossoming; becoming aware of changes in her body for the first time. She's my virgin, and a lot of guys get off on doing someone the first time."

Paris was Couch Dancing, and Lysette could see the customer's tongue flicking at the girl's tiny nipples as she bent over him. Paris had accentuated the positive, and little as she was would be a crowd favorite.

It took all kinds, she thought. All kinds.

Again, the talk was about the mystery woman. She even heard a number of them refer to her as the Nightwatcher. Yes, she thought, the name would stick. So much for the Inky's Angel of Death.

Unlike the night before, though, there was a positive electricity in the air. It was as if the Nightwatcher were on the prowl right now, protecting them from the animals that stalked the streets.

The night before, the emphasis had been as much on the subway mugger, and how it could have been any of them who were attacked. Tonight, they joked and kidded how those pricks better watch out or *they'd* have a third eye in their head.

With spirits soaring, the tipping was better and Cassandra—all the girls, actually—were in hot demand.

When Cassandra Table Danced, she would sometimes have fantasies of her own. She would imagine herself having sex with a particular studly customer. Her hand in her panties, she would fantasize him thrusting himself within her. With the paranoia of AIDS, this was most definitely safe sex.

Tonight, though, she had far different, far darker fantasies. Towering over a young college kid, out alone and very intimidated, she saw the boy in the subway. Midway through her Table Dance she pointed a finger at his head and shot him dead, blowing imaginary smoke from her finger after the execution. Unaware of her thoughts, he giggled self-consciously.

She Couch Danced with what could have been the twin of the man from the playground. All right, she said to herself, not *exactly* his twin, but close enough. He was Hispanic, shorter and pudgy. But Cassandra saw the man from the playground advance toward her. Bent over, with her pussy within inches of the man's face, she whispered, "I'm going to kill you."

"Oh yeah, baby!" he said, misinterpreting her remark. "Any closer and my heart will burst right out of my chest."

As the song came to an end, the man from the playground disappeared, and she was looking into the glazed eyes of the middle-aged Hispanic.

—Nothing like the guy in the playground.

—But a girl had to to have her fantasies.

The images continued. Just before six, little Paris was center stage, writhing on the floor in mock masturbation. She wasn't Paris, though, but Laura, and with each cry of orgasmic joy Paris uttered, Lysette saw a man—his face shrouded—bashing her head with a marble lighter. It seemed so real, Lysette wanted to race toward the stage to save her . . .

—"Don't blame yourself," the psychologist had told her, "that you lived and Laura died. There was nothing you could do." But irrational as it seemed, Lysette did blame herself.

. . . but Cassandra stopped her. They were one. Lysette controlled Cassandra's excesses; Cassandra protected Lysette from the demons of her past.

And the night would have been incomplete without a visit from Rose. An elderly couple often frequented the club. The girls, while changing, would proffer theories why they came.

"It loosens her up," thought Katrina. "Makes her young again. They go home and get it on. Yeah!"

"No, *he* can't get it up without the fantasy," was Jackie's theory. "He sees all this young pussy and when he's humping her, he's humping us."

Tonight, Table Dancing with a regular, the two of them watched her. She saw only the woman. Saw Rose, standing behind her car. Saw the car backing into her . . .

—Run to her, push her out of the way, Lysette thought.

—It's an illusion. Run with it, then let it go, Cassandra interjected.

. . . hitting her, lurching forward, dragging her like a Raggedy Ann doll. She saw Rose at her viewing, which would be held in two days, her face that of a porcelain doll. Lysette bent down to kiss her, and the face cracked under the weight of her kiss.

—Just an illusion, Cassandra told her. Let it go. Let it go!

She did as she was told.

At midnight, she was exhausted. Never had the images seemed so real, so horrific. Were these the images that played through her mind when she slept, she wondered? So terrifying, she would leave her bed and cower in the corner. . . .

—Her nest.

Seeing them now, did it mean she had cleansed herself for the night and could sleep in peace?

—Don't overanalyze, Cassandra told her.

Yeah, Lysette thought, Cassandra was right.

Driving home, Lysette flipped to WWDB. During the 4PM–midnight shift, she was able to listen to her favorite talk show, "Just Talk," with Tisha Collins.

The show's format was unique in that the host held round-table discussions with those who called in. It wasn't just Tisha and a caller. She would open up a number of lines and allow three, even four callers to discuss an issue, acting as a referee or directing the conversation only when necessary.

Sometimes a caller would have his say and hang up. Just like a poker game, Tisha would let someone new at the table. When they went to commercial, she'd clear the lines and a new set of callers would hold sway. "It's Just Talk," she would say. "You're not up to hear me, so why not call and join in?"

Tonight they were talking about her and crime and the helplessness they all felt. But mostly about *her*, and when they spoke of her they didn't seem so lost or hopeless.

"Honest to God," a middle-aged woman said, "I went shopping today, came home and almost forgot to lock the door. When I was young we didn't have to lock the doors, you know."

"Where did you live, out in the country?" another interjected.

"In South Philly, you putz."

Everyone laughed.

"Then you must be *old*," the other caller shot back.

—Saving face, even on the radio, Lysette thought.

There was more laughter.

"I mean, I felt safe," she continued. "You know, with *her* out there."

"You did lock your door, I hope?" asked a haughty man, who must have thought the woman mad.

"Of course. I'm not senile and I'm no fool. But the point is, I hadn't felt so safe in years."

Lysette smiled. She had never meant to become a symbol. She had just wanted to get home . . .

—But what about the playground? Cassandra asked.

—Shut up and go to sleep, Lysette answered.

. . . and now people envisaged her patrolling the streets, watching out for their safety. What a crazy world, she thought. Talking about *her*. If she came forward, she could imagine some cop looking at her and telling her to get lost.

"You're the fifth nut in here today claiming to be the Nightwatcher. Go home and get a life."

The truth was, she was becoming larger than life. Lysette Ormandy, even with a healthy dose of Cassandra Knight, was bound to disappoint. She could never live up to the image of the pistol-packing mama. No one could.

At home she and Cassandra compromised. She hadn't bought new sheets yet, so she tossed her nightgown aside. She lay with the gun between her breasts. But she set her mental alarm for six-thirty. She wanted to read the papers, then get an early start to the beach.

—To sandsculpt.

—To Angel.

Chapter Twenty-one

Briggs surprised Vivian, arriving home a little after four in the afternoon. Ballistics had confirmed the same gun had killed his two perps. Victims they weren't, he thought, the holier-than-thou-press notwithstanding. They were hardened criminals, killed in the act of preparing to kill.

The jogger had proven worthless. Briggs had been tempted to pay a visit to Isiah Hayes. Zeke was holding back. Yet, Briggs instinctively knew today wasn't the day to press the man. With the second killing he would be even more protective than before. Briggs had to come up with a way to crack the old man.

He knew better than to dwell on it, though. In the shower, or taking a crap in the can; hell, even making love to Vivian—if she would have him—*that's* when inspiration would strike. That's the way it had been for him more times than not, though if his wife found out, he would be sleeping on the couch for sure.

Vivian was initially aloof when he arrived so early and unexpected, but he could sense her warm up after seeing him reading to Alexis; the youth's head nestled against his shoulder, his arm wrapped around her protectively.

Briggs knew his wife had come to accept the demands forced upon him by the department. At least now, when he wasn't at work, the focus of his life was his family. Their tragedy, ironically, had drawn them closer together.

Only now did he clearly see the path he had been traveling before Alexis' attack.

He had seen far too many cop marriages go sour for any number of reasons. In his case, bringing his work home with him—*not* sharing, but brooding and becoming self-absorbed—could have been fatal. He *had* taken both his wife and daughter for granted.

They could—would—talk later, was his fallback excuse. Now he had some important case to ponder.

He had missed Alexis in a school play a year earlier. It was unavoidable; he couldn't be blamed. And he would catch her the next time. Promise.

Only now, there might be no next time, for Alexis might never fully recover.

His wife had wanted to talk about moving out of the city. She would show him articles about black-on-black crime. Only recently had the media, and vocal national black spokesmen like Jesse Jackson, come to grips with what he knew daily. Black-on-black crime. *His* people were killing and victimizing their own. Blacks were feasting on blacks.

While Penrose Park was mostly middle-class, crime hadn't taken a vacation. Burglaries, car thefts and drug dealing were up in his neighborhood. He thought he had left that behind when they'd bought a house in Southwest Philly, but a nice house couldn't insulate you from crime.

But it was something he couldn't deal with at the moment, he had said time and time again. He had more pressing matters on his mind.

Looking back on all he had missed and his inane excuses, he wondered if his daughter's attack in some ways was a blessing in disguise. He immediately chastised himself when he looked at her dull, unfocused eyes. But the attack had made him look at his life and his marriage in a different light. Long after he retired he wanted his wife by his side. He didn't want to realize that years after they had divorced. And his daughter. He had missed so much of her growing up. He would be there now, he vowed, when she needed him the most.

Being able to leave early had been a boon. With the unexpected time he had considered running down some leads . . .

—What leads? his mind asked.

. . . on Alexis' attacker after dinner, but thought better of it. He didn't know just how many days like this he would have with his wife and daughter before the Nightwatcher struck again.

He *wanted* to be home. He read to his daughter, knowing deep within she could hear him, even if she couldn't understand the words. And after she went to sleep, he'd make love to his wife. He felt almost like a newlywed. They had become so complacent, so wrapped up in their own workday lives, one almost needed a calendar to *plan* ahead for sex. And it had become devoid of passion.

Alexis' attack had been like cold water thrown in their faces. Each day became more important, because crime being what it was, that day could be their last. What had seemed important now seemed trivial. They both seemed to grasp the need to seize the moment. Share their love for one another, *now*. Both learned to compartmentalize their work from their life at home. They *were* still in love. They just had to reach out for one another. *Now*. The case—any case—could wait until later.

Briggs saw his wife looking at him as he read to Alexis. Their problems now seemed inconsequential. They had one another, and pessimist that he was, deep down a part of him believed they'd have Alexis; the daughter of his *before* the attack.

Chapter Twenty-two

Deidre walked into Carter Hastings' office at six in the morning, and tossed a computer printout on his desk.

"You were right, Carter. Gauging the mood of the city has put this in an entirely different perspective. At the moment, I haven't the foggiest idea how to find her, but I think I'm worming my way into this woman's head."

Hastings read the story quickly, then leaned back in his chair, a smile on his face. "Taking some of your colleagues to task, aren't you?" he said almost gleefully.

"Hey, they deserve it. Deadlines are no reason for some of the crap I read today. When in doubt lay out the facts. These two creeps as victims of society won't wash with the public. The Inky spouts it every time a kid kills a kid. It's nauseating."

"This," he said, holding up her copy, "is what the people really think?" he said a bit uneasily.

"I went to bars, to malls, to fancy department stores and roach-infested pizza parlors. I listened to cops—off the record, of course—talked to high-school kids and retired businessmen in the parks. This is the pulse of the city. *She* is the pulse of the city. She's just taken it a step further."

She ran her hand through her hair, and stifled a yawn. She hadn't gotten much sleep, she thought.

"Talk is cheap, Carter, and this woman is sick of platitudes. I'm in her head. *I want her now*."

"You think she'll come to you?"

Deidre shrugged. "She's acting on instinct. There's no master plan. I've opened the door. Who knows what the fuck she'll do?"

Hastings took out a red pencil and made some changes—correcting punctuation and a few misspellings—then handed the piece back to her.

"You should use the spell checker. They come with our state-of-the-art computers nowadays. And as usual your grammar sucks. Other than that, I wouldn't change a word. Go and piss off your colleagues. I agree. They deserve a kick in the ass."

They exchanged goodbyes. Deidre headed to the hospital to see Jonas.

Chapter Twenty-three

Surprised at being sent home early—actually on time—Nina decided to get some home cooking. Driving through West Kensington, she saw the normal collection of dealers on the streets. Cars would drive by, stop at a corner; money and drugs would change hands. Some things never change, she thought.

But she sensed a different mood; subtle, but there nevertheless, among the riffraff. They were antsy, all jangled nerves, like *they* were wired on the crack, heroin or PCP they sold.

After her brother had been killed, she'd had nightmares for weeks. The backfire of a car or a cat knocking over a trash can brought panic attacks. She would race into the house, screaming for everybody to get down, and hide under her bed.

Sometimes an hour would pass before her father or one of her brothers could cajole her to come out. Other kids reacted in a similar fashion, and a minister decided it would be a good idea to get the kids out of the city for a few days.

He had raised enough money for a three-day trip to the Poconos. There, Nina had seen her first deer, and it reminded her of the dealers she now saw.

It had been by a creek. One minute it was sipping water, the next it sensed her presence. Its ears twitched trying to locate her. It sniffed the air. Its legs quivered as if torn by its desires to quench its thirst and flee. Self-preservation finally won and it bounded into the forest.

The dealers were still out, but they sensed a change in the air and didn't like it one bit.

Over dinner, she heard gunfire and jumped, knocking over her glass of wine. Her father and brother didn't bat an eye at the sound. Her mother closed her eyes in silent prayer. They had become im-

146

mune. It was the only way to survive in a war zone, Nina had learned from psych classes she had taken, but it saddened her to see the emotional toll violence had taken on her family.

Her father reached over, picked up her glass and silently refilled it. She remembered him consoling her after her panic attacks as a child.

"Hush, my little Nina, don't cry. Papa will protect you."

She smiled at him now. She had put aside a good portion of each paycheck. Soon, within the next few months, she would have enough to move them to a safer neighborhood. Her fear, when she went to sleep each night, was violence would strike before she could save enough. Worse, there was nothing—even as a police officer—she could do.

She loved them so, but in a male-dominated family outward signs of affection meant weakness. She sighed. It was tough being a woman in the Rios household, but except for the violence that intruded, she wouldn't trade places with anyone.

She blocked out the violence outside, and basked in the warmth of her family.

Chapter Twenty-four

The people in town talked of the violence in Philadelphia as if it were a foreign country, equating the city to Haiti, Rwanda or Bosnia, where anarchy prevailed. "It could never happen here," was the prevailing—no, *the near universal* sentiment.

Shara felt more isolated than ever. *Could never happen here*—bullshit, she thought. In Allentown, not far away, a rapist had struck twice in the past year, killing two children after defiling them.

Shara knew it wasn't the city, but human nature. She had become a killer, herself, not because of where she lived, but because her brother had tormented her, and her mother wished she had never been born.

Incest, abuse and neglect weren't confined to big cities. Small-town America had its share of atrocities as bad as any in Philadelphia. She would be the first to admit that in big cities there were mitigating circumstances that magnified the crime rate. Poverty, drugs and broken families were the norm and the state and federal government had turned a deaf ear.

But drugs had already invaded this town, though attempts were made to nip the problem in the bud. Broken families were on the upswing here, too. One day this town could very well stare down the barrel of a rapist, serial arsonist or killer in their midst, and they'd never be the same. It had already happened in Allentown, and until a suspect had been arrested, suspicious eyes were cast everywhere. Doors for the first time had been locked to keep the real world from intruding. It could—probably would—happen here, as well.

But their current smugness made her feel even more an outsider than ever. She could never be one of them.

148

She had read recently that two boys had been banished by an Indian tribe after robbing and savagely beating another man.

Her banishment was self-imposed, but she felt as alone as if she were on a deserted island. She longed to return to Philadelphia.

—She couldn't.

She craved to be with her own, ruthless though they could be.

—She couldn't.

The challenge of a hunt beckoned her.

—She couldn't.

She was being driven insane.

—She couldn't.

—She couldn't.

—She couldn't.

—She *must*.

Chapter Twenty-five

Lysette awoke in bed at six-thirty in the morning. Her fantasies at the club *must* have cleansed her mind for the night. She was comforted that the Cassandra in her didn't object to the early wake-up call.

She was achieving balance; becoming one with herself.

She dressed, bought the papers, and over coffee and cigarettes, read.

The Inky seemed taken aback by the mood of the city. Their lone story was relegated to the bottom right-hand corner of the first page, continued deep into the paper. An editorial chastised the public for making the Nightwatcher a hero; though its tone was more subdued than normal.

Lysette laughed aloud how they'd dropped their Angel of Death tag and accepted the moniker used by talk show callers and television stations.

"Today we appear to be in the minority," the editorial preached, "but the lives of even the most heinous of drug dealers and muggers must be respected. To applaud the snuffing out of two lives— victims themselves, lest we forget—is to get in the gutter with those they condemn."

Self-righteous schmucks, she thought. Let the editorial writer stare down the barrel of a gun or have a knife flashed before his eyes and see how he feels.

The *Daily News* had a straightforward report. The writer was cautious, though acknowledged the Nightwatcher had captured the collective attention of the city.

Below was a commentary by Deidre Caffrey, which immediately caught her attention. The reporter recounted her journey through the city the day before and told of the Nightwatcher's cathartic influence. Strangers gathered in parks and bars were talking with one another, relating horror stories of inner-city life. Blacks and whites intermingled. Blacks and Asians, each wary of the other, found common ground. Hispanics, intentionally isolating themselves from other ethnic and racial groups, were eager to share their stories.

Even though only two criminals had been eliminated, Caffrey said, "I sensed a collective sigh of relief that here was *someone* doing *something*. No idle threats. No sanctimonious spiels. No one-day marches, rallies or meetings—all bluster with no results."

She criticized certain members of the media— "You know who you are," she said—for getting on their "bully pulpits" trying to generate sympathy for hardened criminals because "life had kicked them in the balls."

Lysette had never seen that expression in a Philadelphia daily, and thought this lady must have pull to be able to say what was on her mind without someone toning it down.

Then this Deidre Caffrey talked about her, as if the two had had a conversation.

"So who is the Nightwatcher? Let's not delude ourselves. She is no Robocop or larger-than-life hero we see in the movies who singlehandedly rids the city of all that ails it. No," she went on, "this was a woman going home from a tough day at work who instinctively acted to help her fellow man."

Lysette lit another cigarette and continued to read.

"This is a woman who has suffered, for why else would she set herself up to be attacked a night later? This is a woman who's mad as hell and deciding not to take it anymore. For her this is personal. And she is an intensely private woman; probably someone single and without children."

Jesus, Lysette thought, how could she know?

"She's not going to boast to her girlfriends. She has no desire to face the glare and scrutiny of an adoring public and suspicious press. She will be caught eventually, if she doesn't become a victim herself first, because she is no professional. Or, she may come in voluntarily to further mock the inability of the police to get the job done.

"And, one more thing. Before we put her on a pedestal, it must be acknowledged that this is one sick cookie. Not for the subway killing; for that she had no choice. But that somehow triggered something within that has propelled her to act recklessly. She has been lucky so far. Let's hope her luck doesn't run out. This city is not ready to mourn the death of its Nightwatcher."

Lysette sat stunned. How could she know so much about her, she wondered?

—Conjecture, Cassandra responded.

She'd never considered her vulnerability, nor, after the first night, the possibility she would be caught by the police. And what about going to the police voluntarily *before* they closed in? They would look pretty stupid, wouldn't they? Something to consider . . .

—But not yet, Cassandra interjected.

No, not yet. She didn't know why, but there was unfinished business to take care of. She would know, somehow, when it was time to fold her tent. Maybe she would turn herself in. Then again, maybe she would just fade back into the woodwork.

She tore the article out of the paper. She'd want to read it again. This Deidre Caffrey had correctly gauged the pulse of the city, and somehow crawled, ever so briefly, into her head. She felt vaguely uncomfortable, even threatened. Maybe this . . .

—Don't overanalyze, Cassandra piped in.

Lysette laughed. Right, don't overanalyze. Anyway, it was time to get to the shore.

Once on the Atlantic City Expressway, Lysette turned to WPHT-AM to see what Don Imus was ranting about that morning.

Don Imus, considered a shock jock by those who probably never listened to his show, was based in New York, but syndicated around the country, "at more than a hundred stations" he'd boast proudly almost daily. He'd just recently been picked up in Philly on an AM station that had changed from all sports to a talk show format.

Lysette could only take so much of the man at one time, but she found him intriguing and illuminating, unlike Howard Stern, a true schockmeister who was just crude and rude.

She found the Imus show something of a paradox. During his four-and-a-half-hour morning-drive program he informed, infuriated and antagonized—sometimes all within a single sentence.

Neither liberal nor conservative, the issues themselves shaped his views. He'd pillory President Clinton one day, then admit grudging admiration for him the next. Guests of varying political persuasions were a daily staple, but he never upstaged nor made fools of them—one reason so many high-profile politicians and journalists popped up regularly. On the contrary, his guests often made jokes at his expense, which he took with good humor.

She admired the fact that he admitted he didn't know it all, even though he was obviously well read, and thoroughly researched the issues of the day. He made her feel *he* was learning from his guests; that he genuinely wanted their opinion and didn't have them on simply as windowdressing.

On the other hand, for much of the rest of the show, the listener was exposed to Imus' unique brand of bawdy humor. A good deal of the man's repartee was sophomoric, even vindictive. Insults flew fast and furious: fat goober, schmucks, losers, fat weasel, moron, nitwits, maggot, transparent worm, creep, geek, wuss, dork, jerk, clowns, mealy mouthed . . . some of his many putdowns, repeated more times than she could count or tolerate.

And there were his alter egos—mimicked appearances by the late-George Patton, Richard Nixon, Paul Harvey and Walter Cronkite, among others who spewed forth venom Imus had articulated without the spite. They pulled no punches in their often tasteless tirades. With Beavis and Bubba, a take-off on MTV's Beavis and Butthead, Bubba was President Clinton at his raunchiest. However, as it wasn't Imus himself venting, these characters allowed him to get in his digs while seemingly remaining above the fray.

Lysette felt this detracted from the show and was what probably earned him the undeserved reputation as a shock-jock. Still, she had to admit, sometimes the sketches made her both wince and laugh aloud, at the same time.

All in all, she found him refreshing . . . albeit in measured doses.

She was surprised *she* was the topic *du jour*.

"It's time for the national news with Charles McCord," Imus said, introducing his straightman. "Good morning Chuck."

"Well, I-Man, there's been another vigilante slaying in Philadelphia, by the woman who's been dubbed the Nightwatcher by the media—"

"Wasn't she the Angel of Death yesterday?" Imus interrupted, which, Lysette thought to herself, he did often. It was the Imus show, after all, so he could do as he damn well pleased. And he did.

"That she was, I-Man," Charles intoned. "But, today she's the Nightwatcher."

"I wish they'd make up their mind. Fat weasel pencil-pushers sitting at their typewriters. 'Let's try this and see how it flies. No, that didn't work. How about the Nightwatcher?' " he mimicked sarcastically. " 'Maybe folks will like that better.' So what did this Nightwatcher do now?" he asked.

Charles briefly explained the details of the playground shooting.

"It must be the water down there in Philly," Imus deadpanned, when Charles was done, to the laughter of McCord.

"Seriously," he added, "I think it's being a woman that's driving this story. The weaker sex, you know, having more cojones than the toughest of men. A man does what she has and he'd be vilified, like that little weasel Bernard Goetz. But a *woman . . .* " He paused, as if not knowing what to say next—another Imus trademark. "I just don't know," he finally said, and Lysette could imagine him shaking his head in resignation.

"And she's a mystery—an enigma," Charles added.

"Most definitely," Imus agreed, seemingly back up to speed. "Pick up a blonde, in a Philly bar, and the first question you ask is 'Are you packing, honey?' instead of 'Your place or mine?' "

Again, there was laughter in the background.

"In other news," Charles continued.

"Guess it wouldn't be too smart to criticize her cooking," Imus interjected, ignoring his sidekick.

"Oh, I-Man," Charles responded, as if shocked.

"Well, I don't know where I come down on this. On the one hand, I applaud her moxie—especially coming to the rescue of the man in the subway while everyone else wussed out. On the other, well, vigilantism makes me a wee bit squeamish."

"Like you may be next," Charles cut in, with a dig of his own.

"As a matter of fact, I don't plan on visiting Philly anytime soon," the host shot back, with a laugh. He paused for a beat, then added, "I don't think we've heard the last of her. This is one story that's not going to die."

There was a collective groan from Charles and their producer Bernard McGuirk, at Imus' unintentional pun.

"Maybe that was a poor choice of words," Imus responded, as if only then aware what he'd said was in particularly poor taste.

"So, what else is going on, Charles?" Imus asked, seemingly either tired of this story, or fearful he was sinking fast and his cohorts were about to turn on him, as they so often did.

Tired of hearing about herself, she popped in a tape for the remainder of the ride.

She got to the beach . . .

—Angel's beach.

. . . shortly before ten. Late September, but with the temperature in the low eighties, summer didn't seem to want to let go. Lysette dipped her toes in the ocean and shivered involuntarily. The temperature was summerlike, but the ocean was having no part of it. Even Angel wouldn't go in, she thought. She'd freeze her ass off.

But Angel wasn't there. Lysette felt a bit foolish. What made her think she would find the young girl here, waiting for her without knowing when she might come? Why was she so disappointed at her absence? Before Cassandra could scold her she said aloud, "Don't overanalyze, I know," then laughed. The becoming of one. Lysette had analyzed *everything*, and old habits died hard.

With a sigh, Lysette got her tools and began to lay the foundation for her sculpture. What would it be today—the young lovers . . .

—Or the attack by the faceless man?

She worked expertly, savoring the texture of the sand, and the absolute solitude, save for the calls of the seagulls.

She was startled by the sound of music, blaring from a boombox, and looked up to see Angel, naked, dancing to the Pointer Sisters' "Only Sisters Can Do It."

As much as she loved the Pointer Sisters, this particular song made her uneasy. She'd had a sister . . .

—But Laura had been killed.

. . . and so missed the talks they'd had and secrets they'd shared. They were right. "Only sisters can."

The beat of the song was fast, and Angel seemed swept up by its rhythm, seemingly unaware Lysette was staring at her. As the song ended and the next began, Angel turned to her.

"You blanked out again. For a long time. I kinda borrowed your boombox from your car."

Lysette was suddenly angry. "You had no right to go into my car without permission."

"Sorry," Angel answered testily, "but with you staring into space, I could have driven your car away and you wouldn't have noticed. What was I supposed to do anyway, sit here and wait for you to wake up?" She favored Lysette with a pout.

Lysette smiled tightly. "Aren't we bitchy, today."

"Don't mock me." *She* was angry, now. "From all I've read, at my age I'm supposed to have these mood swings. Aren't I supposed to be giddy one minute and brooding the next? My hormones are screwing me emotionally."

Lysette laughed, and this time it was genuine. "You sound just like a magazine article."

Angel relaxed, then shrugged. "Really, I was only borrowing your boombox, like you with the sand. I didn't—"

"No need to apologize," Lysette said. "I was just startled. One minute I was alone, the next you're dancing to the Pointer Sisters."

"They're my favorite group," Angel said. "I'm not into grunge, like most of the other kids."

"This is scary," Lysette said. "They're *my* favorite group, too. You could be the little sister I never had."

"You gonna look at your sculpture?"

Lysette had completely forgotten about it. Looking at it now, she got that lightheaded feeling again. It was much like the last time she had been here—only worse.

She had again carved herself into the bas-relief, being attacked, and the same figure towered over her ready to pounce. But his face wasn't totally blank this time. There was no detail, but there were two red marbles where his eyes should have been, and though the eyebrows didn't have the detail of the chest hair, she had sculpted them to make it appear he was squinting.

—*A face only a mother could love*, popped into her mind again.

"Where did I get the marbles?" she asked.

"You asked me if I had any. I had plenty at home, and brought them."

"Why red? Who has red eyes?"

"You asked for red marbles," Angel answered. "I asked if you wanted blue or brown or green and you said, 'No, red marbles. Red marbles.' You stuck them in, played with the eyebrows, then stared like before."

"Red eyes?" Lysette said, aloud, but she was talking to herself. Then to Angel. "You know, somehow they fit. I mean, the guy's still a blur in my mind, but for some reason when I see him now he has red eyes."

"Weird," Angel said.

"Yeah, weird."

They both stared at the figure for a few moments, then Lysette tore herself loose.

"I've got something for you in the car," Lysette said, breaking the gloom that had settled upon them. "Let me get it."

"So, you've been thinking about me," Angel said smugly.

"Kinda," Lysette said, as she rummaged through her glove compartment, and brought out a tape.

She slipped the tape into the boombox. "A few weeks ago I

bought this CD by War. Listen." It was a slow R&B song, with a lot of bluesy instrumental between verses.

> *My life was just a lonely thing*
> *I never used to laugh or sing*
> *You gave me hope and you made me strong . . .*

Angel, listening intently, smiled at the chorus:

> *Angel*
> *You are here*
> *You are mine*
> *Sweet and lovely*
> *Angel*
> *Please be near*
> *Please be kind.*
> *I was blind I could not see*
> *You came down to rescue me.*

An extended instrumental followed, and Angel got up and began to dance. She moved slowly, her hands gliding up her body, caressing her breasts . . .
—Like Cassandra at the club.
 . . . her lips in a mock pout . . .
—Like Cassandra at the club.
She seemed somehow older, no longer gangly, when she danced now. She was sensuous and erotic . . .
—Almost like a young Cassandra, Lysette thought.
Lysette, sitting on the sand, felt like one of the customers at the club. Standing, Angel towered over her, drawing nearer so Lysette could see every curve in the adolescent's rapidly changing body.

> *Angel*
> *You are here*
> *You are mine*
> *Sweet and lovely*
> *Angel*
> *Please be near*
> *Please be kind.*

157

As the final instrumental chords tapered off, Angel sat on the sand cross-legged. Lysette thought she could see tears in the girl's eyes.

"I love it, Lys. I really do. The words are perfect. It's me."

"Really?" Lysette said. "I thought the lyrics referred more to me. I mean, you're hardly lonely. You must have tons of friends."

"If I have so many friends, why am I out here alone?"

"Why *are* you out here alone?" Lysette asked.

"I'm not," she said with a giggle. "I have you."

"You must have friends your age."

Angel shrugged. "No best friend. Nobody I'd dance for. Nobody I'd bring to *my* beach. Is that the way you dance at the club?"

"What do you mean?" Lysette asked. "I never—"

"Yes you did," Angel interrupted. "Last time, you told me you were a stripper.

"I don't remember—"

"You don't remember lots of things. You make sand sculptures, then look at them like they formed themselves. You ask me to get red marbles, but don't remember . . . "

"All right, already," Lysette said with a forced laugh. "You've made your point. I must be getting senile in my old age."

"So, is that the way you dance at the club?" Angel pressed.

"Sometimes," Lysette said, not wanting to admit how much like herself . . .

—Like Cassandra.

. . . Angel's dancing reminded her.

"Will you dance with me to *my* song?"

"I don't know . . . "

"You can keep your bathing suit on. C'mon, please."

"Okay, already. Once. To *your* song."

The two of them danced, and Lysette could feel Cassandra taking over, her inhibitions slipping away. Angel kept her eyes locked on Lysette's and mimicked her every move; her hands caressing her breasts, moving slowly down her body to her genitals, then up again.

A little Cassandra, Lysette thought.

"Wow!" she said, as the song ended. "You're a great dancer." She gave Lysette a hug, and Lysette was acutely aware of the youth's breasts pressing against her.

"It's such a beautiful song. Thank you, Lys," and she kissed her on the cheek. "Will you do me a favor?" she asked.

"Not another dance. You said only one," Lysette answered.

"Not a dance, though I could dance to *my* song all day. Can you teach me how to sculpt in the sand?"

"Sure. Why not," Lysette said, relieved. "We'll start off with something simple, though."

She saw the beginning of a pout form on Angel's face.

"Not because you're not good enough or too young. When I started I built sand castles. You start off slow, master the technique, then go on to more advanced figures. Okay?"

Angel smiled. "Sorry, it's my hormones."

"You do too much reading, young lady," Lysette said with a laugh.

For half an hour Lysette went over some basics with Angel, telling her she had to make sure her base was good and wet, then formed a hard mound with a wooden block.

After a while, Angel got the hang of it and began working alone. Lysette put on the Pointer Sisters tape again, and watched Angel immerse herself in her sculpting. When she was done, Lysette could tell she had created a room, but wasn't sure just what it was.

"It's not too good," Angel said, looking at Lysette's expression. It wasn't a question.

"That's not it at all. It *is* good." She laughed. "Don't jump all over me with your hormones, but I know it's a room, but just what room is it?"

"An attic, silly. When I'm home, I spend a lot of time in my attic. It's more private than my room. It's where I go when I want to get away from *everything*." Looking a bit embarrassed, she abruptly changed subjects. "You want to go in the water with me?"

"It's freezing!" Lysette said. "I stuck my toes in and just about died."

"I like it cold, but that's okay. I'll go in alone."

Lysette looked at her watch and saw it was two o'clock. She'd be cutting it close to get to the club on time.

"Angel, I'm sorry, but I gotta go. My hours change at work each week. That's why I got here so early."

"That's okay. I'm going to stay and watch the waves take our sculptures away. I mean it's not *our* sand."

Angel helped Lysette put her tools in the car, then went back to get the boombox.

"Do me a favor, Angel."

"Sure."

159

"Keep the boombox at your house. It's too big to schlep around and I don't want to forget it next time."

"I'm glad you'll be back."

"Hey, I want to see how that dude's face turns out," she said jokingly, but just thinking of his red eyes made her uneasy.

Angel handed Lysette her War tape.

"No, that's for you to keep. I made a copy for myself."

Angel was beaming, holding the tape to her chest. "You're something else, Lys," she said.

"I was thinking the same about you."

Lysette got in her car, and before driving away watched Angel pop the tape back into the boombox and play *her* song. She was dancing again. The thought recurred to Lysette—this definitely wasn't the same gangly girl she had seen two days before. She was going to break many a heart . . .

—And cause boys to take many a cold shower, Cassandra joined in.

A lot of cold showers, Lysette agreed.

With the Pointer Sisters in the background, Lysette looked back on the day as she drove home. She hadn't enjoyed herself so much since . . .

—Since before the attack on her family.

Yes, since before the attack. She could talk so easily with Angel, and was surprised by how much they shared in common.

She still couldn't believe she had told Angel she was a stripper the first time they'd met. It wasn't that she was ashamed of her job. On the contrary, she found her job rewarding. She was an entertainer, not a prostitute, whore, slut or strung-out junkie as some feminists labeled those of her profession. You paid your money and lived your fantasy. It wasn't lurid or dirty because it was all a fantasy. If men left the club feeling better after a hard day's work or a relationship gone sour, she had done *more* than her job.

But, there are certain things an eleven-and-a-half-year-old might misconstrue. There was, after all, a stigma attached to what she did; prancing around 'ne-kid.' And, with a shudder, she could imagine Angel bounding into her house.

"Hi, Mom. I met this neat stripper at the beach today," and her mother having apoplexy.

She *had* to have told her, though. These blackouts she was hav-

*Experience the Ultimate in Fear
Every Other Month...
From Leisure Books!*

As a member of the Leisure Horror Book Club,
you'll enjoy the best new horror by the best writers
in the genre, writers who know how to chill your
blood. Upcoming book club releases include
First-Time-in-Paperback novels by such acclaimed
authors as:

*Douglas Clegg   Ed Gorman
John Shirley   Elizabeth Massie
J.N. Williamson   Richard Laymon
Graham Masterton   Bill Pronzini
Mary Ann Mitchell   Tom Piccirilli
Barry Hoffman*

SAVE BETWEEN $3.72 AND $6.72
EACH TIME YOU BUY.
THAT'S A SAVINGS OF UP TO NEARLY 40%!

Every other month Leisure Horror Book Club brings
you three terrifying titles from Leisure Books,
America's leading publisher of horror fiction.
EACH PACKAGE SAVES YOU MONEY.
And you'll never miss a new title.

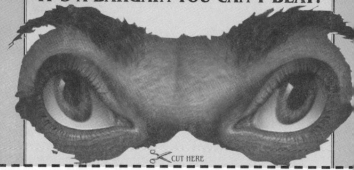

ing disturbed her. It wasn't anything physical, she was certain. Were there times, she wondered, when Cassandra completely took over? But that made no sense either. What did Cassandra know of her attacker? Then again, maybe Cassandra *did* know her attacker; someone Lysette had locked away, but her other self—the Cassandra in her—was fully aware of.

"Red eyes," Lysette said aloud. "He *did* have red eyes," or at least they appeared red to me. She also recalled he squinted, as if the light bothered him when her father had turned on the lights upon entering the house. Piece by piece, a long-lost puzzle was coming together.

Tomorrow was Rose's viewing and Sunday the funeral. Monday, she would go back to the beach and see if she could remember any more about her attacker.

—And see Angel.
—Mostly to see Angel.
—*Sweet and lovely*
—*Angel.*

Lysette stopped by her house and absently packed her bag. Next time why not take your bag with you, she scolded herself. Save you fifteen to twenty minutes.

At the club, she kept her eye on Paris. She was a lot like Angel physically. At least she had taken on the persona of a young, not-yet-fully-aware-of-the-ways-of-the-world girl. In the dressing room, a cigarette dangling from her mouth, she didn't talk like a child. While Lysette maintained her Cassandra persona the entire time at the club, Paris appeared to be like Angel only on the dance floor.

Angel, moreover, was far more sensual than Paris. Lysette knew it came from acting out the part daily, for months in Paris' case; years in hers. But between songs, Lysette could see the Angel in Paris disappear. It happened with many of the girls. The end of a song meant the end of a Table Dance. You have to put your bra back on, then look for another mark. Some girls dropped their facade.

Lysette was always *Cassandra* at the club, but Paris became all business once a song ended, not the impressionable teenager that was her calling card. She had to hand it to Paris, though. She knew what her customers were after and made the forbidden possible. Jil was right. Where Lysette had seen a scrawny twenty-one-year-old, Jil had seen a young teen coming into bloom.

After her shift, Lysette was surprised to see she had packed Cassandra's clothes again; the same black leather skirt, red top—even the black jacket, blonde wig and glitzy jewelry. Lysette put on the skirt and top, but kept on her brunette wig. She was glad she had worn her red coat to work. The black one remained in the bag.

Home, a hot shower, and sleep beckoned. She didn't look forward to the viewing the next day. She wanted to remember Rose as she'd been in life. She recalled the fantasy of the night before. . . .

—Rose's porcelain face.

—Bending down to kiss her.

—The face cracking.

She would go, though, but wouldn't stay long. Wouldn't talk to Rose's friends or relatives. She wasn't, after all, part of the immediate family, though Rose always treated her as another of her grandchildren.

"I miss you, Rose," she said aloud. "Seems everyone I love is taken away prematurely."

—*Not Angel*, her mind screamed.

—I'll protect you, Angel, she thought to herself.

—*Sweet and lovely*

—*Angel.*

Her hands gripped so tightly on the wheel, they almost cramped up, and she was suddenly aware she had passed her house.

—Another blackout? No, her mind had just strayed, she told herself.

She drove up Broad to Lombard, took Lombard almost as far as it went and parked at 24th Street. The Schuylkill Park lay before her. Before the attack, she remembered a new kid in school who had lived near the park. Only then, Kimberly had told her, it was called Taney Park; named after a gang of white trash who claimed it as their own. Mothers didn't take their kids to Taney Park. Sometime in the last seven or eight years, though, the city had somehow reclaimed the park, added tennis courts and a state-of-the-art playground, along with lots of grass and benches, along with added security. Now it was quite popular. Schools brought kids to the playground. Gays sunbathed with the skimpiest of bikini briefs at its northern tip—away, for the most part, from the eyes of children—and area neighbors brought their dogs to romp in the spacious grass.

Something, though, had happened a few weeks earlier. Lysette couldn't recall what, but someone had been badly hurt.

At twelve-forty, the park was not quite empty. She went into the playground and sat on the swing. On the corner, next to the tennis courts, was a fidgety young white man; a dealer. He smoked a cigarette and was constantly on the move, his eyes darting back and forth. Maybe watching for the police. He looked like a rabbit, with his constant twitching.

—Watch out for the big bad fox, she thought.

Lysette had donned the blonde wig, gold crucifix and black coat. She began pumping on the swings . . .

—Her mother not there to caution her.

She was aware that Cassandra was reaching for the heavens. Cassandra might want to go dangerously high, might even want to leap, as children often do, but Lysette would protect the reckless side of herself. The wind slapping against her face was exhilarating. It was much better than kicking her feet into the ground, making sure she didn't draw attention, as she had when she was younger; after her grandmother taught her to behave.

She saw a boy—a young white man, about twenty, actually— score from the man at the corner. He put the drugs in his pocket, watched Lysette on the swings and came over.

He took the swing next to hers and began to pump. He was more cautious than she, and soon slowed down, his eyes fixed on her.

Soon, she too slowed down.

"Man that was something," he said.

—She put her hand in her coat pocket.

"I'm kinda afraid of heights, myself. Not too good at amusement parks, either."

—Felt the cold metal of the gun.

"Like at Dorney Park. Those rides make me nauseous, but I bet you love them."

—Her hand on the trigger.

"My name's Charles. Not Chuck or Charlie. Charles," he said with pride. "What's yours?"

"My mama told me never to talk to strangers," she answered.

Charles was a decent enough looking guy, Lysette thought, though his thick horn-rimmed glasses gave him a nerdy quality.

They were loose, constantly slipping down his nose, and he kept readjusting them.

"Then what are you doing out alone so late?" he asked.

"Any reason I *shouldn't* be out late?" she answered with a question of her own.

163

"It's dangerous, in case you haven't heard. A girl alone, you know. Lots of perverts out here."

"Are you one of them, Charles?" she asked, lighting up a cigarette.

"No, of course not. I'm just making conversation. Are you waiting for someone?"

"Are you making a pass at me?"

He flushed, and looked bewildered. She didn't think he fared too well with girls.

"No. I mean, I saw you alone. Thought you might want some company, you know. But if you're waiting . . ."

"Run along, Charles. I am waiting, as a matter of fact. But not for you."

—She loosened the grip on the gun.

"Didn't mean no harm," he said, hopping off the swing, putting his hands into his pockets, and with his head down he began to shuffle off.

"Charles," she called after him.

He looked back expectantly.

"Those drugs you bought. If I *wasn't* waiting for someone, I wouldn't have gone with you."

He flushed, again.

"Nothing personal, but a woman not on drugs doesn't want to share her man with that kind of shit. If you didn't have the drugs, maybe we could have had a good time."

He began to answer, but Lysette put her fingers to her lips.

"Sorry, Charles, but it's too late. You scored your drugs, *then* tried to score with me. You got your priorities fucked up. Think about it next time." She began to pump again, ignoring Charles, who stared at her for a moment, then disconsolately turned and shuffled off.

You're a nasty girl, Cassandra, Lysette said to herself. She knew it was the Cassandra in her talking at the end. Lysette had no intention of going with Charles, drugs or no drugs, and she knew Cassandra felt the same way. You're a tease, Cassandra, acting like you were still at the club. She'd made her point, though. Poor Charles would probably be jerking off tonight, thinking of his missed opportunity with the almost-slutty-looking blonde.

She got off the swing, lit up another cigarette, took off her coat and sauntered over to the man on the corner. As she got closer, she could see he was a user as well as a dealer. He looked a bit like

Mick Jagger—his cheeks sunken in, his lips too big for his long, thin face. His eyes had that glazed quality of someone who had recently scored. He wore a long brown leather coat that came past his knees. Expensive. But it couldn't cover his unwashed long straight hair, the back tied in a ponytail. He reeked of cologne, but even that couldn't mask the fact that he was in need of a shower. He had been talking on a cellular phone, but cut short his conversation when she approached.

"What can I do for you, sweet thing?" he asked, when she got to the corner.

Lysette took a drag from the cigarette, dropped it and crushed it under her pumps.

"You sold some shit to my friend, over there," she said, pointing to Charles in the distance.

"What's it to you?"

"I like my men clean. Know what I mean?"

"Look, bitch, I'm no social worker. The boy's got a free will. Now, if you'll excuse me, I got business to do and you're hanging around ain't good for business. Know what *I* mean?" he said, mocking her.

"Why don't you get the hell out of here, and sell your wares somewhere else. This is a public park and *I'm* not the one who's leaving."

"What, you a hooker who's choosy?" he asked, misinterpreting her. "This is a big park. Why not make like a banana and split."

"You're a laugh a minute," she said. "I already told you I'm not the one who's going. Sorry if you got a problem with that."

"You're the one who's gonna be sorry, bitch." He opened his coat and reached for a gun in his belt.

Before he could get it out, Lysette raised her hand that had been covered by her coat and shot him once in the head. As he fell, he dropped his cellular phone, which had been in his other hand. Without knowing why, Lysette picked it up and slipped it into her coat pocket. She gave him a last look.

"Guess you *won't* be leaving, after all," she said and walked to her car. She heard running, turned and saw Charles exiting the park like he'd been shot out of a cannon.

She drove a block, removed her wig and turned to "Just Talk." She had tuned in to the middle of a heated discussion.

" . . . can't take the law into your own hands," a cultured-sounding black man was saying. "You become part of the problem, not the solution. Say you get into an argument with a neighbor who has loud parties. Are you going to shoot him and justify it on the grounds the police had been too slow to respond?"

"We're not talking about petty arguments, man," another black male responded. "We're talking about the safety of our children, of our wives. A kid in my daughter's kindergarten class brought in a crack vial for Show and Tell. Imagine that. Told how her brother had such a *good* job he had bought a fancy new car and drove her to school everyday so she'd be safe. There's something wrong with that picture, isn't there?"

"Are you going to shoot the brother?" the first man asked.

"The police ain't done nothing," he said evasively.

"I'd shoot the punk," a third man, with a thick South Philly accent, interjected. "Look, if the police won't do nothing, this little girl may think his stash is candy. If she found an empty vial, who's to say she won't find one that's full? Who's gonna speak for her at her funeral? *If* the police won't step in, it's up to us."

The other two tried to jump in, and Tisha Collins had to regain control.

"Sorry, gentlemen, but we've got to pay the bills. We'll go to commercial, but don't go away. When we come back, we've got *Daily News* reporter Deidre Caffrey on the line, whose commentary today has stirred up a lot of controversy. We'll get some of you on the line with her and Just Talk." She gave the station's phone number, and went to commercial.

Lysette was almost home by this time and put her hand absently in her pocket, touching the cellular phone. She wanted to hear this Deidre Caffrey; wanted to see how she would handle some hostile callers.

Chapter Twenty-six

Deidre expected her commentary to generate an angry response. She expected hostility from her colleagues, who would take her criticism personally. And she expected negative reaction to calling the Nightwatcher "one sick cookie." She had pondered over that phrase long and hard.

She fervently believed most readers would respond favorably to the bulk of her article. She didn't think they'd object to her suggestion the woman, herself, might become a victim. They didn't *want* to read it, but they'd have to acknowledge the possibility. But calling her "sick"—was it worth the flak she would get? In the end, she left the phrase in her article for two reasons.

Most importantly, she believed it to be the truth, and she was not about to pull punches for fear of a negative backlash. Secondly, she wasn't writing the piece *just* for the public, but for the Nightwatcher herself. While this woman hadn't yet contacted the media to explain her rationale for the park killing, and wasn't trying to mock the police, as some killers had done with notes that decried their impotence, Deidre believed the woman had something to say. If she pushed the right button, the Nightwatcher might possibly come to her to get it off her chest. It was unlikely, but worth using the harsh language. After all, it had worked with Shara, though the police were never aware Deidre had been contacted.

Reaction had indeed been swift, and a bit unsettling. She had fielded the first dozen or so phone calls personally from angry citizens and their vehemence rattled her. *They* took it personally that she had labeled the Nightwatcher "sick." They told her this woman was doing what they all wished, but lacked the balls to do.

"How dare you presume to call her sick," an angry Hispanic woman had exploded. "My children, they cannot play in the streets because of goddamn drug dealers with their guns. *That's sick.* The police, those bastards who won't come when we call, *that's sick.* This woman, God bless her, like you said, she's fed up. And you call her *sick*! My little Maria, nine years old, she hear about this woman, and she feel all warm inside. *Someone* is protecting her. She not so scared when she go to school, now."

And that had been one of the more polite calls. She couldn't count the times *she* had been called a bitch, cunt, or dyke, usually followed by "fuck you" or "go fuck yourself." There were other equally crass suggestions:

"Go stick a broom handle up your fucking ass . . . "

"If your man had any balls, he'd slap some sense into you."

"Stick a piece of dynamite up your cunt, light it . . . "

She had hung up on that one, and Carter prevailed on her to stop taking calls.

"You certainly touched a visceral nerve," he'd said, a forced smile on his face. "At least you know you're read."

"Some solace," she had responded, with a weak smile.

How could one phrase, she thought, trigger such raw emotions? Simple, her mind answered. She had attempted to knock *their* Nightwatcher off her pedestal, and they didn't like it one bit. She had correctly gauged their support for this woman, but not its fanatical intensity. They envisioned this invincible woman protecting their backs, and didn't want reality to intrude.

It was in the midst of the frenzy that swirled around her that she got the idea to appear on "Just Talk."

Carter was dubious.

"You can't reason with fanatics, and that's what they are."

"I don't want to. In my gut, I know this woman wants to speak to somebody. Imagine her bottling this all inside. Imagine the turmoil within her."

"You're assuming she hasn't discussed what she's done with anyone."

"I'd bet the house she hasn't. I've spent the last year getting into the heads of people just like her. They don't brag to friends or relatives. For her, for so many of them, it's too personal. That's why so many of your serial killers end up contacting the press. You can hold it in just so long, then you need an outlet."

"So now she's a serial killer?" he asked.

"Not in the classic sense, but by setting herself up, she's exerting the same need for power and control. It only seems like she's allowing herself to be stalked, when it's *her* that's doing the stalking. She's just waiting for someone to pull a weapon, so she can justify her kill."

"Sounds to me like a lot of psychobabble."

"Trust me, Carter, I may not be one hundred percent on target, but this woman needs an outlet; a spokesperson to give words to her actions. Maybe, just maybe, my story got to her like it did to some of the psychos who called today. If so, all she needs is one more push. I go on 'Just Talk' and who knows? She may not respond immediately, but she just might get in contact. I'm the only one who's reaching out."

"I hope you know what you're in for."

"I'll prepare myself. Anyway, I know how Tisha Collins controls her show. She won't allow the crude vulgarity I've heard on the phone."

Carter had reluctantly agreed, and Deidre had called Tisha Collins.

"I want to come on *after* the people have had a chance to vent their spleen. Your last hour."

Tisha Collins had willingly agreed.

"And, no advance warning. The spontaneity is important."

Here, the talk show host had resisted. "At one o'clock, without prior notice, you'll end up talking to an audience of a few dozen," she said, trying to convince her to allow her to announce the one o'clock appearance.

"Bullshit, Tisha. I've stayed up the past few nights, coming to work bleary-eyed. You won't have lost many listeners, and once I'm on you'll have them scurrying to the phone to wake up their friends."

Deidre was adamant. Tisha accepted half a loaf. It was better than nothing at all, Deidre consoled her.

"Look, if things get hot, the station will jump at the chance of running the segment any number of times the next few days, with advertisers lining up to jump on board."

Chapter Twenty-seven

Tisha Collins longed for TV stardom. Unfortunately, factors beyond her control all but made that impossible, so she gladly settled for a career in radio. She now fervently hoped her unique "Just Talk" format might catapult her to stardom. If "Just Talk" could be syndicated, she thought, she just might be up there with Rush and Howard Stern as far as earnings and notoriety.

Tisha looked like Oprah Winfrey before one of her famous diets. Actually, she tipped the scales anywhere between two hundred and two hundred and thirty pounds, depending on her moods. Part of the problem was glandular, part hereditary—her mother and grandmother were both "big" women; but she loved to eat and that didn't help matters.

Talk all you want about equal opportunity, but with few exceptions, television reporters, anchors and talk show hosts were not fat, obese, humongous or two tons of fun; all terms Tisha used in referring to herself. Not the politically correct type, she didn't consider herself "overweight" or "vertically challenged," nor "portly" or "pleasantly plump." She was *fat*, and if not proud of it, she had come to terms with her reality.

She was also black—*very* black—as in dark-skinned; the color of tar. Again, some would protest otherwise, but the majority of blacks on television news and talk shows were light-skinned or coffee-colored, especially if they were women. She was as dark as a black person could be, and doors closed, hitting her in her fat ass, because of her color, as much as because of her weight. So she reluctantly said goodbye to a career in television.

On the other hand, she had a sensuous voice that, she had been told on more than one occasion, had led men to jerk off while listening to her. And jerk off she imagined they did, as for five years

170

she had hosted "Let's Talk Sex," in which she dispensed advice to teens and adults alike.

A psych major in college, though often criticized as a pop icon, she thoroughly researched her area of expertise and took her role seriously. She knew intuitively which were crackpots, who had minor insecurities and who had serious emotional problems. Those last she would ask to hold on after their call, and try to steer them to a therapist for the help they so badly needed.

She viewed herself as an entertainer first, a therapist second, and while she would freely dispense advice on how to achieve the ultimate orgasm or new techniques for masturbation, she was not about to jeopardize someone's life if they seemed severely depressed or unbalanced.

Sex talk shows, however, were too controversial to generate the exposure she desired. Based in New York, she had been syndicated in six other markets, including Philadelphia, but stations all too often bent to uptight parents and the religious right. Jittery advertisers were quick to pull the plug when groups began picketing a station to generate publicity. A station in Philadelphia had even bowed to "community" pressure just two years earlier.

Ironically, she had hit upon "Just Talk" while watching the now svelte *Oprah Winfrey*. She couldn't recall the topic, but three couples were on stage arguing with one another while Oprah acted as referee. The audience had really gotten off on it. Thus was born "Just Talk," where three or four callers could debate one another at the same time.

While she had yet to land a plum morning or afternoon drive period, her 10 PM–2 AM show ranked just behind the urban dance station's "Quiet Storm" format in the Philadelphia market. Syndication had recently been broached, and now out of the blue the Nightwatcher had given her the opportunity to hit the motherlode.

Everyone had an opinion and everyone seemed transfixed by this woman and urban crime in general. Baring their innermost fears and finding them universally shared made "Just Talk" a must-listen.

While she wished she could have promoted Deidre Caffrey's appearance to death, she had been more than happy to accede the reporter's demands. Numbers told her Philadelphians in great abundance were listening even at one in the morning, and the publicity the segment would generate would only add to the show's growing popularity.

Barry Hoffman

Deidre was taking a beating the first fifteen minutes of the show, though she more than held her own. She had hit a raw nerve calling the Nightwatcher a "sick cookie." The Nightwatcher belonged to the community. She was doing what others only fantasized. That she shunned the public eye made her even more endearing to her admirers, and they bitterly resented Deidre's characterization of her as sick.

Callers didn't even attempt to mask their hostility. Deidre was challenged to venture out at night herself, *unarmed*, and see how long it was before she was mugged or raped.

At one-sixteen Tisha's producer frantically signaled to Tisha. She went to commercial and over her headset heard the magic words. "The Nightwatcher's on line one, and wants to talk to Caffrey one-on-one."

Two thoughts struck Tisha at the same time. An exclusive with the Nightwatcher meant syndication; the big-time. The pessimist, who still secretly yearned for TV stardom, assumed this was another crank. There had been any number of them the past two days; each and every one a phony. But Carl, her producer—a twenty-year radio veteran who rarely showed emotion, much less excitement—looked like he was in the throes of an orgasm.

"Carl, why is this one different from any of the others?" she said with mild irritation.

"She says she just killed a drug dealer and can provide details," Carl blurted out. "I called the police and—get this—they said keep her on. 'Get her to talk. Give details.' Their words, not mine, honey. They wouldn't confirm, but they ended up patching me through to Lamar Briggs, you know, the dick handling the Nightwatcher case. I've got a direct line to him. No intermediaries. If I want I can have him on the line in a minute. Need more convincing?"

"Fuck no," Tisha said. "Let me speak to her privately, for a minute, and for God's sake tape our conversation."

Before the commercial break ended, she hurriedly told Deidre she might have the Nightwatcher on the line.

"I hate to leave you in the lurch, but I've got to confirm it's her."

"You want me off the air?" Deidre asked in exasperation.

"No. No! She wants a one-on-one with you. What I mean is you'll be on your own for five minutes or so with the next group of callers. I won't be able to bail you out if they get nasty. My producer will monitor things, and go to commercial—"

172

"Don't worry about me," Deidre interrupted, and Tisha could hear the excitement in her voice. "I can hold my own."

Tisha then got on the line with the Nightwatcher.

"This is Tisha Collins. I don't mean to sound skeptical, but I've been up to my ass with cranks the past two nights. Convince me you're the Nightwatcher."

Lysette provided Tisha Collins with a host of details. "There may even have been a witness. A guy named Charles. Said don't call him Charlie or Chuck. It's *Charles*. He was harmless. Made a drug buy and tried to pick me up. A bit of a geek. Handsome enough, but had these thick horn-rimmed glasses that kept slipping down his nose. He saw me shoot the fucker, then ran off."

Tisha said nothing. She didn't need confirmation to know this was the real thing. Dollar signs flashed before her eyes. Syndication. Print interviews. Talk show appearances. Maybe, just maybe, if she handled herself well, a TV gig wasn't out of the question, after all.

"Don't freeze up on me now, honey," Lysette said. "Get on the horn to the police. Confirm and then make your decision."

Tisha slowly recovered. She remembered meeting Michael Jordan at a benefit. She had been tongue-tied and had nearly peed in her panties. This woman was making her behave in a similar fashion. Get a hold of yourself, she commanded, and told the woman to hang on.

"Get Briggs," she commanded. Paul had contact within seconds. Tisha fed back the details the Nightwatcher had given.

"Is she the real thing?" Tisha asked and held her breath.

"She's the real thing," Briggs said, and Tisha could feel the electricity in his voice, though he tried to sound controlled. "What is she like?"

"Sounds a bit like a bimbo, but that may be the heavy South Philly accent. And bossy. I know I'm contradicting myself, but she doesn't sound anything like I expected."

"Welcome to reality," Briggs said. "Maybe that's why she's kept such a low profile. A knockout on the outside, but when she opens her mouth all your preconceptions are shattered. Get her on and keep her on as long as you can. I hear she wants to talk to Deidre Caffrey, right?"

"One-on-one."

"Deidre can handle her. Just tell Deidre to try to pump her for as much information as she can. Tell Deidre to let the Nightwatcher do the talking. This could be our first big break."

Tisha filled Deidre in, took a deep breath and tried to sound calm as she addressed her listeners.

"I want to apologize to all the callers on hold, but we've got a special guest and I'm sure you'll understand. We've just got a call from the Nightwatcher herself, asking for a one-on-one with Deidre Caffrey. I know what you're thinking. It must be a crank. I assure you we've been in contact with the police, and she's the real deal. As a matter of fact, you might as well be the first to know the Nightwatcher has struck again. A dealer at the Schuylkill Park pulled a gun on her and was shot once in the head. The details that the Nightwatcher has given us have been confirmed by the police.

"We're going to run without commercial interruption, and I'm going to be listening with the rest of you. So then, Nightwatcher, what should we call you?"

Chapter Twenty-eight

"Angel," Lysette said, after a pause. The question had startled her, and she wondered what the hell she was doing. But, then she knew. The attacks on the reporter had been unmerciful; the tone of the callers downright ugly. For some reason this troubled her. Lysette didn't want to go public, but maybe it was time to address some of the questions that were on everyone's mind.

Before calling she had decided to mask her real voice with the thickest South Philly accent she could manage. At the club, the first year, she had used such an accent, though not as thick. As her Cassandra persona developed, however, she had refined the accent, so it was there, but subtle; still nothing like when she was Lysette.

She had always had the uncanny ability to mimic the speech patterns of others. She could have been Hispanic. She could have been black. But, she'd never spoken for any length of time in one of those accents, and was afraid she would slip into her own voice if she were angered or rattled. So, she decided to be a young Rose. Many times in the bakery she had taken on Rose's inflection when dealing with customers, to the woman's delight.

The very first question—"What should we call you?"—reinforced her decision. What should she call herself? The question was so totally unexpected. Lying on her bed, naked, her gaudy Cassandra jewelry around her neck, the gun next to her for comfort, she intuitively chose Angel.

"Does that refer to Angel of Death?" Tisha Collins had asked her.

"Not at all. I'm no Angel of Death. I'm simply Angel."

"Deidre Caffrey has been defending herself for calling you sick. Would you like to address that with Miss Caffrey?"

"That's why I called. Miss Caffrey," Lysette began. "You say I'm sick. Well, I am, but not like you suggest. I'm sick of muggers

175

beating old men on subways. I'm sick of being told how to dress and where not to go so I don't become a target of urban crime. I'm sick of being told to hole up at night; that the night belongs to the scum who sell drugs or steal for money to buy drugs. If that makes me sick, we should all be so sick." She could feel the anger rising with each sentence.

"So the mugging on the subway was the last straw for you?" Deidre asked calmly. "A real mugging. Something you had to respond to?"

"Where I work everything's a fantasy. How can I put it so you understand?" Lysette asked. "It's not the real world. It's a total escape from reality. Like going to a movie, play or concert. For a few hours the real world doesn't intrude. You forget your problems with relationships, bills coming due, the rut you're in. Even I get caught up in the fantasy. Reality intrudes as soon as I leave. And reality sucks."

"Are you an actress?" Deidre asked.

Lysette laughed. "Hey, give me a little credit, Miss Caffrey. Why don't you ask for my name, address and phone number? If you want to understand me, listen and ask the right questions. If you want to play cop, we're both wasting each other's time, and I might as well hang up."

"No, don't," Deidre rushed on. "Sorry, it's my instinct as a reporter. Please go on. You were saying reality sucks," she said with a chuckle.

"Reality sucks. Reality bites. Reality can mean death. In the subway, I saw a man being beaten. I saw other passengers look away. They were afraid they'd become a victim, a statistic, if they helped. So they allowed this punk to pistol-whip a defenseless old man. They didn't understand there's strength in numbers. I couldn't stand by and watch the man savagely beaten. It's as simple as that."

"I understand the subway incident," Deidre said, "but why did you go to the playground and then the park tonight?"

"Because it's my right as a citizen. I lost my virginity that night in the subway, so to speak. Fears we all have living in this jungle of a city evaporated. I decided to go where I pleased when I pleased. I ain't gonna allow myself to be a prisoner in my own city anymore."

"Why the gun?"

"I'm no fool, girlfriend," she said in her thick accent. "I'll go where I please, when I please, but I'm not about to make myself a defenseless target. Understand this, though. I was never the aggressor. Tonight, for example, a young man tried to hit on me. I basically told him to get lost. And he did. The men I've killed have only been in self-defense. That, too, is my right as a citizen."

"So you're saying this is personal. You're not out on any crusade to take back the night?"

"*You* said it's personal in your column today. And you're right. I'm not trying to be no symbol. I'm making a statement for myself. Nothing more."

"What would you have others do?" Deidre asked.

"Who am I to tell others what to do or how to live their lives? I just know I'm sick of living in fear."

"You know you'll eventually get caught."

"Not necessarily," Lysette said.

"Or you may become a victim yourself," Deidre added.

"I admit that's possible. I'm not invincible."

"Don't you want to live? Isn't it suicidal to set yourself up night after night, hoping you'll get the upper hand?"

"Is hiding out in your home at night living?" Lysette answered with a question of her own. "If we let fear drive us what message are we sending to them criminals who think they own the city after dark?"

"So you would have all law-abiding citizens arm themselves and reclaim their neighborhoods?"

"I'm only speaking for myself, you know, but if the police and courts can't protect us, ain't it time we look out for ourselves?"

"Won't there be many casualties as the criminal elements fight back?" Deidre asked.

"Casualties are inevitable in any war. And we are engaged in a war. The crime rate is spiraling in inner cities. Drug dealers, car thieves, even rapists spend little or no time in jail because of fool prison caps. These hoodlums rule the night and are beginning to steal the day, as well. We can let it occur, or we can fight back."

"There must be some other way?" Deidre asked.

Lysette was surprised the reporter herself seemed to be searching for an answer; hoping Lysette would provide it.

"What other way?" Lysette asked, putting the onus on the reporter.

"As much as I hate to agree with my colleagues at the *Inquirer*," Deidre said, "isn't poverty, broken families and despair at the root of the problem?"

"Maybe so, but do you think the city, state or even federal government is going to do anything about it? Get real, honey. We all know what the problems are, but ain't no one going to do anything about it."

Lysette was purposely spicing her language with street slang. Throw in a honey, girlfriend and some poor grammar to solidify the masquerade of a South Philly beautician who'd barely made it out of high school.

"Look, sweetheart, in a perfect world we'd create jobs for everyone, train those who are laid off and make the city livable. But it ain't going to happen. So what do we do? Surrender? We've been doing that for too long and what does it get us? Kids are killing kids. Dealers are becoming role models. Any punk who wants to can get hold of a gun and terrorize an entire neighborhood. You offer no alternative. As for me, I won't live in fear anymore, and I'll protect myself when I venture out into the jungle."

"Were you or your family the victim of crime when you were young?"

Lysette didn't respond.

"Listen . . . Angel," Deidre said, "The people want to know about you. Won't you fill in some blanks without betraying your identity?"

"Your kind dubbed me the Nightwatcher. You've stirred up interest in *me*, instead of focusing on why I refuse to be held hostage anymore. Who I am and details of my past and my family ain't nobody's business. It's also irrelevant. What's important is I'm taking control of my life. Maybe it's time we all looked in a mirror to see if we like what we've become."

"Angel—"

"There's nothing more to say, dear," Lysette interrupted. "Except that I'm sick—to use your word—of people coming down on you for saying what's on your mind. You shouldn't be their scapegoat when they're too afraid to take control of their own lives. I've listened to decent people vent their hatred against you. *That's* sick.

"You're not mugging, raping and killing. You're an easy target. It's the thugs that hold them captive they really fear, but they won't do what's necessary to protect themselves and their loved ones. Remember that mirror I talked about?"

"Yes," Deidre said.

"Those who criticize you should look into that mirror and take stock of themselves before attacking you. That's really all I got to say."

Lysette hung up and turned off the radio. She had no desire to hear herself analyzed. How many more nights, she wondered, would she venture out to prove she was in control of her life?

And was she in control? Why was she attracted to the playground in Fairmount Park? Why had she gone to the Schuylkill Park tonight? It wasn't mere coincidence. She knew she had been lying to herself and lying on the radio, too. No, not lying. *Deceiving* herself. But for the life of her, she didn't know what was driving her.

She suddenly felt weary and afraid. With the gun tucked between her breasts, she began to shut down. She wondered where she'd awaken in the morning.

Chapter Twenty-nine

Shara hadn't been asleep when she'd heard the gunshot tonight when the Nightwatcher had claimed her third victim. It was earlier than before, so she decided to turn on "Just Talk."

She had stayed in touch with the rhythm of the city by listening to talk radio. "Just Talk" was her favorite, for the host allowed more than one caller on at a time to argue with one another.

These people with their short fuses and heavy accents were so different from the bland vanilla-ice-cream people she encountered daily.

At one in the morning, she just about peed in the PJs she wasn't wearing when host Tisha Collins said Deidre would appear on the show. Shara had read Deidre's column and knew it was as calculating as the ones the reporter had written to infuriate her, when she had been on her spree a year and a half before.

Deidre tried to push buttons; worm her way into your head. She wasn't writing for these people calling in to crucify her. She was writing for the Nightwatcher. Calling her sick might irritate her enough to make contact. That was Deidre at her best.

She listened to Deidre defend herself, and was tempted to call in herself to give some aid and comfort. Deidre would recognize her voice instantly, though, and *she'd* be the one doing the peeing. Deidre didn't need her help, though. She slipped every thrust, went on the offensive to defuse venom heaped upon her, and wouldn't allow herself to be bullied.

Shara interacted just as she had when she watched television. Oblivious that no one could hear, Shara talked to the radio. She scolded callers who tried to land low blows and cheered when Deidre scored. "One for Dee," she said aloud more than once.

When the Nightwatcher came on, Shara sat up in her bed to get closer to the radio . . .

—To get closer to the Nightwatcher.

"The woman speaks," she said to the radio. "Deidre, you've done it again."

Listening, Shara found her way out of the idyllic town that had been her living hell. Listening, she found her way to repay Deidre.

She didn't know this woman—this Nightwatcher—but she *knew* who she was. More precisely, she corrected herself, she knew *what* she was. Certain words . . .

—*"Everything's a fantasy . . ."*

. . . and phrases . . .

—" *. . . not the real world . . .*"

. . . clues that would slip by Deidre, good as she was . . .

—" *. . . total escape from reality . . .*"

. . . because she hadn't lived the life. . . .

—*"Even I get caught up in the fantasy."*

"She's a stripper!" Shara yelled aloud at the radio, then put her hand over her mouth. In Philly, you could yell bloody murder and be ignored. Here, half the town might end up at her doorstep if she got carried away.

Memories came flooding back. Washing glasses at the strip joint, the first Shara danced at. She was under age, so she had to remain in the kitchen.

Watching. Listening. Learning.

She relived the first Shara's beating by a customer who wanted her to put out for him after work; something she would never do. The first Shara's death. Her *becoming* Shara. Her constant nagging of the club's owner to allow her to earn a living dancing . . . *dancing naked*.

"Look kid, what am I to do? You're sixteen. *Under age*. Cops find out and my license is yanked. Sorry, but it's out of the question."

Frank Gianetti looked like the stereotypical owner of a strip joint, with his too-shiny suit, paunch, and heavy jowls from too much pasta, and an ever-present cigar in his mouth. In his case, looks were deceiving. He was a gentle, caring man who took the first Shara's death hard; took it personally.

She had manipulated him before, and now, having taken Shara's place, she would badger him until he relented.

"Look, Frank, Shara died because you couldn't protect her,"

she'd said, laying on the guilt. "You owe it to her to make sure I stay off the street and finish school. Without the money she brought in, I'll be homeless within a month."

"Read my lips. You're under age," he'd repeated. "I get busted and I may end up in jail. I'd trade the streets for that anytime."

"What is this busted crap, Frank? We both know you pay off the cops to stay off your back. We both know some of the girls do more than just dance. And you get your cut."

Shara pulled off her sweatshirt and undid her bra. "Look at these, Frank, and tell me I *look* sixteen."

"It's not a life for you," he said, his resistance crumbling, as he stared at her breasts. "Shara wanted you to finish your education."

"It is *the* life for me, *if* I'm to finish my education. I'm Shara now. If I don't dance I've got to drop out of school for a nine-to-five minimum-wage job. Letting me dance is what Shara would have wanted, and you owe her—owe her big time."

"What the fuck," he said, throwing his arms up in the air. "You're as stubborn as she was. Maybe more so. Tell you what. You work with Jil for a week before opening. We both abide by her decision."

Jil had worked her way up from one of the dancers to helping manage the bar. She had a head for business Frank lacked, trained the new dancers, and made sure they kept their noses clean—*literally*. Prostitution Frank could live with, even condone as long as he got a piece of the action. Drugs he wouldn't tolerate, and Jil had taken it upon herself to assure any girl even sampling a drug got kicked out on her ass.

Frank's Place was no upscale strip club. There were few of them eight years before, when Shara began her dancing. You literally danced on a bar, and customers would slip bills in your panties, sometimes trying to cop a feel or slap you on the ass.

But even then, men were there for the same reasons . . .
—The fantasy.
—Escape from the real world.
—Replacing their reality for a few hours.

And when you left, reality intruded, just as the Nightwatcher had said. Deidre had been close when she asked if the Nightwatcher was an actress. Strippers were entertainers. The Nightwatcher hadn't allowed Deidre to pursue the line of questioning. And she was certain Deidre wasn't thinking she might be a stripper. Only someone intimately familiar with stripping could understand.

It was all Shara could want. There was the hunt. There was the lure of the city. There was Deidre; repaying her debt and maybe, just maybe, establishing a real friendship.

She no longer had any secrets from Deidre. There would still be resentment at being used, but that was a challenge Shara would easily accept.

Tomorrow, she would ask to use vacation days she had never taken.

Tomorrow she would return home.

Tomorrow she would see Deidre.

Tomorrow the hunt would begin.

Tomorrow couldn't arrive soon enough.

Chapter Thirty

It was two in the morning, and officers were literally tripping over one another in the less than spacious homicide squadroom.

For the second day in succession, Briggs and Rios had left for home when their regular four PM shift ended. Leads at this point were nonexistent.

Then all hell broke loose.

The killing at Schuylkill Park.

A man running down Lombard Street right into the arms of a uniform. He'd been screaming, "She's after me! She'll kill me, too!"

Then there was Nightwatcher's radio appearance.

So, they were back in the squadroom, bumping heads with the night shift for space.

The dealer, one Brian Diorio, had been shot in the head. Briggs had no doubts it was the work of the Nightwatcher. The witness, Charles Dawson, had been left sitting in a sparse interrogation room. He had been carrying a small amount of crack cocaine. Briggs knew with the prison cap the man would be back on the streets before Briggs had a chance to take a shower, but he didn't think Charles Dawson knew the rules of the game.

Tisha Collins' producer had sent over a copy of the tape of Tisha and the Nightwatcher talking before she went on the air, and the first ten minutes of her conversation with Deidre. They'd get the rest of the tape later.

While Briggs was tempted to interrogate Charles-don't-call-me-Chuck-or-Charlie, his gut told him Rios might have more success. The man was clearly intimidated by women, and Rios just might rattle his cage. They had discussed strategy before they both went

184

in, Briggs standing stoically by the door. The heat had been purposely turned high, and Charles was sweating profusely.

"You think maybe I should have a lawyer?" Charles asked.

"That's up to you, Charlie—"

"*Charles*," he interrupted. "Not Charlie, not Chuck . . . "

"*Charlie*," Rios said scornfully, "Don't fucking interrupt me again," she commanded. "Let me lay it out for you. We can get you a lawyer right now, but once we do we can't help you . . . "

"Whadda you mean help me?"

Rios pointed a finger at him. "What did I tell you about interrupting me?" she asked, bullying him. "You got shit for brains, Charlie?"

He began to reply, but thought better of it and stared at the bare table.

"Look at me, Charlie, when I'm talking to you."

Briggs thought she sounded like a damned dominatrix, which was exactly the way to handle this guy who had never had a brush with the law. Dawson looked at her when commanded.

"Where was I?" Rios asked, unbuttoning the top two buttons of her blouse.

She had his number, Briggs thought. She *was* good. They'd always interviewed witnesses separately. It was the first time he had seen her in action.

"Something about helping me . . . " Dawson said in a hushed whisper.

"Right. All right, let me lay it out for you, okay? You been caught with crack. *And*, you witnessed a murder. If you don't cooperate that's accessory after the fact," she lied, "and we're talking serious jail time, Charlie. But we're after the woman who did the killing. You cooperate and all you are is a helpful witness. Be straight with us and we can make the possession charge disappear. Or . . . you can ask for a lawyer. Then"—she shrugged—"unfortunately, our hands are tied."

"But I didn't see nothing," Dawson said.

Rios put a small tape recorder on the table and played the Nightwatcher's conversation with Tisha Collins.

" . . . have been a witness . . . "

" . . . Charles—said don't call him Charlie or Chuck . . . "

"Made a drug buy and tried to hit on me . . . "

" . . . horn-rimmed glasses that kept slipping down his nose."

" . . . saw me shoot the fucker, then ran off."

Rios cut off the recorder. "Now who's she describing, Charlie?"

"That's not her," Dawson said. "I don't know how she picked me out, but it's not her."

"What the fuck you mean it's not her?" Rios asked.

Briggs had all he could do to remain still. What the *fuck* is going on, he wondered?

"Doesn't sound nothing like the girl I tried to pick up. Girl I spoke to hardly had any accent at all. This girl . . . "

Rios didn't miss a beat. "Forget the accent, Charlie. Did you score from the dealer she shot?"

"Yeah, I scored from Slim," he said, hardly above a whisper. "First time I ever bought drugs, honest to God. A friend told me he was called Slim. Don't know his real name."

When they opened up, Briggs thought, sometimes there was no shutting them up.

"You saw the woman shoot him?"

"Yeah. It was his own fucking fault. I couldn't hear what they were saying, but all of a sudden he went for his piece. She had a gun under her coat she was carrying and shot him once. Then I ran. Didn't know what that crazy bitch might do if she saw me."

"You tried to pick her up?"

"Yeah, but she said something like she don't go with guys who think more of drugs than of women."

"You think she was a hooker?"

"Had to be, way she was dressed and being out there alone at that time of night."

"How was she dressed?"

He described her clothes; the same as the other two shootings.

"She have a good body?"

"Tits that'd knock your eyes out," he blurted out, then flushed. "Sorry, ma'am, didn't mean to sound . . . "

"That's okay, *Charles*," Rios said, emphasizing his name.

Now that she had his full cooperation, Briggs knew she wasn't about to antagonize him. He was Charles now, as long as he was a good boy. Subtle, Briggs thought, but the sign of a good instinctive interrogator.

"And the clothes accentuated the body?"

"She had on a gold necklace. Probably cheap shit, but she had this cross . . . " He stopped, then flushed again.

"Don't be bashful, now, Charles."

"Well, her top was tight and lowcut. You could see a lot. Know what I mean?" He went on, assuming Rios understood. "This cross—a gold crucifix—was tucked right between her . . . her boobs. Like you couldn't *not* look at them, you know."

"And her face?"

Charles turned even redder than he had before. "I really wasn't looking at her face. Know what I mean?"

"Concentrate," Rios said forcefully. "When you first saw her, you must have checked out her face. Was she the type with a great bod, but you had to put a paper bag over her face before you'd bang her?"

"No. No. She wasn't ugly. Like I said, I didn't get a good look at her face. It was dark, you know." He gave a vague description that jibed with that of the subway passengers and jogger, then lapsed into silence for a moment. "I'm not holding back, honest. It's just those knockers and the crucifix, you know, sorta grabbed my attention."

"And you say she didn't sound like the woman on the tape?"

"Nah, not at all. I wouldn't have known she was from South Philly from her accent. But she was cocky, like on the tape. You know, someone who don't take no shit."

"Self-assured and confident?" Rios asked.

"Yeah . . . and . . . " Silence again. He looked to be searching for a word that wasn't part of his limited vocabulary.

"Arrogant. That what you looking for?" Rios helped out.

"Yeah, arrogant. That's it."

Rios shot Briggs a look, as if to ask if he had anything to ask. Briggs shook his head no. They had gotten everything they could.

"Look, I cooperated," Dawson said. "Are you going to cut me some slack? Help me out, like you said?"

Rios was noncommittal. "We have to talk to our sergeant. We'll be back soon. Meanwhile, you think *real* hard and see if there's anything else about her you can remember. Like her face. Okay, Charles?"

"Yes, ma'am."

Outside they both cracked up.

"Was hard to keep a straight face in there, Nina," Briggs said. "When he started describing her tits, I knew we'd hit a brick wall."

"No way in hell we were going to get much on her face," Rios agreed.

"You did a good job," Briggs said. "Hit all the right buttons at just the right time."

She did a curtsy for her partner. "Glad I passed muster."

"Don't go bitchy on me, now. Shit, I gave you a compliment. Same as I would a male officer."

She smiled and Briggs felt the fool for not seeing she was trying to hide her pride at the compliment with sarcasm.

"So, do we let Charlie walk?" she asked.

"Let him stew in there for half an hour. Tell him we had a tough time with our sarge, but in the end he came around. Put the fear of God in him about buying drugs and send him on his way. For all we know maybe we *have* scared the shit out of him. I wouldn't bet on it . . . " He trailed off.

"The eternal optimist," she said, shaking her head. "Like the woman said, he's kind of a geek. My money says it's the first time he's tried to score. He thinks he almost got killed; saw his connection shot in the head; went through a police interrogation *all* in one night. I don't think he has the balls to try again."

Briggs merely shrugged.

"So, what's next?" she asked.

"I'm getting copies of the tape of the entire interview. Let's listen independently and then get together and compare notes. At least we found out she was faking the South Philly accent. And we got a good description of her body," he said, laughing. "Wonder if he could pick her tits out of a lineup?"

"Even if he couldn't, he'd have fun trying," Rios added, and she too was laughing.

Rios went off to complete the paperwork for Dawson's release.

There were two other loose ends Briggs had to clear up that had nothing to do with his partner. Before listening to the tape, he went outside to get some fresh air.

Tomorrow he would talk with Isiah Hayes. Now that the Nightwatcher had struck again, he had a game plan, and this time he intended to get the upper hand on good old Zeke, and not be played like a rookie.

And then there was Deidre. Like it or not, she was part of the case now. She had gotten the Nightwatcher to contact her once. She probably could again. The problem was getting Deidre to cooperate fully; not hold back, as he was certain she had with the Vigilante case. He would talk with Morales. The Sarge could be very persuasive, and Deidre could be a help. He had the feeling she had somehow gotten to the Nightwatcher.

They were getting close, Briggs thought. Zeke could provide a crucial piece to the puzzle; he was sure of it—had seen it in the man's eyes. And the Nightwatcher was getting more brazen. Talking to Charlie and allowing him to witness the killing was sloppy—or maybe just arrogant.

It was all starting to come together. Briggs knew each case presented its own momentum. The Nightwatcher was a wild card, unlike the average perp. An enigma wrapped in a mystery, he remembered reading somewhere. For the past two days they had been stuck in molasses; getting nowhere fast. Tonight, though, Briggs could sense the momentum building. He hadn't felt so jazzed, so energized, since . . .

—The attack on Alexis.

Chapter Thirty-one

By the time Nina was able to come up for a breath of fresh air, at around noon, she looked back on the long night with pride and contentment. She had wanted to be viewed as one of the guys, a homicide detective with a lot to learn, but also with a lot to offer.

She hated to admit it, but she felt she had passed an important test with Briggs. Since their confrontation at Cavanaugh's he had become more open, less aloof. And his praise of her interrogation of Charles Dawson burned in her brain.

She had come back from taking a leak at the john to find a blonde wig and an oversized bra filled with toilet paper for padding on what passed for her desk. Attached to the bra was a note, in Briggs' handwriting. "You, too, can be a Nightwatcher."

Caught up in the spirit of the moment, she donned the wig and put the bra with its padding over her blouse, went up to Briggs and said in a heavy South Philly accent, "Detective, I've come to confess. I'm the Nightwatcher."

The whole squadroom, Briggs included, cracked up.

She wouldn't delude herself. She was not yet one of them, but she was gaining acceptance—and damn, it felt good, she told herself.

She saw a stoic Morales taking in the scene. When she caught his eye, he nodded, ever so slightly.

Yes! she thought, a barrier *had* been breached; a test passed. Maybe soon she would be judged on her ability, and not be resented because she was a woman in the man's world of homicide.

The morning itself had been filled with the grunge work of any investigation where the killer wasn't quickly identified. A great majority of homicides were clear cut. Domestic quarrels that had gotten out of hand. Grudges over money owed. An addict sold bad shit out for revenge. The killer, in each case, knew the victim.

190

These cases were usually cleared quickly, even if the punishment handed out by the courts often didn't fit the crime. That wasn't her worry, anyway, Nina knew. Justice was not always served by clearing a case, but the department ran on statistics. Capture the perp; score one for the good guys. What the courts did was basically irrelevant to her work.

Today, she and Briggs would supervise a canvassing of the neighborhood that bordered Schuylkill Park. It was a residential area with a lot of ground to cover. As the Nightwatcher and the dead dealer had no ties, what they were looking for was a break; someone who had seen the blonde leave the scene; someone who could identify the car she had driven. Six uniforms had been assigned to assist.

They had been met with silent shrugs and even overt hostility. These people often hid the truth because of fear of reprisal. Now, they didn't care to cooperate because they didn't want the Nightwatcher caught. The woman had rid the neighborhood of one piece of scum, and for that they were grateful.

Nina couldn't really blame them. The Nightwatcher in one night had done more than the police in a month. The police were quickly becoming the villains; trying to apprehend someone the people felt had done nothing wrong, instead of ridding the city of *real* criminals.

She and Briggs had gone over the tapes of the Tisha Collins show after a quick lunch. He had told her of his hunch about Isiah Hayes, and how exasperated he had been to find the man out of town when, unannounced, he had sent a squad car to pick him up.

"A relative died in North Carolina," he said between bites of a burger he'd ordered at Roosevelt's on 22nd and Walnut. "Some dot on the map outside of Fayetteville. He took a fucking bus and won't return until Monday morning," he said shaking his head.

"Tell you this, though. I'll have a car outside his house bright and early Monday. Minute he gets home, we pick him up. He'll be tired. You can't *really* sleep on the bus. Won't even let him take a shower. I'm gonna get him here, stick him in an interrogation room and let him stew for half an hour. He'll tell me what he's holding back. Guaranteed." The last word he strung out slowly.

"Doesn't it make you feel like shit when you have to browbeat an innocent man—a victim himself?" Nina asked.

He looked at her quizzically.

"I'm not condemning you. It's got to be done. It's just that it's so

191

adversarial. He's the enemy, just like Charlie Dawson was last night. You know what I mean?"

"Poor old geezer gets pistol-whipped, and now I want my piece of him. Is that what you mean?" he asked, sounding pissed.

She shrugged, not wanting to antagonize him further.

"Look Nina. He has made himself the enemy by withholding information. Hell, I respect . . . I *like* the man. But he knows something that could help break this case. And he knows *I* know."

He took a bite of his burger, then continued. "It's almost like a game to him. She saved his life and he's not about to dime on her. So, hell yes, he's the enemy. I need every advantage I can to crack him, and I won't apologize for doing what's necessary."

"You're right," she said, without passion. "It's just that everything's so fucking ass backwards. That's all I was saying. Maybe that's why this woman is such a hero. It's all black and white for her. Defend *only* when attacked. We deal in gray areas the people can't or don't want to understand."

She sipped her coffee, trying to put her thoughts into words. "Why didn't we arrest Diorio, even though uniforms knew he was a dealer, and the park was his turf? That's what *that* neighborhood wants to know. We're shackled by the system, but they don't want to hear about it. Now we're the enemy."

He was silent for a minute, then offered her his fries. "You're all skin and bones. You need these more than I do."

"Thanks for the compliment," she said sarcastically, but took the fries nevertheless. "Just because I don't have the tits of the Night-watcher . . . "

"Your tits are fine," Briggs interrupted, then flushed. "I mean, don't be so damn self-conscious and defensive. You're thin, scrawny, but that doesn't make you any less of a woman. I offered you my fries, that's all. No ulterior motive. I wasn't comparing your tits to those of the Nightwatcher."

Nina smiled. "I've got reason to be defensive, but let's not get into that. So, tell me, how are you going to get the old man to talk?"

He told her. She made a suggestion or two, and they finished lunch in comfortable silence.

Afterwards they compared impressions about the tape of Deidre questioning the Nightwatcher.

"Caffrey's good," Nina said. "That question about being an actress."

"Dee *is* good. Too damned good for herself, sometimes."

"You know her?" Nina said with surprise.

"Oh yeah, we go way back." Briggs told her of their first encounter, then working together on the Vigilante case. How they had come to respect one another, but how in the end, Briggs was certain she had held out on him. He also told her he was going to speak to Morales about getting her cooperation on the case.

"I trust her," Briggs concluded, "but I wouldn't turn my back on her, if you know what I mean."

"Then she *must* be good," Nina said and laughed. "Okay, what about the phony accent?"

"She's clearly got a job, the way I see it. That was why she was on the subway the first night. So, she can't go on radio without masking her voice. A friend, relative or co-worker might recognize her."

"Granted, but does it say anything about her? Is she around people from South Philly a lot? Does she live in South Philly? Did she have the accent as a kid, and weaned herself off of it to join the mainstream?"

"All good questions," Briggs said. "For now, we just know it's phony. Only that's our secret. We won't even tell Caffrey. If the Nightwatcher finds out Deidre knows the accent is phony, she may put two and two together and know she's working with us. *We've* spoken to Charlie, but we haven't made it public. So Deidre can't know."

They talked for a bit longer, but there were no further revelations. Briggs told Nina he was going to speak to Morales about Deidre. "McNally is working on the canvassing, if you want to give him a hand."

"Is that an order?" she asked with suspicion.

"I don't give my partners orders. If I want you to do something, I'll ask. Just didn't want you sitting around twiddling your thumbs. I may be a while. Shit, Nina, when are you going to start trusting me? Partnership is a two-way street. Don't look for hidden meanings in everything I say."

She smiled. "Sorry. I can be an uptight bitch sometimes."

"And I can be a stubborn bastard. So what else is new?"

"I've got to clear my mind. You know, take a step back and see if I'm missing something. Go talk to Morales. If I get bored, I'll help out McNally."

"Right you will," Briggs said with a smile.

Nina *did* want to step back and look at the big picture. She felt she was missing something important; something that was staring her right in the face. Then again, maybe she just didn't want to do any more canvassing.

She found a copy of the *Daily News* on Briggs' chair and decided to take it along with her to the john. At least she would have some privacy.

A story on page five caught her attention. A viewing was being held for Rose Santucci, the victim of a carjacking. The name, the *incident*, rang a bell. "Think. Think," she said aloud.

"Doesn't *stink* too bad, Rios," a male voice yelled, then laughed. "Hope you don't have shit for brains, Rios, cause when you're done you won't be any use to us at all." Now two cops were laughing.

"Fuck off, Stavinsky," Nina replied, then thought to herself that was a pretty lame comeback.

Laughing, the two detectives left.

There weren't separate lavoratories for men and women in homicide. Until recently, there had been no need. Nina could have gone up or down one floor, as her predecessor did, but she had spoken to Morales, instead. The next day, he ushered her into the locker room and on one of the two stalls that still had doors was a cardboard sign, "Rios' Stall."

"Sorry, Nina, but with our current budget it's the best I could do," he'd said with a smile.

"At least you gave me one with a door," she replied in kind.

"Least I could do. Unfortunately, if you want to shower, you'll have to go to another floor."

"Who needs a shower when I have my own stall," she'd replied. She wasn't thrilled, to say the least, but she had more important battles to fight than a private shower.

She had learned patience in her battle for equality in the department. In this case, she knew there wasn't much Morales could do. She could make a stink, file a complaint and probably win a small battle. But she would also lose an ally. She would fight tooth and nail when necessary, but she had to choose her battles carefully. More important, if she gained her co-workers' respect, they'd fight *for* her, not against her.

Her mind in space, she suddenly recalled where she had seen the story about the Santucci woman: the newspaper the Nightwatcher had been reading in the subway.

She finished her business in *her* stall, hustled down to the evidence room, and checked out the paper the woman had been reading before the attack on the old man.

There were scattered prints of the Nightwatcher on pages one, two and the back page, like she'd been holding the paper. But page three was littered with her prints. Page three told of the carjacking and Rose Santucci, and below a rapist in the midst of a trial. The trial had concluded, and Rose Santucci's viewing was just about over. But the funeral was the next day. A blonde with big tits in her mid-twenties. How many could there be?

She mentally rehearsed her pitch to Morales. If Briggs agreed, she wanted to stake out the Santucci funeral, take photos of anyone remotely fitting the description and get Charlie, the jogger and the subway passengers to take a look. To be on the safe side, she figured she would have to check out the case of the rapist, as well. Both the victims and assailant had been black, so unless there was a blonde witness her best bet was the funeral.

Sitting at what passed for her desk, she waited for Briggs to come out. A woman she assumed was Deidre Caffrey had entered Morales' office just as she got back from the evidence room. If she was right, if she had come up with the missing piece, Lamar-Fucking-Briggs would be kissing her scrawny ass.

Chapter Thirty-two

Morales had been on the phone when Briggs knocked. He gestured for Briggs to take a seat. While Morales chatted, Briggs thought of Rios and how fond he'd become of her. She was . . .

—*Like the daughter he no longer had*, his mind screamed.

. . . something special. He could help make her a good cop, if she wouldn't be so damned insecure and defensive. But, he told himself, she had every right to be suspicious of motives. The department was still dominated by men. Rios was tolerated by some of the detectives in homicide, but most harbored resentment at her rapid rise. Hell, he had resented her, and wouldn't give her a break just a few days before. If she won him over, though, given time, most of the others would come around.

And now, waiting for Morales to finish, he was aware of the irony of yet another woman becoming part of this case. For someone who had had precious little respect for women involved in policework, he was suddenly surrounded by them.

Briggs became aware Morales was staring at him, and Briggs started.

"Sorry, Sarge—"

Morales raised a hand to silence him. "It's been a long night and day. I know the feeling when a case begins to come together. There's the rush, and it propels you just so far. You take your breaks when you can. So fill me in."

There wasn't much to tell. Morales already knew about the interrogation of Charlie Dawson and the Nightwatcher's phony accent. He told Morales the radio tapes had revealed little, and canvassing hadn't produced a single lead. Then he got to Deidre.

"I've worked with her before. She got the Nightwatcher to contact her, and I think there's a good chance the woman will get in

196

touch with Deidre again. I'd rather not read about it in the papers. I'd like to bring her in on the investigation."

"I can live with her, if you can," Morales said, giving his approval. "I'm sure you'll use discretion as to what you share."

Briggs fidgeted in his seat. Morales waited. "Sarge, Deidre and I have a history. Not *that* kind of history," he quickly added when he saw the incredulous look on his superior's face. Then he laughed.

"I'm sorry, Sarge, but I know what you were thinking, and you should have seen the look on your face."

"Just what sort of *history* do you two have?"

"Adversarial initially, then cooperative, then . . . I don't know, but I think somewhere along the line it became adversarial again."

He told Morales his initial antagonism when she came after him for helping a dirty cop who was a friend. How they'd gained respect for one another during the course of the Vigilante investigation. Finally, how that case had soured.

"She held out on me. I'm sure of it. What I don't understand is why. She got no exclusive, left her job with the Mayor, and has never written word one about the case. I guess what I'm saying is I'm gun shy; kind of leery about getting her full cooperation."

Before Morales could respond, Rios knocked. "Sorry to bother you, but Deidre Caffrey's on the phone for Briggs. Says it's important."

The two men exchanged glances, then each shrugged. "He'll take it in here, Nina," Morales said.

Briggs told Deidre he was with his sergeant, and they were on a speaker phone.

"You did a nice job last night, Dee," Briggs began. "So what gives?"

"An envelope was left downstairs this morning. No one can remember who dropped it off. It was just sent up to me. There's a cellular phone and note from the Nightwatcher."

"You sure it's from the Nightwatcher?" Briggs asked.

"I'm sure you'll be able to find out. The note, written in block letters, is pretty short. 'Took this from the dealer I shot. I'll be in touch.' It's signed 'One sick cookie.' "

"Did you touch the phone?" Briggs asked.

"Same old Briggs. What kind of fool do you take me for?" She didn't wait for a response. "We worked together long enough for me to learn a lot. I can have the phone and letter sent over, and you can check for prints."

Now Morales spoke. "Miss Caffrey, why don't you bring it over yourself? Detective Briggs has a proposition for you. And I think we should meet. Now, if possible."

"I can clear my calendar, Sergeant," she said with a laugh. "Give me fifteen minutes."

Briggs made introductions when Deidre arrived. She gave Briggs the envelope and he put it on Morales' desk. Morales read the letter, which Deidre had put in a plastic bag, and passed it to Briggs.

"Your ears must have been ringing, Miss Caffrey," Morales said.

"You've got me at a disadvantage," Deidre said, looking at both men.

"Detective Briggs and I were talking about you when you called."

"Really," she said with a slight smile.

Morales nodded to Briggs.

"Look, Dee," Briggs began, "You obviously have connected with this woman. We'd like your cooperation."

"What kind of cooperation?" she asked suspiciously.

"Anything that can help us locate her, if she contacts you. You know the questions to ask."

"And what do I get in return?" she said without hesitation.

"We'll share whatever we have with you. You might surprise her with your knowledge and she'll let something slip."

"Can I use what you give me in the paper?"

"Within bounds."

"What's that supposed to mean?"

Morales took over. "I won't mince words, Miss Caffrey," he said stiffly.

Briggs could see he felt awkward. He knew his boss liked to feel out people in his own way, and he had only what Briggs had told him to go on. He must have felt at a disadvantage, and he knew his sarge hated not to be in control.

"There may be a few details we don't want to divulge outside the department; for the sake of the investigation. We have to be able to sift the cranks from the real thing. However, you're free to dispute anything we prefer to keep in house. You'll find I'm reasonable and flexible. When it's time to make an arrest, you get the first call. And, if she's willing, you get an exclusive interview."

"I can live with that," Deidre said.

"Fine." Morales picked up the envelope and gave it to Briggs. "Take it down to forensics. Then you and Rios can discuss coordinating efforts with Miss Caffrey."

* * *

After Briggs left, Morales got out of his chair and came around to Deidre. He talked softly, but firmly.

"I wanted to discuss something with you privately." He paused, and when Deidre said nothing he went on.

"You and Briggs have a history, as he puts it. It's ancient history, as far as I'm concerned. But understand this. There will be no personal agendas with this case. We'll share *all* information; no holding back. No empathizing with the victim that will compromise the investigation."

He bent down so their faces almost touched.

"Fuck with my squad—with Briggs—and I'll have your ass. Make book on it. I'll harass your sources so they dry up. I'll call in markers and make sure no inside information comes your way or to other reporters at your paper. You'll be a pariah. I'll have you up on charges, and tie you up in court so working will be impossible. I don't care about the outcome. But I'll be a bug up your ass."

He was about to go on when Deidre interrupted. "I think you've made your point," she said just as forcefully.

He ignored her. "I didn't choose you. This Nightwatcher woman did, but if you can't make it work, tell me now and we'll both go our separate ways. But understand where I'm coming from. I could give a rat's ass about the Nightwatcher. Sooner or later we'll catch her or some mugger will beat us to the punch. I want her off the streets before someone innocent gets killed."

"Is that all?" she asked stiffly.

"One more thing. The most important. Briggs is very vulnerable now. You know about his daughter?"

Deidre nodded yes.

"He doesn't need you fucking with his mind. Here's your first bit of information and it's for your ears only. I didn't assign Briggs to this case. He should be spending as much time as he can at home with his wife and daughter. *I* was told this was Briggs' case. I had no say in the matter. Just don't fuck with him." He said the last sentence slowly, emphasizing each word. "Do we have an understanding?"

Deidre looked at him, then spoke as softly and firmly as he had.

"I didn't ask *this* woman to contact me—"

"Like fuck you didn't," Morales interrupted, raising his voice for the first time. "Can you honestly tell me you didn't craft your article to strike a nerve with this woman?"

Deidre looked nonplussed. "I'm not the one asking for cooperation. I'm not looking to share information. You came to me. You
got some fucking nerve threatening me."

She held up a hand when she saw Morales ready to interrupt.

"But I don't want a war with you. I'll play by your rules. I just
want *you* to know one thing. Briggs and I have had our differences,
but I genuinely respect and like the man. I've seen his daughter,
since the attack, and it makes me want to cry. I will never—*never*
do anything to harm Briggs. Do you understand where *I'm* coming
from?"

Morales looked at her with a combination of hostility and respect. His thoughts were in disarray, but he wasn't about to let her
know.

"I think we've cleared the air," he said.

Deidre got up, walked to the door, and turned back. "I admire
the way you stand up for your men."

Without waiting for a response, she left.

Chapter Thirty-three

Morales prided himself on judging people accurately and handling people in an appropriate manner. However, with Deidre he felt he had fumbled the ball in his effort to protect Briggs. He had read Caffrey's work occasionally. He recalled the overly sympathetic stories she had written about victims of crime and natural disasters. He recalled now, too, that lately there had been a subtle change in her perspective. In the past year she had written about victims who had gone astray when they became adults. There was a definite lack of empathy in her portrayals of twisted minds that preyed on others.

She was clearly a much more complex woman than he had imagined. She also had an inner strength he usually associated with men like Briggs. She would not be bullied. Worse, he now knew there had been no need to bully her. Whatever problems she and Briggs may have had, she was clearly fond of him.

Later he would apologize. Not to get her in his good graces, but because he had misjudged her.

Forty-five minutes later, there was a knock on his door, and Briggs stuck his head in again. Rios was with him.

"You and Caffrey on the same page?"

"We're square," Briggs answered.

"Want to tell me why you're grinning like the cat that ate the canary, or are you just going to stand there all day?"

"Nina may have come up with the break we've been looking for."

"Come in and bend my ear," Morales said.

Briggs deferred to Nina. Morales saw the pride in the man's face. A few days ago he had been fuming at being assigned this woman. Now he seemed to have taken her under his wing. . . .

—Almost like a daughter, he thought.

Morales had mixed feelings. He didn't want Briggs to give up on his own daughter. At the same time he could see a new self-assurance in Nina that could have only come from being accepted by Briggs.

He heard Rios out and thought her idea a good one. It was important to keep moving forward. The adrenaline produced by the sudden deluge of information would last only so long. They really weren't any closer to the Nightwatcher than a day before. Rios' suggestion, even if it didn't pan out, would propel them for several days.

"Good job, Nina," he said when she had finished. "Clues invariably fall through the cracks in a case like this. I'm impressed by your initiative."

Nina flushed with pride, and Briggs looked just as content.

—Like a proud father, Morales thought.

Morales looked at his watch. "It's after four. You've earned a rest. Nothing more you can do till tomorrow anyway. I'll make sure there's someone here tomorrow to develop your photos. Hopefully, someone who doesn't give a shit about the Eagles."

Morales could swear the two of them swaggered out. He didn't want them too high. The fall would be that much harder if the lead turned to dust. Happy as he was to see Briggs caught up in a case, the Briggs he knew kept things in perspective. Briggs was recovering. He hadn't recovered, though. He'd have to keep an eye on him.

Chapter Thirty-four

Deidre spent over an hour at the hospital, telling Jonas about her mindboggling twenty-four hours.

"It's strange how Morales saw right through me when I told him I didn't choose the Nightwatcher; that she chose me. We both knew I meant to provoke her by trying to get inside her head. He's not someone I want to fuck with."

During some of her talks with Jonas, she imagined him answering her, playing devil's advocate.

"Maybe I did underestimate Briggs, Jonas," she responded to an unspoken comment. "*He's* the one who knew I tried to make contact with the woman. What I don't understand, though, was Morales' hostility."

She listened to Jonas, reading what his thoughts would have been.

"You're right. Briggs knew I hid something. Sure, he confided in me and I let him down."

She paused, as if listening.

"Okay, he took it personally. God, you men have such fragile egos. *I* found Shara. *I* made her a promise I vowed not to break. What the hell did I owe Briggs? Nothing more than he got; advice when he asked for it, and shelter from the media."

Jonas asked her to put herself in Briggs' shoes.

"I gave him hope, and let him fall without a safety net. I guess it would make me wary next time, if someone did it to me. . . ."

—Shara did it to me and I don't trust her one bit, she thought to herself.

"I thought when we talked months later that Briggs had come to terms with losing the task force. We both knew it was best for him.

Shara wasn't going to strike again. He would have sat on his ass for six months without another lead."

She listened again.

"Okay, he doesn't trust me, and told his superior, who laid me out."

She brushed his thick gray hair, and noticed that like wheat in a drought, his hair was losing its luster. And each day she found more strands of his hair in her brush. And he was so pale. No, worse, his face had that waxen sheen of someone who had died and been made to appear decent for the funeral.

"Don't slip away, Jonas. You can fight it. You've never quit in your life. Don't now."

He spoke to her again.

"Hell, yes, I'm feeling sorry for myself. You're all I've got. I'm a selfish bitch, I admit it. What will I do? Oh, you mean about Briggs."

She paused in thought.

"I have to gain his trust. No holding back this time. Why should I, anyway? I have no vested interest like with Shara."

She felt better after their talk. He always helped her put everything in perspective, even in his current state.

She gave him a kiss. "Like always, you're not letting me off easy. Sure, we'll talk more tomorrow."

She walked the fourteen blocks to her apartment, painfully aware how utterly alone she was. She had never been one to hobnob with other reporters at work. She'd had her husband and son. When they were taken away from her, she totally lost contact with those she might have considered her friends. They were colleagues and acquaintances, not true friends. And now she didn't even have Jonas to speak to. He had been her best friend of all.

She would have to confront Morales, Briggs and his partner, Rios, alone.

She felt so empty. Alone. Without anyone to turn to.

She let herself into her apartment and met her past.

Shara was holding the fishbowl that held her goldfish; the one Shara had sent after she had inadvertently killed Deidre's first fish. That time, too, Shara had broken into her apartment. That time she had rearranged her furniture to unravel her. She had been closing in on Shara before she had completed her mission, and Shara couldn't let that happen.

Now she was back; like Freddy Krueger of *Nightmare on Elm*

Street, Shara *always* came back. Deidre was furious at this invasion of her privacy.

"What the fuck are you doing? Put him down," she yelled.

"Such language," Shara said calmly. But she put the bowl down. "Not at all like the Deidre Caffrey I knew a year ago. I'm glad you kept him—the fish. I thought you might resent any reminder of me. What's his name anyhow?"

"Get out of here, right now," Deidre said with undisguised hostility. "I never want to see you again."

Shara shrugged, and began to leave.

"Leon, Too," Deidre said before Shara reached the door.

Shara kept walking.

"Not Leon the second. Leon, T-o-o," she spelled it out. "Like this one is Leon, too."

Shara had her hand on the doorknob.

"You infuriated me by mocking me for naming my fish. You know that."

Shara opened the door.

"Wait. Don't go," she said just above a whisper. "You surprised me, breaking in. Damn you, Shara, it's like being mentally raped, having someone rummaging through your house. This house is *me*. It holds my memories, my secrets, and your going through what's mine . . . "

Shara turned. "I haven't gone through anything. I've been standing here for an hour, looking at Leon, Too. Remembering us. I'm sorry I upset you. I'll leave."

"Dammit, I said don't—" She stopped in mid-sentence, seeing a suitcase Shara had brought with her under a mirror far from the door.

"You cunning bitch. You had no intention of leaving without your suitcase."

"Whoops," Shara said. "Really, I forgot it." She went to pick it up.

"Stop playing me for a fool. You're not going anyplace. *Not* until I say so."

"Didn't you tell me to leave?"

Deidre glowered at her. "Why do I get tongue-tied around you? Why do I feel like a schoolgirl caught doing something wrong by a teacher? Why are you back in my life?"

"You need my help," Shara said.

"The fuck I do. What arrogance. What an ego. What . . . "

"I need *you*," Shara said softly. "I owe you."

205

"Give me a break, Shara. I don't need your pompous bullshit. My life's—"

"I've been thinking about you a lot lately," Shara interrupted. "How badly I treated you. How I used you. What a shit it makes me feel like. How lucky I am you saw something in me that prevented you from turning me in."

"I've regretted it more than once," Deidre said with a pout.

"So you've been thinking about me, too," Shara said with a forced smile.

"Don't flatter yourself." But she smiled as well. "Well, maybe a little. I'm naturally curious. Have you . . . " She didn't know how to put it.

"Killed anyone lately? Only once since I left."

Deidre looked crestfallen.

"I'm kidding! Jesus, you never had much of a sense of humor." Then seriously. "I told you I wasn't a serial killer. It was all premeditated to conceal having to kill my brother. And they were brutal animals, each and every one of them, out of the reach of the law."

"I never bought that crap," Deidre said. "I think you enjoyed killing the others."

"I enjoyed the *hunt*. There's a difference. Truthfully, it's one reason I'm here. The stalking is like a narcotic. The killing." She shrugged. "It's closure. In that sense I'm like most serial killers. They don't get off on the kill. Unlike serial killers, I don't need to kill. I don't get off on making someone feel powerless and impotent. But I do enjoy the hunt. And hunting doesn't have to be illegal."

"What are you getting at?"

"Your Nightwatcher. I can hunt her down. I have no desire to harm her. See, it's a legal hunt. In that sense police are no different than serial killers. They get jazzed by the hunt. As they're closing in, as the pieces all start coming together, it's as good a high as any narcotic."

Deidre was watching Shara, who was talking as much to herself as she was to her.

"When the capture's made, a confession given, or the evidence overwhelming, the letdown is little different than an addict coming off a high. Cops will drink themselves into a stupor, the depression's so deep. But there's always the next case. Another hunt."

"What's come over you?" Deidre asked. "You stir crazy?"

"Stir crazy and then some. Don't get me wrong. I needed this past year to come to terms with myself. Since the day I ran away at twelve until I killed my brother last year; for eleven years I was totally consumed by my need for closure. With Bobby's death, I thought I was released from my own personal prison."

"Thought? You weren't?"

"I went from one prison to another. Only it didn't dawn on me immediately. For a while I basked in being free; free of the Hungry Eyes of my brother; free of being hunted by you, and the police. I needed a lot of healing and the one-horse town I went to healed me."

"But? Something's happened?"

"I found I was in another prison. My life was a sham. A slip of the tongue and everything could unravel. Close relationships were impossible. Even friendships. And I was bored to tears."

"So you're back," Deidre said

"I can help you. No shit. I would have been back sooner, but the time wasn't right."

Deidre looked at Shara. She seemed sincere, but Shara had fooled her before. She was changed, though. Looked healthier.

"You've put on some weight," Deidre said. "I mean you're still thin, but it's a healthy thin."

"I had more to worry about than food the year and a half I was stalking."

"And now you want to hunt down the Nightwatcher to feed another need of yours. You have nothing to offer," Deidre said, dismissing her.

"But I do," Shara said with a broad smile. "Not until last night, but I know the Nightwatcher."

"Get real."

"No. Listen. I know the Nightwatcher because she was me. Not the me who stalked and killed," Shara rushed on before Deidre could interrupt. "But a part of me you know very little about."

"Go on. You've piqued my interest," Deidre said, without hiding her curiosity. She *knew* she was being sucked in again. But she couldn't help herself.

"Do you have the tape from last night?"

"Sure," Deidre said. "I've played it half a dozen times for clues. Girl, there ain't none."

"You're wrong. You were close. You asked her if she was an actress. Remember?"

"She was talking about losing herself, like being in a play or a movie. You take on a part in a play, so I thought she might be an actress."

"An *entertainer*, not an actress. A stripper."

"A stripper. Get off," Deidre said.

"Get the tape," Shara commanded. "Please."

Deidre played the tape back. At several parts Shara made her stop, and replay key phrases.

"Everything is a fantasy . . . "

" . . . total escape from reality."

"Even I get caught up in the fantasy."

"Reality intrudes as soon as I leave."

"Then you asked her if she was an actress. You were close, and she sensed it and pulled back. Remember I told you I danced—I was a stripper—after the first Shara died. When I danced, I built a fantasy world. I got caught up in my fantasy. And when I left the club at night, reality intruded."

"A stripper?"

"I'm not making any guarantees, but it all fits. She was talking about herself, but it could have been me. Not only that, but even the words she used were words told to me. It was creepy. I was hearing phrases told to me eight years ago."

"You're saying you personally know the Nightwatcher?" Deidre asked incredulously.

"I don't think so. This person would be in her mid-thirties. The papers say the Nightwatcher is my age. But it's possible she was trained by the same person who trained me."

"Strippers have trainers? This is too much," Deidre said.

"Silly girl. That's why you need me. The world I'm talking about is totally foreign to you. Look, experienced dancers break in new girls. Train them. Trainers. See?"

"And the girl that taught you is still a stripper?"

"That would make it too easy. No, she's the manager of several clubs." She held up a hand before Deidre could ask her a question.

"I read about a controversy her club was involved in a few years ago, when I was a cop. I always knew she would get into management. The good news is I'd bet the house she hired the Nightwatcher."

"And the bad news?"

"There's a tremendous turnover among strippers. We're not talking about choosing from two or three girls. The Nightwatcher could be one of several dozen. Maybe more."

Shara had been pacing about the room . . .

—Like a caged animal, Deidre thought. Do I dare let her loose?

"You are . . . jazzed. A predator ready to stalk; to pounce."

"Prepared to offer you the Nightwatcher on a silver platter," Shara said.

"And what do you want in return?"

"Nothing." She paused. "That's a lie. Forgiveness. Redemption in your eyes."

"Then you can return to your one-horse town?"

"I'm through lying to you, Dee. I don't know if I can ever return. Let me do this for you—for *us*. One step at a time. I don't want the limelight. You know that as well as I. This time there are no hidden agendas. I need you, Dee, to make me whole. I need you . . . "

Deidre wouldn't say it, but she needed Shara as much as Shara needed her. Someone to confide in who, unlike Jonas, would answer back. She had been living in a vacuum since Jonas' stroke. It hadn't made a difference until the Nightwatcher contacted her, and then Briggs asked for her cooperation. She could tell Shara about Briggs and Morales. She could share her doubts and fears. If . . . *if* Shara was for real. If this wasn't just another ploy.

"Can I trust you, Shara? Don't be hasty or flip. You admitted you strung me along from the day we met after your kidnapping. It's become habitual. Can. I. Trust. You?" she emphasized every word.

Shara looked Deidre in the eye, making sure she made contact before she spoke. "The eyes, Dee. They don't lie. I was haunted by my brother's eyes. I saw the evil in the eyes of those I killed. I kept a veil over my eyes from you from the day we met. Look at me now. I've nothing to hide. I need you, Dee. And, yes, you can trust me."

Deidre saw the truth in Shara's eyes. She remembered Morales' words—"Don't fuck with Briggs." She wouldn't admit it—not yet at least—that Shara had changed, but she knew she had to take the chance.

"Don't fuck with me, Shara. Deceive me and I'll doubt myself forever and it'll be on your head. So don't fuck with me."

"I love it when you talk dirty," Shara said, and smiled. "So you going to show me to my room?"

"You've got to be kidding," Deidre said. "Go to a hotel. Better yet, stay with your foster parents."

"You know I can't. The child that stayed with them committed suicide. If I stay with them, there will be questions."

"Then a hotel," Deidre said, sullenly. "I like my privacy."

"You don't fool me for a moment," Shara said. She went over to Leon, Too and held the bowl so it was eye level. "He needs a companion, you know. He's lonely. You're lonely. All you have is your father-in-law . . . what's his name?"

"Jonas. And I don't have him. He had a stroke and can't speak. Can't move. Can't do anything. He's . . . he's dying," Deidre said, her eyes welling with tears. It was the first time she'd said the words aloud.

Shara put the bowl down and put her arms around Deidre. At first she resisted; then she put her head on Shara's shoulders and began to sob. "He's dying . . . and I'm all alone."

"I'm sorry, but you're not alone. Not anymore." She looked Deidre in the eyes. "Face it, girl, we need one another. But hey, I'll get a hotel, if you insist."

Deidre smiled. "Manipulated me again. You can stay here. I want to get into the mind of the Nightwatcher. If she's a stripper, you can tell me about her world. If she contacts me, I can use it to trap her."

"You like the hunt, too. Don't deny it. You tracked me down without telling the police. A personal challenge." She growled like a lion. "A predator, just like me. Well, sorta."

Deidre ignored the comment and showed Shara to her guest room.

"Get settled. I'll make coffee and we can make our plans."

"The hunt begins," Shara said, with a broad smile.

"You *have* changed," Deidre said. "The Shara I knew—the Renee before her—I can't remember her ever really smiling."

"The Renee and Shara you knew had little to smile about. They hid their emotions. They were under enormous pressure. This Shara has been released. I haven't found happiness, yet, but I can be happy."

"Just don't fuck with me," Deidre said, and this time they both smiled.

Over coffee they talked.

"When do we go see your former trainer?"

"*We* don't go. This is my world we're talking about; something totally alien to you." She put up a hand to stop Deidre from protesting.

"Strippers are equated with hookers, and almost universally reviled. They insulate themselves from outsiders. You're an interloper, the enemy. Even if you're sympathetic, they'll be wary of you."

"And you can just waltz in and gain their trust?" Deidre asked skeptically.

"I've got to speak to Jil—my trainer. If *she* trusts me, I'll get her cooperation and that's paramount. What I need from you is hard information on what to look for. How to narrow down the list of suspects."

For the next half an hour, Deidre told all she knew of the Nightwatcher, including information she had just gotten from the police that day.

When they were done, Deidre smiled. "You were right, you know. I'd be totally out of my element. Maybe I was a bit jealous. *Your* hunt has begun."

"And you?" Shara asked. "What will you do?"

"What I do best. Write. She came to me once; she'll come again."

"What's your pitch this time?"

"A story dealing with my appearance on "Just Talk," with some juicy tidbits thrown in."

"This is going to be good," Shara said. "When you were after me, you got into my head and under my skin. I don't mind telling you I didn't like it one bit. How are you going to rattle her?"

"First the phony voice. The police didn't want to tell me, but we both agreed there would be no holding back. It makes sense; the phony voice, I mean. Without it someone would recognize her. Then there's the theory the trigger was a recent tragedy. The police will be photographing those attending the funeral of a woman killed in a carjacking. Apparently, the Nightwatcher may have been reading about it on the subway before she struck. It may not be the *right* tragedy, but something set her off." Deidre paused.

"Anything else?"

"You. Actually your angle. Not being a stripper, per se. Not yet. An entertainer. I'll quote the woman herself. End it with something like, 'How am I doing? You know how to reach me.' "

"You know how to read people, I'll give you that. You're a worm. In a positive sense," she added hurriedly. "Burrow in around and through barriers set up for protection. A rat's more like it, but that would sound offensive."

Deidre frowned. "A low-down dirty rat. I do act like that, sometimes. It worries me. I got you mad. You killed my fish—"

"By accident, for God's sake," Shara piped in.

"Nevertheless, you lost control . . . for a bit. Should I be worrying about the Nightwatcher?"

"I doubt it. You were a threat to me. You're not to her. All you have is speculation. If she's angry, she'll ignore you, and you're left high and dry. And she has principles. I didn't."

"Past tense?" Deidre asked.

Shara laughed. "Still wary. Look, I'm not going to fuck with you. Back to our friend, by showing you understand her she may confide in you. She isn't going to come after you."

Shara got up. "I'm going to get changed and see an old acquaintance."

She had been wearing jeans and a shirt tied at the waist. Ten minutes later, she emerged from the guest room in a tight clingy skirt that revealed a lot of leg, and a halter top that left little to the imagination. The tattoos—six pairs of unseeing eyes—that covered her breasts were not visible.

"Do you regret them?" Deidre asked. "The tattoos."

"They're inconvenient, but no, they're a part of me."

"If Briggs saw them . . . ," Deidre began.

"He would know instantly," Shara finished. "It's one reason why intimate relationships may be impossible. I can see myself in bed, naked with someone and that someone putting two and two together. Maybe not then, but it preys on my mind."

"You wouldn't part with them, though." It wasn't a question.

"They kept me sane; at least *saner*, when Bobby's eyes were haunting me. The insecurity they cause now is a small price for helping me get through a tough time." She paused. "Enough already. Wish me luck."

"Not luck. Good hunting."

Shara smiled. "I like that. Yeah, good hunting."

Chapter Thirty-five

The Genesis Club was a far cry from Frank's Place, Shara thought, as she looked around. She had asked for Jil, and been told she wasn't seeing prospective dancers that night.

"Honey," she told the hostess, "just tell Jil a friend from Frank's is here and let her decide."

The woman shrugged, spoke into a walkie-talkie, shrugged again, then told Shara Jil would be down shortly.

The club was mammoth. While Frank's had one bar on which the women actually danced, Shara counted five here; none of which were for dancing; all dispensing soft drinks. There was a stage in the center of the room, instead, surrounded by tables.

Shara couldn't believe the number of security guards; men with white shirts, black pants and red or black bowties. Each wore a headset. At the slightest hint of trouble, they could be summoned immediately. Frank's, on the other hand, had one bouncer: Frank, himself.

A Hispanic girl danced center stage, discarding her bra, then her panties to the delight of customers who sat at tables closest to the stage. Shara could see bills in their hands, which would soon adorn the woman's garter belt. At least six other women in her direct line of vision were performing Table Dances.

"Can I help you?"

It was Jil, behind her. Shara turned.

"I'm impressed," Shara said. "You've come a long way."

The other woman frowned. "I'm afraid you have me at a disadvantage," Jil said stiffly. "A friend from Frank's, I was told?"

Shara said nothing. Jil looked management, in a conservative pant suit. Her straight blonde hair didn't quite reach her shoulders, but was professionally cut. She had a confident, almost smug look about her. Her all-business attitude evaporated, though, when a flicker of recognition came to her hazel eyes.

"Oh my God. Shara? Is it really you?"

"In the flesh."

"My God. It's been, what . . . five years? You're a sight for sore eyes," and without another word she hugged Shara like a long-lost relative.

"Come to my office. You can't hear yourself think with the music blaring."

In a spacious, tastefully decorated office, Jil stared at Shara, as if she had returned from the dead. Shara knew a slew of questions would follow and waited.

"I thought something awful had happened to you," she finally said. "I mean, I've followed most of the girls from . . . from the early days, but you just up and disappeared."

"How are the girls?" Shara asked.

Jil frowned. "It was different then. A rougher time. We don't serve booze here and drugs, well, you know I never tolerated them. We also discourage prostitution. Seriously," she said, when Shara looked skeptical. "It leads to too many problems. We're a lot different from Frank's.

"Carla," she sighed, "and Geena died of drug overdoses. Wanda and Terri went into hooking full time. Wanda was found stabbed in an alley two years ago. Terri's still on the streets. Life's been tough on her."

Then Jil brightened. "Gretchen's married with *four* kids, two twins. And, Justice is an assistant manager at one of the other clubs."

"And Frank?"

"Lung cancer, a year after you left. He left the bar to me, which was a bittersweet blessing."

Shara gave her a puzzled look.

"He never actually owned it. A corporation did, so he left me nothing. But the same people that owned the bar owned an upscale club. They knew all about me and let me manage Frank's for a year. Suggested I take a couple of business and computer courses, then put me in charge of a second upscale club they'd purchased."

"Then this club," Shara finished for her. "I read about how you defused the protestors. You were management material from the get go."

"So, what about you?" Jil asked.

"I became a cop, if you can believe that," she said, and laughed.

Jil looked shocked. "A cop! You're not here to bust me, are you?" she asked with a smile, but her eyes had narrowed.

"Hardly. I left the force a year ago. I'm working for a reporter now. Deidre Caffrey."

"Girl, you do get around." Then her eyes opened wide. "*She's* the one that talked to the Nightwatcher. You're kidding me. You work for *her*!"

"The very same. Did you hear the show?"

"Not til this morning. One of the girls on the day shift told me to listen. They've rebroadcast it several times."

"What was your take?"

"Not much." Jil looked uncomfortable. "I mean she makes a lot of sense, but Caffrey's right, she is one troubled woman."

"If you had to hazard a guess," Shara began, "what do you think she does for a living?"

"I haven't the foggiest," Jil answered, a bit too quickly, Shara thought, and she looked even more unsettled than before.

Shara decided to digress a bit; put her at ease.

"I remember when Frank gave me to you," Shara said. "It was a risk. I was sixteen, and while I had watched, I had never danced . . . you know, butt-naked. All those eyes were on me. You told me to fantasize, pick out one customer and dance only for him. Told me no matter how crass the guys were, they were escaping their reality for a few hours. Remember?"

"Course I do. I've got others to do training for me now, but every once in a while, I like to work with someone who strikes me as needing an experienced hand."

"Your words to me, Jil, were the very same words the Nightwatcher used," Shara said, coming out from left field.

"What are you getting at, Shara?" Jil asked, all business now.

"There's a good chance the Nightwatcher is a stripper. One you hired. One you might have even trained."

"Bullshit." There was hostility in her voice now.

"I'm not here to cause trouble, Jil. On the contrary, I don't want this woman to take you down with her."

"What do you mean?"

Shara could tell she had piqued her interest.

"The cops are closing in. It's only a matter of time now. I mean, this woman's no professional killer. Thing is, I picked up on her fantasy life. Caffrey came close. 'Are you an actress?' Remember that?"

Jil nodded affirmatively, but said nothing.

"The cops aren't assholes; least not the cops on this case. It'll take them longer, but they'll come to the same conclusion. There are two ways this can play out."

Shara paused.

"Go on," Jil said.

Shara smiled. She had her. "Okay. One, the cops figure it out and come in force, bringing a lot of bad publicity to your operation; hassling girls who want to remain anonymous; asking questions of customers who might not want it known they frequent a strip joint—even an upscale club."

Another pause.

"And the other scenario?" Jil asked.

Hook, line and sinker, Shara thought. "Deidre Caffrey's not working for the police. She wants a scoop. Maybe convince the girl to give herself up."

"And you want to see if it's one of my girls," Jil finished for her.

"Look, I pose no threat, Jil. I'm a former stripper, writing a book to shed a positive light on the profession. Just a few questions here and there. Sure beats the police swarming all over."

Jil visibly relaxed, sitting back in her chair. "You always were a tough kid. You weren't going to succumb to drugs or become a hooker. No, something else drove you. You seemed to carry the weight of the world, but you were one determined girl."

"You're stalling," Shara said.

"Just considering my options," Jil answered, with a smile.

"You have none."

"You're right. If I help you, and you find the woman or decide it's not any of them, there will be no cops. That what you're telling me?" Jil asked.

Shara shook her head. "*If* I find her, no cops, that's all I said. If I don't, I can't guarantee anything, but I won't plant the seed. Promise."

"I'm glad you didn't try to bullshit me," she said with a smile of her own. "So, tell me what you want."

Shara took out a paper. "Here are the times of the killings. It will help eliminate a lot of the girls. I need to know who worked on the fourteenth—the subway shooting—anyone who got off your midnight shift. Girls who live in South Philly or Center City. Girls who sometimes take public transportation. Anyone who's quit or not shown up since the night of the first shooting. Anyone who's called in sick the past two weeks, with dates corresponding to the last two shootings. Which girls may have been abused either now or as a child or suffered from a traumatic experience. And anyone acting different the past few weeks. You know, overly quiet or given to tantrums, unexplained outbursts or crying jags. Girls customers have complained about. Not just this club, all three clubs. Her description will make it easier. Medium height, twentyish, big tits, long blonde hair. Be loose though. Someone six feet or overly heavy you can scratch. Not the others."

"What about her accent?" Jil asked. "I can eliminate—"

"Forget the accent," Shara interrupted. "This is not for public consumption, but it's a phony. Don't ask me how I know, I'm not at liberty to say."

She lit a cigarette, which prompted Jil to light a cigarillo of her own.

"I'd like two lists," she went on. "Give priority to those who fit the description. List the others separately."

Shara stopped to catch her breath.

"Hold it," Jil said with a laugh. "This alone will take me hours. Please don't add another dozen variables."

"Sorry, I got carried away. Take all the time you need. In the meantime I can circulate and get a feel for the place and the girls."

"You get off on this, don't you? I mean, you're jazzed. I can't *ever* remember you being so excited." She laughed. "If you could see your eyes. Put it this way, I wouldn't want you after me."

Suddenly, she brightened. "Look, I've got a great idea," Jil said. "Why not do a set? It would make the girls feel more comfortable. They'd know you were one of them. What do you say?"

"I wish I could," Shara said thinking on the fly for an excuse, "but I had to leave the force due to a hip injury. Too much dancing and you'll have me out on a stretcher."

"What a bummer. You've still got the body."

"Jil, I talk the talk and walk the walk. I don't have to prove myself to them."

"All right," she said with disappointment. "Go do your thing. One of my floor managers will buzz you when I'm done."

217

Shara got up. "Jil, I appreciate everything. Not just this, but . . . you know, *everything*. I'll do what I can to keep the cops off your ass."

Jil smiled. "Out now, if you want this list." As Shara got up to leave Jil added, "I'm glad to see things turned out as they did. You made good."

If you only knew, Shara thought. If you only knew.

An hour and a half later, at seven-thirty, Jil gave Shara a list of twenty girls.

"Ouch," Shara said.

"And, there may be more. Most of these girls work here. Actually, many of the girls circulate between clubs. The customers get to see fresh girls every week. I've hired them all, but as to mood changes, how they get to and from other clubs, I've got to speak to my assistants at those clubs. I'll probably have three or four more."

Shara saw the list broken down into two categories. Looking at the lists, she had to admit Jil was a good record keeper and capable with computers. Probably, unlike her, she couldn't hack worth a damn, but organization was her bailiwick. She had prioritized the data Shara needed in a way that made some girls stand out from others.

"Ten no longer here?" Shara asked, seeing a notation.

"Turnover's not that high, but with what you wanted, this is what you got. I've listed the real names and addresses of those who've left."

"Any here now?" Shara looked at her watch. Eight-twenty-five already.

"Three. I've marked those on the other shifts. Looks like you'll be spending a lot of time here."

"What does your gut tell you?" Shara asked. "Is there one or two that stand out; who are capable of playing out a fantasy on the streets?"

Jil pondered the question. "Someone like you. Tough as nails who's lost someone. But you're not on my list, unfortunately, or you'd be right at the top. Ummm, Tori's a lot like you. She was raped six weeks ago; during her off week. Her lesbian lover left her three weeks later. Couldn't emotionally handle the situation.

"Tori's had mood swings and there have been days she's called in sick. It's understandable. She'll work through it though. In time.

Like I said, she's tough, like you. Her shift's over. She'll be in tomorrow at four P.M."

She shrugged. "No way it's her, though, but then, no way it's any of the others, either." She lapsed into silence.

"Let's start with Violet," Shara said. "Is she the one with the tattoos of violets high up on her thighs?"

"Observant little bugger, aren't you? That's her. Let me get her and tell the other two you'll be interviewing them."

She got up to leave. "I hope you're wrong, Shara. Not for what it might do to the business. We can stand the heat. I just can't see any of my girls being this Nightwatcher character."

"Maybe one of your girls has gotten caught up in their fantasy; their stage persona. We both know it's happened. Then again, maybe I'm barking up the wrong tree. We'll know soon enough."

Chapter Thirty-six

Shara let herself into Deidre's apartment at eleven-forty-five. Deidre had kidded Shara about not needing a key, since she had gotten in so easily without one. She had given her one, nevertheless.

Shara was bushed, to say the least. She and Deidre had had an emotional tug-of-war earlier. Seeing Jil had brought back memories, both good and bad. The interviews had drained her further. And the din of the music—Shara recalled the pounding headaches she sometimes got when she danced. Nonstop music, pulsing and undulating. There were days the body rebelled. She had gotten used to it after a while. But she hadn't been to a strip club in five years, and wasn't prepared for the barrage.

She had planned to visit one of the girls who had quit, on her way back to Deidre's, but had absentmindedly passed her block, and not noticed it for another dozen. She had given up. She desperately needed sleep.

Deidre was up and eager to learn what had transpired.

"If I don't take a pee, I'll be dribbling over your carpet. I must have had twenty cups of coffee tonight, if I had one. Okay, if I do my business and take a quick shower? This way I won't fall asleep on you."

Half an hour later, she and Deidre talked over yet another cup of coffee.

"What of the three you spoke with?" Deidre asked, after Shara had told her about her meeting with Jil.

"Washouts. Two of the girls were together the night of the subway shooting. Violet drove Clarice and stayed the night. That left Spike."

"Spike? Is she some sort of bully?" Deidre asked.

Shara noticed that Deidre was taking a vicarious thrill in her progress. Details. She wanted *all* the details. Nothing abridged.

"Her hair," Shara laughed. "When she began working, her hair was short and spiky—hence, Spike. Even though she let it grow, she kept the name. Customers are curious, just like you were. Using your assets, Deidre, that's the name of their game."

"So, could Spike be the Nightwatcher?" Deidre began to giggle. "Imagine if she were?" Deidre cupped her hand like a microphone and mimicked a TV reporter. "Police confirmed that Spike . . . " She gestured to Shara for a last name.

"Mallory," Shara said, beginning to giggle herself.

"Spike Mallory confessed to being the infamous Nightwatcher. Spike . . . " She couldn't go on further, breaking down in laughter. Finally, "Sorry, I'm just punch drunk. So tell me about Spike." She bit her tongue to keep from laughing.

"Well, *Spike*," Shara said, emphasizing the name, which set Deidre off again. "*Spike* . . . "

"Shara, stop before I split a gut."

Shara smiled. "The lady in question had an alibi for two of the killings."

"How did you get that out of her without arousing suspicion?" Deidre asked, stifling a giggle in mid-sentence.

"I heard on television how on the anniversary of John F. Kennedy's assassination, just about everybody could recall where they were. I told her as a stripper, when a major news story broke, I could associate it with some incident where I was dancing. Like, 'Do you remember where you were when the Nightwatcher killed the punk in the subway?'

"She played along. Told me she hadn't seen her boyfriend in a week. He picked her up, and they began balling right in the parking lot. Can you picture our . . . *Spike* doing it right in the . . . " She burst into laughter, unable to finish, and Deidre followed suit.

After several minutes Deidre held up her hand, and between ebbing giggles got her question out. "How (giggle) will you (giggle) prove it?"

Shara took a deep breath and explained. "While Jil was compiling the list, I cozied up to some of the security guards. Just like a secretary knows all that goes on at a business, security guards and hostesses know all the house secrets at the club. Cultivate them, and you've got a good source.

"I told them we had no hired bouncer at Frank's; how if things got out of hand Frank had this big old baseball bat which he wasn't afraid to use. After I spoke with . . . our friend," she said, smiling, "I casually brought it up to one of the guards. He confirmed it. He escorted . . . our friend out, and waited for the car to drive off. And waited. And waited. After fifteen minutes, he said fuck it and went inside. The whole time the car was shaking."

There was another spasm of laughter from the two of them.

"Tomorrow," Shara finally said, "I'll visit the homes of those who quit and in the afternoon hit the club again."

She paused, taking a breath. God, she thought, the laughter was good. When was the last time . . . ? There hadn't been *any* last time. This was the *first*.

"So, how did your story turn out?"

Deidre gasped. "Forget the story. Did you hear the news?"

"Did the Nightwatcher strike again?"

"No. No. A mob began a march in North Philly protesting a crack house. It was an abandoned building that had been boarded up half-a-dozen times. Each time crack addicts had reclaimed the building within a day.

"It began peacefully enough, but at some point someone decided to solve this problem once and for all. They set the building ablaze. When the fire department came, some blocked the way. Others pushed abandoned cars in front of fire hydrants. They had live reports on television, and here was this mob making sure no other addicts would ever use the house."

"So the Nightwatcher *did* strike in a manner of speaking," Shara said.

Deidre shook her head in agreement. "And get this," Deidre went on. "The police arrested two men for starting the fire, and within half an hour others came forward claiming *they'd* started it. Demanded *they* be arrested."

"Holy shit," Shara said.

"My instincts tell me this is only the beginning. I mean, here's this woman that most of the city has now heard saying *she's* taking back the night for herself. She's shamed others to action. Not just peaceful marches with demands that end up ignored, but *action*. One less building. It's going to spread. Mark my words."

"Is the story you were going to write old news, then?" Shara asked, stifling a yawn.

"No. I lead and end with the fire, but the Nightwatcher's still the story." She gave Shara a printout to read.

Shara smiled when she had finished. "You are *soooo* bad, Deidre Caffrey. *Sooooo* very bad. She'll respond only to tell you you're on the wrong track."

"That's good to hear, since you've had firsthand knowledge of my writing directly to you."

"You pissed me off with your story about my poor grieving mother. I knew what you were doing, on one level, but it got to me anyway."

"I've got a feeling I'll have to update the beginning tomorrow before I send it in for Monday's paper. This city's like a volcano that's been rumbling so long, it's ignored. It's about ready to erupt."

Shara leaned back in the kitchen chair. "It's good to have someone to talk to without having to watch every word."

Deidre smiled. "It's good to have someone to talk to who answers back. Pissed as I was, I *was* glad to see you. I'm glad you're here."

Tired as they both were, they were loath to end the conversation. They talked volumes for another twenty minutes.

Saying nothing.

Saying everything.

Chapter Thirty-seven

Lysette sat glued to the TV set Monday morning. She had been both damned and praised for what some called mob hysteria, and others, community empowerment. The Sunday *Inquirer* had run excerpts of her chat on "Just Talk," while radio and television commentators analyzed it to death, much like a pivotal presidential address.

On Saturday, on her way to the club, KYW, Philly's all-news station, described the gutting of a haven for addicts earlier that evening, adding how over one hundred people had confessed to the crime, for which two had been arrested.

That same night, scant attention was paid to the rape of an eleven-year-old in West Philly. On Sunday, though, it was big news. The child had been able to describe her assailant, and her parents and relatives had gotten a neighborhood artist to render a sketch of his likeness.

It was plastered around for blocks. The rapist happened to be in a WAWA convenience store as the father was taping the picture to the front window. The Asian clerk, in halting English, pointed and yelled, "That him!" and the father and his brother pursued and captured the man.

Without calling the police, they'd taken the man to the youth's house where she had identified him as her attacker. They then delivered him to the police, much worse for the wear.

Seemingly out of the woodwork, a dozen, two dozen, then close to a hundred neighbors and strangers had converged on the station for the man's arraignment. They were perfectly peaceful—polite to a fault, and the police decided not to antagonize them by forcing them to disperse.

A judge, sensing the mood of the silent mob, set bail prohibitively high, without any objection from the alleged rapist's public defender.

It was later learned that the assailant told his lawyer he had no desire to be released on bail. Freedom, his lawyer later told the media, in this case, meant death.

That night three other havens for addicts and dealers were torched. Dealers had gone underground, cynics saying they knew the mania would pass and the streets would be theirs in a matter of days.

A Take Back the Night Coalition had been formed headed by Reverend Calvin Whitaker, a black Baptist activist, and Father Diego Negron, his counterpart in the Hispanic community.

They not only condoned the torching of abandoned homes that had been taken over by dealers and addicts, but called on families to go in groups to reclaim playgrounds long ago lost to thugs, gangs and dealers.

Whitaker, himself, led one group of men, women and children to a West Philly playground, sweeping up crack vials and lighting the playground with the eerie glow of flashlights, while their children played on swings, slides and seesaws.

Negron had led a similar group in West Kensington, telling his followers: "We must stand before we walk. We must walk before we run. This is a symbol of our resolve. *Together*, we shall take back the night!"

And, in every report Lysette—the Nightwatcher—was given her due; by most, given credit. One TV reporter, Lysette thought, best summed up the feeling of a city held hostage to crime: "This woman told the people of this city to look in a mirror. Apparently, they didn't like what they saw, and now they have joined together as one to regain their self-respect."

"I said that?" Lysette said aloud to the television screen. I guess I did, she thought, but she never anticipated being taken literally.

Why not? the Cassandra in her asked. They looked to you . . .

—Us, no, *me*, Lysette corrected.

. . . for action and heeded your words.

There had been ominous signs personally for Lysette. She didn't know if it was paranoia or if she took Deidre Caffrey's column too seriously, but she felt the police closing in.

They had been at the funeral. She hadn't noticed them at first, as

Barry Hoffman

the media had come out in full force. Rose Santucci, because of the timing of her funeral, had become, in death, a symbol of a city gone astray.

As family and friends exited the church, Lysette overheard one of Rose's sons talking to his wife.

"See the black man over there?" he said pointing. "I've seen him on television. A goddamn cop, taking pictures of *us*. Why the hell aren't they out looking for the man who killed Mama?"

Lysette saw the man, and a Hispanic woman with him. At first Lysette felt terribly exposed; almost as if she were naked.

"Lady, come with us," she imagined them saying. "Thought you could elude us, but you're no match for Philadelphia's finest."

But she was all but ignored, and she knew why. Without her wig, wearing a floppy hat to cover her scarred temple, and dressed conservatively in black, she didn't remotely resemble the Nightwatcher. They were looking for blondes, and there were a hell of a lot of them at the funeral.

Their very presence, though, was unsettling.

Then, at the club on Sunday, a woman claiming to be a former stripper researching a book on upscale exotic dancers was talking to a number of girls; *all* blondes. It could have been merely a coincidence . . .

—Coincidence my ass, Cassandra chided.

. . . but she was glad she was wearing the brunette wig.

Closing in on her.

Why did it so unsettle her?

Something deep within told her there was unfinished business to attend to. What, she had no idea, but capture now would be premature.

And, finally, there was the recurring dream of the past two nights. She was at a playground. Something had been placed over her head, and she could barely breathe. She could see nothing. She began to panic. Reached for the gun in her pocket, but it wasn't there. She saw herself dying, and woke up in a cold sweat in her nest in the corner of her room.

Where are you now, Cassandra? she asked. She knew. Cassandra was within her. Had always been. A balance had been struck. This dream, so powerful, so lifelike, was too much for even the new Lysette.

Upon awakening, both times, she had checked the gun. Two bullets.

226

—For him.

For who?

—For *him*.

When she went to the beach today she thought she might stop by a gun shop and purchase additional bullets. . . .

—You won't need them, some inner voice spoke.

Why not? She wanted to ask, but knew there would be no answer. It was all coming to a head. The police. The woman at the club. Her death. The two bullets.

And she couldn't forget the article in today's *Daily News*—Deidre Caffrey's article. Saturday, on a whim, she had put the cellular phone in an envelope with a short note and taken a bus to the building that housed both the *Daily News* and *Inquirer*.

She'd had no plan. She wore a pair of baggy jeans, an oversized sweatshirt and a Phillies cap. Getting off the bus, she saw a teenager washing car windows when the light turned red. Reluctantly most drivers gave the youth some change or a bill. He was good-natured. If they ignored him, he didn't rant, rave or curse them out. There were plenty of cars and, she imagined, he pocketed a tidy sum before going home.

She walked up to him when the light turned green, holding out a five-dollar bill.

"I'm in a hurry, and I need this delivered to the main desk in that building," she said pointing to the *Inquirer* building. She held up the five-dollar bill. "Interested?"

Without saying a word, he plucked the bill from her fingers and held out his hand for the package. "No sweat," he said, as he turned and made his way into the building. When he entered, she made her way to a subway station.

Caffrey's new article only added to her malaise. The reporter knew the South Philly accent was phony, but her explanation made sense; unaltered, her voice might give her away to a listener.

She talked, again, about what may have triggered the Nightwatcher to set herself up and "kill with impunity. It could have been a recent tragedy, such as the carjacking that lead to the death of Rose Santucci."

How did she know? She didn't, the Cassandra in her answered. She's guessing. Speculating. She's right, but only because the funeral was the day before. Coincidence. Of course, but too close to home, nevertheless.

And lastly, the possibility she was an entertainer. "It didn't occur to me at the time, but when I asked if she was an actress, she became evasive; defensive, as if I might have stumbled onto the truth."

The article ended with a challenge. "So, Nightwatcher, how am I doing? You know how to reach me."

Without thinking, Lysette picked up the phone and called Deidre Caffrey at the *Daily News*. She had to go through several menus, but finally the reporter picked up her line. "Caffrey, here."

"You got my package?" Lysette asked in her heavy South Philly accent.

"I get lots of packages," the reporter had answered coyly.

"A telephone."

"You want to talk?" she asked. "You're not on the radio, you can drop the accent."

Lysette ignored her. "Not now. Give me a home number I can reach you at. I may want to talk later."

The reporter gave her the number.

"We'll talk," Lysette said, and hung up.

—Closing in on you from all sides, she told herself.

It was time to get out of town. At least, until she had to go to work. She needed to clear her head.

—See if the sand sculpture revealed anything more.

—See Angel.

—*Mostly see Angel.*

Chapter Thirty-eight

There was a chill in the air at nine-thirty, when Lysette reached the beach. The surf crashed with the same turmoil that was boiling within her. She kept on the Temple University sweatshirt she had worn, and began building the base for her sculpture.

As before, she was startled awake by the sound of music, and knew she had once again been in one of her fugues. This time, though, she ignored Angel, dancing to the hip-hop club version of Mariah Carey's "Anytime You Need a Friend."

She stared at the figure. The sculpture was a carbon copy of the others, but there was more detail in her assailant's face. The hair was close-cropped and wiry, like Brillo—a blackman. Yet, she had covered the face and hair with white powder. The red eyes—two marbles—stared at her, the eyebrows still protecting him from the glare of the light.

Looking at the face, she saw herself on a set of swings. Felt a presence behind her. Felt the bag placed over her face, as she was yanked backwards. This time she heard the gun fall to the ground from the coat on her lap. Land close to her. The man was on top of her, his hand exploring underneath her dress, then ripping her panties off . . .

Angel interrupted her thoughts.

" . . . I said you're the Nightwatcher, aren't you?"

"What?"

"I hate it when you go into those . . . trances," she said haltingly, as if searching for the right word. "I thought we were friends."

"What are you talking about?" Lysette asked, still having difficulty separating the dream from reality.

"Friends don't keep secrets. You should have told me you were the Nightwatcher."

229

Lysette had recovered. "You haven't told me much. Actually anything *at all* about yourself."

Angel ignored her. "Why use my name—on the radio show?"

Lysette smiled. "I don't know. It came naturally. Maybe I was thinking of you. Friends do that, you know."

"I almost didn't come today. I was mad."

"But you *did* come. Friends get mad at one another, but they don't stay mad."

Angel picked up a canvas tote bag and took out a gun.

"Teach me to shoot," she said.

"Where did you get that?" Lysette asked, shocked. It was a .38 caliber, much like the one she had taken from the boy in the subway. It seemed like ages ago, but it was just a day shy of a week.

"A girl needs to protect herself." Angel said, running the barrel of the gun up her naked body.

Lysette looked at her closely for the first time that day. Her breasts seemed fuller, the thatch of pubic hair darker and more prominent. *Older*, Lysette thought. It was as if she had aged a year or more in less than a week.

"How old are you, Angel?"

"I told you, twelve. Actually twelve and a half."

"No, you told me your were eleven and a half," Lysette said emphatically.

Angel laughed "Closing in on thirteen, I told you. You must be getting senile in your old age."

"I'm serious, Angel. I *know* you told me eleven and a half."

"You don't know what's going on half the time you're here, so what do *you* really know?" she shot back. "Always demanding . . ."

"Demanding?"

"See, you don't *know* what you're doing. We have conversations you forget. How do you think you got the powder? Last time it was marbles. Today you sent me home for powder."

"Powder?" Lysette asked, bewildered. "*I* asked for powder?"

"You were looking at his face," Angel said, pointing to the man holding the lighter. " 'It's not right,' you said, over and over, and then, 'Powder. I need powder.' "

"And you went home to get powder?"

"Sure," she shrugged. "You were upset. It gave me goosebumps. I want you to be happy."

Lysette smiled.

"So you see, half the time you don't know what's going on. You think I said 'Going on twelve.' I said twelve, *going* on thirteen. It sounds so much more mature than twelve and a half."

What did it matter, Lysette thought. Going on twelve, going on thirteen. Big deal. And, she had asked Angel to get the marbles and powder without being aware she had asked. Still . . . she did *look* older than a week ago, and that wasn't her imagination. Or was it? Angel brought her back to reality.

"So, will you teach me to shoot?"

"Oh, I don't know . . ."

"I'm not a child," Angel yelled scornfully. "What if *I'm* attacked?"

"It's not that. The shots might draw someone. You know, like the police," she laughed. "I really don't need the police poking around."

"Deep in the woods," Angel countered. "No one will hear a sound. The woods are like . . . walls. Inside of them no one can hear a thing. Watch."

Without waiting, she bounded towards the woods. A few minutes later she returned.

"I called out for you. Did you hear?"

"Not a thing. Did you really call?"

"Friends don't lie to one another."

"I'm sorry," Lysette said. "All right, but won't your parents be upset? I should get their permission."

"It's my father's gun. I took it. He doesn't know, and he'll be pissed if he finds out. C'mon, teach me to shoot, like your grandfather taught you."

"I told you that?"

Angel put her hands on her hips. "No, I read your mind. Of course you told me. How else would I know?"

Without waiting for an answer, she grabbed Lysette's hand and pulled her into the woods.

Lysette allowed herself to be led. Sometimes there was no use in arguing, she thought. Entering the woods was like leaving one world for another. The screech of the seagulls was replaced by utter silence. She again thought of a nuclear holocaust. Not a living thing could be seen or heard. And it was much warmer here. A comfortable warmth, though. It had looked foreboding from afar, but once inside, she felt an inner calm replace her churning emotions.

Angel led her to a fallen tree with cans on top.

"See, I have everything ready." She handed Lysette the gun. "Show me. Then teach me."

Lysette fired off four shots; the first one missed—the next three knocked cans off the fallen tree.

Angel applauded, ran to the tree and replaced the cans.

Lysette again noticed her body, her gait, her very presence seemed altered. There seemed to be the curves of a young woman where there had been skin and bones just days before. Angel moved with self-assuredness and poise that was missing when she dashed into the ocean the first day they met. There was almost something predatory about the way she moved, as if she spent her life in the forest. And an erotic grace surrounded her like an aura. Yes, Lysette thought, teach her how to defend herself. Like a lioness with her cubs. Give her the tools and she'll never fall prey to those who yearn for her body without consent.

For the next forty-five minutes, Lysette instructed her, much as her grandfather had taught her. "Gently squeeze, don't *pull* the trigger."

"The gun is an extension of your arm. Be aware of the recoil, but don't control it and don't let it control you."

"*Never* aim to wound. If you need to use a gun, shoot to kill. The head if close enough. The chest if further away."

Angel learned quickly and well.

Exiting the forest, the din of the surf and the seagulls' incessant yelling assaulted Lysette's ears.

"Practice," she told her pupil. "A few times a week in the beginning. Then it's like riding a bike. Remember, though, it's not a toy. Guns don't kill. People do. People with guns."

Angel ran to the boombox Lysette had given her and danced to the song Lysette had heard when she had come out of her fugue, "Anytime You Need a Friend."

"I bought it for *us*," Angel said, as she sang the words of the chorus, about never being alone again, everlasting friendship. "Is there something wrong?" she asked, seeing Lysette looking troubled.

"Wait here. I'll be right back."

Lysette went to her car and came back with a tape, put it in the boombox and watched Angel as the song played; the *same* song they'd just listened to, except it was the original version from Mariah Carey's album; slower, much more soulful and impassioned.

"I didn't think anything of it when I came out of my fog," Lysette said, when the song ended. "But it's creepy. The *same* song, different versions. But the *same* song. Like the other day with the Pointer Sisters."

Angel danced to the slow version, as if she were a stripper and Lysette thought, again, how much this child—this young woman, she corrected herself—reminded her of herself now. She wondered if Angel was dancing for Lysette or herself. Her eyes were fixed on Lysette, as her hands caressed her breasts, then journeyed down to her pubic hair. She rubbed herself down there, then journeyed up her body again. A sensuous creature, Lysette thought . . .

—And now deadly with her gun.

. . . her body a weapon in itself.

Then it was time to leave.

"How's your sculpting coming?" Lysette asked. They hadn't time for Angel to sculpt what with her teaching Angel how to shoot.

"I'm all thumbs," Angel laughed, "but I'm getting a little better. I love watching the water swallow up my room. Like I'm sharing something with the goddess of the sea. A sacrifice. That's what I mean."

"A sacrifice," Lysette said. "I never thought of it that way, but I like it."

As Lysette was going to get in her car, Angel came towards her.

"Thanks, Lys," she said. "You know, for teaching me how to shoot. And . . . for being my friend." She gave Lysette a quick kiss on the lips, then flushed.

Lysette took her into her arms and hugged her. "You don't know how I look forward to coming out here. Coming to you."

Lysette got in her car.

Angel came up to her window. "Lysette," she said, and paused. "Be careful tonight."

Before Lysette could ask her what she meant, Angel had turned and run into the surf. Lysette shivered. She didn't know if it was thinking how cold the water must be or what Angel had said. She just knew she loved the child like a little sister. . . .

—Like Laura loved you.

Chapter Thirty-nine

Every war has its casualties, and the club was abuzz with the first in the battle to take back the streets. At noon, three members of Reverend Whitaker's flock had been killed in a drive-by shooting; another four wounded, one critically.

The day before, the Coalition, as it had been dubbed by the press, had laid claim to six vacant stores. Each was to be a neighborhood headquarters.

Reverend Whitaker had told the press who had gathered at the opening he personally attended that if addicts and dealers could take over buildings to ply their illicit trade, the forces of those seeking to restore law and order could do the same.

Area businesses were more than willing to lend a hand. Bell Atlantic had provided free phone service and equipment; PECO Energy, electricity without cost; Staples office supplies, furniture and supplies, to name just a few.

The drive-by shooting in North Philly at 25th and Columbia had been a not-too-subtle message that the targets of the Coalition were not about to sit idly by watching their profits turn to ashes.

If they thought they could intimidate the Reverend, however, they were dead wrong.

Reverend Calvin Whitaker *created* bandwagons; he didn't jump on them. A high-school track star, he had been shot in the knee when he had gotten too tight with the girlfriend of a gang member. He had been sent a message that ended his dreams of competing in the Olympics.

Tall, lean and dark-skinned, he had grudgingly followed his father's footsteps into the ministry; but not until he, himself, had succumbed to drugs.

His addiction had started innocently enough. The pain in his knee refused to quiet, and his doctor prescribed stronger and more addictive painkillers to ease his torment. Young Calvin eventually became totally dependent. Ever resourceful, he had stolen his doctor's prescription pad, and kept increasing the dosage as the effects of the pills began to wear off.

His father had finally confronted him after money from a church function had come up woefully short.

Always a believer in self-help, Reverend Calvin Whitaker, Sr., didn't send his son to a drug rehab center, though he could have easily afforded to, if he desired. He stayed with his son in the church basement for five days, as the youth fought the demons of withdrawal.

Eight years later, the son succeeded his father as pastor when cancer claimed the minister's life. As he lay dying, the father told his son there were some battles that just couldn't be won, and the "Big C" was one of them.

Calvin jettisoned the junior that followed his name, though keeping faithful to his father's beliefs. He soon built a reputation equal to that of his father, as an activist minister. Long before Jesse Jackson made it fashionable to crusade against black-on-black crime, Calvin Whitaker had been preaching the word to his flock, saying the black community must come to grips with itself and not rely on outside assistance.

Now he had taken on the challenge the Nightwatcher had thrust upon the populace to take back the streets and had seen three of his followers slain.

Within hours of the shooting, the Coalition responded. Four buildings used by pushers and addicts were torched. In one, addicts had been ushered out; some too strung out were even carried. Yet, two dealers were later found to have perished in the blaze. While the Reverend was publicly remorseful at the loss of life, speculation was rife that the dealers had been knocked unconscious and left to die in the inferno; a message sent.

Both sides had dug in their heels, and as the probability for further bloodshed loomed, everyone at the club had an opinion on the subject.

Lysette soaked it all in.

"Every pusher taken out makes the streets safer."

"Don't be naive. For every pusher who falls, there's another to take his place," another countered.

"Kids are finally seeing their parents standing up to these hoodlums. They're beginning to look at their parents through different eyes."

"Yeah, but their parents are still poor, and the pushers still have fancy cars, jewelry, women and money to burn," was one of the many retorts.

Lysette tried not to get caught up in the debate. Her job, after all, was to take their minds off of the mayhem outside.

She was also all too aware of the continued presence of the writer, Shara Farris, who, word had it, had completed her interviews and had been sequestered with Jil in her office for forty-five minutes.

Lysette noticed the woman again had interviewed only blondes, and only girls who fit her general description, with the exception of her hair color. She spoke with none of the black, Hispanic or Asian girls. Lysette didn't believe in coincidences. This was no writer researching a book. Possibly a reporter, but more likely an undercover cop. But why here? Lysette wondered. She thought back to Deidre Caffrey's article.

—An entertainer.

But why a stripper? Why here?

Lysette also noticed the woman looking at her, earlier in the evening, when she thought Lysette wasn't aware. Once, Lysette defiantly returned her stare, though later she chastised herself for her foolishness. Why draw attention to herself? she asked herself. Surprisingly, this woman hadn't turned away. Something about the woman was familiar. She was . . .

—A hunter.

—A predator.

. . . on the prowl, after something . . .

—After *her*.

Then it came to her. She seemed like an older version of Angel, when they'd entered the forest. She was a hardened Angel, to be sure; someone who had lived a harsh life. Like Angel though, she seemed like a wild, untamed animal. And like Angel, in the forest, in the club this woman was in her element. Lysette almost thought she could detect the woman sniffing, as if trying to identify some scent of guilt or fear she might be giving off. It was Lysette who broke eye contact.

The woman was gone when Lysette left the club at midnight.

She wasn't surprised to find she had packed her black skirt, red

op and the rest of her paraphernalia, along with the gun and its
wo remaining bullets.

Wasn't surprised she took a different route home; one that
would take much longer than her normal drive. She drove through
Upper Darby, made a right onto 63rd Street, parked on Chestnut
street and made her way past Walnut and Spruce to a small playground on Cobbs Creek Parkway.

It was a playground in the loosest sense of the word. It consisted
of a set of swings and a slide.

She remembered the dream . . .

—The swings.

—Approached from behind.

—Her face covered.

—Unable to breathe.

—Unable to find her gun.

. . . and the vision at the beach . . .

—The gun falling from her coat.

—A man straddling her.

—His hands groping under her skirt.

—Her panties ripped off.

. . . and the dream again . . .

—*Her death.*

She could flee. Should flee. *Must* flee, if she was ever going to
see Angel again.

She didn't.

She got on the swing and waited. The man who attacked her
tonight—and she had no doubt the attack would come—was it the
same man who had killed her mother and Laura, and left her to
die? Was he here to finish what he had started? Was the dream a
glimpse into her future or a warning?

Regardless, could she alter the outcome?

She was so into herself, she didn't hear his approach, and was
taken by surprise when a canvas bag covered her head, and she was
blinded. He roughly pulled her backwards off the swing, the wind
being knocked from her as she landed on the ground.

In her mind's eyes, she saw her gun slip from her coat pocket as
she fell to the ground. If her vision had been accurate, it was within
her grasp.

He was on top of her now, his arms pinning her down. His breath
smelled of onions . . .

—And death.

. . . as he spoke. "Struggle, cunt, and you die. Die hard. Accep
the inevitable, and you'll see tomorrow."

It sounded rehearsed, Lysette thought, like he had used it before
even practiced saying it in front of a mirror, trying to give eac
word the proper inflection. She had no intention of fighting him—
just yet. Her arms pinned, there was no chance of her reaching th
gun, and with the bag over her head, she was blind. She relaxed he
arms. He took notice, and she could imagine the smile on his face

"That's a good bitch," he said, and his hand went straight to he
thighs, and up her dress. There was to be no foreplay. He yanked a
her panties, and they tore away—just as they had in her dream.

She had been breathing heavily, and felt faint. She fought t
calm herself before she passed out. His fingers were now inside o
her, and he was talking to himself. She was an object, nothin
more.

She felt him change positions slightly, and knew he was unzip
ping his pants.

Slowly, her right arm canvassed the grass. She recalled the vi
sion. The gun was at four o'clock on an imaginary clock. If i
wasn't there, she'd be lucky if she were only raped. If it wasn'
there, she knew intuitively, she'd be beaten and killed, *after* th
rape.

He moved again, and hiked up her skirt. In so doing he pushe
her back six inches, and her hand grazed the cold metal of her .38

As her fingers grabbed the gun, he entered her, grunting wit
satisfaction.

Her hand on the trigger, she decided, without her sight, sh
couldn't go for a head shot.

He thrust once.

A second time.

Once again.

She shot at his midsection.

"What the fuck!" he yelled in pain.

One bullet left, she told herself. Just one. Not yet, she thought
She'd be aiming blind.

She swung the hand with the gun wildly, connecting with hi
head on the third swipe, then pushed with both hands against hi
chest, and was able to roll free.

She yanked off the hood, and in the darkness of the night was in
stantly able to see him.

An albino! A black man in his twenties, but an albino. The eyes shone red. His face was white, though not quite the color of the powder she had used on the sand sculpture. His short-cropped wiry hair was blond.

She took this all in in an instant, because, while surprised by the wound in his side, he was hardly disabled. She hadn't gut-shot him and he had a rock in his hand . . .

—Like the lighter.

. . . and was going to hit her in the head . . .

—Like he had done twelve years earlier.

"You fucking bitch. You goddamn fucking bitch." He lunged, and she raised the gun and shot him through his left eye, not in the temple, as she had the others. He was so close to her his blood and brain matter sprayed her like water from a sprinkler.

She rolled to her right as his downward momentum propelled him forward, just missing her. He lay still, facedown on the ground.

She wanted to turn him over and get another look at him. *Could it be the same man who had attacked her twelve years earlier?* She'd thought this man to be in his mid-twenties, even though she had only gotten a quick glimpse. Had her attacker been a young teen? She couldn't be sure. His face swam before her—so much like this man's—but she couldn't be sure. Just one more look, she told herself.

—Get your ass out of here, Cassandra commanded.

Lysette obeyed.

In her car, she was assaulted by a barrage of thoughts and images. Her genitals ached and itched. That vile creature had been *in* her, and she felt soiled. She had to concentrate to keep from speeding—so intent was she to get home to cleanse herself.

The dream. The vision at the beach. They had saved her life. She had seen what *could* have been her future, but had been able to alter it—*only* because she knew where the gun would be.

And Angel. *Be careful tonight.*

Had she sensed some sort of danger?

She knew one thing for sure. There was no more Nightwatcher. Whatever had propelled her the past week was sated. There had been some inner need to prowl the streets. There was a destiny, for want of a better word, she'd had to fulfill. It had nothing to do with taking back the night. She *hadn't* been in control. At least Lysette hadn't been in control. Was it Cassandra? She didn't think so. Cassandra was a part of her. Cassandra was an exhibitionist, outgoing and aggressive, but not reckless. Cassandra had never exposed herself to danger at the club. On the contrary, for all her abandon, she was cautious. Maybe, she thought, the combination of the two— Lysette and Cassandra . . .

—Let it rest, the Cassandra in her said. At least for now.

Again, she obeyed.

But what now? Would she just drop out of sight? More important, *could* she? The police, Deidre Caffrey and the woman at the club, Shara Farris. They *had* been closing in. Should she give herself up to the police? Were there any other options?

—Let it rest. Cassandra again. *This* is not the time to make hasty decisions. We've been raped.

At home, Lysette ignored the locks on the door and headed right for the shower, discarding her blood-soaked clothes as she walked to the stairs.

Hot water only. She needed the pain. Soaped her genitals, rinsed, then soaped again, trying to rid herself of him. After half an hour, she could still feel his presence. He hadn't come, but like tiny insects, he was within her. She longed to stick her hand deep within her and pull him out, regardless of the damage it caused.

Washcloth in hand, she scrubbed again and again, until she was raw.

Then, in the mist of the shower, his face emerged. Smiling. "Go you. *Again!*" He was there with her; his face blown off, gray matter seeping from the wound in his vacant left eye. She looked down and saw the wound in his side; blood cascading down his leg. His penis was hard. He came toward her, and she bumped her head against the tile to avoid him.

She had dropped her gun on the floor when she had entered the house. Two bullets had been left. She'd used two bullets to kill him, and it hadn't been enough. Empty. Useless. She crouched down, knees up to protect her genitals, head between her knees so she couldn't watch his assault and waited.

—And waited.

—And waited.

Eventually the water turned cold, but Lysette wasn't aware.

—Waiting.

—She was waiting.

—Waiting, no matter how long it took.

—Waiting for him to take her, as in her dream.

—Waiting for her death.

Chapter Forty

Extra police had been called in to preserve the crime scene. Word had spread the Nightwatcher had struck again. From all over the city, at one in the morning, they'd converged; first a few individuals, then by the dozens and by two o'clock, police estimated well over a thousand had assembled.

Briggs was reminded of a man a few years earlier who said the spirit of Jesus visited his home the third Sunday of each month. He'd forgotten all the details, but soon hundreds made pilgrimages to the sight, though the Church advised against putting stock into the sighting until it had been thoroughly investigated. The Church had been ignored. The people came.

People had a need to believe, Briggs thought, whether it be Jesus or the current symbol of the fight against lawlessness, this Nightwatcher.

With the Coalition and various criminals engaged in a bloody slugfest, news of the presence of the Nightwatcher brought people out in droves. When all looked bleak, she somehow gave them hope; rallied them on.

There was no carnival atmosphere, however. It was almost surreal; it made Briggs' flesh crawl. Like the *Night of the Living Dead*.

The gathering was almost reverential and spontaneity ruled. The Nightwatcher had taken yet another thug off the streets. Diego Negron appeared and, seeing the near-silent procession, began handing out candles. When the crowd continued to grow and there were not enough candles, others lit cigarette lighters and pocket flashlights.

There were attempts at song from the Hispanic priest, but the people seemed to want none of it. *They just wanted to be there.*

Feel the Nightwatcher's presence. No speeches. No rallying cries. No song.

The police made no attempt to disperse the crowd. They patrolled the ever-expanding perimeter solely to assure safety; no further retaliation from criminals. A riot could have easily broken out had the two mixed.

Despite an early-evening address from the Mayor calling for calm, the Coalition had been active that night. Acting on tips, neighbors had broken into two chop shops, depositing hundreds of car parts and a dozen bruised and battered car thieves at the closest police station.

A child molester, released on his own recognizance, had been castrated and was in serious condition at an undisclosed hospital. A carjacker had been chased by a caravan of cars. Using walkie talkies, they had signalled ahead and a street had been blocked by a Dumpster. The carjacker had given up; the car returned to its rightful owner. The carjacker, however, had been run over, his knees smashed, and left for the police to scrape off the ground. He'd never walk again, *if* he survived.

Fire, though, remained the main weapon of choice. Drug dealers' cars had been targeted, with over a dozen set ablaze. Four weed-strewn lots, hangouts for addicts who littered them with crack vials and needles, were set on fire. A local contractor volunteered to grade and cover the lots with tar. Modell's Sporting Goods donated basketball backboards, hoops and stanchions, while a fencing company agreed to enclose the lot. Off-duty police volunteered to provide security.

Parents had begun confronting their strung-out children, demanding they identify suppliers. In one case a twelve-year-old had shot and killed his father, when confronted. . . .

—Casualties of war.

But that was the exception, not the norm. Most kids seemed willing, even eager, to dime on those tearing their families apart. For some, it was the first show of concern from their families in years; and it was welcomed with open arms.

Citizen arrests ended with badly injured dealers brought to the police and the police were not about to arrest those turning in pushers.

Sullen but silent mobs gathered in courtrooms as judges finally began setting what was considered reasonable bail. The Mayor himself had decided to defy a federal court judge, and the revolving-door policy at police stations began to slow. Overcrowding might become a problem, said the Mayor, but the people were crying for action and the rights of prisoners were not his top priority at the moment.

On the other hand, there had been an unsuccessful attempt on Calvin Whitaker's life, in which one of his parishioners had been killed. Later, one of the six Coalition headquarters had been firebombed.

But then news spread that the Nightwatcher had struck again. All activity ceased, as the people converged on the crime scene.

While Briggs and Morales combed the area, uniforms nervously watched the silent sea of humanity watching them.

Morales, after conferring with his lieutenant about the massive crowd, came up to Briggs.

"Make sure you get *everything* you need before you leave. There's no way to preserve this crime scene. These people want souvenirs; something to show their children they witnessed the Nightwatcher's work. The Commissioner feels if we keep an armed presence here, it will only provoke them." He shrugged. "What can I say? Politics have entered into this. No one wants to be responsible for igniting the spark that leads to a riot; one in which it's the people against the police."

He paused and scanned the crowd. "I don't like the quiet," he finally said. "It's like they're not even here. And, they won't listen to their leaders, because many of them are just concerned citizens who don't belong to the Coalition." Another pause. "A no-win situation."

He finally looked at Briggs and sighed. "So, what have we got?"

"This one was not as neat as the others," Briggs said. "The ME thinks she was attacked—possibly raped. There were two bullet wounds; one in the side and the fatal one to the head."

"You're sure it's the Nightwatcher?" Morales asked. "Not a copycat?"

Briggs nodded affirmatively.

"Before the crowd arrived," he said, "we were able to conduct some preliminary canvassing. We have a witness across the street who saw a struggle, heard a shot, then another half a minute later. She saw a woman run off fitting the description of the Nightwatcher. We have her cigarette butts near the swings and ballistics will tell us if it's the same gun."

Morales was shaking his head. "I don't know what's worse. The crowd's reaction if we catch the Nightwatcher, or what will happen if some thug gets lucky and kills her."

"We're damned either way, Sarge," Briggs answered, "but if she's killed I can see rioting."

"So, we have to catch her. And soon. I've been authorized to give you additional manpower."

"Sarge, it's not men we need. A little luck would help. Seems like the gods are conspiring against us. The victim from the subway, Isiah Hayes, was supposed to come back home today. He decided to stay with his family another day. He's on a train now. I hope to get something from him tomorrow."

Morales looked doubtful.

"Trust me on this. He's holding back, but I can squeeze him, especially if the woman was raped before she plugged the guy."

"And the pictures from the Santucci funeral?"

"Rios has shown them to all possible witnesses. Nothing. She's taking it hard."

"Don't give her too much comfort," Morales said. "You *are* a married man."

"It's not like—"

Morales laughed. "Don't get so defensive, or I *will* become suspicious." He slapped Briggs on the shoulder.

A uniform came up and Morales looked at him expectantly. "Sorry to bother you, but a reporter named Caffrey says to tell you she's here."

"Send her over," Morales said.

Deidre made her way with a younger woman.

"Sergeant," Deidre said curtly, then nodded to Briggs. Before they could ask, she made introductions. "This is Shara Farris. She used to work for the department, then moved to a small town where there was less crime. She's visiting and helping me out." She looked at Shara.

"Shara, Sergeant Morales and Detective Briggs."

Briggs ignored Shara. "Did the Nightwatcher call back?"

"Not yet, but if she calls now, it'll be forwarded."

Briggs had been thrilled when Deidre had called and told him the Nightwatcher had asked for her home number.

"I expect you'll be hearing from her soon." He filled her in on what they knew of the rapist's attack.

"You mentioned some pictures taken at the Santucci funeral," Deidre said.

"Didn't pan out," Briggs said. "We've shown them to witnesses and nada. Nothing. Zilch. Another dead end. Not worth your time."

"Briggs," Deidre said with irritation, "remember, we share *everything*. Let me waste my time, if I want to." She held out her hand. "The pictures. *Please,*" she added, with a smile.

Briggs shook his head, but called over to Rios, and asked her to show Deidre and her friend the photos. Before they went off with her, Briggs added, "Call me if you hear from her. No matter what the time."

"No holding back, Briggs," she said. "I'll call."

"Don't get paranoid on me," Morales told Briggs when they'd left. "There's no reason for her to hide anything."

Briggs shrugged. "I've been kicked in the balls once. It's tough *not* being suspicious."

Briggs went over and took a last look at the body. Deidre had been right in her columns, he thought. It was a dangerous game this woman was playing. She had apparently been caught off guard or overpowered tonight for the first time. If something didn't break soon, he had the sinking feeling they'd be carting *her* off next in a body bag.

Tomorrow, he thought. Zeke, I'm gonna break you.

Chapter Forty-one

Shara had remained silent as Rios showed Deidre the photos, then passed them to her. She hadn't liked the idea of meeting Briggs one bit. The man, after all, had been after her just over a year ago. Hadn't gotten close, but all the same, some cops never let go of an old case no matter how cold it got.

Then she'd seen the photos, and Briggs was forgotten. She could hardly contain her excitement as they got in Deidre's car.

"I saw her, Dee. She's in one of the photos!"

Deidre looked at her incredulously. "Someone from the club?"

"Yes, though not one of the ones I've interviewed. Matter of fact, she was in the background of one of the pictures. The police didn't intentionally take her picture."

"I don't understand," Deidre said. "You're going in circles."

Shara's hands were moving like a mime trying to communicate. She got that way when she was excited, her gestures as expressive as her voice.

"The police took photos of blondes. The Nightwatcher is *no blonde*."

Again, Deidre looked befuddled, but said nothing.

"Okay. Let me start from the beginning. I finished my interviews at the club. I didn't get the feeling any of them could have been our girl. No need to go into details, now. Just accept it. I mean, it's irrelevant."

"Hey, I'm not asking for details. Go on."

"So, I hung around the club for about half an hour after, for no good reason. Then I saw her. This brunette. *And* she saw me. She didn't panic; didn't do *anything* to give herself away."

"But you *knew*," Deidre said with sarcasm.

"I *knew* she was wary—even fearful of me. How can I explain? You still don't really know me."

Deidre closed her eyes. "Don't tell me you have more secrets to unload," she said, her voice tinged with irritation.

"No, it's not a secret. It's a sixth sense. One animal—a predator—crossing paths with another; one who's both the predator and the prey. Like a snake."

Her hands were all over the place now, helping make her point.

"They prey on others, but are the prey as well. She exuded . . . " Shara stopped, searching for the right word; the right word so Deidre could relate, but could find nothing except the truth.

"It'll sound foolish, but she exuded a smell, an odor of fear."

"You're right. I don't understand."

"When I was hunting the men I killed, I developed a keen sense of smell. Actually always had it, but I refined it, and was more aware of it then. Confidence, fear, jealousy, joy, hate—they all emanate different odors; something animals are acutely aware of."

She paused for a moment in thought. "It's not so hard to understand. A blind person can smell better and hear better than one with sight. He needs that sense to compensate for the one lost."

"*That*, I understand," Deidre said.

"Is it that great a leap then that someone could refine their sense of smell even if they hadn't lost one of their other senses? Remember, Dee, I was—still am—an animal of sorts. Accept the fact I sensed—*smelled*—her fear of me. Saw it, too, when we locked eyes."

"But you said she wasn't on your list."

"I confronted Jil. I was angry, because I didn't get that feeling with any of the other girls. It could have meant nothing. She could have been hiding something having nothing to do with the Nightwatcher—drug use or prostitution, both forbidden fruit at the club—but she was hiding *something*."

Deidre was listening intently now. "And?" she prodded.

"At first Jil told me she was working at the time of the subway shooting. And she wasn't a blonde, of course. But once I'd planted the seed, Jil cursed herself. She checked her calendar and remembered she had sent the girl home early that night."

"She didn't have to punch out?" Deidre asked.

Shara felt like a teacher explaining the ways of the world—*her world*. Frustrating, but that's why *she* had gone to the club instead of Deidre. It was *her world*.

"Strippers don't get paid by the hour. They don't get paid by management *at all*. They're independent contractors. *They* give management a piece of what they earn. So no punching in or out. This woman had been a friend of Rose Santucci, who had died the afternoon before the subway shooting. Jil sent her home early, but had forgotten. She wore a wig to hide some sort of scar. She had been a blonde, but changed wigs the past week. Again, nothing out of the ordinary."

"So why didn't you interview her?"

"By the time I'd finished with Jil, she had left. Jil gave me her name—her real name—and address. I was going to see her tomorrow. While I had a feeling about her, her fear of me didn't mean she was the Nightwatcher. Disturbing her at home after a long night shift would only antagonize her."

"And she was at the funeral?"

"Right next to a blonde. She was in a conservative black dress. *Without* the wig and clothes she had been seen wearing, no witness would recognize her as the Nightwatcher."

Deidre considered what she'd been told. "It makes sense. She disguised her voice so others wouldn't recognize her. Why not her appearance? The police have been looking for a blonde all along, and I bought into their thinking. What I fool I was."

"It didn't dawn on me either," Shara said, "so don't get all bent out of shape."

"So, *we* go to interview her tomorrow," Deidre said with enthusiasm. She purposely emphasized the *we*.

"No and no," Shara answered.

Deidre looked at her darkly.

"*We* don't go. *I* go and tonight."

"Why tonight, and why alone?" Deidre asked, ice in her voice.

"She's in trouble, Dee. She's been raped. She's killed and she hasn't contacted you. There's something wrong. I can feel it. *She's* always been in control. This time things didn't go as planned. She *should* have called you, if only for some other human contact."

"You're right. She wanted to talk. Calling after her latest kill would make sense."

"But something went wrong."

"Why don't we both go?"

"Please, don't take this wrong." Shara took a deep breath before going on. "This woman and I share more than just our profession. Something you've only *written* about. She's killed. I've killed. I was raped—mentally, but it's rape, nevertheless. If she's been raped, she's no longer the person she was. You and I going—it would be overkill. She'll withdraw. Only one of us can go. *Must go*. And now."

Deidre looked at Shara hard and long, then shook her head.

"You're both strippers. You're both killers. You've both been victimized. Even before tonight, I knew she had been victimized." She paused.

"You're right," she said finally, almost in a whisper. "Damn you to hell, but you're right. I'm out of my element. A goddamn fish out of water."

"You don't want to be where we've been, Dee," Shara said. "It's hell and then some."

Deidre smiled. "That's supposed to make me feel better?"

Shara shrugged. "It's the truth."

"All right, but I'm going to wait outside in the car."

Shara was going to protest, but thought better of it. "It may be a long night, or if I'm wrong she'll kick me out on my ass in five minutes."

"I've no better place to go. I'll wait, and I'll be there if you need me."

Chapter Forty-two

Shara rang the bell, then knocked, but nobody answered. She could have been taking a shower, Shara thought. Or maybe, she hadn't gone directly home after her last kill. Or, face it, another part of her chided, maybe she's *not* the Nightwatcher and had plans after work.

—She's in trouble, her mind screamed, *and in the house*.

Shara was going to pick the lock. Without thinking, though, she tried the doorknob and it was unlocked. Not a good sign, she thought. *Everyone* locks their doors in Philly. Her suspicions were confirmed by the three locks on the door. Lysette was here. Something *was* wrong.

She took a step and almost fell over something. To hell with caution, she thought. She turned on a light. High-heeled shoes, like the ones worn at the club, were on the floor. She had tripped over one. A black coat, black leather skirt and red blouse made a path to the stairs.

Lysette wanted to get out of them fast, and Shara knew why. She smelled blood. Picking up the coat by one finger, she saw blood stains; still wet. There was even more blood on the blouse. She didn't bother with the skirt, but bounded upstairs.

Lysette could be waiting up there with a gun; waiting to blow the intruder away, but Shara knew, intuitively, that wasn't the case.

The door at the top of the stairs was open, but totally dark. From within, she heard the sound of a shower. That would have made her pause, except for the clothes downstairs.

The room was devoid of light, not just dark, Shara realized as she tried, unsuccessfully, to get accustomed to the blackness. She felt around for a light switch. Even with the light, the room was surreal. Everything totally black. Even the light seemed to be

250

sucked in by the darkness, like a flashlight whose batteries were dying.

Shara made her way into the bathroom. Lysette was huddled in the shower. Shara touched the water. Icy cold, but Lysette wasn't shivering. Huddled . . .

—Catatonic.

. . . with cold water cascading over her. Shara tried to turn off the cold water, but the knob wouldn't budge. She turned the hot water knob and it gave. She gave an involuntarily shiver. The hot water had been on long enough to have depleted all the water in the heater. How long had Lysette been huddled there?

"Lysette, don't be frightened," she said and waited for a response.

There was none.

She touched the woman on the shoulder.

Still no reaction.

Shara thought of getting Deidre. There was definitely something wrong. Something within her, though, told her only she alone could get the woman out of her shell.

She took Lysette's hand and lifted her up.

Lysette didn't resist, but still did not respond to Shara's presence. She covered Lysette with a robe that hung on the bathroom door and led her to her bed.

Still nothing.

She sat her down on the bed. Her eyes were open, but vacant, like she had gone into hiding.

Again, panic welled within her. What if she had taken drugs? Should she call for an ambulance? She went into the bathroom, but found only Tylenol and the jar was almost full. She breathed a sigh of relief.

Not an overdose, she thought. Shock. She was in shock. Raped and in shock. Had killed the fucker, gotten back to her home, into the shower, and then been hit by what had happened to her.

She saw Lysette rubbing at her genitals; though her face was expressionless and her eyes still unfocused.

Strippers who took off all their clothes shaved their pubic hair, Shara knew, to give customers a better view. Lysette had rubbed herself raw; like a baby with a severe case of diaper rash. She was rubbing again, as if trying to rid herself of something. Rid herself of *him*, she knew. The monster who raped her. Even in death, he was tormenting her.

Shara moved Lysette's hands away. No resistance, but when she let go, the woman began rubbing herself again. Shara moved her hands away again, and this time held them lightly.

No resistance.

No response.

"Lysette, can you hear me?" She paused. "I'm Shara. We met at the club."

No response.

"Come on, girl," she said. "You've been through hell, but it's no time for hiding. If you don't snap out of it, I'll have to call for paramedics. Then your secret will be out. Work with me."

Still no response.

Fuck, she thought. Big lot of good she was doing. She considered slapping her, but couldn't bring herself to do it. The woman in front of her seemed so frail. A good slap and she'd break.

Shara saw a CD player. What the fuck, she thought. Music had always been her outlet when she was mad, upset or depressed. "Private Dancer" by Tina Turner. The *only* song she had played during the period she stalked and killed. Maybe Lysette had a song she'd respond to. With one hand, Shara turned on the CD and pushed play; holding Lysette's hands with the other. Whatever was on would have some meaning to this woman. A song by Mariah Carey, "Anytime You Need a Friend."

Did Lysette have a special bond with someone, a friend to share with? Shara didn't know, but waited for some response from Lysette.

Nothing.

Friendship? Never being alone? Love? All foreign to Shara, as she listened to the words. She watched Lysette for any response.

Eye movement. Almost imperceptible, but she'd seen it.

The chorus boomed—*everlasting friendship*.

Lysette's body began moving to the music, spasmodically at first, as if a tug of war was going on within. Face reality and all its horrors, Shara thought, or stay buried within her cocoon. She did nothing; just held Lysette's hands and let the music weave its magic.

Shara knew this wasn't a song Lysette played for herself, but shared with someone special. As the chorus was repeated, Lysette seemed to finally free herself from the fog that had engulfed her.

"Angel," Lysette whispered. "Angel, are you there?" Her eyes began to focus. Color returned to her face.

"I'm your friend, Lysette, and I'm by your side," Shara said.

Lysette looked at her, confusion clouding her face.

"You're not Angel."

"No, but I *am* a friend," Shara said.

Recognition dawned. "You're *no* friend."

Shara saw panic in her eyes. "Saw you at the club. Spying. Spying on *me*," Lysette said.

She began to shiver uncontrollably, and Shara hugged her, holding her tight, whispering, "I'm no spy." It was a lie, but the thing to say. "I'm a friend, someone you can trust." And Shara knew she meant it. Knew, too, there was another friend she might now have to deceive.

"You can let go, now," Lysette said.

She sounded calm. Shara looked at her. She *was* back.

"Had me worried there for a while. You were deep within yourself."

Lysette's face clouded over. "Yes, somebody calling me." She concentrated, as if to remember, then shrugged. "But I'm all right now."

"You want some coffee or tea?. Maybe a stiff drink?" Shara asked.

Lysette laughed. "Coffee and a cigarette. C'mon, let's go downstairs."

Walking down, Lysette saw her clothes scattered near the stairs and looked at Shara.

"You know, don't you? You know I'm the . . . " She hesitated.

"The Nightwatcher. Yeah, I know. Knew when I saw you at the club tonight."

"I'm not, you know. The Nightwatcher."

Shara looked at her with concern.

Lysette laughed. "*They've* named me the Nightwatcher, but I'm not."

"That's right," Shara said, playing along. "Just exercising your right to be where you want, when you want."

Lysette shrugged. "Not even that." She said no more.

Over coffee, having finished her second cigarette and having lit a third, Lysette began to relax. She had been gazing at Shara.

"Are you a cop?"

"Was," Shara said, "but I'm not here as a cop."

"Then what?"

"I'm helping Deidre Caffrey."

Lysette laughed. "Stupid of me. To call that show."

253

"Not so stupid," Shara said. "If you stayed in that shower all night, you may never have returned."

"Would that be such a terrible thing?" Lysette asked, but Shara sensed it was as much a question to herself as to her.

"So, what now?" Lysette asked. "You and Deidre take me in? Headlines for the both of you," she said bitterly.

"No headlines for me," Shara said instinctively, the words coming out in a rush. "No one's turning you in," she added more slowly.

"Caffrey agree to that?"

"She'll do what I say. I can be very convincing. Look, I sense you need someone to talk to. A friend. Why not dump on me?"

"So you can use what I say in your story? Look, I don't know you. Can't trust anyone . . . except. . . . " She paused.

"Angel?" Shara prompted.

Lysette looked at Shara sharply. "How do you know about Angel?"

"I don't. You called for her when I played the song. Is she a friend you can confide in?"

"Hardly," Lysette laughed. "She's a twelve . . . no, an *almost* thirteen-year-old. A friend, but still, just a child," she said and shrugged. "I'm not about to tell her I was raped. That he'll always be with me, haunting my nights. I won't try to explain the humiliation, the terror. Bad enough it could happen to her. I'm not about to make her live *my* torment."

"So confide in me."

Lysette shook her head no. "I appreciate what you did, but I need to be alone."

"You don't want to be alone. You shouldn't be alone right now. You want to confide in someone. *Must* confide in someone," Shara said.

"How do you know what I want? You a goddamn shrink, too?" she said derisively.

"I've been there. I had Deidre to talk to. I went seven years without a friend. I mean *no one*. Seven years with everything bottled up inside. I know what it did to me. You don't want to go through that."

Lysette stared at her, but said nothing.

"This may sound crazy, but I heard you shoot the dude in the subway."

"You weren't there," Lysette said.

"No, I was seventy miles away, and the shot awakened me."

Lysette looked at her oddly, but again remained silent.

"I heard it when you killed the next two men. Don't ask me how. I'm no psychic, but we've been drawn together. I knew who you were—at least your occupation—when you appeared on the radio show."

"How?"

"Jil trained me. Years ago. I was a dancer . . . a stripper. You used words Jil used with me. I came to help Deidre. I owed her. But I also think I came to help you, even though I didn't know it then."

Again, Lysette shook her head now. "Sorry. No sale. You're smooth . . ."

"Dammit, woman!" Shara interrupted. "I'm not the police. I don't need to hear your confession. Deidre's outside right now." She saw Lysette tense. "Don't worry. She's waiting for me. What I'm saying is, I could have brought her in when I saw the clothes. Could have called the cops. Use your head. Why am I here sipping coffee with you?"

"An exclusive interview."

"Cynical. And hardheaded." She pondered her next words for a moment. "You want convincing. You want something *you* can hold over *my* head? Fine. You remember the Vigilante? Someone who killed six rapists and child molesters last year?"

"Of course. You know who he is? You're going to tell me the Vigilante confided in you, and you kept his secret. That what you're going to tell me?" she said scornfully.

"I'm the Vigilante," Shara said, then went silent.

"Get out. *You* the Vigilante?"

"And only Deidre knows."

"Prove it," Lysette challenged. "Give me the sordid details."

Shara shook her head no. "I'll do better."

She unbuttoned her top, took it off and removed her bra. Lysette was staring at Shara's tattooed breasts.

"Six pair of eyes," Shara said. "One for each of the men I killed. After each kill, I got a tattoo. It was like a puzzle; a mosaic." She pointed to the most colorful one. "With the last kill, the mosaic was complete. I haven't killed since."

She put her clothes back on.

Lysette looked dumbstruck.

"There's more, isn't there?" Lysette said.

"Plenty. But I'm not here to bare my past," she said, then

laughed. "*Bare* it, I just did, I guess. You want to know if you can trust me. As I said, *only* Deidre knows my secret. I. Am. Your. Friend." She said each word slowly and forcefully. "Anything you tell me stays between us. I won't tell Deidre. Won't tell *anyone*."

Tears welled in Lysette's eyes, and she wiped them with a napkin.

"I don't want to die," she said finally. "It's over, you know. No more Nightwatcher. No more jaunts in parks and playgrounds at night. No more killing. Like you were drawn to me, I was drawn to that man who . . . who raped me tonight."

"Do you know why?"

"I'm not certain." She told Shara of the attack on her family when she was eleven. Told her she had never been able to recall the faces of the men who killed them; the one who beat her.

"Lately, though, I think I've begun remembering. Bits and pieces. He was an albino. I knew that only this afternoon."

"The man who attacked you, who you killed, was an albino. The same man?"

"I honestly don't know. But I've been drawn to him. That's what my late-night excursions have been about, I'm certain. Not exercising my rights. I've been searching for him. Like you, I can't explain how. I didn't know he would attack me tonight."

She was quiet for a moment, then shivered.

"I dreamed of my death the last several nights, of his attack. But not when. He surprised me. Took something *more* from me. He'd already taken so much, but he wanted more. *If* it was him. Now I've killed him. It's over."

"Is that your story, if you're caught?" Shara asked.

"I said I want to live. Not be committed to a mental hospital. *If* I'm caught, I'm the Nightwatcher, exercising my rights. Self-defense. They *were* self-defense," she emphasized.

"You want to disappear, though." It wasn't a question.

"Yes. I think I can."

Shara shook her head no. "I was closing in. Deidre's closing in, even without my help. The cops are closing in. You will be caught. Not with my help, though," she added.

"I don't want the notoriety. I don't want to be part of a media circus, probing in my past, into what I do now. I want it to go away."

"It won't. You're a symbol, whether you like it or not. Whether you wanted to become one or not. Look what's happening around you," Shara said.

"The people responded to you. You have to come to grips with the possibility you'll be caught, because the heat's on the police, and they won't give up."

"What would you have me do? Turn myself in?"

"It's an option. What's important is maintaining your dignity. If you come in, it's on your own terms. You set the agenda, not the police."

"I'm not ready," Lysette said, sounding tired. "I've been raped, Shara. I must come to terms with that first."

"All right. How about this. You lay low. Go on with your life, as best as you can. If the police close in, I'll let you know. *Then*, turn yourself into Deidre. Let her negotiate with the police."

"She'll do that?"

"You've made her your go-between. It would be natural."

They sat in comfortable silence for a while, Lysette smoking her fourth and fifth cigarettes, plying herself with another cup of coffee.

Shara just sat. She was good at waiting. She and Lysette were alike, yet very different. Both had been victimized, Shara thought, when young. Both had responded to some triggering mechanism that sent them on a spree of violence.

Lysette, though, was not street smart like she was. Shara had lied and deceived all her life. Lysette, on the other hand, had coped with her tragedy. She bore scars, for sure, but she was as normal— more so—than probably half the population. Lysette was good people, and there were too few of them around.

Shara would help protect her.

Lysette broke the silence. "Thank you for saving my life, or at least my sanity, tonight. And for being a friend. *Your* secret's safe with me."

She paused, seemingly not sure how to say what she wanted to next.

"Can I call you? To just talk. I'm only now realizing how terribly lonely and isolated I've become."

"I'd like that," Shara said. "There's things I need to get off my chest, too. Deidre and I have a weird relationship. I want to open up to her, but I spent a lot of time deceiving her. I get the feeling she has to weigh everything I say to decide what's true. And I can't say I blame her."

Lysette lit yet another cigarette. Later, Shara thought, she'd have to wean her off; if only a bit.

"We may get over that hurdle," Shara went on. "Then again, I'm not going to be completely straight with her now. It's never going to be easy with Deidre and I. So, yeah, I'd like the two of us to chat. I'll be at the club; probably interview you, like I told Jil. And you can reach me at Deidre's, when I'm not at the club. That's where I'm staying for the moment."

Shara got up to leave. "A piece of advice from someone who wished it had been offered to her: If you can't get over the attack tonight, see a rape counsellor. You can talk to me, but I'm no expert. Don't let him eat away at you. Take it from one who knows."

She left, somehow more at peace with herself than she'd been in a long time.

Chapter Forty-three

Deidre was dozing when Shara got to the car. Shara watched her for a few seconds before getting in. She didn't particularly like herself at that moment. The problem with life, she thought, was there was too much gray. She owed Deidre. She needed Deidre. The woman could have turned her in. Yet, she felt closer to Lysette. Lysette needed her. To protect Lysette, she would have to deceive Deidre. *Again.* Life sucks, she thought.

Deidre awoke with a start when Shara got in.

"At least someone got some sleep," Shara said with a tired smile.

Deidre looked at her watch. "Jesus, it's four-thirty. It's been over three hours. So, is she the one?"

"Yes, but there's no proof," Shara said. Real good of you, Shara, she thought to herself. Start right out with a lie.

"What's that supposed to mean?"

"She admitted she was the Nightwatcher, but won't come in, and there's no hard proof to go to the police with."

"Briggs isn't looking for hard proof from us. We tell him what we know and *he* digs up evidence."

"You didn't ask me about her," Shara said evasively. "You *have* changed. You're one tough lady, now. Did I do that to you? Rob you of your compassion? I mean, this woman was raped."

"And she's also killed," Deidre said.

"In self-defense."

"And will do so again," Deidre countered, "Unless we help stop her."

"No," Shara said. "I'm going to dog her. Told her as much."

"You want me to ignore what I know?" Deidre asked, incredulously. "Go back on my word to Briggs?"

"No. I want the police to prove it's her. I want to alert her *before*

259

she's arrested. I want her to turn herself in to you. This way she can come in with dignity, and you break the story."

"Are you hiding something?"

"I told you about the hunt, Dee. The high the hunt provides. Well, the hunt's over, and I'm feeling down . . . and tired." Shara paused, deep in thought. "She's not like me, Dee. Yes, she set herself up, but each time *she* was attacked. She is not your common criminal."

"How are the police to locate her?"

"With your help," Shara said with a smile. "They'll find out soon enough, but call Briggs and plant the seed she's not a blonde. She wears a wig. I'm sure they found hair fibers in the bag her attacker used, and with the rape, there will be pubic hairs. Then maybe he'll look at those pictures again."

"And how do I tell him I stumbled on this?"

"She disguised her voice, right? To assure no one recognized her. Well, why not the hair color? Hair style? Hair length? Tell him it's just a hunch, but let him play with it."

"And with that he'll catch her?"

"That's not what's important. We have to convince Lysette the police are closing in. I told her if I could catch her, the police couldn't be far behind. She's not ready to come in. She just needs a bit of a push, though."

Deidre looked at her closely.

"You're not playing me *again*, are you? It would destroy anything we had."

"It's you I owe, Dee. Trust me on this. You'll come out smelling like a rose."

"Trust you? Trust *you*. It's like being in bed with a black widow."

Shara smiled. "You have toughened. This time, though, I'm not going to bite you in the ass. Call Briggs. Maybe you'll get lucky and wake him up just as he's going to bed." With that she laughed, laid back and closed her eyes.

Deidre smiled. "Like when you called me." She shook her head. "You can be a bitch."

If you only knew the half of it, Shara thought, but with the hunt over, she *was* tired. As Deidre called Briggs on her car phone, she fell asleep.

Chapter Forty-four

Lysette sat in the kitchen long after Shara left. She recalled the shower. Recalled the albino's presence, though she knew it had been in her mind. Knew, too, she had gone deep within herself. *Almost* to the attic. If Shara hadn't been there, she would have gone in. As it was, she vaguely recalled a voice. . . .

—*Stay with me.*

Was it Laura? The voice from her childhood. It wasn't Cassandra. Cassandra was a part of her. Or was it just her mind playing games?

Shara had brought her back before she had answered the summons. The song—hers and Angel's—had brought her back. She had to see Angel. She looked at her watch. Four-forty-five. Today. She had to get some sleep, though. But could she sleep without thinking of the albino?

She went to her room, picking up the clothes on the floor as she went. She would burn them at the beach. And the gun? Empty. She *had* needed both bullets. She didn't need the gun any longer. She'd give it to the ocean. Be done with it and hope the police *didn't* close in.

The blackness of her room was suddenly intimidating. The room which had once shielded her *from* the albino, now seemed to hide the creature from her. He could be here. Anywhere.

—He's dead, Cassandra told her.

Then why do I see him? Sense him? Smell him? *Everywhere.*

She pulled the black shade off the window. She'd redecorate the room. No more black. Sand. The colors of the beach. She felt safe at the beach. It would help her feel safe at home.

She set her mental alarm for eight. She didn't want to hear the news, read the papers or listen to the talk shows. They would be talking about the Nightwatcher. A symbol of the fight against crime. Not flesh and bones and emotions. They wouldn't be talking about her.

She fell asleep.

When she opened her eyes, she was staring into the albino's face. Part of his head was shot off, and blood was streaming down his face. Yet, he was smiling.

"Hello, baby. Here to finish what I started."

He had only one eye, but she saw it glide down and stop at her naked breasts, then dip lower to her genitals.

He wore the same clothes from the night before. His erect penis was sticking out of his unzipped jeans. His smiled turned to a leer.

"I'll always be with you, sweet thing."

" . . . always be with you . . . "

" . . . always . . . "

She screamed, rolled off the bed, and reached for the gun she had dropped on the floor. Fired once.

Blank.

Again.

Blank.

And again.

Blank.

She scampered to the corner, to her nest, and watched him on her bed. Like wax, he began to melt, his body seeping into the silk of her sheets. A fetid odor of death and decay permeated the room.

She lay in the corner, awake, her eyes on the bed. Watched and waited.

" . . . always be with you . . . "

" . . . always . . . "

She heard the words, and knew she wouldn't sleep.

Chapter Forty-five

The weather had turned. The beach seemed nowhere as inviting as before. Unable to sleep, Lysette had left the city just after seven. A dense fog made the going slow. She couldn't find music to fit her mood, or alter it for that matter. She felt so out of sync; almost spastic, there was no rhythm to her movements.

Still in shock, she thought to herself. Still wondering when she'd see the albino again. If he appeared next to her now, she knew she'd lose control of the car, crash and burn. She wondered why the thought didn't terrify her; why it was almost comforting.

At the beach, a mist hung in the air. The waves seemed to crash like thunder. Uninviting. *Stay away*, they seemed to echo. Enter at your own peril. She wouldn't let Angel venture in today, even if she wanted. The ocean wanted a sacrifice. Wanted Angel.

Lysette began her sculpture close to the shore. Whatever she created, she wanted it swallowed by the sea sooner rather than later.

Would it be the albino? The attack on her as a child or the night before? As always, her hands moved with a will of their own. She didn't go into any trance, but was nevertheless unaware of the nature of her sculpture until it was completed.

Lying on the ground was a female figure; her clothes ripped and tattered, her hands above her head as if held in place by some other unseen figure. Her face was contorted in terror; a silent scream was on her lips.

A woman being raped. She thought it was her, from the night before, but then had to stifle a scream of her own.

—*Angel*.

Had something happened to Angel? *Would* something happen to Angel?

She became aware of a presence behind her. She turned and saw

Angel staring at the figure. She wasn't naked. She wore a long coat that came to her knees. Her left eye was swollen. There was dried blood at the corner of her mouth. She looked even older than the day before. Older because of something that had happened to her. Older because . . .

"I was raped last night," Angel said, without emotion. "That's me," she said, pointing at the sculpture.

Lysette tried to hug her, but Angel moved away.

"Have you told anyone?" Lysette asked.

Angel shook her head no.

"What happened?"

"I don't want to talk about it." Again her voice was flat; lifeless.

"You must," Lysette said. "It will fester and spread like a cancer if you keep it bottled inside."

"You wouldn't understand," she said, staring at herself sculpted in the sand.

"Yes I will. I was raped last night, too. By the man in my sculpture. I know how you feel. I came here to flee him. But I can't. He's here. He's *everywhere*."

"Yes, he's here," Angel said. "He wants more." She took her gun out of her coat pocket. "I was going to end it. Go into the ocean. Shoot myself, and give myself to the sea."

"That's not the answer," Lysette said, panic rising within her. "Life's shitty. But it's precious, too. With all its horrors. *You* saved me last night."

Angel gave her a quizzical look.

"Our song. 'Anytime You Need a Friend.' I'd gone into myself, after the rape. Deep within myself. Almost didn't come out. The song. Knowing you were there with me, though you were nowhere near, brought me back."

"It was a mistake," Angel said. "Within yourself, no one could hurt you."

Lysette took Angel in her arms. At first she resisted, but finally gave in. She began to sob and held on to Lysette tightly.

"I can't keep him away from me," the youth said. "He's long gone, but still by my side."

"I know," Lysette answered. "Me, too. I killed the man who raped me, but he returned. A part of him is in me. I don't know if I can ever escape him. But we must go on. We can't let him win. We mustn't let him destroy us. He'd be raping our soul, not just our bodies."

They held on to one another for a good while. Finally, Angel broke free. The waves were licking at the sand sculpture—at her.

"I want to see her destroyed," Angel said. "Let the sea have *her*, and maybe I can find peace."

They both sat down, each with their own thoughts, and watched the ocean claim the child of sand. Soon the figure was gone. Some color had returned to Angel's face.

"Remember the Nightwatcher?" Lysette said.

Angel nodded yes.

"She's no more." Lysette got up, took the empty gun from her pocket and threw it into the sea. "She never was. A Nightwatcher, I mean. We both have to come to terms with what happened to us."

Angel was shaking her head no, and began to speak, but Lysette put a finger to the child's mouth.

"Not now, I know. But when you're ready, I will be here for you. We both need to talk it out. Exorcise our demons. But only when you're ready. Okay?"

Angel smiled weakly. "Thanks for not pushing. Probing. Making me relive it. I'm *not* ready. Not yet. One day, though. Just you and me."

Lysette knew she had to go. Had to get to work. Then later, might have to face the albino again. She'd deal with him. For herself. For Angel. She had to be strong.

—For herself.

—For Angel.

"You going to be all right?" Lysette asked.

"All right? No. Better." She paused. "Better. Yes."

"One day at a time," Lysette said. "It won't go away. It's a part of you. But you've got to learn to live with it. And, I'll be there to help when you feel it's time."

They hugged again; then Lysette got into her car. She couldn't help Angel anymore, now. There was someone who could help her, though. She would tell Shara about her recurring visions of the albino. "Talk it out," she had told Angel. She was ready to share with Shara, just as she hoped Angel would soon be willing to open up to her.

Chapter Forty-six

Briggs could feel the momentum propelling him at the dizzyin
pace of a roller coaster. Having reached the apex of its journey, th
rush downward was unimpeded. There had been bumps along th
way; he had been sidetracked; despair had settled in at times. Bu
all was forgotten with the death of Keith Lowell.

The crowd that had continued to grow through the early-morn
ing investigation had been suffocating. The people with their can
dles and lighters had watched in near total silence, which ha
unsettled him more than anything. As dawn approached, and th
police prepared to leave, the crowd began to disperse as one, of i
own accord. There had been no announcement. It was just time
Eerie could hardly describe it, Briggs thought.

The Nightwatcher had become careless or sloppy or overconfi
dent; possibly all three. It had almost literally led to her demise
While she had escaped, the police had a crime scene teeming wit
evidence that would certainly lead to her arrest.

The bag that had covered the woman's head had yielded numer
ous strands of blonde hair, and there was skin under Lowell's nails
A witness, not located until after eight in the morning, saw
woman fitting the Nightwatcher's description flee up towar
Chestnut Street and drive away in a red car.

He hadn't gotten the license number, but he was pretty sure i
was a Dodge Charger.

"Got one myself. Makes a hell of a racket, just like the one th
lady drove, but you can't beat it in the winter."

At five AM, Deidre had called and told him her theory that th
Nightwatcher was no blonde.

"This a stab in the dark, Dee, or are you holding somethin

266

ack?" He couldn't help himself. She just naturally aroused his uspicions, with her little tidbits. Just a bit, but not quite enough.

"I'm sorry you can't trust me, Briggs. Call it intuition, but like I aid, if she disguised her voice, why not her appearance? Run with t or forget it. Your call."

"I remember similar words from you before, and look where it got me."

Deidre said nothing.

"And you haven't heard from her?"

"No."

"Why not?"

"I haven't the foggiest," she said with irritation.

"I mean," Briggs amended, "why don't you think she called?"

"She was raped," Deidre said. "Calling me may not be her top priority at the moment."

"Point taken. She may still call, though. You *will* let me know if he does."

"You've got a way with people, you know that? Inspires confidence and trust."

"I'm an asshole, okay. I admit it, at least when it comes to you. You will call me, though."

"Scout's honor," she said, and hung up.

Briggs was angry with himself when he hung up the phone. Sure, he harbored suspicions about the reporter, but why alienate her? To hell with your bruised ego, he chided himself.

He called her back and apologized. Hung up the phone and hated himself for what he'd been forced to do. Apologize to her, he thought. She owes me big time. And she knows it.

He called forensics, and told them to let him know if the blonde hair was from a wig.

"And look carefully for pubic hairs. I can't believe there were none."

Half an hour later, Jack Tierney of forensics called back.

"I've got good news and good news," he said, and waited for Briggs' response.

Tierney was an irritating character. Thorough at his job, at five feet one, he had a Napoleon complex. He was brilliant, according to him, the rest of the department, dolts. He was a sanctimonious son of a bitch who loved making others feel inferior. Piss him off, and he'd be cooperative to a fault; telling you his findings in terms men with doctorates in medicine would find difficult to follow. Briggs checked his anger and kissed the man's ass. . . .

—A lot of ass kissing, for so early in the morning, he thought. First Deidre and now Tierney.

"That was quick, Jack. You know I appreciate it."

There was a pause. Briggs could sense Tierney's disappointment.

"The blonde hair was from a wig," he finally said, without driving Briggs crazy with details. And we *did* find pubic hairs."

Briggs could hear the triumph in the man's voice.

"She shaved." He paused, and again Briggs could almost hear the man waiting for Briggs to snap at him.

Briggs said nothing.

"Shaved her pubic region," he finally went on. "We recovered few small hairs. The woman's natural hair color is black."

Briggs wanted to tell the man *he'd* planted the seed. Would Tierney have been so meticulous without Briggs' call? He doubted it, but swallowed his pride, lavished praise on the man, and rang off.

An hour later, at nine, he got a call from the 30th Street Station. It was from a uniform he had sent to intercept Isiah Hayes as soon as he arrived. Briggs had decided he wouldn't even let the man go home.

"We have your witness, but he's no happy camper. Says he'd like to shave, shower and shit and come down in the afternoon."

"Tell him he can shit at the station," Briggs answered. "Bring him."

The other man laughed. "Shit at the station. I like that." He rung off.

Briggs let Isiah Hayes sit in an interrogation room for forty-five minutes. This time he was going to do it right. Play the man, not be played. He had to scare the man. Make him feel the Nightwatcher and others were in danger. The man knew something. Something important. It could break the case wide open. He felt it in his bones.

"How ya doing, Mr. Hayes?" Briggs asked, entering, as if the wait had been five minutes, not forty-five.

Hayes smiled and shook his head. "You're playing hardball now, Detective. Pulling me right off the train. Making me wait." He shrugged. "I'm an old man, Detective. I got nowhere to go. Ain't in no rush at all."

"You aware what's been going on since you've been out of town?"

"I read the papers." He picked up the *Daily News* on the other

se bare table in front of him. "This just happened to be here," he
id with a smile. " 'Bout time, I say, people started fighting back.
l account of that little lady."

"That little lady, Zeke, got raped last night. Something that
sn't hit the papers yet. How do you feel about that?"

He saw Hayes was taken aback, just as Briggs had planned.

"Saved your black ass, and because of *you*, she's been raped," he
id, his voice rising. "Nothing worse for a woman than to be
ped, Zeke."

"Because of me?"

"Because of something *you* know *you* haven't told me. She's sit-
g at home now, alone, reliving some creep jabbing his cock into
r. You think she feels safe now?"

Hayes looked down.

"And what next, Zeke? She goes out again, and maybe gets her-
lf killed. Mind preoccupied with being raped. No longer in con-
l. And dies. Because of *you*," he yelled, slamming his palm on
e table. "When are you going to take some responsibility and do
e right thing? When are you going to help her, like she helped
u? Because I'll tell you, Zeke, she's in a world of hurt now.
ight get careless. Then get killed."

"I don't know nothing," he said, but he couldn't look at Briggs.

Good, Briggs thought. Time now to let him think some. He
uched his left ear, a sign for Rios to interrupt. She came in on cue.

"Sorry, Detective, but there's a call for you," she said.

"Excuse me, Zeke," and without another word he left.

Outside he and Rios kept an eye on the old man.

"Any progress?" Nina asked.

"I shook him up. I haven't played my full hand yet. We'll let him
 and stew some, then I'll go after him again."

Twenty minutes later he reentered the room. Briggs offered no
nall talk, and there was no banter from Hayes. Briggs put a
onde wig on the table.

"Yeah, Zeke, we know she wore a wig. You knew, too, didn't
u?"

The old man said nothing.

Briggs put the wig on and stood over Hayes.

"Look at me, Zeke."

The old man looked up. For the first time he looked his age.

"Just like in the subway car, wasn't it? You sitting down and she
anding over you. You didn't tell me she wore a wig."

"Couldn't see," he said, sullenly. "Blood in my eyes. Woozy was woozy."

"Bullshit, Zeke. You saw something else, didn't you? I saw it your eyes the last time."

Hayes averted his eyes now.

Briggs produced an envelope.

"You're not protecting her, Zeke. Here's the man who rap her." One by one he dropped photos on the desk. "Look at the Zeke."

There was the head shot. Gruesome, but not the one Brig knew would shake the old man. Then some wide angle shots. nally closeups. A photo of Keith Lowell's penis sticking out of unzipped pants. And another, and another; each an enlargeme of the last. Enlargements Briggs had the lab make solely for t interrogation.

"Raped her, Zeke. With *that*, he said in disgust. "Imagine h she felt? How she feels now? There was no one to help her. Su she killed him, but not *before* he stuck that in her. She's going die, Zeke." He paused. "Unless you help. Help her, Zeke, befor have to bring you in to identify *her* body."

"What'll happen to her? You know. If she's caught?"

Briggs took off the wig and sat down for the first time. The t men locked eyes. "Want the truth?" he said conspiratorially.

The old man nodded his head yes.

"Just between the two of us—nothing. Not a goddamn thi I'd bet the house on it. She'll be arrested, sure. But she'll get help she needs. You don't get raped and come out sane withe help, Zeke. Then she'll go to trial. And you know what? We b know no jury will find this woman guilty."

"Then why are you after her? Why not let her be?"

"Because she's going to get herself killed, Zeke, and in part i be on your head."

He knew he had the old man. He wasn't particularly prou Felt no triumph in beating him down. But he needed what the c man had.

"Right here," Hayes said, touching the left side of his forehe "Looked like an egg been cracked. Not a scar. Looked like son one took a hammer and knocked her upside the head a few tim Her hair, the wig, covered it up pretty good, but I seen it. Ha scar, too, over her left eye." Then he was silent.

"You did the right thing, Zeke," Briggs said.

The old man looked at him, with tears in his eyes. "Ratting on the woman that saved my life. That's doing the right thing?"

"Saving her life," Briggs answered. "That's doing the right thing."

When Briggs came out of the interrogation room ten minutes later, Rios congratulated him.

"You did good."

"Then why do I feel like such a shit?" he asked.

"Because you're a decent guy," she answered without hesitation. He looked at her sharply.

"Don't worry." She smiled. "No one will hear it from me. Anyone asks, you cracked the guy and enjoyed every minute of it."

"Don't be making fun of me, Nina," he said, but he was smiling.

Now he decided to put Deidre to the test; see if she could *really* get in the Nightwatcher's head. With all the new information he had, Deidre could smoke her out. Or, someone would recognize her and come forward.

After his call to Deidre, Briggs went outside. He was feeling slightly claustrophobic in the crowded squadroom. Normally, he didn't mind the lack of privacy; today he felt all eyes on him, and he didn't like it one bit. He *knew* his colleagues weren't staring at him. They *had*, just after the attack on Alexis. He knew it wasn't curiosity, but concern. He'd withdrawn. Their eyes were on him a long time, gauging his mood, his frame of mind. He had always been part of the squadroom banter; one of the guys. Hadn't wanted it any other way. Until Alexis had been hurt. When he'd felt powerless. Even responsible. It was irrational, but he hadn't been completely sane.

He now knew how difficult it must have been working with—actually *around*—him. You had to watch your tongue; anything could set him off. Even when some of the guys would ask about his daughter, he would snap at them.

—Were they blaming him? The thought went through his mind more than once.

At some point they had given up, all except Morales. It was up to him to make the next move. Show he was again one of them. Nina had broken through his shell. Morales made him look at himself. He *hadn't* been responsible for what had happened to Alexis. Sure, he could have given in and moved to the suburbs. He'd take responsibility for that. But there were animals in the suburbs, too. It *could* have happened anywhere, and he would not have been

able to do a thing about it. He had to accept that. Alexis was grow
ing up. Neither he nor her mother could watch over her twenty
four hours a day. Unless he had been with her, which was absur
he couldn't have prevented the attack.

As far as not being able to catch her attacker, that wasn't h
fault either. There was precious little to go on. He needed to g
after the animal who had hurt her. But there were limitations o
what he could do.

So, it was time to give up the search; time to allow his co
leagues—his *friends*—back into his life.

Soon, he thought; when he'd wrapped up this case. For the m
ment, he needed some privacy. He wanted to savor the satisfactio
of knowing his gut feeling had been on target; Isiah Hayes *had* ha
something important he had hidden. He wanted to replay the inte
rogation. *This time* he had done good. Had been the cop he kne
he was. But there was less satisfaction in breaking the old ma
than a good-for-nothing perp.

He had to come to grips with that, too. Outside he could escaj
their stares. Good cops, he sometimes thought they could read h
mind, as he sometimes could theirs. He didn't want anyone
know how bad he felt about breaking the old man.

There was a chill in the air. He breathed it in deeply.

It wouldn't be long now, he thought. Then he remembered wh
he had told Hayes; no jury would convict the woman. It had bee
the truth. It was a bit depressing in a way. All the work. All th
manpower. And for what? Nothing. She'd get off.

Didn't matter, he tried to convince himself. His job was to fir
her, and give the DA the evidence needed to build a case. It was u
to the DA to convict. Still, conviction was a pipedream.

He saw Rios come out the front door with another man, ar
point toward him. She went back inside. The man approache
Briggs recognized him as he got close. Dan Mathias; workir
rape. Mathias was in his late twenties. Tall, lean, dark-skinned ar
impeccably dressed. A young cop on the rise.

"How's it going, Briggs? Hear you're closing in on the Nigh
watcher."

Briggs shrugged. "We're making progress, Dan. You're not he
to socialize, though, are you?"

Mathias smiled. "Right to business, huh? All right, then. Th
man your Nightwatcher killed last night. Keith Lowell. He's a se
ial rapist I've been after."

"You know where to find him," Briggs said. "You caught a break."

"The two playgrounds your woman struck," Mathias said, ignoring Briggs' comment. "The week before she was in each playground, Lowell raped a teenager at each one. I don't believe in coincidences, do you?"

Briggs suddenly looked interested. "No, I don't. What are you getting at?"

"Two things. I don't know what to make of the first. Why was your Nightwatcher drawn to my rapist last night? The other rapes were reported in the papers. For some reason, your Nightwatcher could have innocently chosen those locations to make her statement. But, he hadn't attacked anyone at this playground. It makes no sense to me, but I thought it only right to tell you."

Briggs smiled. "You mean lay your puzzle on me."

Mathias shrugged. "Not my puzzle anymore. Like you said, I know where to find him, and he ain't going noplace, nor telling no one why he did what he did."

"And the second thing?"

Mathias shifted, and looked uncomfortable, Briggs thought. "It's not my case, but I took an interest in your daughter's . . . attack. Professional courtesy."

Briggs stiffened.

"We know Lowell committed four rapes; all in playgrounds. Your daughter doesn't fit the pattern. But the method of the attack was similar. All the victims were beaten in the head with a rock. Officially, she's not part of my investigation. Understand?"

"But unofficially?"

"I listed her as number five. His first, actually. At least that I know of. The Nightwatcher was number six. The skin found under your daughter's nails matches Lowell's. Aside from the Nightwatcher, she was the only one to get a piece of the bastard. I know it's little consolation, but she put up one hell of a struggle. It may be why he beat her so much more severely than the others. And, after your daughter, he began using a bag so he couldn't be identified. The other attacks were carefully planned. I get the feeling that with your daughter it was impulse. He had a craving. Saw your daughter alone . . . " He stopped, as if uncomfortable going into details with the father of a victim.

"The woman I'm after killed the scum that attacked my daughter?" Briggs said incredulously.

273

"Yeah. Ain't that a bitch." He paused a moment, then went on. "Look, I'm not listing your daughter as one of his victims. The press will have a field day when word gets out the Nightwatcher killed this fucker. I don't think you want them camping outside your house waiting for you or your wife's reaction. Anyway, I've dealt with enough parents of rape victims to know how this must have been preying on your mind. Closure and all that shit. Must have been hell on you." He stopped, seeming to know he had said enough.

Briggs nodded. "I owe you one, Dan." He wiped a tear that had formed at his eye. "What can I say? Thanks doesn't begin to express my gratitude."

"Enough said. I know where you're coming from."

The two men shook hands and Mathias headed back into the building.

It's over, Briggs thought. He wanted to call Vivian with the news, but it wasn't a message you deliver over the phone. He looked at his watch. Almost noon. Morales would let him go home for lunch.

A second thought intruded, one he didn't want to consider. The woman he was after had killed the man who had attacked his daughter. Been raped by the bastard herself. He knew how relieved his wife would feel. The news might even help his daughter. He didn't know how much Alexis understood, how serious the brain damage was. But he was sure a part of her feared her attacker might return. It could only help her recovery.

Now he was dead. Killed by the woman he hunted. A woman he now owed. He couldn't deny it complicated matters. Hunting someone he owed. Somehow it didn't seem right. Suddenly he knew how Isiah Hayes felt.

He remembered Mathias' words: "Ain't that a bitch." Damn right, Briggs thought.

Chapter Forty-seven

Shara watched Lysette dance listlessly for forty-five minutes. She should have taken the night off, Shara thought, but understood that might arouse suspicion.

She had come to work, but Shara could imagine Lysette dancing, thinking each customer a potential rapist.

Shara had told Jil she wanted to interview the woman. Deidre had gotten a call earlier from Briggs. Her indentation and scar. Lysette would be shocked how close they were. She'd have to make a decision soon. Tonight, Shara thought. As one song wound down and another took its place, Shara made her way over to Lysette.

"We've gotta talk. Jil thinks it's my interview with you."

Without a word, Lysette followed Shara. There were a number of small offices on the second floor, where the blare of the music, though still present, was muted.

"How you holding up?" Shara asked.

Lysette averted her eyes, holding back tears.

"Sorry to say, it's not going to get easier," Shara said.

Lysette recovered. "It's been that kind of day. You might as well add to it."

Shara didn't bother to probe. Lysette would tell her when she was ready.

"The police know about your scar and indentation on your forehead."

Lysette closed her eyes. "How?" she said, her voice filled with suspicion.

"The old man you saved in the subway. The detective in charge of the case finally broke him." She paused. "There's more."

Lysette said nothing, just shook her head, so Shara went on.

"They know the blonde hair is a wig from the fibers at the scene.

Know you drove a red Charger, from a witness. Deidre's supposed to write the story for tomorrow's paper. Jil will know immediately it's you. Others will too, I imagine."

Lysette let out a hollow laugh. "Thought I had a few days to sort things out. You know, get my affairs in order."

Now Shara was silent.

"What do you suggest?" Lysette said after a moment.

"You can ride it out; hope for the impossible until the cops come knocking. You could wait until Deidre's story and turn yourself in. Or . . . " Shara paused. "There's the preemptive strike."

"Preemptive strike?"

"Call Deidre *now*. Tell her you meant to call her after the attack last night, but you'd been raped. You can fill in the blanks. Tell her we've spoken, and you want for her to arrange your surrender. You go in quietly without any media frenzy. Deidre gets her exclusive. You get to go in on your own terms."

Lysette seemed to ignore her. "I've seen him. The albino. Three times, now. The shower before you came. In my bed after you'd left, and here at the club."

She lit a cigarette, then continued.

"I was Couch Dancing with one of my regulars. Turned my back and bent down to give him a good view, looked between my legs, and there he was. Sitting there leering where my customer had been. His face was a bloody mess. One eye gone. He reached for my . . . my genitals."

She paused and shivered.

"Then his hands turned to wax and were gone. His face began dripping, like wax in a fire. Then I was staring at the customer again. Only, there was his smell. Like in my bed last night. His smell. And death. And decay. And *his* smell."

Again, she paused, wiped her eyes and composed herself.

"These are my conditions. I want to see him. The albino. Want to see him *dead* on a slab. I want a rape counsellor present; someone I can see after the police question me. I want a lawyer. Any lawyer. I don't plan on being coy with the cops, but I'm no fool. I want Deidre present so I can tell my story. I *won't* be talking to reporters except through Deidre."

Shara shook her head in agreement, and went to Jil's office to use her phone. Fifteen minutes later, Lysette had her deal. She would go to Deidre, answer the reporter's questions and then, with Deidre, turn herself in to the police.

Deidre would contact a lawyer while they drove to the paper. Her attorney would hear what Lysette told Deidre and provide counsel. After questioning, she would get to see the albino and then a rape counsellor. There would be no public spectacle.

Lysette told Jil she was the Nightwatcher before they left.

"I owe it to her," she had told Shara. "Once it gets out I work here, the press will flock here like flies on shit. Jil shouldn't be taken by surprise. She's done right by me."

Lysette smiled. "I expect some of my adoring public to abandon me once it's known I'm a stripper. Fuck 'em. But, I don't want Jil caught in the crossfire unaware."

They drove to the *Inquirer* building in silence. A few blocks away, Lysette finally spoke.

"Did you really mean what you said? We could talk. Or, have you completed your job?" She shook her head. "I'm sorry, that didn't come out right. It's just—"

"You've got to think about yourself now, girl," Shara said. "Not about hurting others' feelings. I'm here whenever you need me. I wasn't playing you. We'll talk. Whenever you're ready."

Lysette smiled. "Deidre gets her story. The police collar the Nightwatcher. What do you get?"

Shara considered the question. She didn't want to be flip. "Maybe a new start. Locating you has been a blast. Not *you* personally. Finding the Nightwatcher. It's something I've been bred for. Or acquired," she said with a shrug.

"Anyway, I'm good. And you can't believe the rush of the hunt. I know I can't go back to my old existence. So, yeah, maybe you've given me a new lease on life."

"We *do* have to talk," Lysette said. "You talk in riddles. Not intentionally," she added quickly. "I want to know *everything*. And I want to tell you everything."

"Like I said," Shara answered. "Just say the word."

Chapter Forty-eight

Lysette was oddly detached the next few days, through the blur of activity that surrounded her. Closure had come with the killing of the albino. Yet she had become some sort of bigger-than-life symbol, and had to go through the motions with the police, the media, fans and critics.

She felt like the two-headed woman at a freak show. Everyone wanted a peek. And everyone wanted a piece of her.

From the minute she stepped into a private office provided by Deidre's editor, she felt the Cassandra in her emerge; was glad for her presence. *She* would guide her through the minefield that loomed. With the Cassandra that was her leading the way, Lysette exuded self-confidence, even if she didn't feel it. She was, after all, an entertainer, and this was the biggest show of her life.

Deidre introduced her to Hillary Bankhead, a take-charge criminal attorney Deidre's editor knew. Matronly and conservative in appearance, the forty-nine-year-old woman dispensed advice in a tone that brokered, in no uncertain terms, her wisdom was gospel.

The Cassandra in Lysette wanted to punch her lights out. Lysette put the kibosh on that.

Shara was also present, but said nothing.

—*A fly on the wall*, Lysette thought to herself.

Lysette told her story. The subway incident, the report on the news that had so irritated her; how women had to dress and act in a particular way so as not to be victimized.

Each time she went out, she recounted, it was to exercise her rights as a citizen. She protected herself *only* when attacked. Her being raped had convinced her it was only a matter of time before she'd end up a statistic, herself. Much as she desired her privacy, she had been thrust into the public eye. But her actions, she em-

278

phasized, were simply her own personal response to what the city had become. She was leading no movement; had no agenda.

She had committed no crime and was voluntarily going public to answer police inquiries. She fully expected to be exonerated, and wished only to get this over with and be left alone.

"Do you condemn or condone the actions of the Coalition?" Deidre asked, when she had concluded.

"No offense, Miss Caffrey, but I'm not here to be interviewed. You've got your exclusive. You'll hear more details, I'm sure, when the police question me." She looked at the lawyer, then continued.

"Miss Bankhead, I'm confident, will advise me just what questions from the police I'm obligated to answer."

She looked at the lawyer. "What will I be charged with? Just what have I done?"

The lawyer cleared her throat, then spoke in a condescending fashion; a teacher lecturing a recalcitrant student.

"It's up to the DA—the District Attorney," she began. "But I assume the charge will be murder generally."

"Which is?" Lysette cut in purposely to interrupt the woman's train of thought.

—*Like to punch her lights out*, the Cassandra in her said.

"In Pennsylvania, Miss Ormandy, murder generally means the jury can choose from a whole host of charges from murder one—premeditated—to third degree to manslaughter. There are any number of defenses we can put up: diminished capacity, for example."

"How about self-defense?" Lysette asked.

"That of course is an option . . . "

"Not one you would recommend," Lysette said, reading her tone of voice.

"In the end, I think we'll be offered a plea bargain—a deal. They will want to save face, justify their massive manhunt—"

"I think not, Miss Bankhead. No plea bargain. No deals. No diminished capacity—a euphemism for temporary insanity, if I'm not mistaken. Not guilty. Self-defense. *I insist*."

The lawyer bristled. "I'm not sure if you know what you're up against, young lady. You will be tried three times, once for each homicide. They'll attempt to wear you down—"

"No jury will find me guilty," Lysette interrupted.

"You're guilty of a weapons offense, at the very least," the lawyer said haughtily. "You could get one to two years in prison."

Lysette hid her fear. "Is that likely?"

The lawyer pondered the question, then answered with resignation. "Probation is more likely. A first-time offender. You *are* a
first-time offender, I assume."

"You assume correctly," Lysette said. "So, I have nothing to fear,
do I?"

"I wouldn't be so arrogant if I were you, Miss Ormandy. No
everyone concurs with your actions."

"You're appalled by what I've done, isn't that right?"

"It's not my job to judge you—"

"And I'm a stripper. A tramp. A whore. An *embarrassment*." He
voice rose, and she stared directly at her attorney.

The lawyer flushed. "Your profession will not aid your defense
I can assure you."

"I think I'm prepared for the police," Lysette said rising. "I'm
sure Miss Bankhead will zealously guard my rights," she added
with a wink to Shara.

In the interrogation room at the Roundhouse twenty minutes
later, Lysette recounted her story once again. A detective named
Rios conducted the interrogation. Another detective in the room—
Briggs was his name—seemed strangely subdued, though his eyes
were fixed on her the entire time.

Unlike Shara, though, his gaze wasn't predatory. He wasn't bid-
ing his time ready to pounce at just the right moment. There was
something else in his eyes, something Lysette couldn't read.

As Lysette told her story, Rios pressed her for details which she
gladly provided.

"Why did you flee the subway?" the woman detective asked.

"I was in a state of shock. The old man who had been pistol-
whipped told me to go. Something about it being turned into a
racial incident by certain rabble-rousers."

"Why didn't you come in the next day when you were exonerated, then?"

Lysette again told about the television reporter whose story had
so infuriated her.

"So you went out looking to be attacked?" Rios asked.

"You don't have to answer that, Lysette," her lawyer quickly
interjected.

Now that they were with the police—the criminal attorney's natural adversary—she took on a totally different demeanor with Lysette. Protective. Almost like a grandmother.

—Lysette hated her grandmother.

She despised this woman, but she knew the attorney was no fool. She let Lysette talk freely, interrupting only when there was a question meant to entrap her. Those questions she would answer carefully, saying as little as possible, or not answer at all if she wished.

"I'll answer," she told her attorney. Then to the detective. "I just went out. I certainly didn't want to be attacked."

"You took a gun, though, expecting to use it."

"Detective!" Bankhead fumed.

"That's all right," Lysette said to her attorney. She saw the trap. "I took a gun for protection. Would *you* go out at night without one?"

Later, Rios asked her how she chose the parks she visited.

"To be perfectly honest, I don't know."

Rios pursued the questioning from many angles, but Lysette wouldn't budge. Finally: "Why turn yourself in now? Why not continue to *exercise* your rights?" she said sarcastically.

"I was raped, Detective. It changes one's perspective. Suddenly I felt even more vulnerable. I have no death wish. It's even more dangerous out there than I'd thought."

Rios parried a bit more, then looked at Briggs, who merely shook his head no.

"If you'll excuse us for a moment, Ms. Ormandy," Rios said. "We'll be back shortly."

She and Briggs left.

"What now?" Lysette said after they had gone.

"I assume someone from the District Attorney's office has been listening."

The grandmother in the woman was gone, replaced by the dour professional.

"You'll be charged with murder generally, as I said previously. Spend the night in jail and be arraigned tomorrow. We'll ask for reasonable bail—"

"How did I do, Counsellor?" Lysette interrupted. She enjoyed making the woman uncomfortable. So used to total control, she didn't respond well at all to someone not completely subservient.

"You did little damage," she conceded, "if you insist on pleading not guilty by reason of self-defense."

"What if I can't afford 'reasonable bail'?" she asked.

"You'll remain in jail until your trial," she said, and Lysette could detect a trace of sadistic glee in her voice.

Barry Hoffman

Lysette had an idea, but she didn't want to broach it to the attorney.

"May I see Miss Caffrey and Miss Farris for a few minutes? Alone."

She stood up stiffly. "I'll see what I can do."

She left and a few minutes later Deidre and Shara came in.

"Your attorney thinks you're a bitch," Shara said, with a wry smile. "Given her druthers, she'd love to be the DA in this case."

Lysette returned the smile and shrugged.

"You're a real thorn in their side," Deidre said. "The police and District Attorney's office, I mean. If word gets out—"

"I want word to get out," Lysette interrupted.

"I thought you wanted to shun the glare," Deidre said.

"Listen," Lysette said. "As a reporter, I don't think you should be involved in what I'm going to ask. I do have a request of Shara, though."

Deidre and Shara exchanged glances.

"Ask," Deidre said. "I understand, I think."

"You will. From what my esteemed attorney tells me—who, by the way, I'll be firing after the arraignment—I'm to spend the night in jail and post bail or remain locked up until trial. I've got money for reasonable bail, but why should I be treated worse than those who attacked me? I rot in jail, while pushers walk in and out of here like there's a revolving door."

Shara laughed. "It's a fucked-up system. You sound just like the good Reverend Calvin Whitaker, you know."

"I *do* know. Look, I need reinforcements. Shara, will you call the Coalition and tell them I came in voluntarily? Tell them I'm to be locked up and if I can't make bail, *rot* in prison until my trial. Use those words. Rile them up."

"I see why you didn't want me to handle this," Deidre said. "It would be awkward."

"To say the least," Lysette said. "You might suggest, Shara, they mobilize immediately. A show of force for the Nightwatcher might have some impact at my arraignment."

"It might," Shara said with a smile. "I've got another idea. Why spend even one night in jail? When you talk to the rape counsellor, tell her about the albino—his return. Suggest a hospital might be a better place to spend the night."

"You are bad, Shara," Deidre said.

282

"Yes, she is," Lysette added, "but she's right. Deidre, one last favor."

"If I can."

"With my change in plans, if I do get out, I'll be hounded by reporters, and ordinary people who are curious about the Nightwatcher. I *won't* have it. My life will be an open book; dissected, analyzed and picked apart. I won't be able to go back to my home. I need someplace to stay. Away from it all."

Deidre thought for a moment, then snapped her fingers. "I know where you can stay, away from their prying eyes. But I do have a suggestion. It's well and good to use me as an intermediary to the media. But they'll resent it and hound you no matter where you stay. After your arraignment, why not give the press one opportunity?"

Lysette was shaking her head no.

"Listen," Deidre went on. "Make a statement, but stress how difficult it has been coming to terms with your rape. You need privacy. You're getting counselling. Your attorney advises against any further contact with the media, so you can't answer questions about what you did or why you did it. They'll respect your wishes. They'll have to. You let the people know of your torment. Any reporter who invades your privacy, then, will not only answer to his editor, but to the people as well."

"All right," Lysette said. "I'm not doing cartwheels, but I'll give the press, and the people, their pound of flesh. So, where are you going to put me up?"

"My father-in-law's apartment. He's in the hospital. He'd offer, if he could. I know him."

Rios returned soon after, and the fun and games began.

Rios informed Lysette she was under arrest. Bankhead asked if they would honor their agreement: Lysette would see the albino and a rape counsellor.

"Of course," Rios said. "Detective Briggs will take your client down to the morgue. The counsellor you brought can wait in here."

Briggs escorted Lysette to the elevator. Once in, he pressed the stop button.

"You've put me in a very awkward position," he said, his first words since the interrogation began.

Lysette said nothing.

"The albino—Keith Lowell. I . . . Well, I found out today he was the man who beat and raped my daughter. We should be adversaries. I can't condone what you've done, but I can't condemn you, either. You're a very brave, very foolish young woman. It's good you came in. You'd just about used up all your luck."

He pulled the stop button, and the elevator descended.

"Why do you want to see him?" Briggs asked, before the elevator came to a stop.

"I know he's dead, but I can't shake him. Have you talked to your daughter about the attack?"

"I talk to her all the time. There was brain damage. She hasn't uttered a word in over four months."

"I'm sorry." She paused, searching for a way to describe her torment. "He's like Freddy Krueger. You kill him, but he keeps returning. Intellectually, I know he's dead, but emotionally he's just around the corner. Doesn't make a whole lot of sense, does it?"

"Makes perfect sense," Briggs said. "I told my daughter earlier today. That he was dead. She said nothing. No miraculous breakthrough, but her eyes focused for a moment. She understood. I'm sure. She seemed less fearful when I left, though it might just be wishful thinking on my part." He lapsed into silence.

"I'd like to talk to her, Detective, if possible. Couldn't hurt," Lysette said, as the elevator completed its descent.

"Thank you for offering."

She looked at him carefully. He hadn't agreed, yet he hadn't dismissed her, either.

He led her to the morgue, where a chubby attendant opened the door to a refrigerated drawer and pulled the body out, wrapped in a plastic body bag.

"Leave us alone, please, Charlie," Briggs said to the man who pattered away.

Briggs unzipped the bag so Lysette could see the face.

Lysette closed her eyes for a moment, trying to shake the light-headed feeling that struck her. Felt herself shaking. Felt Briggs' arm around her shoulder.

"He's dead," Briggs said. "Not going to hurt anyone ever again." He paused. "*Because of you.*"

Lysette opened her eyes. There was no blood. He had been cleaned up. He looked pale, even for an albino. Her mind flashed back to the man who attacked her as a child. Was he the one? She had no answer.

"Pull the zipper all the way down. I need to see his penis."

Briggs looked at her, but did as she asked.

It was small and shriveled up. Not at all like the man of her dreams.

"Stay away from me, you bastard," she said to him, as he lay there. "Stay the fuck away from me!"

Chapter Forty-nine

An hour earlier, Morales had been one happy camper. Not only was the Nightwatcher in custody, she had been totally cooperative. That she had surrendered and not been apprehended didn't faze him in the least. They would have had her within a day, he knew.

Briggs' cracking the old man had been the clincher. That, the witness who had seen her car, and finding out she had worn a wig made her apprehension inevitable.

There had been other benefits, as well. Briggs had his second wind. He had finally thrown off the blanket of despair that had looked to smother him since his daughter's attack. Her assailant, moreover, was dead; another weight off Briggs' shoulders. And not only had pairing Rios with Briggs worked, he could see tangible evidence Nina had learned a lot from Briggs and gained a good deal of self-confidence; possibly even some acceptance by the rest of the squad.

But there was a cloud to every silver lining, he now told himself. For the past hour a crowd had been gathering outside the Round-house. First, supporters of Calvin Whitaker, followed by those of Diego Negron. Others, with no affiliation, had joined. There were at least a thousand people outside, with more coming as word spread that the Nightwatcher was in custody.

While they assembled peacefully, they were in an ugly mood. Many held photos taken by Coalition members of drug dealers, car thieves, vandals and others who had been arrested the past two days, then released on their own recognizance.

Two of Whitaker's supporters unfurled a banner—words hastily spray painted on a sheet—that simply read PHILADELPHIA JUSTICE. One by one, those with photos walked up to the sheet and spoke.

"This pusher is selling crack, as I speak. The Nightwatcher sits in jail."

"This car thief," said a second, "is back on the streets. The Nightwatcher sits in jail."

Soon, as each came up and spoke, the rest of the crowd joined in the second sentence: "The Nightwatcher sits in jail." Angry voices filled with venom over an outrageous injustice.

"The Nightwatcher sits in jail."

"The Nightwatcher sits in jail!"

"The Nightwatcher SITS IN JAIL!"

That the Nightwatcher wasn't in jail meant nothing. Perception was everything. Lysette Ormandy was still in the interrogation room talking with a rape counsellor. The counsellor had come out a short time before and suggested Lysette be hospitalized for the night.

"She's still in shock," the woman told Morales.

Morales had rolled his eyes to the ceiling.

"Do you want to risk putting her in a jail cell in the same building as her assailant?"

"The difference," Morales told her, "is her attacker is dead."

The woman shook her head. "Not in that young woman's mind."

"Let me make some calls," he'd told her, muttering under his breath.

Before he had a chance to contact his superior, *he* received a call, which completely dampened his earlier contentment. One of the Commissioner's deputies.

"Sergeant. It's been decided it serves no purpose to hold the young woman in jail for even one night."

He had then been given orders, and knew it pointless to argue.

He called Briggs and Rios into his office. Told them to close the door. Take a seat. Have some jelly beans.

The two officers looked at one another.

"Our guest," Morales began sarcastically, "is to be put under house arrest for the night. While a spokesman for the department informs the crowd, you're to take her home. Nina, you stay with her in her house. Lamar, you stay in your car across the street in case anyone ferrets out her identity before her arraignment. Bring her in at nine AM tomorrow. Then it's in a judge's hands, and *he* can be told what to do," he ended bitterly.

"Told what to do?" Nina asked.

"From the very beginning, someone's been pulling strings. Briggs was assigned the case over my objections. I've shielded you both, but there have been calls daily demanding quicker results."

He shook his head as Briggs tried to speak.

"No one's being critical of the investigation. Someone out of the loop, though, is applying pressure. It comes down the chain of command. Now that we've got the Nightwatcher and word is out, someone fears mob violence if she spends one moment in jail."

"Who?" Briggs asked. "The Mayor?"

"Someone with even *more* clout. I've made calls, and been told in no uncertain terms my career, my *health* and that of my family is best served by not asking questions. This is not coming from the Mayor, I can assure you. So," he said, and leaned forward. "We do as we're told. It'll be out of our hands tomorrow morning, thank God. You've both done an outstanding job."

"Do I search the house while I'm there?" Rios asked.

"Tomorrow, Nina. We'll get a warrant and clear up the loose ends. If she insists on giving you the gun, however, I can't see the harm," he said with a tight smile.

They got up to leave.

"Almost forgot." He handed Briggs a folder. "Some background on Ms. Ormandy. She's had it tough. Make the best of tonight," he said with a rueful smile. "No more overtime for either of you on this case."

They left and so did his smile.

    "... pulling strings."

    "... out of the loop ... "

    "... career ... health ... not served by asking questions."

    "... your family ... "

    "... your family ... "

    "... *your family!* ... "

He slammed his fist on the table in frustration.

Chapter Fifty

Lysette averted her eyes from the sand sculpture. It was almost two in the afternoon and she had finished it an hour before, hoping to wake from her trance and see Angel. But there had been no sight of her then, nor in the intervening hour.

The last two days had been filled with one surprise after another. One minute, two days before, she had been talking with a rape counsellor, expecting hospitalization for the night. The next, Briggs told her she could go home; she was under house arrest. She had looked at him quizzically.

"Someone's looking out for you," he said with a shrug.

Though Nina Rios seemed pleasant enough, once at home, Lysette felt drained and went immediately to bed, setting her mental alarm for five-forty-five in the morning. She had fallen asleep almost as soon as she hit the pillow, and awoke from a dreamless sleep.

Already, she felt better. It was just one night, but the albino hadn't returned. Opening up to the rape counsellor had helped. So, too, she felt had been seeing her assailant on the slab. He seemed so much less threatening in person than in her dreams. When she thought of his shriveled-up penis, she almost laughed. This *thing* had been terrorizing her.

Over coffee and a cigarette, she watched the morning news. A sleepy-eyed Rios joined her, along with Briggs, whom she had fetched from outside.

The crowd, a reporter said, in front of the Roundhouse, had grown to three thousand. Had remained long after being told the Nightwatcher had been allowed to go home under house arrest.

"And for the second consecutive night, there was peace in the streets," he continued. No abandoned buildings set ablaze; no shots

289

fired, and most importantly, no casualties as the criminals who just days ago owned the streets at night once again maintained a low profile.

"Today, we get to meet the Nightwatcher. Her arraignment is set for nine this morning, followed by a press conference. The Coalition has called on their supporters to encircle City Hall to send a message to the arraigning judge to see the Nightwatcher gets the same treatment afforded thugs who prey on the innocent."

He went on to provide information, obviously gleaned from Deidre's article, though neither Deidre nor the *Daily News* was given credit.

Deidre called at eight, telling Lysette that after the arraignment, if she was freed, Shara would drive her to her father-in-law's apartment. Shara would stay with her for protection.

There were additional surprises at the arraignment. Bankhead had been shocked the DA's office had sent one of its least experienced ADAs to handle the preliminaries.

"They must have something up their sleeve," she told Lysette, in a conspirational tone.

When the judge asked the ADA for his bail request, all he asked was a paltry $25,000. Bankhead was almost at a loss for words. As she got up, Lysette whispered.

"Tell him we want *no* bail."

Bankhead looked at her incredulously. "Young lady, the ADA's asking a pittance. If I protest, we may anger the judge. He does have the discretion to ignore the ADA's request and demand more."

"No bail," Lysette said again.

Bankhead had scarcely begun describing the trauma Lysette had been through, and how she wasn't a flight risk, when the judge shushed her.

An elderly man, who looked about to fall asleep or drop dead right on the bench, curtly interrupted her in mid-sentence.

Lysette liked him immediately.

"You've more than made your point, Counsellor, and I concur." He now ignored Bankhead, and turned his attention to the crowded courtroom. "Daily, hardened criminals are allowed their freedom with only their signature to guarantee their appearance at trial. No reason I should require more here."

As Bankhead gathered her papers, Lysette whispered to her.

"By the way, Hillary, you're fired."

"You little bitch," the woman said, in outraged annoyance. "You don't know what—"

"Oh, I do," Lysette interrupted. "You're not capable of handling my defense. More importantly, you've shown me no respect. You may be a fine attorney, but you're a lousy human being. I don't want anyone in my corner ready to plunge a knife in my back."

Lysette had gotten up and left. She was escorted by Briggs, Rios and a phalanx of police, who kept admirers at bay, to a cavernous room where she met a fawning Calvin Whitaker and Diego Negron for the first time.

Shara stood inconspicuously in a corner while introductions were made. Lysette hardly had time to light up a cigarette.

Whitaker took out a prepared statement and handed it to Lysette. "I'm sure you've been much too busy . . . "

Lysette ignored him and read the text, endorsing the actions of the Coalition and pledging her support, then balled it up. Much as she hated to admit it, she was pumped. The Cassandra in her had taken over, like at the club.

"I'm sorry, but I don't have time for subtlety. I appreciate your efforts on my behalf, but I'm not about to endorse anything right now. I'm no puppet on a string. As you can see, my attorney is not present. She was a pompous ass, so I fired her."

She turned to the priest.

"Father Negron. What bothers you most about me? Please be candid."

The priest looked uncomfortable and tongue-tied.

"My occupation. Right?" Lysette answered for him. She had finished her cigarette, and lit a second one with the first.

"It is worrisome," he said.

"And you, Reverend?"

"The same."

She saw the Reverend sensed her determination. Sensed, too, the good Reverend would not be as easily cowered as the priest.

"Good. We'll get that out in the open at the press conference, and until my trial I'll disappear from public view. I certainly won't condemn what you've done, but I won't be a part of it either, or by my endorsement give you free rein to do what you want in my name. Now, gentlemen, we've got a press conference to attend."

Lysette got up to leave.

"You're not going out there with a cigarette," Whitaker said.

"There will be impressionable youngsters watching. You're a role model whether you like it or not."

Lysette took a long drag on her cigarette. It was all she could do not to blow smoke in the man's face. "You best hope I'm no role model, Reverend. If I am, a hell of a lot of young girls in this city are going to end up strippers."

Whitaker glared at her, but said nothing.

"I'm human. One with flaws. I want people to see me as a human being who got sick and tired of being afraid. Not a symbol of all that's righteous and good. I smoke. It's a nasty habit, but no one's perfect. The people will accept me for what I am or not at all."

She left, police in tow, lighting a third cigarette with the second.

The press conference was brief and to the point. Over the course of a five-minute statement and fifteen minutes of questions she made a number of points, the gist of which she had scrawled on index cards:

"We all have the right to go where we please, when we please, without fear of intimidation. I did what I thought necessary. I'm not advocating that others follow my lead. Let's not forget, I did get raped and almost killed."

To a follow-up question: "The rape has had a traumatic effect on me. For that reason, I ask that you respect my privacy, while I heal physically and emotionally."

To a question from a prissy reporter from the *Inquirer,* who could have been Hillary Bankhead's younger sister: "A stripper isn't a prostitute or a tramp. I entertain with my body. It's not dirty. It's not degrading. It's pure fantasy; an escape from the real world. And it's quite lucrative. Let me emphasize, where I work there's no alcohol, no drugs, no prostitution.

"I'm proud of my profession, though there will be many among you who will condemn it. If you're looking for a hero without flaws, you've got the wrong person. Accept me for what I am or not at all."

She walked off stage to wild applause from members of the Coalition who were part of the audience. A few members of the media applauded as well. Whitaker and Negron looked grim. As she was leaving, Whitaker took to the podium to manage damage control.

At Jonas' house that afternoon, Lysette listened to WWBD's talk shows to gauge reactions to her comments. The vast majority were favorable, though a few were chagrined at her profession.

On "Just Talk" there were a number of noisy interchanges.

"I'm certainly not thrilled to find out this woman is a stripper. I expected more," from a middle-aged woman.

"What does her job have to do with her standing up for her rights?" a youngish-sounding man responded. "It's her courage and resolve that's most important."

"But what kind of role model is she?" the woman continued.

"She's not to be a role model," a young Hispanic woman chimed in. "She said as much. This was *her* response to what the city had become."

On and on it went. Lysette eventually became detached from the entire debate. She wanted her freedom and privacy, though she had no illusions the press wouldn't track her down. For now, though, she was comfortable in the cozy and cluttered womb of Jonas Caffrey's apartment.

She went to the beach the next day to see how Angel was handling *her* ordeal. But Angel hadn't shown up.

Now she looked at her sand sculpture. She had chiseled the figure of a female in bas-relief. The left side was of a woman; herself under attack. There was the indentation on her forehead, a firm breast and a hand splayed in search of her gun. The other half of the figure was Angel. There was a look of terror on her face, as opposed to the anger and resolve on her own. Her breast was smaller, her hand covering her genitals.

Lysette didn't know what to make of the figure, and Angel's absence only added to her trepidation.

Then she heard the boombox, and the opening chords from the club version of "Anytime You Need a Friend"; Angel's version. She looked toward the woods and saw two figures emerge from the mist. As the weather had gotten cooler, the forest had become bathed in a fog. She could barely make out the lifeless trees. She expected Angel, and perhaps her father, but instead saw Briggs leading a young black girl; obviously his daughter. The girl held the boombox by her side.

"Where did you get that?" she asked in irritation as they got within earshot.

"I took Alexis, my daughter, into the—"

293

"That's mine. I gave it to a friend. Where did you get it?" Lysette demanded, ignoring Briggs' banter.

"I'm sorry," Briggs said, flustered. "I didn't know—"

"Where did you get it?" Lysette could barely control the panic that gripped her.

Briggs was clearly nonplussed. "It was in the woods. We went in. It was deathly silent. Eerie—"

Lysette glowered at him.

"Sorry. Then we heard the song, and saw the box."

"Did you see anyone else?"

"No one," he said, shaking his head.

Briggs now spoke to his daughter, while reaching for the boombox. "Let me have it, honey. It belongs—"

"No," Lysette interrupted. "Let her keep it." She paused, then looked crossly at Briggs. "I assume you followed me here, Detective. I don't appreciate the intrusion."

"I'm not here as a police officer. My friends and co-workers, just about everyone, calls me Briggs, by the way. Feel free, if you want."

He paused, as if waiting for Lysette to respond. When she didn't, he continued.

"I followed you so we could talk privately. Off the record. And so you could meet Alexis. She can sit by the dune while we talk. She won't wander off."

"Can I take her?" Lysette asked.

Briggs nodded. "Sure. If she'll go with you."

Lysette grasped the limp hand of the young girl, and led her to a sand dune. They both sat down. Alexis reminded her of a doll. She seemed to respond only to outside stimuli. If Lysette lifted her hands above her head, she was certain they would stay there until she put them down. Turn her head to the left and there it would remain.

Brain damage or shock. Brain damage *and* shock. Alexis reminded her of herself when she was in a coma, as a child. Inside, aware; outwardly, a shell.

On an impulse, Lysette turned Alexis' head so their eyes met. She picked up the girl's hand and put it to the indentation on her head.

"I was hurt as a child," she told the girl. She moved the hands over the indentation. Ever so slightly, the girl's fingers moved on their own, tracing and probing the old injury.

Then Lysette gently touched the side of Alexis' head, lightly caressing the young girl's scars. For a brief second Alexis' eyes seemed to come alive, then clouded over again.

Lysette put the boombox in Alexis' lap and pressed the play button.

"You don't fool me, Alexis. Inside, you're aware. I've been there. It'll be our secret. Listen to the music while I talk to your father."

She walked over to Briggs, who had been watching them, captivated.

"She's wary of strangers, but she seemed totally at ease with you." He shook his head. "In the woods." He paused. "I can't explain it, but when she heard the music, she responded. Not much. But she responded. She doesn't do that at home. And, she seems more at ease since I told her her attacker was dead."

He suddenly stopped talking.

"Wouldn't you feel better if someone who harmed you was caught?" Lysette asked. "Your daughter's no vegetable. I'm no doctor, but she's retreated into herself."

"Like you did?"

Lysette eyed him suspiciously.

Briggs took out some folded papers from his shirt pocket.

"There was a file on your attack . . . as a child."

"Thorough, aren't you, *Detective*," she said with disdain.

—*Briggs to his friends*. To her he was a cop; probing, trying to entrap her.

Briggs pointed to the sand sculpture. "Is that you as a child; the other half your being attacked at the playground?"

Lysette wasn't about to tell him about Angel. "Possibly. I don't consciously sculpt figures. I go into a sort of trance, I guess, and my subconscious expresses itself."

Lysette turned and looked at Alexis, swaying ever so slightly to the music. When the song ended it would rewind and repeat unless you pressed the stop button.

"What are you doing here, Detective?"

"Briggs," he said.

"What are you doing here, *Briggs*?"

"I'm not reading you your rights. Nothing you tell me is admissible in court, and anything I learn as a result of our conversation is also inadmissible—fruits of the poisonous tree."

"Am I supposed to confess something?" she asked.

"Just listen. The first two playgrounds you went to were ones

295

where the albino had raped a young girl the previous week. Can you explain that?"

"I'll be honest with you, Briggs, though I don't buy for a minute the inadmissible crap you mentioned. Without a lawyer, it could be a crock. Anyway, I have no idea whatsoever what drove me to those particular playgrounds. That's the truth. I'd read of the rapes, and maybe subconsciously went to the same parks. It wasn't intentional," she added with a shrug.

"And the last playground. Where you met the albino?"

Lysette shrugged once more. "Happenstance. Coincidence."

"I don't buy it," Briggs said.

"So arrest me," Lysette said, then laughed.

"I'll be straight with you," he said. "First, no way in hell you'll be convicted. I know it and you know it. Second, I admit I have a grudging respect for what you've done. The thug in the subway and the next two—all had long rap sheets. All belonged in prison. As a cop I'm powerless at times, and I feel impotent. *You* got them off the streets. *Permanently.* Lastly, you killed my daughter's attacker. I'll always be in your debt for that."

"What's this leading to?"

"A theory. No one ever caught the man who killed your family and left you in a coma. I've checked the record of the albino. He would have been twelve, but he already had a well-documented criminal record. He *could* have been your attacker."

"You're reaching," she said.

He ignored her. "Somehow, you found out and went searching for him. Hoped he'd return to the scene of one of his earlier crimes."

"Then my killing him would be premeditated," she said.

"It's a theory."

"With holes."

"Like Swiss cheese," Briggs said. "The biggest being how you knew he would be at the playground when he attacked you."

"So what are you going to do? Pitch it to the DA?"

"He'd think it insane. And it is. Or is it?"

"It's whatever you want it to be, Det— Briggs."

"Whatever it is, it's between the two of us," Briggs said. "It's a puzzle. A loose end. I like things tidy. You don't always get what you want in my profession. I guess this is one of those times."

He paused, looking a bit uncomfortable.

"You said you would talk to Alexis," he said finally. "Would you? I mean, if you're right . . . "

"I'm no doctor, as I said. Her wounds are far greater than mine were. You can't reverse brain damage. *But*, I saw what you did when you told her the albino was dead. Recognition. Yes, I'll talk to her. Can I take her to the woods? You said she seemed to feel comfortable there."

"Go ahead."

Lysette led Alexis into the woods. She never ceased to be amazed by the transformation. It was like going into a soundproof room. One minute she heard the roar of the ocean and the screaming of the gulls; the next they were gone. A deathly stillness. No insects. No wind. Total silence. Yet not foreboding. Once in the woods, the fog dissipated.

"I'll tell you a secret, Alexis. Something I didn't tell your father." She held the girl's hand as they walked.

"I came here today to meet a friend. Someone your age. Angel. I gave her the boombox. Don't imagine you'll be telling anyone my secret, though."

They came to a clearing, and she sat Alexis down, then sat opposite her.

"The man. No, the *animal* who attacked you, he attacked me."

Lysette looked into Alexis' eyes, searching for recognition. There was none.

"He put a bag over my head. Raped me. I had a gun, but it fell out of my coat."

Alexis' eyes focused on Lysette now.

"I found the gun. Shot him with the bag still over my head. Just wounded him, but I was able to get away from him."

Alexis *was* listening, Lysette was positive. Taking it in. Her eyes were alive.

"He came at me with a rock. Like he did to you. I shot him in the face. Killed him. Saw him at the police station. The morgue. He really is dead, and not near so terrifying as I thought."

A tear fell from Alexis' eye.

"You're safe. He can't hurt you ever again. A part of you has gone into hiding. I call it my attic. When I was a child, my family and I were attacked. *Maybe* by the same man I killed. I hid in my attic for a month. There's no need for you to hide any longer. He's gone. For good."

Tears flowed down Alexis' cheeks.

Lysette bent over and kissed the girl's scarred face, then pressed the button on the boombox so the song played.

"I'll be your friend, Alexis. If you want to come out of hiding I'll be there for you."

She hugged the youth, and she too began to cry. Cried for this child who would never lead a normal life. For Angel, who she missed dearly, and feared she would never see again. For herself, for all she had lost.

"Time to go, Alexis." She grasped Alexis' hand. Alexis let go of the radio. Lysette looked at her.

"You *did* understand, didn't you? It's Angel's boombox. Maybe she'll come back for it later."

Lysette brought Alexis back to her father.

"We had a nice chat. We'll have to do it again."

"The ocean's closing in on your sculpture," Briggs said, taking his daughter's hand.

"Want to sit a bit and watch the sea claim her?" Lysette asked. "The three of us."

"I'd like that," Briggs said.

They sat and watched. Fingers of water clutched at the figure. Then the water slapped like a hand. Soon the figure began to topple against the onslaught.

Lysette was thinking of Angel. She knew Briggs was thinking of his daughter. And Alexis? Hopefully thinking about what she had told her. The big bad wolf was gone. It was safe to come out of the attic now.

Chapter Fifty-one

As a stripper, Lysette worked six weeks, then received a full week off. Some girls splurged and went on vacation, but many spent their off week catching up on mundane chores that fell through the cracks after exhaustive eight-hour shifts. Lysette had worked four straight weeks before surrendering to the police. Jil suggested she take a week off—more if necessary—to attend to her legal problems, and heal physically and emotionally from her rape.

The week flew by, yet Lysette hungered to get back to work.

Each day, without fail, she had gone back to the beach, in hopes Angel would show. Each time she had been disappointed. The boombox, in the forest, was untouched. There were no tracks in the sand.

On a whim, on her fourth visit, she drove to houses that bordered the beach to search out Angel. She was worried sick. It was bad enough for an adult to face the emotional traúma of rape, but what must it be like for an adolescent? Especially one who probably wouldn't confide in her parents or seek professional help.

She had seen what it had done to Alexis, and feared Angel might have retreated into herself, as well.

Oddly, no one at the three houses closest to the beach knew, or had even heard of Angel. Thinking she might have used a fictitious name, she described the youth, but still drew blank stares. She tried a few houses further back from the beach, but they proved fruitless, as well.

Upon her return that day she met for several hours with her new attorney, Tyra Ferrel. Deidre had been amused at Lysette's dismissal of Hillary Bankhead, and suggested a way to find a more compatible attorney.

"She's a pompous ass," Deidre had said when given the news of

Bankhead's dismissal. "You've got to be comfortable with whoever represents you. I can make a few more calls . . . "

"No," Lysette said. "You've done more than enough already. This apartment is a wonderful retreat. Jonas has a scrapbook of all your stories. I hope you don't mind my having read them?"

"Jonas saved my old stories? Sentimental old goat," Deidre said, shaking her head. "I had no idea."

She picked up and thumbed through one of the two large scrapbooks. She wiped a tear from her eye.

"Of course I don't mind," she said, and gave the books back to Lysette. "What are you looking for in an attorney?"

Lysette gave the question some thought. It was a good question. You don't shop until you have an idea of what you're looking for.

"Someone who will treat me with respect," she said finally. "Someone who will argue my case as I wish."

"A mouthpiece, then," said Deidre. "What do you have to offer?"

Lysette looked at her quizzically. "Their fee, of course."

"What about instant recognition? Notoriety. Media coverage—*national exposure*—no money can buy."

"What are you getting at?" Lysette asked.

"A recent graduate from a local law school. Someone hungry. Your lawyer will get exposure far more valuable than any fee. I know the dean of students at the Temple Law School. Why not let him recommend some of his recent graduates? You can pick who you want without being deluged; without having to sacrifice your privacy."

"I like it. If it's all right with you, I can interview them at your office." She smiled. "You get another exclusive."

"That's not why—" Deidre protested, but Lysette cut her short.

"I know. It was your idea, though, and you should reap some reward."

The next day Lysette interviewed five applicants. The second was Tyra Ferrell, and after speaking with her, the others were mere formality.

Tyra Ferrell was a short, slight, dark-skinned black woman with close-cropped hair. On her resume, Lysette noted she had three children, though she was only twenty-seven.

"You've been busy," Lysette said, purposely goading the woman to measure her response.

"I made some mistakes," she said without hesitation. "I got

regnant in high school; graduated two days before the birth of my
rst child. I've been in a gang, taken drugs and slept around with-
ut regard to the consequences. It's a wonder I'm still alive."

"Yet you went to law school. Did you have some divine revela-
on?" Lysette asked.

"Hardly." Again, there was no embarrassment. "I was going to
narry the father of my third child, but he began to abuse me. I went
o a shelter for abused women, and they helped me get a restraining
rder. My boyfriend was on parole, so the court order actually
vorked. Why abuse me and risk prison, when you can get fresh
neat to batter around? I was hooked on the law, cleaned up my act
nd graduated last year."

"What if I said you wouldn't be paid?"

"I would expect you to pay expenses, but, yes, I'd represent you
or free."

"Because you believe in my case?"

"Hardly," she laughed. "With my background, most doors are
losed to me. Unmarried mother of three—who wants to take a
lyer on someone with a family and no husband? I even agree with
hem. I would be leery of hiring me."

Tyra's voice resonated from her petite body. She radiated confi-
lence, dignity and commanded attention.

"As your attorney," she continued, "doors *will* open for me.
From what I've read about you, you value your privacy. I'll be your
oice to the public. I see this as a unique opportunity for career ad-
ancement. Like a free commercial; one long infomercial," she
aid, smiling.

"I'm pleading self-defense. No mitigating circumstances," Ly-
ette said. "No diminished capacity crap. I did nothing wrong. Do
ou have a problem with that?"

"Hardly. In this case, it's the best defense. The only defense, in
ny opinion. Why confuse the jury with a lot of psychobabble?"

"You don't have much experience," Lysette said.

"It's a Catch-22, Miss Ormandy."

"*Lysette*. My former attorney called me Miss Ormandy, and
nade me feel like a tramp."

"Lysette," she said, shaking her head in understanding, "you
an't get experience unless you're given the opportunity. I'm not
given a chance because I lack credentials—experience. Your case
s a no-brainer. No great experience *in the law* needed."

Lysette looked at her curiously.

301

"No offense, but I can't see a jury convicting you. I'll be persuasive. I'll be prepared. I'll win your case and preserve your dignitBeing black and a woman won't hurt either."

Lysette had no doubt Tyra Ferrell would do a superb job.

Her vacation over, she called Jil and told her she would be rturning. Jil seemed somewhat distant on the phone. Lysette wodered just how much flak she had received once it came out shworked at the club.

On her way to the club, Lysette listened to the news on KYWThere had been another aborted attempt on the life of CalviWhitaker.

"Reverend Whitaker is resting comfortably at an undisclosehospital, after an unsuccessful attempt on his life. The Take Bacthe Night Coalition cochairman was shot in the thigh in a drive-bshooting that killed two of his followers and wounded four otherone critically.

"Two men fleeing the scene, in a stolen car, crashed into a fihydrant and were severely beaten by Whitaker's irate supporterBoth are in serious but stable condition. No arrests were made iconnection with their beating."

Lysette tuned out the rest. The two-day calm that had followeher rape and surrender had given way to increased activity by thCoalition—seemingly energized by the Nightwatcher's havincome forward—followed by violent retribution by those targeteby the group.

The torching of abandoned buildings reached near epidemiproportions in the days that followed Lysette's arraignment. ThCoalition organized nightly playground events, calling on peoplto flood neighborhood playgrounds; their very presence woulmake it persona non grata for both dealers and addicts.

Car thieves who stole for drug money, when apprehended, werfollowed to police stations by Coalition Ministers of Justice. Thosset free without bail were followed and beaten. Word spread anthieves caught soon refused bail.

After a child was killed in the crossfire between two dealertheir bodies were found floating in the Schuylkill River.

Even though Lysette had distanced herself from the Coalitiorher name was invariably linked to the vigilantism that "plagued thstreets," as one *Inquirer* columnist exhorted. The Mayor, PolicCommissioner, and many in the media called for calm, but werignored.

Like a wild animal who had tasted human blood and no longer
~ared two-legged creatures, the people had tasted success in their
~attle against crime, and were not to be denied.

And Lysette couldn't blame them. *No one* was looking out for
~eir interests. They had finally had enough, and taken the bull by
~e horns.

Hadn't she done the same? She sometimes wondered. She *had*
~een after the albino, as Briggs had theorized. But just as he had
~uestions that he couldn't answer, so did she. Had she somehow
~onnected with him when their paths had finally crossed? Or was it
~ere coincidence they'd finally met?

Had the urge to go out at night been extinguished by her rape
~d near death, or had she fulfilled some destiny? And was the al-
~ino the same man who had attacked her as a child or just a look-
~like? With his death that last question would remain
~nanswered.

Lysette walked into the club to kisses and hugs. Here, among the
~aff, no one condemned her, though many were surprised.

Jil was on the phone when Lysette knocked. Still talking, she
~eckoned her in. Another minute and she hung up.

"So kiddo, how ya doing?"

"Better each day. You don't get over being raped, but you gotta
~o on. And I've got some friends who have been really supportive."

Jil shook her head. "*You*, the Nightwatcher. I wouldn't have
~uessed in a hundred years. Know what I think?"

Lysette said nothing and Jil continued.

"Cassandra, your stage persona. *She* could be the Night-
~atcher—not Lysette. I think you got your wires crossed. Cassan-
~ra left the club, Cassandra exposed herself to danger and
~assandra killed. Lysette woke up in the morning, but what was
~he supposed to do? Turn herself in? What do you think?"

"No worse than other theories I've heard."

Actually, she'd considered the possibility, but it was too simplis-
~c. There *was* some truth to it, but it wasn't Cassandra acting with-
~ut Lysette's knowledge or approval. They had become one. It *was*
~e Cassandra in her who had the stones to act, but Cassandra was
~ysette. It wasn't something, though, she would discuss with Jil.
~Iaybe with Shara.

"I think it's time I got back to work," Lysette said, getting up to
~hange, but Jil gestured for her to sit.

"I can't have you dancing, Lysette."

Lysette looked shocked. "What? You feeling heat from th press? From the township? From your bosses?"

"That's not it at all. Well, to be honest, my bosses have som concerns, but I could handle them. There are two valid reason First, you'd be a freak show. Customers getting up close and pe sonal with the Nightwatcher. Once word spread, God knows wh would show up. It could be dangerous."

"C'mon, Jil—" Lysette began, but her boss cut her off.

"There's a more important reason; one I'm surprised yo haven't considered. You dance and, guaranteed, someone from th media will snap a photo of you. Maybe it runs in the paper, with black bar over your tits. And it'll be exhibit one at your trial. Yo don't need that."

Lysette hadn't thought of the possibility, and had to admit J had a point. "So, what am I supposed to do? Get a job at McDo ald's? I mean, I've saved money, but not near enough to open th art gallery I want. What if I host?" There was desperation in he voice.

"Look, girl, I'm not about to leave you high and dry. You're n gonna dance, and hosting will still draw hordes of gawkers wh could cause trouble, but I do have an offer."

"Go on," Lysette said, unable to keep the skepticism and disap pointment from her voice. The last person she expected to abando her had been Jil. If she caved in . . .

Jil's voice cut off her train of thought.

"We're opening a fourth club in Havertown—Aphrodisia. I nee an assistant manager. Interested?"

"Am I qualified?"

"Course you are. You've trained your share of girls. You can sp talent. What you don't know, you'll learn. You would spend month here learning the ropes, then we open up."

"What can I say?" Lysette said, stilled awed by yet anothe change in her life wrought by the Nightwatcher.

"You can say yes."

"All right. Yes. Yes. Yes!"

At Jonas' apartment that night, she told Shara the news.

"You don't sound thrilled," Shara said.

"I don't know. I'm overwhelmed, that's all. And I liked dancing When I gave it up, I wanted it to be on my terms. Here I'm bein forced into decisions against my will."

"Look, it's a good opportunity, Lys. You had a good run, but yo knew you wouldn't dance forever. Not many dancers get the opportunity to move up into management."

"I know. It's just, it's so sudden. And what of Cassandra? She was more than just a stage persona. She was—*is*—a part of me."

Over the past week, Lysette and Shara had shared many of their secrets. Shara knew all about Cassandra.

"She is part of you," Shara said, now. "I've seen Cassandra when you were interrogated, when you met with Whitaker and Negron, and at the press conference. And you'll need the Cassandra in you in your new job. She's gotten a promotion. The both of you have. Look, you can't consider her a separate entity. That's schizophrenia, and that's not you."

Lysette lit up another cigarette, and leaned back in her chair. "I'm glad you're here, Shara. I've *never* had anyone I could confide in. Air out my fears and have someone tell me they're unfounded."

"Ditto," Shara said. "There's just so much I can tell Deidre. We're from totally different worlds. I had forgotten that when I was in that hick town recovering; dying to get back to Deidre. You and I. We've shared a lot of the same experiences.

They talked for another hour.

—About everything.

—About nothing.

—Just talked.

Chapter Fifty-two

Morales was present at each session of the five-day Nightwatcher trial. Like the media, Morales thought it was a foregone conclusion Lysette would be acquitted of all but the weapons offense. The DA's office had offered a plea bargain of voluntary manslaughter, but had been rebuffed. According to Lysette's new attorney, Tyra Ferrell, Lysette was intent—even eager—to go to trial, to validate her actions.

"Anything less," said Ms. Ferrell just prior to jury selection, "would be a clear signal that law-abiding citizens have no right to protect themselves from our crime-infested streets.

"This trial," she concluded, "is not about Lysette Ormandy, but the first test in the ongoing fight to reclaim our city."

Morales had to hand it to Lysette. Her new attorney was made to order for the media attention the trial would attract. The woman was brash, yet dignified. She possessed a droll sense of humor that contrasted to the dry platitudes against vigilantism of her adversary. And she was a master of the sound bite.

Meanwhile, she had shielded her client from the probing eyes of the media. "A budding star," *Newsweek* had commented, Ferrell seemed to thrive on the media attention she generated. A natural, this trial propelled her into the national spotlight.

Nationwide polls indicated over 70 percent of those questioned accepted Lysette's innocence. In the Philadelphia area, one poll had 87 percent favoring acquittal; 72 percent felt *no* charges should have been leveled at all.

Morales' attention was focused, though, on the judge, jury and ADA. The someone who had been pulling strings during the police investigation for the Nightwatcher wouldn't be content, he was certain, to sit idly by during the trial.

306

The problem was, he wasn't certain which side these powerful interests would take. *Someone* had reached out so Lysette was put under house arrest that first night. *Someone* wanted bail set low so the Nightwatcher wouldn't be jailed the six weeks prior to her trial. That same *someone* may have gotten to the arraigning judge, who had shrugged off bail entirely.

Just what the agenda was of this someone, Morales had no clue. But that *someone* had orchestrated the Nightwatcher investigation from the start didn't sit right with him. He had fought against political interference from above as a homicide detective, and was in a foul mood that with his promotion to sergeant he was little more than a piece on a giant chess board, being manipulated at someone else's whim. His problem was he was shadow boxing. There was no one of substance he could go after. Worse, he had been told of the consequences if he continued to pursue the matter.

—" . . . your career . . . "

—" . . . your health . . . "

—" . . . *the health of your family* . . . "

He couldn't even speak of his misgivings to friends in the department. Once or twice he had broached the subject casually, and could see the discomfort in their eyes.

"More powerful than the mayor," he had told Briggs and Rios. Money he concluded. Money was the root of power. The power behind the throne was calling the shots.

The Nightwatcher trial had been assigned to Judge Richard Cassells. The man was no trailblazer, but he was more than competent. He had been on the bench for nine years, and was considered tough on crime.

Has *someone* gotten to you, Judge? Morales thought to himself. If so, was it to convict or acquit?

And what of the ADA, Mark Grissom? Also competent, but with his bowtie and lack of charisma, he was out of his league compared to the inexperienced but vibrant Tyra Ferrell. For this *was* a media event, and the stuffy Grissom was ill-suited in such a forum.

Had *someone* reached down to have him assigned? Or would this someone *manipulate* the man himself?

And what of the jury? Did Morales' *someone* have the arrogance to co-opt an entire jury or just one or two jurors?

This was what intrigued Morales. The game within the game. For if Lysette Ormandy was found guilty, it could only be because *someone* had manipulated the process. On the other hand, would this *someone* merely want to insure Lysette was acquitted? He couldn't begin to fathom a reason this *someone* would favor conviction or acquittal.

The trial itself was unremarkable, with the notable exception of Lysette's testimony. Tyra Ferrell led her through the sequence of events; drawing on the sympathy of the jury first by having Lysette describe the attack on her family. She then told how she had been devastated by the carjacking that resulted in the death of her good friend Rose Santucci. It had triggered her reaction on the subway.

The jury was emotionally sucked in.

Ferrell then went to work on the jury's outrage at the helplessness of those living in inner cities. She played for the jury the video of the story that had so infuriated Lysette; how *not* to be a victim.

"It disgusted me," Lysette said, at its conclusion. "Telling me how to dress, when and where not to be on the streets. I was the inmate, with the criminals running the asylum. And I said, '*No way.*' No way will I live my life running scared."

Ferrell quickly led Lysette through the first two killings at the playgrounds; then had her describe in lurid detail her encounter with the albino.

She was being charged with the death of the albino at this trial; the one for which the police had the most evidence. Morales, though, pondered the wisdom of attempting to convict her the one time she had been caught off guard. She had been raped. Emotionally, the jury had to be sympathetic to the victim; and the victim was Lysette.

Had *someone* dictated she be tried first for the killing of the albino? Morales wondered.

Morales could see the jury hanging on every word. Lysette, who had been so composed at the start of her testimony, whose anger flared when she discussed how criminals ruled the streets, now showed herself to be a vulnerable woman. Even a gun had not prevented her rape.

"Why did you turn yourself in to the police, Lysette?" Ferrell asked.

"I didn't want to die. That night . . . when I was raped, I saw my death. I'd been lucky. I'd been a fool to think I could go where I pleased, when I pleased. Alone I was as vulnerable as anyone else who ventured out at night, even with a gun."

Grissom made a half-hearted attempt to plug holes in Lysette's testimony, but he was clearly antagonizing the jury. She was viewed as the victim. He abruptly ended his cross-examination, apparently seeing with each question he was only further alienating the jury.

Morales wondered if a better prosecutor would have handled Lysette's cross-examination differently. He wondered if Grissom had intentionally angered the jury with his cross.

He wondered if his paranoia was impeding his judgment.

Grissom had been ineffective, but had *someone* planted the seed or was Grissom just in an impossible situation?

The jury took less than an hour to deliberate, and returned with an acquittal on all but the weapons offense. The judge's instructions on Lysette's possession of a gun without a permit had been clear. To exonerate her on the weapons offense would have been inexcusable.

Sensing a restlessness within the courtroom, Judge Cassells decided against a delay in sentencing. After admonishing her for possessing a gun without a permit, the judge gave Lysette two years' probation; a typical sentence for a first-time offender.

The courtroom, filled with members of the Coalition, broke into wild applause. Morales could see Tyra Ferrell applying all of her self-control to keep from joining in the festivities. Lysette looked relieved, he thought. There would be two more trials, however, and while Lysette would certainly be acquitted in those as well, it would be exhausting.

Briggs and Rios, joined by two uniformed officers, escorted Lysette and her attorney out of the courtroom, to a press conference outside City Hall. Neither of his two officers had to be there, but they had requested the assignment.

Morales knew Briggs' loyalties weren't with the prosecution. Briggs had told him the albino had been his daughter's attacker. He had decided against removing the detective from the case; and his confidence in the man's integrity proved justified. Both he and Rios had been thorough in gathering evidence after Lysette's surrender. Briggs had been an exemplary witness.

There was just no case . . . unless *someone* pulling strings wanted a conviction.

As they left the courtroom, Morales was filled with self-doubt. The trial seemed clear cut. The judge, ADA and jury all seemed to have acted properly. So why, then, did he feel someone had co-opted the legal process? With popular sentiment running as it was, why did he feel someone had assured that Lysette would not be found guilty?

Even worse, he was alone. He wouldn't involve Briggs; the man had a family and enough problems of his own. Friends and colleagues had already cautioned him. The one man he could turn to was out of the question. Disgraced five years earlier, Morales hadn't spoken to him since. His pride wouldn't allow him to compromise his principles and speak to him now. So Morales walked out of the courtroom alone, surrounded by a feeling of impotence.

Chapter Fifty-three

Nina could feel the hostility of the crowd focused on her as she led Lysette out of the courtroom. *They* were supposed to be the good guys, but the police had become the enemy. She was as pleased with the outcome of the trial as they were, but dared not show it. Had she been on the jury, she would have voted to acquit.

This woman *had* done something concrete to fight crime; had galvanized the city—the *entire* nation—to look at inner-city crime in a way they had stubbornly refused to before.

Nina didn't believe in vigilantism, but the politicians, courts and police had proven totally ineffective in curtailing crime. Lysette's actions, if nothing else, had exposed the cancer of inner-city life for all to see. The nation could no longer merely pay lip service to the problem with empty platitudes.

Nina and Briggs would help Lysette navigate her way through the phalanx of reporters in the corridor, so her lawyer could address the press. It was the least she could do.

Lysette was bombarded with questions from those trying to impress their editors or get a quote those outside wouldn't be privy to.

"How do you feel, Lysette?" one asked.

—Asshole, Nina thought. How would *anyone* feel being acquitted?

"What do you have to say to your fans?" from another.

—*Fans?* Nina thought. Yeah, *fans.* There were no longer supporters, but those who idolized Lysette. Nina had read that dozens of parents had named their newborn daughters Lysette. One forty-five-year-old woman, in Ohio, had her first name legally changed just the day before. A fucking crazy world, she thought.

Out of the crowd of journalists that grudgingly parted before them, Nina saw the glint of metal. A microphone? Camera? Tape

311

recorder? No. Someone was coming toward them. A gun. Pointed at Lysette.

In slow motion, Nina saw the arm rise. Saw the barrel of the gun. Saw another arm inadvertently nudge the hand with the gun. Saw the flash of a shot fired before she heard the explosion that followed.

Instinctively she lunged at the gunman. . . .

—Must save Lysette, she thought.

The arm steadied as she drew closer. . . .

—Can't let her die.

Fired before she could knock it from his hand. Nina felt an explosion in her head.

Everything faded to black.

Chapter Fifty-four

"I take it this ain't heaven," Nina said weakly.

Briggs awoke with a start from a seat in the small hospital room.

"I doze for a moment, and you pick that time to awaken from the dead," he said with a weak smile, then stifled a yawn.

"How long?" She seemed to want to say something more, but her mouth couldn't quite get the words out.

"Almost twenty-four hours. You—"

"Is Lysette all right?" she interrupted, her eyes showing the terror of remembering what had happened.

"Wasn't hit, thanks to you."

"Why so glum, then? Is there something wrong with me?"

"No. Bullet grazed your forehead. You hit the ground face first, and that did more damage. Concussion and a broken nose. But nothing permanent. Always said you had a thick skull."

Briggs went silent.

"Then what?" Nina asked.

"Tyra Ferrell. She was killed. The first shot—"

"Oh my God! What happened after I got shot?"

"You were quicker than me. You lunged before I even saw the bastard. Your thick skull deflected a bullet meant for Lysette. I wrestled the fucker to the ground."

"Who was it?"

"A no one," Briggs said bitterly. "Small-time pusher out to make a name for himself."

Nina was silent.

"There's more," Briggs said.

Nina looked at him glumly.

"Fifteen minutes after the attempt, Lysette's house was fire-bombed. Her house and two adjacent burned to the ground."

"Bastards," Nina said. "Goddamn fucking bastards."

"There's more. Nothing gruesome," Briggs added quickly. "Two hours after the shooting, the DA dropped all charges against Lysette."

Nina said nothing. She closed her eyes, as if exhausted by the news.

"And Lysette's joined the Coalition," Briggs added.

"What?" Nina was totally awake again. "I thought she wanted nothing to do with them; wanted her privacy back."

"She did, but she lost her lawyer and friend, then her home. She held a news conference just after the charges were dropped against her. She still wore the blood-soaked clothes from the trial."

Nina looked confused.

"I'm sorry. You were hugging the floor," he said with a wan smile. "Ferrell was shot in the head. Once we had the gunman restrained, Lysette cradled her attorney in her lap. She was blood-soaked, but refused to change clothes. She wore them at the press conference, waving a gun."

"But the judge told her—"

"No guns. She's on probation. I know. She challenged the judge and the police to arrest her. Said someone just tried to kill her and she'd be damned if she wasn't going to protect herself."

"Will she get away with it?"

"Looks like it. The judge isn't saying a word, and Morales says word's come down from above not to hassle her. Matter of fact, the department offered her twenty-four-hour protection, but she declined."

"Crazy bitch."

Briggs laughed.

"I'm scared for her," Nina said.

"Me, too. She's not leading marches or anything like that. From what I gather, she's going to provide direction and some inspiration. It's not a full-time job with her like for Whitaker and Negron. But she's indicated she won't be cowered by the attack on her life. Said to retreat would mean Tyra Ferrell died for nothing."

Nina closed her eyes, and this time fell asleep. Briggs had one more thing to tell her, but it could wait.

Alexis had been watching the television during the attempt on Lysette's life. She had spoken for the first time in over four months.

"Don't die, Lysette." Over and over a dozen or more times. Then she'd begun singing the song that had played on the boombox in the woods, "Anytime You Need a Friend." Haltingly at first, then stronger. Over and over again, rocking back and forth. Briggs had gotten a message through to Lysette, who had been driven over just after dinner.

Shara Farris, acting as a bodyguard, waited in a car outside while Lysette came in.

Alexis' eyes had focused on Lysette immediately, and tears streamed from her eyes. Lysette had hugged her.

"I'm all right."

Alexis sang the song once for Lysette, who smiled weakly.

"I'll be here for you, too," Lysette told her. "We're gonna be all right, Alexis. The both of us."

Alexis hadn't said anything else, but Lysette kept up a monologue for another twenty minutes. When she rose, Briggs saw his daughter's eyes follow Lysette.

Briggs felt awkward. "Look. Thanks. You know. Thanks for coming. For helping Alexis."

"Thanks for saving my life," she told him.

"It was Rios—"

Lysette put a finger to his lips.

"Thanks for saving my life, Det—Briggs."

Briggs hadn't argued with her, and she soon left.

He had come back to the hospital soon after, waiting in vain for Nina to awake, and the next morning had brought Alexis to see her doctor.

"I don't want to get your hopes up," the doctor had told Briggs, after conducting numerous tests, "but there has been a definite breakthrough. I don't know how much she'll recover, but the next few weeks should tell us a lot."

Briggs sat by Nina now, an emotional wreck. He thought he had lost Nina the day before. There had been so much blood. At the hospital he had been assured she wasn't seriously hurt, but until she woke up he hadn't dared believe them.

There was no question in his mind, now, that Nina belonged. She had proven herself. *She* had seen the gunman before Briggs. *She* had acted instinctively to save Lysette without regard for her own safety. *She* had saved Lysette. There were many ways to pay your dues, Briggs thought. Slow, steady advancement was one.

315

Taking a bullet in the fashion Nina had was another. He was certain the rest of the squad would accept her as well; an equal. *One of the guys*, as Nina liked to say.

Then on the heels of the shooting there had been the break-through with his daughter.

" . . . don't know how much she'll recover . . . " But at least he had hope. And, again, Lysette had connected with Alexis. For someone he had hunted and helped bring to ground, he had an awful lot to thank her for.

Two things were certain.

He'd be there for Alexis.

And he'd be there for Nina. His *partner*.

Chapter Fifty-five

Tommy Rosati was angry. He had been waiting in a checkout line at an Acme Supermarket for ten minutes while a shopper and checker kibitzed. He was in the *express line*—eight items, max— but the old bag in front of him had twelve. He had counted them; *three times*. And the bitch wouldn't even bag her own groceries. There oughta be a law, he thought, simmering.

"How are you today?" the perky checker asked when the old cow finally left.

He glared at her, but held his tongue.

Tommy Rosati was angry a lot lately. Driving around ten minutes to find a parking spot, while three earmarked for the handicapped stood vacant; cavernous spots beckoning to him like a bitch in heat at a bar—her clothes literally painted on—waiting to be picked up, and screwed to death.

Female drivers and old farts slowing down traffic on the expressway, as they hovered right at or below the speed limit, in the left-hand lane, gnawed at him bigtime.

No newspaper to read that morning—because delivery had once again been late—had started the day on a sour note.

Each episode fueled his anger.

Some clown collecting for some fool charity was outside the supermarket as he exited. He was a captive audience, and it bugged him. . . .

—*There oughta be a law*.

"Would you care to make a donation to . . . "

"Go fuck yourself," he said to the man. "Shouldn't allow fucking solicitations outside the market."

"What's your problem?" the man asked, testily.

Tommy ignored the fool, and made for his car, being pelted by a

317

hard-driving rain the whole way. Behind the wheel, he was tempted to run the fucker down. Let's see who has a problem then, he thought, but had to be satisfied with honking his horn as he passed and giving the man the finger.

These minor irritants, which so angered him, he knew, were not at the root of his malaise.

All his life he had wanted to be a cop. His father assumed he would join the family water ice business, but Tommy had defied him for one of the few times and gone to the Academy.

Seven years he had been on the streets; a good cop. Tough when he had to be, yet compassionate when the need arose. His problem was he had been born twenty years too late. He was white and Italian. Twenty years earlier, that alone would have made for a speedy ascent. That he was a good cop would have just made the climb that much more rapid.

But, fucking affirmative action had stood in his way at every turn. First it was the niggers, spics and gooks who were promoted ahead of him, though they were not nearly as qualified. Now it was bitches. Goddamn skirts, who wouldn't walk into an abandoned building unless someone held their hand, were promoted ahead of him, solely because they *didn't* have balls. Literally. Who would be next? Faggots and dykes, he thought. Gotta have *diversity*. To fuck with diversity, Tommy thought.

Tommy could no longer check his anger when he entered the squadroom or locker room. He railed against the injustice of it all to the few other whites who shared his fate. Commiserated with them at a South Philly bar after work. He was vocal. Eventually he was heard.

At home, after returning from the market, the phone rang just as he hit the can. He cursed, almost stumbled over his pants and clumsily made his way to the phone.

"Yeah," he said, one hand holding the phone, the other his pants, which he hadn't had time to fasten.

"Tommy Rosati."

"You got him." If this were a phone solicitation from some charity he'd chew the fucker's ass out. His time in the can, reading *The Sporting News*, was his quality time.

"You remember Linardi?" the voice asked.

Ralph Linardi was a slightly older version of himself, Tommy recalled. Ten years on the force, passed over time and again for promotions because he was a heterosexual male Caucasian. A bitter man and rightly so.

Then two years ago a promotion had unexpectedly reared its head. A year later, he'd heard, Linardi was in vice with yet another promotion. The gods must have been smiling on his ass, Tommy had thought, more than once.

"He get another promotion?" Tommy asked sarcastically.

The voice at the other end of the line softened.

"He was asked to do a small service. Promised *nothing* specific in return. Only that he would be taken care of. You want to be taken care of, Tommy?"

Tommy was wary of being entrapped. He remained silent.

"Smart man," the other said. "This ain't got nothing to do with the mob, Tommy. No tampering with evidence or shit like that. If you want to travel the same path as Linardi, be at the corner of Broad and Locust at six-thirty tonight," the man said, and hung up.

This wasn't the first time the temptation had been there to turn dirty. Too many cops he knew were corrupted to some degree. So far he hadn't given in, no matter how angry he got. And to his knowledge, Linardi hadn't, either. The man was a straight arrow. He knew that was why the caller had dropped his name.

—" . . . do a small service."

—"Promised nothing specific in return."

—" . . . he would be taken care of."

Tommy returned to the can, but couldn't focus on sports.

" . . . a small service."

—" . . . be taken care of."

—*Like Linardi.*

Tommy was on the corner of Broad and Locust at six-thirty. The rain had changed to a fine mist, which Tommy didn't mind at all. A nondescript gray, late-model Ford stopped and the back door opened. Tommy got in. The interior was pitch black; the windows so heavily tinted he couldn't see out of them. There was only a driver; a man who said nothing.

They drove for over an hour. At first, Tommy tried to memorize the route, but gave up after ten minutes. He listened for familiar sounds, but the driver had turned on the radio to an urban dance station, and turned up the volume so Tommy could hardly hear himself think. Conversation with the driver was clearly out of the question.

When the car stopped, the driver, without turning around, reached back and gave him a hood.

"Put it on."

Tommy did as he was told. What the fuck had he gotten himself into? he thought.

" . . . be taken care of."

—*Just like Linardi*.

He was led through a door and down a set of stairs, then into a room. The driver led him to a seat and helped him sit down.

"Please keep the hood on," another voice said. "I apologize, but it's for your own good." The man paused. "Relax, son. There's nothing to be afraid of," the man added, as if reading Tommy's thoughts.

Chapter Fifty-six

Unlike his three colleagues, to Richard Ashley, life's unpredictability was a constant source of comfort. There was no challenge, after all, if all went according to plan. And while stability was at the core of The Fist's existence, Ashley wasn't fazed, in the least, by the potholes that gave the others heartburn.

All had seemed to fall into place with the surrender of the Nightwatcher, Ashley had incorrectly thought. The goal all along had been to neutralize her impact. He and his colleagues had done just that once the woman was in custody.

House arrest instead of jail; freed without bail until her trial; probation for the weapons offense. All had been their doing. Defuse a potentially volatile situation.

Even before the tragic shooting of the woman's attorney, the DA's office had been told to drop all remaining charges. Lysette Ormandy was no threat. She wanted no part of the glare of public attention. No part of the Coalition. She had made her statement and now only wished to disappear.

The fragile balance, though, had been thoroughly upset with the shooting that followed the trial. Instead of fading from public view, the woman was now again the focus of attention, as she openly endorsed and became a spokeswoman for the Coalition.

Both Judge Cassells and the police had been told to ignore her illegal possession of a gun, though this was but a cosmetic solution to the larger problem.

The Coalition and those involved in the drug trade were now more than ever on a collision course. This could not be allowed to occur. Lysette Ormandy was the glue that held the Coalition together. She had to be neutralized; taken out of the game.

Ashley glanced down at the photo of Tommy Rosati. A hand-

some young man with short-cropped jet-black hair, his tempe
made him something of a liability. On the other hand, he wa
shrewd, ambitious and loyal. Through all the indignities of bein
passed over by members of minority groups with inferior creden
tials, he hadn't turned dirty. He had internalized his frustration, bu
it was only a matter of time before it bubbled over and ruined
promising career.

Ashley could restore the man's equilibrium, if Tommy Rosa
was willing to step over the line just once for the greater good. Th
irony didn't slip past him; restoring the balance by ridding them
selves of the Ormandy woman would reestablish Tommy Rosati'
stability, as well.

"Officer Rosati," Ashley began. "We are acutely aware you hav
been denied advancement due to, let us say, the politics of diversity
We can remedy the situation, if you'll do us a service."

He paused, now, for effect.

"Ralph Linardi faced a similar career decision in this very room
I needn't say more. You're an intelligent man."

Ashley explained to Rosati how Lysette Ormandy had become
thorn in the side of those who deplored the current anarchy on the
streets. He told Rosati the woman had to be eliminated. He told the
man exactly how.

"If you agree, you'll have a week to complete your task. Do you
have any questions?"

"What if there are suspicions concerning my involvement?"

"There won't be any," Ashley said, in a tone indicating this wa
not something to be debated.

"When will I be, uh, compensated? How will I—"

Ashley didn't let him finish. "You'll be compensated, much a
officer Linardi was. That is your desire." It was a statement, not a
question.

"As to when, you will have to show patience. Officer Linard
waited a year before he received his . . . compensation. To avoid
the appearance of impropriety, you will have to be patient, as well
Do not question our sincerity. Your ascent, once it begins, shal
more than repay your patience."

"And if I don't take you up on your offer?"

"Then this meeting never took place. You won't be offered the
opportunity again, but there will be no retribution . . . as long as
you remain silent. Speak to *anyone* of this meeting . . . " Ashley

aused. "I don't think it's necessary to go into details. Anything lse?"

"One last question. I don't mean to be skeptical, but I want to be lear. You said this is the *only* service I must perform. I have only our word, and don't even know who you are."

"I appreciate your candor and understand your concern. You nay be called on again, but only to convey a message, much as the ne you received. We do not abuse our power. This extraordinary equest we make, we do so only once. You must take that at face alue. The decision, of course, is yours."

There was silence for several moments before Rosati agreed.

"What if I need to get in contact with you? If there are compli-ations," he added hurriedly.

"You have a week," Ashley said tartly. "When you leave you hall receive certain tools you will need. Should complications rise after the event, we will intervene on your behalf. Otherwise, ou are on your own. We have not chosen you hastily, cavalierly or rbitrarily. You will not need our assistance to complete your task. t is your area of expertise."

The door opened and a man guided Rosati out of the room.

After the door closed, Ashley addressed his colleagues.

"If things don't work according to plan, perhaps we should re-cruit Ms. Ormandy to join our little group," he said lightheartedly.

The meeting was concluded. The others laughed and rose to eave.

Chapter Fifty-seven

"What did you think you were doing?" Calvin Whitaker said, unable to keep his anger in check. "This isn't a strip joint, Ms. Ormandy."

"You're familiar with strip joints, Reverend?" Lysette asked without a hint of backing down.

The cofounder of the Coalition glared at her. "Don't mock me, young lady. I asked a question and expect an answer. You had thirty women strip naked. If the press . . . "

"If the press questions my methods," Lysette interrupted, with irritation, "I'd have a perfectly acceptable explanation. If you weren't so fucking condescending, I'd have an explanation for you, as well. Your moral indignation will be no help to these women if mugged or attacked, and certainly won't intimidate me.

The Reverend closed his eyes. Lysette could imagine him counting to ten or saying a prayer, trying to compose himself.

"What's your explanation then?"

Lysette was aware he hadn't apologized, but his tone had become more mollified.

"These women were having fun, dressed in leotards and cutoffs. They were learning self-defense techniques, but there was a party atmosphere. I envisioned them giving high-fives to one another when we were finished."

"I don't see the problem," the Reverend said.

"There was no tension; no sense of danger. So I upped the stakes. Naked, they were exposed. Embarrassed of their bodies. Glancing around to make sure no men were stealing peeks at the doors. They ceased enjoying themselves and saw themselves as the vulnerable women they are."

"I won't have it. It's scandalous," the Reverend said, his voice booming again.

"Loosen up, Rev," Lysette said, aware she was enjoying his discomfort. "You agreed I would teach these women self-defense techniques, *as I saw fit*," she said, emphasizing the last four words. These aren't martial arts classes. Take it from one who's been raped, self-defense requires a certain state of mind. Panic must be suppressed. Fear overcome. You don't like my methods, tell me to get the hell out."

"You know I can't do that."

"Then I'll go back to my lessons."

Lysette turned, leaving an exasperated Calvin Whitaker to stew.

It had been a week since the shooting. She had wanted nothing to do with the Coalition and the politics that went with it, but she owed it to Tyra to get involved; to maintain the momentum and cohesion of the fragile alliance of egos.

And she wasn't going to be simply a figurehead; a symbol—a trophy to be shown off at events. Be seen, be heard by the masses, but remain silent when it came to decision making.

She volunteered to teach women self-defense and close-quarters shooting. Her methods, she knew, were unorthodox, but if they saved even one life, that was her only concern.

At the shooting range, she first taught the rudiments, much as her grandfather had taught her. When the women were smug with their ability to hit a stationary paper target, she changed the rules.

The women were given guns with dye pellets, and men attacked them from the front, rear, sides and above. The women, forgetting they carried no live ammunition, had to first learn what it meant to fire at another human being.

"Don't view them as human. They're animals. They want your body. Want your purse. Want to injure, maim and kill." She slapped herself in the chest. "Aim for the chest, the torso. You'll have time for one shot if you're lucky. Stop the fucker in his tracks. Then run for help."

"What if he's badly hurt?" one woman asked. "You're telling us to leave him?"

"What if he still has the strength to plunge a knife into you while you check his vitals?" Lysette answered, and was rewarded with laughter.

"There's no such thing as fair play when you're attacked. You go

325

screaming for help. And I mean *screaming*. Forget your goddam
dignity. Get the hell out and let the cops see how badly the poo
darling's hurt."

There was more laughter.

Today, she had told the women to strip during their self-defens
lessons.

"Rapists don't hide in bushes checking you out, looking for
choice piece of meat," she had told them.

She walked up to a heavy, light-skinned black woman. "A rapis
would just as soon have your fat ass, as some chick with all th
curves in the right places."

Lysette moved to a self-conscious, flat-chested, coffee-colore
young woman. "You think he's going to care you have no boobs?"
Lysette pointed to the woman's genitals. "He wants in. *There*
Don't think for a minute you're immune."

She turned to the rest of them.

"Anyway, it takes all kinds. Some men like their women fat; oth
ers scrawny. You're all potential victims."

If the good Reverend was mad at her now, he'd be apoplectic in
week, when she'd bring a fully-clothed man into the class of nake
women. He'd attack, say vile things and they'd have to respond.

Lysette had also suggested the invasion of high schools by con
cerned parents. By the dozens, they would march in unannounced
and demand lockers be opened by a cowering administrator.

With hand-held metal detectors, they'd barge into classroom
and frisk students. With whatever contraband they found, alon
with locker numbers and names of offending students, they woul
wait outside the principal's office while he called the police an
bureaucrats at the administration building to find out what to do.

Word soon spread that any school was fair game. Anytime. Ly
sette demanded there be no pattern. Some schools were "invaded"
two days in succession, just to keep the kids off balance.

A majority of students cheered them on; some even called the
Coalition hotline with information where drugs were stashed t
elude the "invaders": boiler rooms, janitor supply closets, fire ex
tinguishers, to name but a few.

And each day, Lysette spoke to the press, displaying the photos
of offenders arrested but let out without bail, due to the infamous
prison cap.

"Momentum," she told the Coalition's board. "These are voluneers. Their initial anger can be fueled only so long. We have to be creative to keep them coming back."

Reluctantly Whitaker and Negron agreed.

At home—Jonas' apartment actually—Lysette battled depression. Fortunately, she had Shara with her. She had told the Coalition he needed a bodyguard, and funds had been raised. Shara took a leave of absence, and with a job that paid, was feeling more at ease.

The two women talked daily of Lysette's feelings of guilt.

"How long will you work for the Coalition?" Shara asked. "The bureaucracy nauseates you."

"If it wasn't for me, Tyra would be alive . . . "

"Bullshit," Shara interrupted. "You can't blame yourself. You didn't force her to be your attorney. She did it willingly, and her defense would have catapulted her into big bucks. And, you've established a trust fund so her children will never have to worry about their next meal or education."

"You don't understand. I would have been acquitted with Bankhead as my attorney. I had this need to control. My ego got in the way of my common sense."

"So, you wouldn't feel guilty if Bankhead got killed, right?"

"You bitch," Lysette responded, then paused. "Truthfully, no. I know it sounds callous, but Tyra had her whole life ahead of her, and three children now without a mother or father; faced with growing up as I did."

"So now you dream of Tyra getting shot instead of the albino attacking you."

"Every night. Holding her in my hands; her blood gushing from her head onto my hands. Accusing me."

"It'll pass, Lys. It'll pass. She wouldn't have blamed you. You have to come to terms with that reality."

Lysette got by, keeping her days full. She put in six to eight hours at the new club—Aphrodisia—and found she was a good manager. While Jil had final say, she interviewed girls and Jil invariably concurred with her recommendations. She was getting a handle on the minutiae that went with the job, and was fair—but no pushover—with the dancers and staff.

And each day she made time to see Alexis. Several days a week, she drove her to the beach. At first she hoped to spot Angel, but she was gone. It was too cold—the mid-December wind biting—to spend time on the beach itself, but the forest was something else.

Lysette and Alexis would enter the forest and be transported to parallel universe. That was how Lysette viewed it. No matter how cold it was outside, in the forest it was almost balmy. She suspected there was some sort of greenhouse effect as, looking up clouds kept the elements away like a roof. The ground was always dry and the boombox, there for over six months now, was in perfect condition.

Alexis seemed most comfortable here. At home she spoke little seemingly exasperated by her inability to string thoughts together at anything but a snail's pace.

Something about the forest, though, seemed to clear her mind. While she grudgingly allowed Lysette to expand her musical horizons, she insisted on hearing *her* song . . .

—Angel's song, Lysette's mind corrected Alexis.

. . . two or three times each visit. She now sang along with it without so much as missing a beat.

Briggs had gotten her a private tutor to teach her to read and write again. The doctors were astounded by her progress. There would always be a slight limp and weakness on the right side of her body. She would never be college material, though in this regard Lysette didn't concur. But she could be taught to read and write, they told her parents. And with time, her speech, they said should return to near normal.

In the forest, though, she spoke much more coherently, read the newspaper with ease, and wrote in a diary she kept under the boombox. Crazy as it sounded, Lysette felt the forest had some sort of regenerative effect on the girl. Could it be, she thought, the girl's brain was *healing*?

Alexis was also perceptive as hell; to the point of being down right scary.

"You miss Angel, don't you?"

"Miss her and fear for her," Lysette admitted. She had long ago dropped her patronizing attitude toward the girl. Yes, she needed help, but Lysette would treat her as an equal.

"You're angry at her," Alexis said.

"Of course not," Lysette answered, assuming it had been a question, knowing it had not.

"Oh yes. You feel she . . . she abandoned you, when . . . when you needed her most."

"That's . . . " *Ridiculous*, Lysette was about to say, but Alexis was right. She was pissed at Angel. She had needed Angel after

Tyra had been killed. Angel had always been there, since all the craziness had begun. Where the hell had she gone?

"Maybe you don't need her. Not like before. You have Shara. You have me."

"It doesn't make me miss her any less or stop me from worrying," Lysette responded.

Alexis said nothing, but took the Pointer Sisters tape out and put in "Anytime You Need a Friend."

"I know it's her song, but can it . . . can it be ours, too?"

"Of course. You *are* my friend, and coming here with you—just being with you—does wonders for me."

Alexis sang along with the song, as if she were in church. It was the only time there was real life in her voice. Lysette couldn't explain it—hell, she couldn't explain half of what was going on with this girl—but while intellectually she had regained her faculties, she was still emotionally crippled. Her voice, except when she sang, was flat; everything stated as a fact, without any change of inflection.

It would have made more sense if she didn't spring to life when she sang. If Briggs could only hear her now, Lysette thought. It gave her hope that she might regain her emotional faculties, instead of sounding like an android. Something therapeutic about this forest, Lysette knew. Something that chased the demons away. One day, Lysette knew, Alexis would get up and dance. Not like Angel; Alexis wasn't *that* type of girl, but she would dance.

How long it would take her to recover *outside* the forest, Lysette didn't know. With time, though, she would be all right; far better than the doctor's best prognosis.

Before bringing Alexis to the beach, Lysette would go to the Coalition headquarters at 52nd and Chestnut Streets. Actually, what with many of the women's work schedules, she began classes at six-thirty in the morning, ending around seven-fifteen so the women could shower and get ready for work.

Today she planned to have one of the male instructors attack the women while they were naked. She was glad Whitaker was not present. He wasn't up this early, except when there was an emergency. Once word got out what she had done today, he would be there bright and early the next morning. He'd throw a fit, but truthfully, Lysette didn't care. Today the women would face reality and learn to come to terms with it or flee.

Albert Toomes came crashing through the back door fifteen

minutes after they'd begun, grabbing one of the girls from behind, dragging her to the ground, and planting himself on her stomach.

Several woman screamed and two hurriedly dressed. Muttering under their breath they left. Lysette doubted they would return.

Chanel, the scrawny girl, so self-conscious about her flat chest, was the first to recover. She approached Albert from the side, and with her heel kicked him in the head.

Though momentarily stunned, he quickly got to his feet, just in time for Chanel to kick him in the balls. As he bent down in pain she drove a knee into his nose, which began gushing blood. Then as instructed, she fled to the other side of the room.

The room filled with applause and catcalls. The other women crowded around Chanel, the embarrassment of their nudity forgotten as they congratulated the blushing but radiant young woman.

Lysette checked on Albert, saw except for a possible broken nose he was ambulatory, and sent him on his way.

"All right, ladies. Gather around and take a seat."

Still caught up in the excitement, the women slowly complied.

"I don't want to rain on your parade, ladies, but let's look at your reaction to our little . . . interruption."

The women laughed.

"Jasmine, if this were the streets, you would have been raped, beaten and possibly killed. Don't feel bad," she rushed on. "The purpose of these lessons is to learn from your mistakes, so you won't make them again. Vigilance, ladies. You can't panic. You can't freeze. Two women were embarrassed at being seen naked and fled. The rest of you, except for Chanel, froze. Your attacker expects weakness, panic and fear. Counts on it. That is *his* weakness. Exploit it. Attack him where he's most vulnerable, then like Chanel, flee."

Lysette smiled. "I think we've had enough excitement for today. Think about what I've said. Get dressed. I'll check on poor Albert."

She exited to muffled giggles, at the mention of "poor" Albert.

Lysette found Albert with a bag of ice on his nose.

"Sorry," Lysette said.

Albert put up a hand and shook his head. "No need. She caught me off guard. Good for her. Good for *you*. I've had worse. Go on and let me soothe my wounded pride."

Lysette needed a cigarette and some air. Smoking was frowned upon at the headquarters, so she and Shara spent a lot of time outside. Shara had gone across the street to a McDonald's to get some

reakfast for the two of them, thinking the lessons would last their
sual forty-five minutes.

Lysette wandered outside alone. She felt good. She had accom-
lished something just now. Possibly saved one or more of these
women from a future attack.

Chapter Fifty-eight

Tommy Rosati was almost caught off guard when Lysette exite◌ the Coalition headquarters at seven AM, *alone*.

Five days had passed since he had been given his assignment.

—Tick-tock, tick-tock.

" . . . you have seven days."

—Tick-tock, tick-tock.

Time's running out.

He had committed himself after speaking to Ralph Linardi.

The man had refused to speak on the phone.

"Borders Books on 18th and Walnut. Second floor. Mystery sec◌ tion. Be there in half an hour," he'd said when Tommy called, an◌ hung up.

Tommy saw Linardi browsing through the mystery sectio◌ twenty-eight minutes later.

"Tell me about your promotions, Ralph," Tommy had asked.

"Nothing to tell. I'd waited long enough, hadn't I?"

"That's not what I just heard," Tommy said.

Linardi gave him a quick glance and paged through a Dick Fran◌ cis mystery.

"People talk," he finally said. "Jealousy's all it is. I got my pro◌ motions the old-fashioned way. I earned them."

"With a service. One very special *service* with no specific re◌ ward promised," Tommy said. "It was offered to me, tonight."

Linardi considered him cautiously.

"Look, Rosati, there are some things better left unsaid, if you ge◌ my drift. You're talking in riddles."

"So you didn't . . . "

"Take the offer seriously, man," Linardi interrupted. He put the◌ book back on the shelf. "See you around," and he walked off.

Take the offer seriously.

Tommy had.

For two days he loosely tailed Lysette Ormandy to establish her routine. For what was required, only the Coalition headquarters met his needs. She was there from six-thirty to seven-thirty every morning. The first two days he had staked out the headquarters, whenever Ormandy came out she was accompanied by another woman. Ormandy had to be alone for what was required. . . .

—A service.

The clock was running.

—Tick-tock.

Time was running out.

He now sat in a nondescript battered car. The windows were tinted so he could see out, but no prying eyes could see him. The car wasn't worth cannibalizing or vandalizing. No one gave it a second thought.

In the backseat Tyrone Wilkins dozed. Tyrone was a crackhead and a two-time loser. A year earlier, Tommy had walked into a liquor store Tyrone had been robbing. The man panicked, dropped his gun and ran. Tommy had caught him in an alley three blocks away.

"Cut me some slack, man," Tyrone had pleaded.

Tommy had. People like Tyrone were his eyes and ears on the street. All cops had them. It was all unofficial with he and Tyrone. No money had been taken from the liquor store. Tommy told the owner he'd lost the perp; the man accepted his failure as typical and the incident was forgotten.

Now he told Tyrone he had a *service* he needed performed. He'd smiled when he told the man. Using the same words as his future benefactors seemed ironic. He gave Tyrone twenty dollars a day to doze in the backseat of the car. He'd told the man what he needed done, *if* the proper moment arose. Twenty bucks a day for less than two hours of doing nothing had been music to the man's ears.

Now the Ormandy woman was alone, without the other bitch, Tommy thought.

—Tick-tock.

—Tick-tock.

—Time's running out.

"Tyrone," Tommy said, slapping the man lightly on the face with his gloved hand. "It's showtime. Remember what to do?"

"Yeah, man. You'll be there, right? Before—"

"Just like I said, my man. Now strut your stuff."

Tyrone got out of the car and approached Lysette. The street wa quiet. Across Chestnut, on the opposite corner, was a McDonald' but an enclosed plastic slide covered the windows. Three youn black girls, eight to ten years old, were jumping rope; double dutch, they called it, Tommy recalled. They'd be off to scho soon, but for now were intent on their game. Cars drove dow Chestnut Street, ignoring the stores with graffiti-filled iron grate barring anyone from vandalizing the stores during the night. Ther were no cars on 52nd Street.

Tyrone pulled the ski mask over his face, got out of the car an circled around the Ormandy woman.

Tommy watched, intently.

Tyrone had just accosted the woman, was saying something t her, as Tommy approached from the rear. Tyrone took out a switc blade. He kept it shut, though, as Tommy had told him. The woma reached into her coat . . .

—The gun, Tommy knew, she always carried. Before she cou get it out of her pocket, Tommy hit her from behind with a black jack. Not too hard. Just enough to daze her.

Tyrone's back was facing McDonald's. Tommy held out hi hand and a smiling Tyrone, who had been promised a hundred do lar bonus, flipped the knife to Tommy.

Tommy, in turn, threw Tyrone what looked like a switchblad but when you pushed the button a comb was exposed. As Tyron grasped the comb-knife, Tommy swung his free hand, which ha been behind his back, and with a .38 caliber gun shot Tyrone onc in the head; just like the Nightwatcher would.

It was all he *had* to do, but he'd had an inspiration a few minute earlier. Without hesitating, he fired again, aiming at and hitting on of the children across the street.

As she slumped to the ground, the other two kids ran for cove just as their mothers had probably told them.

Quickly, Tommy reached into the Ormandy woman's pocke and took out her .38 caliber gun. He wrapped his gun in her han and walked in the opposite direction, toward Market Street. Walk ing, he pulled his ski mask off, replaced it with an Eagles cap an kept his head down.

He was three quarters up the block before anyone from th Coalition headquarters or the McDonald's began pouring out ont the street. He turned left on Market, then again left onto 53r treet, where he hopped into a second wreck he had stolen and rove away.

—" . . . a service performed."

—" . . . service performed."

—" . . . service . . . "

Now came the hard part. Having the patience to wait for his reward. Fight the demons that would awaken him at night, telling im he had been suckered.

Had killed a man.

Had killed a child.

For nothing.

He'd have to control his temper, too. That would be tough, what ith the games his mind would be playing; waiting for a reward ome part of his brain refused to accept he would ever receive.

At least he didn't hear the tick-tock of the clock in his head anyore. He'd done it . . .

—The *service.*

. . . with two days to spare.

Chapter Fifty-nine

"What happened?" Shara asked, bending over Lysette.

"I . . . I don't know. I just *don't* know," Lysette said, fightin[]
back panic.

A large crowd had gathered; a churning sea of mostly blac[]
faces, eying this white woman with undisguised fury. The shri[]
scream of police sirens could be heard approaching. Lysette sa[]
the uncertainty in Shara's eyes turn to resolve.

"Let's get you inside."

Once inside the Coalition headquarters, Shara took over. Sh[]
ushered Lysette into a small room.

"Listen carefully, Lys," Shara said, making eye contact with h[]
dazed friend. "Don't say *anything* to *anybody*. Understand? Not []
word. I'll be right back."

She spotted Albert as soon as she left the room.

"Albert, guard the door. *No one* gets in to talk to Lysette. Te[]
them she's barely conscious."

She turned to a young woman. "Alisha, call Reverend Whitake[]
Tell him to get a lawyer over here pronto. Someone with clout, wh[]
won't be bullied by the police. Oh, and a doctor."

Shara came back into the office.

"How you feeling?"

"Woozy. Queasy. What happened, Shara?" she asked.

"That's what I want you to tell me," Shara said with exasperatio[]

"No, I mean, why is everyone looking at me like I killed the[]
daughter?"

"Lys, you've got to pull yourself together. The police will b[]
here soon, and we can stall them just so long."

"Shara, what the fuck happened?" Lysette exploded.

336

"You shot a man who apparently attacked you," Shara hesitated.

"And?" Lysette said with growing impatience.

"A little girl across the street. In front of McDonald's."

"Oh my God. Are they . . . ?" She couldn't finish and shivered involuntarily.

"The man is dead. Shot in the head. The girl . . . she was shot in the chest. She's in bad shape. Paramedics hadn't arrived when I brought you in." Shara stopped abruptly, and snapped her fingers, as if she had forgotten something important.

"Wait here. I'll be back in a second."

Again Shara left.

"Alisha, did you get Whitaker?"

"The Reverend's sending over a lawyer and doctor, just like you asked," the woman said.

"Go out, please," Shara said, "and find out how the little girl's doing." Then to Albert, "Let Alisha in the room when she returns. Just Alisha. Okay?"

Back in the room with Lysette, Shara was all business. "Look at me, Lys."

Lysette did as she was instructed, with difficulty.

Looking at Lysette, Shara could imagine what she was thinking. A little girl shot. Shot by *her*. She must be wondering if she'd had another blackout, like those she had told Shara about—in front of the television or at the beach? Did she even know what she'd done? Shara had to shake the lethargy that seemed to grip her friend.

"You gotta tell me what happened," Shara said urgently.

"A man wanted my purse. He had a knife."

"Are you sure?" Shara asked.

"I saw it," Lysette said, without emotion.

"Lys, it wasn't a real knife. Just a comb in a knife. Push the button on the knife and out comes a comb, like a switchblade."

"Not a knife?" Lysette asked. "I saw a knife. I think." Her voice was distant.

"How many times did you fire your gun?"

"I don't remember. Don't remember firing the gun *at all*. Shot a little girl?" she asked, shaking her head, "Shot Alexis? Shot Angel?"

"No. NO! It wasn't Alexis. And not Angel. Focus on me, Lys. It's important. . . . "

337

Lysette had fallen silent. Dimly, while Shara had been speaking to her, she'd been aware of a voice beckoning to her. A voice from within; tentative at first, but gaining strength as Shara told her what she'd done. The voice came from the attic of her mind. She'd ignored it initially, but as the enormity of what she had done struck her, Shara's voice now sounded far away; the voice in her mind tugged at her, with urgency. The voice of a friend; someone who would protect and comfort her, as she had done many years before.

So she ventured back into the attic of her mind, and this time there *was* someone there; someone calling her. Someone who would shield her from the horrors she could no longer confront.

"I'm here for you," the voice said.

It was Angel.

Lysette tuned out the rest of the world.

Epilogue

Lysette was once again a fly on the wall, listening to the buzz around and about her. Shara was by her side. She had been to the hospital daily for the past, what, eight, nine days? Today a man was with her. She recognized the voice. Detective Briggs.

"How is she doing?" the police officer asked.

"No change," Shara said, tonelessly.

"Will she come out of it?"

"Has your daughter? I'm sorry," she added, quickly. "I mean, she's in shock. She's catatonic. There's nothing physically wrong. She could come out of it as we speak. Or . . . "

"Or never," Briggs finished for her.

"Or never," Shara confirmed. Then, "Why weren't you assigned to the case? Instead of . . . " Shara paused, seemingly confused.

"Marsh," Briggs said. "My sarge got a call, not five minutes after the shooting. Under *no* circumstances were Rios and I to be involved. We were too close to her, he was told. It doesn't make sense. *Because* of our involvement, we could have been more efficient. Marsh is with a different squad. They wanted to squeeze my sergeant out, too."

"Why Marsh?" Shara asked.

"He's quick. Unimaginative. Saw the obvious and closed the case within a day. Some clown came after Lysette with a comb. Lysette mistook it for a knife, and shot twice, hitting the man and the little girl. You know she died yesterday?"

"No, I didn't," Shara said. "I've been so caught up with Lysette, I haven't read a paper or heard the news in days."

"The trauma was just too much for her little body. So much loss of blood. Had been on life support until . . . " His voice trailed off a moment. "She never regained consciousness."

"What about the knife Lysette saw?" Shara asked. "Just before she . . . left us, I guess is as good a phrase as any, she seemed adamant it was a knife."

"I saw the comb in the evidence room," Briggs said. "What more can I say? She panicked and fucked up."

"I won't believe that," Shara said testily. "Look, Briggs, it may seem inconsequential now, what with Lysette catatonic and all, but if—no, *when*, she wakes up, she'll be charged—"

"She won't," Briggs interrupted. "Don't ask me why, but the DA has decided against filing charges. The feeling is the quicker the Nightwatcher goes away, the better."

"So that's it, then?" Shara said. "You won't look into it further?"

"I'd like to. So would my sarge. We've been warned off. It's over. Look, I gotta go. My daughter's physical therapy is ending. I'll stop by next week."

"How is Alexis?" Shara asked.

"She had a setback, when Lysette stopped coming. She heard the news, but I don't know if it registered. It's gonna be slow." He lapsed into silence.

"Briggs," Shara said tentatively. "I spent a lot of time with Lysette, while I was protecting her. Some job I did . . . " she said bitterly. "Anyway, she told me about Alexis. They were close. Would you mind. . . . I mean, could I see her? Maybe take her to the beach Lysette took her to?"

"I don't know, Miss Farris," Briggs said warily.

"Ask Alexis. That's all I ask. What's the harm?"

"Let me think about it. I'll give you a call. Look, I've got to be going. I will call, though. Promise."

When Briggs had gone, Shara spoke to Lysette.

"You heard, girl. No charges. I know, it's small consolation, but it is one less worry. I know you can hear me. I need you. Alexis needs you. You're being a selfish bitch, hiding from the world because things got tough."

Nothing.

"I'm not going away, Lys. I'll be here every day to badger you. Till you're so sick of me, you'll wake up just to send me packing."

She paused.

"Got a job yesterday. Your job, actually. Temporary, until you get better. Jil called me. With you ill, she needed an assistant manager for the new club. You did real good. Got an eye for talent *and* character. I jumped right in last night—with Jil hovering at my shoulder—and it was a piece of cake, due to you. So, don't think you can get rid of me easily."

Shara was quiet. Lysette thought she had left.

"I need a friend, Lys. Someone to confide in. Someone who understands what I've been through. I thought it was Dee, like I told you, but she hasn't experienced what you and I share. We talk. But it's not like it was with you."

She paused again, then seemed to brighten.

"Did I tell you I'm going to help Dee with her investigations? Part time. She's no fool. She knows with my background, I can go places and fit in where she can't. I can do my hunting without anyone getting hurt."

Lysette felt Shara kiss her on the forehead.

"Think on it. You're not getting rid of me, so you might as well come out of that shell."

Another pause.

"Stubborn bitch, aren't you? Tomorrow. *I'll* be here. And the day after and the day after."

Another kiss on the forehead.

"I *do* need you, girlfriend."

And she was gone, and it was only Lysette and Angel. The voice in the attic when her family was attacked *hadn't* been Laura. It had been Angel. She had left, but she was back. Lysette wanted to be with her.

With Angel she was safe.

And, it was kinda fun being a fly on the wall.

(2)

Richard Ashley finished reading the morning paper. Expect the unexpected and accept it was his credo. He had never imagined just how successful his scheme to discredit the Nightwatcher would have been when he had given Tommy Rosati his marching orders.

But that was the joy of life; its unpredictability. The young girl's death didn't disturb him, for he was never wracked by feelings of guilt. He also didn't believe in hindsight.

—If you had to do it over again.

341

You didn't, so forget it and go on.

In hindsight, whether by design or chance, shooting the child had been a master stroke on Rosati's part. The Ormandy woman and the Coalition had been pilloried by the press and the public alike; had taken a direct hit that would soon lead to its demise. Guns for protection were fine, until an innocent child was caught in the crossfire. Then, it seemed, most everyone wanted to get off the bandwagon. Fickle, he thought, and so utterly predictable. Sheep, he thought. From a savior to a fiend in the bat of an eye.

And, apparently, the death of the child had been too much even for the Ormandy woman. Catatonic, it was far easier to discredit her activities than if she could articulate her case.

—Expect the unexpected and accept it.

While the Coalition hadn't officially dissolved, it was fragmented and adrift at sea, Negron had attacked Whitaker, and Whitaker had responded in kind. Activities that had attracted hundreds just a week earlier were now attended by just a few remaining diehards.

While over the past two months, over one hundred abandoned buildings had been burned to the ground, others had taken their place for addicts and dealers alike. The night, once again, belonged to the city's criminal element.

The balance had been restored.

The Fist had reached out quickly on two fronts after the shooting. Ashley hadn't wanted a thorough investigation of the Ormandy incident. Detective Briggs, so instrumental in hunting down the woman when she was the anonymous Nightwatcher, was not now desired. A phone call and another detective, more intent on quickly closing an open case, had been assigned.

And what of the Ormandy woman? If she awoke, she could be an embarrassment if she went to trial. The answer, here, too, was incredibly simple. If there were no charges filed, there would be no trial; no forum for the woman to repudiate her guilt. A phone call and it was done.

Most pleasant, as planned, Ormandy was no martyr. The choice had been to kill her or discredit her. He had prevailed. Martyrs furthered causes. Discredit the symbol, and the crusade grinds to a screeching halt. The Ormandy woman would now be merely a footnote in the city's history; not a heroine.

Richard Ashley closed his eyes and exalted in his success. The founder would have been proud.

Miguel Rodriguez's daughter, Amanda, ushered Morales into the living room, where Morales' mentor sat stoically chewing on an unlit cigar.

Morales hadn't seen or spoken to the man in five years. Miguel Rodriguez had paved the way for Hispanics in the Philadelphia Police Department long before it was politically correct.

The first Hispanic officer to reach lieutenant, he had been an outstanding role model until his wife was diagnosed with Alzheimer's. The woman was healthy as a horse and only fifty, and Rodriguez faced the prospect of putting her in a nursing home or hiring a full-time nurse for an indefinite period of time.

He refused to do the former; didn't have the financial resources for the latter. So once, just this once, he had bent and tainted heroin contained in the evidence room in a major drug bust. Just once he had broken his code; not for himself, but for his beloved Anna.

And he had been caught. In one of the inexplicable ironies of his life, he hadn't been prosecuted or held up to public scorn *because* he was Hispanic. Because of the embarrassment the disclosure of impropriety regarding its most prominent Hispanic officer would bring to the department, he was allowed to retire with full benefits. *Now* he could be with Anna literally day and night, and in fact had dedicated his existence to her.

Rodriguez had attempted to contact Morales on numerous occasions after he'd resigned. Morales refused all calls. A proud man himself, Rodriguez abandoned his attempts to reach his friend and pupil.

Both proud and stubborn, Morales had denied his mentor's existence until the Nightwatcher trial. He had decided to swallow his pride *only* after Lysette's shooting of the child. *Someone* had again called. *Someone* didn't want Briggs on the case. *Someone* didn't want meddlesome Morales involved at all. *Someone* wanted everything neatly and quickly wrapped up. And *someone* had decided no charges would be filed against the woman, so if she ever recovered she would be silenced.

He wondered if there was more to the shooting than met the eye. Could this *someone* have set Ormandy up? So many questions without answers.

Morales thought he had been transported back five years when he saw Rodriguez. The man hadn't changed an iota. Trim and fit, as he had always been. Just a trace of gray in his straight black hair. The pencil-thin mustache. The cigar he chewed on, but never lit. Maybe a few extra lines in his still youthful-looking face. Fifty-five, he looked ten years younger. He was reading a Spanish-language newspaper. He ignored Morales as he entered.

"May I sit down, Miguel?" he asked.

No response, so Morales sat across from the man. Rodriguez turned the page and continued to read. Morales could detect a slight tremor in the man's hands. Anger? Age? Some infirmity? He had called before coming. Amanda said she didn't know if her father would speak to him, but told him to come over anyway. Now he was being stonewalled.

Morales told his story, though from the lack of reaction, for all he knew, the other man wasn't listening.

"I've no place to turn," he concluded. "I've been told, no, *threatened* that I risk my career, my health and that of my family if I pursue the matter. I need your help. I need to know what I'm up against. What is everybody hiding?"

Finished, the two men sat is silence for five minutes. Rodriguez continued to read his newspaper. Morales waited. Finally, Rodriguez put the paper down.

"Five years, Estefan. Five years I didn't exist. Five years I'm worse than shit. *Now* you have a problem. *Now* you come running to me. How am I to react?"

"Five years ago," Morales answered, "I felt personally betrayed. *You* talked about being the good cop; not giving in to temptation. *You* hit a rock in the road and then trash your beliefs. I looked up to you, and look what you did."

"You sanctimonious asshole. My Anna is more important than any fucking belief system. It's easy to talk the talk and walk the walk when everything is going your way. Try on your beliefs when a loved one's life is at stake. *Friends* don't abandon friends, Estefan, because one fucks up. Friends understand."

Morales raised his hand as if to say "enough."

"That's why I couldn't talk to you five years ago. We could have argued the rest of our lives. You wouldn't have convinced me. I wouldn't have changed your mind."

"So, I become an outcast," Rodriguez said bitterly. "No, worse, I don't exist. *That's* betrayal, Estefan. I needed your support. Not for what I did. Your support as a *friend*. And you didn't have the decency to return my call. You wouldn't even look me in the eye, even to condemn me. Tell me, why should I help you now?"

"Because we *were* friends. Because you were an exemplary cop. You wouldn't have been intimidated by these people who are manipulating us like puppets. You should help me because it's the right thing to do."

Rodriguez was silent for a moment.

"If I were your friend, I'd tell you to heed the warnings given."

"You've heard of them, then?" Morales asked.

Rodriguez said nothing.

"I'll dig, Miguel. With or without your help. It's become an obsession."

"Your career. Your health. *The health of your family.* It's not idle chatter. You know that, yet you want to sacrifice your family for your holy crusade." He shook his head in sadness.

Morales sat forward in his chair. "I need to know what I'm up against. Maybe that will be sufficient. I can't sit back and do nothing."

More silence. Then a heavy sigh.

"You are one pigheaded son-of-a-bitch, Estefan." He paused, then spoke the next words in a near whisper. "*El Puno.*"

"*El Puno?* The Fist. I don't understand."

"There was a lieutenant, much like yourself. Alan Sharperson. We'd get calls all the time requesting an officer be put on a case or one withdrawn. A lot of it was political. Someone calls their councilman or the Mayor. Sometimes . . . "

He paused and shrugged.

"Sometimes," he finally continued, "there was no logical reason. Good detectives replaced by plodders who would just go through the motions. A cop suspected of being in the mob's pocket assigned to a mob-related case. You try to find out who gave the order or why, and you're told to mind your own business."

"And Sharperson didn't?" Morales asked, excitedly.

"Obstinate, like you. Nobody tells him who's assigned a case, without a damned good reason, he says. So he digs. Too deep. His friends, they stop taking his calls. Soon he's isolated."

"I know the feeling," Morales said.

"Sharperson's a hard drinker, and he'd go to a hangout, get plastered, and say things he shouldn't. 'Someone's pulling strings.' Or, 'Officers promoted without merit.' Nobody specific. Just conjecture."

The man paused and looked at Morales carefully.

"I was there one night. He was sloshed. Pounds his fists on the table. '*El Puno*. The Fist,' he yells. 'They squash you like a bug.'"

"What else did he say?" Morales asked.

"Nothing. Some guy, another cop, picks a fight with him. We made sure both got home before they could do any damage to their careers."

"Is that all?"

"Next day," Rodriguez went on, ignoring Morales, "an eighteen-wheeler plows into his car. He, his wife and three children killed instantly," he said and snapped his fingers for emphasis. "That night his house burned down."

"Jesus," Morales said. "*El Puno*. The Fist. Squashed him like a bug."

"They'll do the same to you, if you get in their way."

"You know I can't drop it," Morales said.

"I know." Rodriguez picked up the newspaper, and Morales could see the trace of a smile. "That's why I told you. I'll send flowers to your funeral. Pity. You'll sacrifice your family to feed your obsession."

"Miguel . . ."

"Go. You're not welcome here. You got what you came for. Now get the hell out of my house. You make me sick with your self-righteousness."

Morales left. What would he do with what he had learned? Who could he turn to for help?

—" . . . his career . . . "

—" . . . his health . . . "

—" . . . the health of his family . . . "

All endangered if he plowed ahead.

(4)

Deidre stood over Jonas, furious with him. He was fading. Fading *fast*. He'd suffered a second stroke the night before.

"You've always demanded I be straight," his doctor had told Deidre. "So, I won't mince words with you. We're talking days. There's only so much we can do. . . . "

He had gone on, but Deidre had shut him out. There were to be no heroic measures; no artificial life support. Jonas had been emphatic; had even executed a living will. More to the point, though, he had made Deidre pledge to allow him to die with dignity, in the event he was incapable of making such decisions.

"You're a bastard, Jonas. You really are," she said to him after the doctor had left. "Selfish. Only thinking of yourself and your precious dignity. You could have fought this. I know. But, if you couldn't recover one hundred percent, you didn't want to recover at all. So you're giving up. Damn you, Jonas. Damn you."

She sat crying for a good ten minutes.

Then he spoke to her.

Not really. She heard his words, as they *would* have been, if he could have spoken, and she answered.

"You say I have Shara. *Right*. I *never* had Shara. I lost her to Lysette, and now to Alexis. We're friends. Good buds," she said sarcastically. "She's going to work with me on some stories."

Deidre shook her head, trying to find the words.

"We're from different worlds, Jonas. I know that now more than ever. I've led a pretty pedestrian middle-class existence. She's a street urchin. The gulf that separates our experiences is too wide. Maybe if I went out and was raped . . . " she started bitterly, but couldn't finish.

"Whatever pain I've suffered, it's nothing compared to that which she, Lysette and Alexis share."

She got up and wiped Jonas' chin. Drooling. Like a baby. No wonder he wanted to die, she thought.

"Shara bought me a companion for my goldfish. She named him Leon, Also." She laughed. "You know, a play on words. I have Leon, Too. Now, I have Leon, Also."

She brushed his hair, then cringed when she saw how many strands remained in the brush. More than yesterday. *Many more*.

"We talk. We share. But there are awkward moments that don't exist between real friends. I could drive with you to a convention and we wouldn't talk for half an hour. It was a comfortable silence. Like between lovers. With Shara and me, there are these pregnant pauses, with each of us searching for something to say."

She opened a window. It was stuffy, nauseatingly oppressive . . .

—*Like in a hospital*, her mind screamed, *where someone is dying*.

. . . in the room. She knew Jonas hated it to be too hot. "Always can put on a sweater, if it's cold," he would say when she complained how cold he kept his apartment, "but it's not proper to prance around in my drawers if it's too hot."

"And there are still secrets and deceptions. It's in her nature.

What's galling is that I'm not talking about the past. She's still deceiving me. I can feel it."

She stared at Jonas, willing him to tell her to stuff her self-pity up her ass, but as usual, he just lay there.

"I'm letting Shara lease your apartment. She's got a job, and it keeps us close. Also gives me an excuse to drop in. I'm just so lonely, Jonas. Even considered going to a singles bar the other night."

She laughed.

"Must be getting desperate."

Jonas spoke to her again.

"Tell Shara how I really feel? I don't know, Jonas. I don't want her pity. Anyway, I've got my work. I'll be closing the Nightwatcher piece tonight. I've already begun research for my next series. Remember I told you about it? It'll keep me hopping and I can use Shara for research. Don't worry about me. I'll be fine."

She stroked his face.

"It's time for you to start fighting back. When I come tomorrow, I want to see some color in your cheeks."

She gave him a kiss and left.

At home she got out her laptop. It *was* time to put the Nightwatcher to bed. She had thought about the events of the past two months for the past several days. She thought she finally had a handle on it.

"A child was buried today," she began typing. "The first victim of street crime in the post–Nightwatcher/Take Back the Night period. It seems appropriate with her death to put the elusive, reluctant Nightwatcher—Lysette Ormandy—into proper perspective."

Deidre took a sip of coffee, and glanced at her notes.

"The child's name is unimportant, for purposes of this article. She's a symbol, just as the Nightwatcher was before she surrendered and we found out her identity. Another added to an already bloated list; one that will get longer still.

"A child, killed by a carjacker trying to elude the police. Just sitting on the steps of her North Philly rowhouse, when some young hood lost control of the car and snuffed out her young life. Cruel as it sounds, just another statistic; another casualty whose name will stay with us for a few weeks and then begin to dim."

She read over what she had written and resumed typing.

"Crime isn't on the rise. So says the Inky in a recent article. Using cold, raw, impersonal data we're told that crime, in fact, hasn't risen to the epidemic proportions we've fantasized.

"Tell that to the family of the latest child raped. Tell that to pre-teens emulating drug dealers, making a quick score for the pusher with the fancy car and fine threads, instead of going to school. Tell that to those who refuse to venture out on the streets at night for fear of being mugged. Tell that to store owners fortifying their properties so they won't end up on a slab in the morgue. Tell that to those who buy the Club and every other new-fangled crime-fighting device in the neverending fight to stay one step ahead of crime. Tell that to the mother of the child run over three days ago, because she had the nerve to be out on her steps, and not locked inside her house.

"It's a jungle out there, plain and simple. We don't need statistics to know life in urban America today is far different from ten years ago. We sense it. We live it. We are the prey and spend our waking hours eluding urban predators."

Deidre was on a roll, now.

"For a week, though, we watched in awe as someone fought back; the anonymous Nightwatcher, who refused to be cowered—refused to live in a bubble. She gave us hope. She gave us courage. She made us act. We, too, could reclaim the streets.

"What a sight to see families mass at playgrounds at night, so their children could play in safety. Those of us who live in the city by choice or necessity were united, as we'd never been before."

She thought of Lysette lying in a hospital, and continued.

"*One* woman brought us together. But she was human. With flaws. Readily admitted to them. Once she had a name and face, detractors appeared out of nowhere. A stripper for a role model. Heaven help us.

"And what of the Coalition that began in response to her actions? A fragile group of bloated egos, each bringing its own agenda to the cause. Without the Nightwatcher, the Coalition was doomed. Lysette Ormandy was the glue that held it together, because all she wanted was safe streets. No hidden motives. No political aspirations. She wasn't looking for a way to line her pockets."

Deidre, as often happened, sensed it was time to tie it all together.

"But I believe even she knew the cause was doomed to failure, because for every dealer arrested there's another to take his place; for every house torched, there's another beckoning addicts. It's been two weeks since Lysette Ormandy left us, so to speak, and already she's forgotten. Yesterday's news. The prison cap remains; the Mayor has retreated now that the pressure is off. Dealers, car thieves and worse are arrested, only to be released within hours.

349

Barry Hoffman

We cringe at the backfire of a car, thinking it's a bullet with our name on it. We're not fool enough to venture out at night alone.

"No matter how things change, they remain the same. Call me a pessimist, but that's the sad legacy of the Nightwatcher. A legacy that brings tears to my eyes as I see a child being buried. Her name's unimportant, for many others will follow."

Depressing, Deidre thought, when she reread it, but except for substituting a word here and there, it remained unchanged.

She looked at her goldfish—Leon, Too and Leon, Also. Round and round they swam, seemingly oblivious of the other's existence. She thought of calling Shara, to get her take on the piece before she filed it, but hung up the phone before dialing.

She was Leon, Too.

Shara was Leon, Also.

—Oblivious to one another's existence.

(5)

Nina read Deidre Caffrey's column, and at first thought it a bit dramatic and overly pessimistic. She was only deluding herself, though, she knew. Not a block away dealers were back on the streets. *Her* people, turning on their own for profit.

A losing battle? Perhaps. No, probably.

She wouldn't admit defeat, though, for to do so would give her job no meaning other than collecting a paycheck. On the other hand, she couldn't ignore reality—the reality Deidre Caffrey spoke of.

She had waited long enough. *Too long.* Tempted the fates. That, too, was folly. This morning she had gone to the bank and taken out a small loan. She'd had almost enough to move her parents and wheelchair-bound brother to a safer neighborhood . . .

—But how much safer? she asked herself.

—*Safer*, her mind answered.

She could have waited another three months. But the dealers were out in droves again. She heard gunshots nightly, as she tried in vain to sleep. A bullet with her father's name on it. Her mother's. Her brother, tied to his wheelchair.

She couldn't chance it. . . .

—But how much safer?

So she took out a loan. Would they be safe somewhere else?

—They would be *safer*.

That was the best she could do.

Shara and Alexis stood at the foot of the forest. Briggs had called two days after they'd spoken at the hospital.

"She wants to go with you. To the forest," Briggs had said.

"Did she tell you?"

"Not in so many words." He paused. "I read it in her eyes. Thirteen years old," he said, as if talking to himself, "and only in the last few months have I really *seen* my daughter. She talks to me with her eyes. I know it sounds—"

"Crazy?" Shara interrupted. "The eyes are the mirrors of the world. I know. Believe me, I know. You can read her eyes, so you can communicate until she speaks."

"Anyway, she wants to go."

Lysette had told Shara about the forest. Shara had seen it from afar, when she had driven Lysette and Alexis to the shore. Up close and personal, though, was another matter. It seemed so out of place; like aliens had plopped it down in the middle of this beach, left and never returned.

Shara held Alexis' hand and they entered. The blast of late-December wind was like being lashed by a whip, but once inside the forest, it was late spring or early fall. A bit cool for swimsuits, but too warm for the heavy jackets they wore.

Alexis had been silent during the trip, and Shara had to literally lead her into the forest. . . .

—"She's had a setback," Briggs had said.

Once in the forest, though, Alexis let go of Shara's hand and walked by herself. Gingerly, at first, with a perceptible limp, but without any help. The farther they went, the stronger she seemed. Shara recalled seeing a horse give birth for the first time, the year she'd spent away from the city. So tentative at first, when it tried to rise, within a short time it was running to and fro.

Alexis went directly to the boombox and pressed the play button. "Anytime You Need a Friend," Shara immediately recognized, the song that had kept Lysette from withdrawing into herself the day she was raped; when Shara found her cringing in her shower.

Shara marveled at the forest. Not a sound. Not a leaf on a tree. Not a bug, fly or gnat. But the forest was alive. Or, Shara thought, the forest *was* life. She couldn't explain it, but she could feel it.

Alexis was singing along with the music, her voice husky and rich. How? Shara thought. She'd been near mute since Lysette had shot the little girl.

Shara sat next to Alexis and put an arm around her shoulder. Her breasts itched. It was the tattoos. They hadn't itched in a long time. The warmth . . .

—The *life*.

. . . of the forest, she thought.

"Can I see them?" Alexis asked, putting a hand on Shara's breast, as if reading her mind.

"My breasts?" Shara asked, taken by surprise.

"No. The eyes," the youth answered.

"Did Lysette tell you about the eyes?"

"No. I just knew. Can I see them?"

Shara took off her sweatshirt and bra. Lysette *had* to have told her, she thought. There was no other explanation.

Alexis touched each eye. The tattoos seemed to fascinate her. She touched the nipple with the tear from her brother's eyes.

"He was the one who hurt you," Alexis said. "Your brother. Bobby. You did what you had to." Her words were halting and flat, but clear.

"Are you psychic?" Shara asked, then felt foolish.

"I see things. What has happened," Alexis answered.

"Have you always seen things?"

Alexis shook her head no. "Only since I was hit in the head. I see lots of things, but I forget most of them."

"Why do you only talk here?"

Alexis shrugged. "Something magic . . . here. I talk all the time . . . at home, but the words don't come out. Here . . . they do."

Shara put her bra and sweatshirt back on while Alexis took out the tape in the recorder and put in another from her pocket. It was amazing, she thought. She had kept her secret—the eyes—from everyone but Deidre, and now in two months she'd shared it with two total strangers.

She listened to the music.

> *You are here*
> *You are mine*
> *Sweet and lovely*
> *Angel*

"She's with Angel," Alexis said.

"Who?"

"Lysette. She's with Angel." Alexis pointed to her head.

"Angel's in Lysette's head. Is that what you're saying?"

Alexis nodded her head yes.

Shara didn't understand. Lysette had told her about the girl on the beach—Angel.

"Angel wants her to stay," Alexis continued.

"Stay where?"

"In the attic. Attic of her mind. She feels safe there . . . with Angel."

This is too much, Shara thought. What's worse, I believe her.

An idea suddenly struck her. She looked directly into Alexis' eyes. . . .

—The mirrors of the soul.

"Did you see what happened when Lysette shot the little girl?"

Alexis nodded her head yes.

"Did the man have a knife?"

"Yes, then no. A knife, then a comb in a knife." With her hand, she made believe she held a knife, pressed a button. "Out pops a comb. No knife."

Talking in riddles, Shara thought, but she pressed.

"Alexis, did Lysette shoot the man?"

"No."

"Did she shoot the little girl?"

"No."

"Who did then?"

Alexis looked puzzled. "*El Puno*. The Fist."

"I don't understand."

"*El Puno*. The Fist," the girl said again. "Not Lysette."

They stayed in the forest for another hour. Shara told Alexis about herself; opened up just as she had with Lysette. It was the right thing to do. She trusted the girl. Knew the girl would better understand her, if she knew of her past. Knew, too, she'd never betray her.

"Our secret," Alexis repeated after Shara, when she had finished.

Shara felt cleansed after she'd unburdened herself. First to Deidre. Then to Lysette. Now Alexis. Careful, she thought, soon you'll go on *Oprah Winfrey* and tell the world.

Alexis laughed. "That was funny. About *Oprah Winfrey*."

It was the first time Shara had heard Alexis laugh. It felt good. Scary, that the girl could read her thoughts, but good to hear her laugh.

When they were ready to leave . . .

—They could have stayed there forever, Shara thought. But, no, the forest was for healing, not for habitation.

. . . Alexis reached for Shara's hand.

"Will you bring me here again?"

"If your father will let me."

"He will," she said with a smile . . .

—*Another first*, Shara thought.

"I can talk to him with my eyes."

"You are something else, you know that?" Shara said. "Hey, I've got an idea. Let's visit Lysette in the hospital. What do you say?"

Alexis' eyes clouded over. "I don't know if I can speak there," she said haltingly. "And . . . " She paused, then shivered involuntarily. "Angel. She scares me. Not bad, but she's . . . " Alexis couldn't quite put into words what she wanted to say, and grew agitated, slapping her sides with her hands.

"That's okay, honey. Let me help? Is she dangerous?"

"Yes. No. She wants Lysette. Needs Lysette. To stay inside."

"Possessive?" Shara asked.

"Yes. Possessive. Possessive. Possessive! *Yes*. And I might frighten her because I know about it. Her being inside Lysette."

"I'll have a chat with Angel. Okay?"

"You're not making fun of me, are you?"

"Not at all. I *do* want to talk with Angel. Real bad."

Outside the forest, Alexis began to shut down. Not completely, but she had trouble getting words out, then halfway to Philly stopped talking altogether.

"I understand," Shara said. "You can hear me. If I wasn't driving, you could talk to me with your eyes. Don't let it bother you. It'll come. If you can talk in the forest, you'll talk outside."

One day, Shara thought, she might bring Briggs to the forest. It was something she'd have to consider. He would be floored, of course. But could he deal with *only* being able to communicate with his daughter in the forest, until she got better? Could he deal with the forest? Something so inexplicable?

(7)

Lysette was aware of someone near her bed.

"Hey, girlfriend."

It was Shara. Lysette smiled within herself.

"I've got someone with me. Alexis. Only she can't talk. Not here. Only in the forest." She paused. "Yes, I've been to the forest with her. Found out an awful lot."

Lysette felt a hand on her cheek.

"It's Alexis," Shara said.

The hand moved slowly across Lysette's cheek, then touched the indentation on Lysette's head.

Lysette wanted to speak to Alexis; to ask how she was doing, but that was against the rules. If she woke up, she would have to leave Angel, and she couldn't.

"Lys," Shara said. "I want to speak to Angel. I know she's in there with you. Alexis told me." Shara paused, and now spoke to the girl within the woman.

"Angel. I know all about you. I know who you are. You're me when I was young. Self-absorbed. A bitch. I used people because I'd been hurt. It's selfish, and it's wrong. We need Lysette. Alexis does. I do. Let her go. Not today. I know you better than that. But soon."

She watched Alexis caressing Lysette's temple; first the indentation, then the scar.

"That beach. That forest," Shara went on. "I know it's . . . how can I put it into words? Magical. Okay. I've said it. Let Lysette out of the attic, and you can see her whenever you want at the beach. I know you're not evil. You're a part of Lysette. You don't want to keep her from those who really need her. I know."

Alexis kissed the indentation on Lysette's temple.

"Enough for now, Angel. We'll talk again. Just the two of us. Make a bet on it."

Finished with Angel, she told Lysette what Alexis had told her about the shooting.

"You didn't do anything, Lys. There's no need for you to hide from the world. You were set up. Come back to us and we'll find out who. Or we won't. It's up to you."

Lysette felt Shara kiss her on the cheek. Then felt another kiss. Alexis.

"Gotta take this child home before her papa pitches a fit," Shara said. "We'll be back, though. The both of us. To speak to the *two* of you."

Lysette wanted to reach out and touch Shara. Touch Alexis. She wanted to hold them. Hug them. They were there for her.

But she couldn't leave Angel, yet. She wasn't ready for the world outside, even with Shara and Alexis beside her.

She'd stay in the attic with Angel.

At least for now.

Author's Afterword

Let's chat.

The publication of my debut novel *Hungry Eyes*, and subsequent decision to write a sequel, raised questions among readers who contacted me and those who reviewed the book, which I'd like to answer.

First, why the sequel? It wasn't planned. I actually feel more comfortable writing stand-alone novels. I pour my heart and soul into the major characters of a book. Holding back for a sequel, I feel, would be cheating the reader. When I completed *Hungry Eyes*, I was satisfied I had dissected Shara to the fullest extent. There were those, however, who felt it would be difficult to try to sell the novel to a mass-market publisher with the novel's ambivalent ending. A sequel was suggested. Rather than dismissing the idea out of hand, I thought of a novel way to write a sequel, of sorts, which could also be enjoyed by someone who had not read *Hungry Eyes*. The book wouldn't focus on Shara. Initially, she was to make what would be considered a cameo appearance. As has happened with each of my novels (Angel in *Eyes of Prey*, for instance, was initially meant to function solely as someone for Lysette to talk to) the best laid plans were altered as the book took shape. Shara is such a dominating figure, she forced herself to become a pivotal character, once again, in the sequel.

After writing *Eyes of Prey*, I considered my exploration into Shara complete. I've since written three stand-alone novels, and immensely enjoyed creating a complete cast of new characters from scratch for each.

Every once in a while, though, I'd come back to Shara. The ending to *Eyes of Prey* made sense *for that book* . . . but I couldn't see Shara settling down to a full-time, nine-to-five job. It goes against everything that defines Shara. And working *for* Deidre? That, too, ang hollow, though not in the context of *Eyes of Prey*. Shara was still feeling her way around. She doesn't have all the answers as to what to do with her life. That's the way it *should* have been left in *Eyes of Prey*. I knew what Shara *should* become, but until recently (over three years after finishing *Eyes of Prey*), I'd put her out of sight, if never completely out of mind.

Shara will return for a third and *fourth* appearance in what now must be called a series. In the third book the focus once again is on Shara. She has left her job and taken another (write me and let me know what you think it is; I won't divulge it here). She confronts someone very much like her, which forces her to look deeper into herself. This is where I feel there is room for Shara to grow. We *know* what happened to her. There is still room, though, for her to explore what it means to her life; to come to grips with who she is. And the fourth book will focus on Alexis Briggs and delve into the supernatural. However, in plotting the book, Shara, right now, appears in two pivotal scenes. And I wouldn't be surprised if she demands even more. I've learned I can't deny her. She won't allow herself to be exorcised from my consciousness.

Second, a number of reviewers wrote that I must have experienced a traumatic childhood to create a character like Shara. In *Pirate Writings*, for example, the reviewer said, "It's hard not to believe Hoffman hadn't experienced firsthand all the terrible molestations described."

So am I venting as a result of childhood trauma? Sorry, but while I've had more than my share of misery, I'm not writing from firsthand experience. Life, at times, has been a bitch. My sister, who was two years younger than me, died from leukemia when she was nine, but unlike other cancers she didn't waste away before my eyes. Both of my parents passed away in their early seventies; my mother from ovarian cancer; my father—also my best friend—from heart disease. I miss them terribly, especially my father, who was my anchor.

While I don't consider my divorce a trauma (actually, a blessing in disguise), my ex remarried, then sued for custody of my three children. A fool of a judge felt a married couple better suited than I, a single parent, and awarded her custody, giving me my children's summers. Her new husband, being in the army, traveled from base to base . . . with my kids moving every few years to such exotic places as Alabama, Texas, Kentucky and North Carolina. Obviously, I'm bitter. There's not much worse than missing out on the childhood of one's children.

Barry Hoffman

So, sure, life's been a bumpy road, but *no*, I was not abused as a child, nor did I face a childhood trauma that allows me to peer from the eyes of tortured souls.

My writing allows me to vent my rage, so I *don't* go postal. find nothing more liberating than creating characters (much a some kids had invisible friends when they were young) and the journey from start to finish is filled with wonderful surprises. don't plot out a book chapter by chapter, with everything etched in stone. My books *are* plotted out, but I welcome the twists and turn that invariably occur; minor characters who emerge as majo forces by book's end. I play fast and loose with the direction I've mapped; even changed endings midway through a book. Tha works for me, though I'm sure some writers would shake thei heads in dismay. That's why writing is an art form, not a science.

Will the story of Shara Farris, and those who surround her, end with the fourth book? I'd be lying if I had the answer. She's got a grip on me, and who knows when she'll let loose? I hope you enjoy the ride with me, whether it ends with four books or forty.

Barry Hoffman
May 16, 1998

Postscript: As this book first went to press, on June 16, 1998, the Philadelphia police in conjunction with the Drug Enforcement Administration, the FBI and the U.S. Marshall's Office began Operation Sunrise—a coordinated effort to rid Philadelphia's Badland of drug dealers and make the streets of the community safe for the populace. The police promise a "twenty-four-hour, seven-day continuous presence" for as long as it takes to rid the streets of crime (estimated at a year to eighteen months). The area targeted is 2.4 square miles of the city, and while a disproportionate amount of crime takes place in the Badlands, the plan seems ill-conceived. A leader of Philadelphia's Fraternal Order of Police put it succinctly "When we do one division at a time I wonder . . . are we looking to eradicate it or relocate it?"

A fortune in money and man hours will be spent in what will be little more than a public relations stunt. The Badlands will be cleansed . . . at least until the police presence lessens. More to the point, this offensive doesn't get at the root of the problem. As long as poverty exists in the inner cities, and as long as the federal and state governments fail to provide sufficient funds to attack the problem, Operation Sunrise will be little more than a placebo. It costs *far too much* to attack poverty, *permanently* add more police officers, build prisons so a "three strikes and you're out" law can be effective (a dealer convicted for the third time would get a minimum sentence of, say, twenty years *without* parole, for instance), improve schools and provide jobs so an Operation Sunrise wouldn't be necessary. This offensive will generate a massive amount of publicity and will bear fruit . . . *in the short run*. But, dealers may simply relocate and when the police leave to attack another area will surely return.

Eyes of Prey focused on another solution, which proved equally ineffective . . . though it cost a hell of a lot less. There are no easy solutions, no panaceas. That is the message of *Eyes of Prey* and will, I believe, be the legacy of Operation Sunrise.

HUNGRY EYES

BARRY HOFFMAN

The eyes are always watching. She can feel them as she huddles there, naked, vulnerable, in an iron cage in a twisted man's basement. Someday she will be the one with the power, the need to close the eyes. And she'll close them all.

___4449-8 $4.99 US/$5.99 CAN

Dorchester Publishing Co., Inc.
P.O. Box 6640
Wayne, PA 19087-8640

Please add $1.75 for shipping and handling for the first book and $.50 for each book thereafter. NY, NYC, and PA residents, please add appropriate sales tax. No cash, stamps, or C.O.D.s. All orders shipped within 6 weeks via postal service book rate. Canadian orders require $2.00 extra postage and must be paid in U.S. dollars through a U.S. banking facility.

Name_____
Address_____
City_____ State_____ Zip_____
I have enclosed $_____ in payment for the checked book(s).
Payment <u>must</u> accompany all orders. ❏ Please send a free catalog.

DOUGLAS
HALLOWEEN
THE
MAN
CLEGG

The New England coastal town of Stonehaven has a history of nightmares—and dark secrets. When Stony Crawford becomes a pawn in a game of horror and darkness, he finds that he alone holds the key to the mystery of Stonehaven, and to the power of the unspeakable creature trapped within a summer mansion.

___4439-0 $5.50 US/$6.50 CAN

Dorchester Publishing Co., Inc.
P.O. Box 6640
Wayne, PA 19087-8640

Please add $1.75 for shipping and handling for the first book and $.50 for each book thereafter. NY, NYC, and PA residents, please add appropriate sales tax. No cash, stamps, or C.O.D.s. All orders shipped within 6 weeks via postal service book rate. Canadian orders require $2.00 extra postage and must be paid in U.S. dollars through a U.S. banking facility.

Name_____
Address_____
City_____State_____Zip_____
I have enclosed $_____ in payment for the checked book(s).
Payment <u>must</u> accompany all orders. ❏ Please send a free catalog.
    CHECK OUT OUR WEBSITE! www.dorchesterpub.com

Max Allan Collins

BRASS

ROBERT J. CONLEY

The ancient Cherokees know him as *Untsaiyi*, or Brass, because of his metallic skin. He is one of the old ones, the original beings who lived long before man walked the earth. And he will live forever. He cares nothing for humans, though he can take their form—or virtually any form—at will. For untold centuries the world has been free of his deadly games, but now Brass is back among us and no one who sees him will ever be the same . . . if they survive at all.

___4505-2 $5.50 US/$6.50 CAN

Cold Blue Midnight

Ed Gorman

In Indiana the condemned die at midnight—killers like Peter Tapley, a twisted man who lives in his mother's shadow and takes his hatred out on trusting young women. Six years after Tapley's execution, his ex-wife Jill is trying to live down his crimes. But somewhere in the chilly nights someone won't let her forget. Someone who still blames her for her husband's hideous deeds. Someone who plans to make her pay . . . in blood.

___4417-X $4.99 US/$5.99 CAN

SHADOW GAMES
ED GORMAN

Cobey Daniels had it all. He was rich, he was young, and he was the hottest star in the country. Then there was that messy business with the teenage girl . . . and it all went to hell for Cobey. But that was a few years ago. Now Cobey's pulled his life together, they're letting him out of the hospital, and he's ready for his big comeback. But the past is still out there, waiting for him. Waiting to show Cobey a hell much more terrifying than he ever could have imagined.

___4515-X $5.50 US/$6.50 CAN

UNGRATEFUL DEAD

GARY L. HOLLEMAN

When Alana Magnus first comes to Luther Shea's office, he thinks she is crazy. Her claim that her mother is interfering in her life sounds normal enough—except that her mother is dead. Bit by bit, Alana sees herself taking on the physical characteristics, even distinguishing marks, of her mother. And the more Luther looks into her claims, the more he comes to believe she is right.

___4472-2 $5.99 US/$6.99 CAN

Dorchester Publishing Co., Inc.
P.O. Box 6640
Wayne, PA 19087-8640

Please add $1.75 for shipping and handling for the first book and $.50 for each book thereafter. NY, NYC, and PA residents please add appropriate sales tax. No cash, stamps, or C.O.D.s. All orders shipped within 6 weeks via postal service book rate. Canadian orders require $2.00 extra postage and must be paid in U.S. dollars through a U.S. banking facility.

Name_____
Address_____
City_____ State_____ Zip_____
I have enclosed $_____ in payment for the checked book(s).
Payment <u>must</u> accompany all orders. ❑ Please send a free catalog.
           CHECK OUT OUR WEBSITE! www.dorchesterpub.com

B|TE RICHARD LAYMON

"No one writes like Laymon, and you're going to have a good time with anything he writes."
—Dean Koontz

It's almost midnight. Cat's on the bed, facedown and naked. She's Sam's former girlfriend, the only woman he's ever loved. Sam's in the closet, with a hammer in one hand and a wooden stake in the other. Together they wait as the clock ticks down because . . . the vampire is coming. When Cat first appears at Sam's door he can't believe his eyes. He hasn't seen her in ten years, but he's never forgotten her. Not for a second. But before this night is through, Sam will enter a nightmare of blood and fear that he'll never be able to forget—no matter how hard he tries.

"Laymon is one of the best writers in the genre today."
—*Cemetery Dance*